By the same author

Redwall
Mossflower
Mattimeo
Mariel of Redwall
Salamandastron
Martin the Warrior
The Bellmaker
Outcast of Redwall
Pearls of Lutra
The Long Patrol
Marlfox
The Legend of Luke
Lord Brocktree
Taggerung
Triss
Loamhedge
Rakkety Tam
High Rhulain
Eulalia!
Doomwyte

Castaways of the Flying Dutchman
The Angel's Command
Voyage of Slaves

The Great Redwall Feast
A Redwall Winter's Tale
The Tale of Urso Brunov
Urso Brunov and the White Emperor
Seven Strange and Ghostly Tales
The Ribbajack

The Sable Quean

BRIAN JACQUES

The Sable Quean

Illustrated by SEAN RUBIN

PHILOMEL BOOKS
AN IMPRINT OF PENGUIN GROUP (USA) INC.

PHILOMEL BOOKS
A division of Penguin Young Readers Group.
Published by The Penguin Group.
Penguin Group (USA) Inc., 375 Hudson Street, New York, NY 10014, U.S.A.
Penguin Group (Canada), 90 Eglinton Avenue East, Suite 700, Toronto, Ontario M4P 2Y3, Canada (a division of Pearson Penguin Canada Inc.).
Penguin Books Ltd, 80 Strand, London WC2R 0RL, England.
Penguin Ireland, 25 St. Stephen's Green, Dublin 2, Ireland (a division of Penguin Books Ltd).
Penguin Group (Australia), 250 Camberwell Road, Camberwell, Victoria 3124, Australia (a division of Pearson Australia Group Pty Ltd).
Penguin Books India Pvt Ltd, 11 Community Centre, Panchsheel Park, New Delhi - 110 017, India.
Penguin Group (NZ), 67 Apollo Drive, Rosedale, North Shore 0632, New Zealand (a division of Pearson New Zealand Ltd).
Penguin Books (South Africa) (Pty) Ltd, 24 Sturdee Avenue, Rosebank, Johannesburg 2196, South Africa.
Penguin Books Ltd, Registered Offices: 80 Strand, London WC2R 0RL, England.

Published simultaneously in Canada. Printed in the United States of America.
Text set in Palatino.
Library of Congress Cataloging-in-Publication Data is available upon request.
Jacques, Brian. The Sable Quean [sic] / Brian Jacques ; illustrated by Sean Rubin.
p. cm. — (Redwall) Summary: The courageous Redwall creatures band together as Vilaya, the evil Sable Quean, and her horde of vermin attempt to make off with the young animals of the Abbey. [1. Animals—Fiction. 2. Kidnapping—Fiction. 3. Fantasy.] I. Elliot, David, 1952– ill. II. Title. PZ7.J15317Sab 2009 [Fic]—dc22 2009002653
ISBN 978-0-399-25164-1
1 3 5 7 9 10 8 6 4 2

To Billy Maher,
Maestro Di Musica
and My Good Friend

A VIEW OF MOSSFLOWER COUNTRY
DURING THE EVENTS OF THE SABLE QUEAN

RAVAGERS' CAMP

WATER
EADOWS

BROCKHALL

MUMZY

ROAD

DITCH

THE
ESTERN PLAINS

UNES

One day when our hearts were young,
we went roving with right good will,
side by side two comrades
to find what lay o'er the hill.
Our spirits never wearied then,
in those high old times gone by.
What friends we made, what perils we faced,
together you and I.
Now eyes grow dim, and paws feel stiff,
even vittles don't taste the same.
You wake one day, with your whiskers grey,
what price then, medals an' fame?
Alas, all we have are memories,
to take out, dust off, and share.
But, oh, my friend, the pride we feel,
just to know that we were there!
We travelled an' fought an' feasted,
we triumphed, we marched and songs were sung,
we faced death, saw life and adventure!
    One day when our hearts were young.

The Ballad of Colonel Meliton Gubthorpe
Digglethwaite (Retired)

BOOK ONE

Travel Is An Adventure!

1

Wreathing slowly through the foliage of a white willow, smoke spiralled into the warm summer noon. Below on the riverbank, two rats and a burly stoat squatted around the fire, roasting roots and wild turnips on sharpened sticks. Scraping away ashes and burnt soil, the stoat inspected his half-raw turnip. He spat sourly into the fire.

"Wot sorta vittles is this fer a warrior? Stinkin' roots an' turnips 'ard as rocks!"

One of the rats remarked hopefully, "If'n ye don't fancy it, then I'll eat it for ye."

Baring his snaggled teeth, the stoat whipped forth a dagger. "Put a paw near my vittles an' I'll gut yer!"

The other rat nibbled at a ramson root, wincing with disgust. He was in agreement with the stoat. "Aye mate, meat's wot we need, a brace o' plump woodpigeons, or even a fish. I like fishes."

The stoat flung his turnip into the fire, scowling. "We don't have ter put up wid this muck. I thought we was Ravagers, not scavengers. Any'ow, wot are we supposed t'be doin', that's wot I'd like t'know?"

The first rat retrieved the turnip from the hot ashes, wiping it off on his tattered sleeve. "Zwilt the Shade sez Sable Quean wants woodlanders, young uns. So we've got t'stay hid in the area an' capture any we sees. That's our orders, mate."

Testing the edge of his blade on a grimy paw, the stoat grinned wickedly. "Young uns would make good meat. Just let me git me paws on a fat dormouse or a chubby liddle squirrel. I'd let Zwilt 'ave the bones to give to the Sable Quean!"

The smaller of the two rats looked fearful. "You'd do that? I wouldn't like t'be you if Zwilt found out."

The burly stoat tossed his dagger into the air, catching it skilfully. "So, wot if'n he did, eh? Lissen, I ain't scared of Zwilt, or 'is Sable Quean. They don't bother me!"

The larger rat whispered nervously, "Be careful wot ye say. They don't call 'im Zwilt the Shade for nothin'—some say 'e's magic!"

The stoat scoffed. "Rubbish! Wot sort o' magic, eh?"

The rat took swift glances up and down the bank. "Nobeast sees Zwilt, unless 'e wants 'em to. They say 'e can come an' go secretly, just as 'e pleases."

The big stoat shook his head pityingly. "Yer a right ole frogwife if'n ye believe that. Shade or no Shade, Zwilt's just a beast like any other. Y'see this dagger o' mine? Well, one good stab of it'd make Zwilt vanish forever!"

The voice came out of nowhere. "How can you do that when you're already dead, fool?"

Brandishing his weapon, the stoat bounded upright. "Who said that—who's there?"

From behind his back, a cloaked figure emerged through the smoky willow foliage. With lightning speed and savage strength, it wrenched the stoat's paw backward, sending the dagger spinning. Dust rose as the stoat's back slammed against the ground. He lay there, staring up into the face of Zwilt the Shade.

The sable was a sight to instil fear into most creatures. Behind the natural mask of dark fur, his eyes were totally black, dead and inscrutable. Zwilt was lean, wiry and very tall for one of his species. Beneath a flowing cloak of dull purple, he wore a snakeskin belt with a broadsword thrust through it. His teeth showed small, white and sharply pointed as he hissed at the hapless stoat.

"You should have believed the rats. They spoke truly."

The burly stoat gulped. "Sire, I was only jestin' . . ."

Zwilt held a paw to his lips. "Silence. You should not be speaking—I've already told you that you're dead."

In desperation, the stoat tried to rise. "No I ain't—"

The broadsword appeared suddenly in Zwilt's paws; he swung it like lightning. As the severed head rolled into the river, Zwilt addressed it.

"Oh, yes you are. Perhaps you'll believe me now?" Without raising his voice, Zwilt the Shade turned his unblinking stare on the two rats. "You believe me, don't you?"

They both nodded wordlessly, in stunned silence.

The tall killer wiped his blade on the headless carcass. "Get this thing out of my sight. Throw it in the river."

The rats scrambled to obey his order. When they turned back again, he had gone. There was only the fire, dying to embers in the bright summer afternoon. The remains of their former comrade drifted slowly away on the current.

None of the vermin band known as the Ravagers dared to disobey Zwilt the Shade. His orders came directly from Vilaya, the one they called the Sable Quean.

2

Waves broke endlessly on the sands of Mossflower's western shore, with the lonely hissing sigh that is the music of the sea. Late noon sun was still warming the beach above the tideline, where the mountain of Salamandastron towered over all. Brang the Badger Lord and his trusty companion, General Flackbuth, sat watching a young hare drilling a group of leverets in the use of the sword. Brang nodded in admiration of the Blademaster.

"I tell ye, Flack, that young Buckler Kordyne is by far the best we've seen here since his grandsire, Feryn. What d'ye think, eh?"

The old officer brushed a paw over his drooping military mustachio. "Hmmph, I don't doubt y'word, sah, not bein' old enough to remember Feryn, wot!"

Brang gave a deep rumbling chuckle. "No, of course not. I'm the only one on this mountain still alive to tell the tale. That's the trouble with living several life spans more than most beasts. Hoho—see that, Flack. Well parried, young un!"

Buckler had just returned the stroke of another hare's lunge. With an expert flick, he sent his opponent's sabre whirling in the air. The blade flashed in the sunlight, landing point first in the damp sand.

Executing a swift half turn, the Blademaster disarmed an attacker who had been stealing up on him. He shook his head at the culprit.

"Never hesitate when you see an opening, Tormy. I felt you behind me before I saw you. Remember, a slowbeast is a deadbeast. You'll have to move faster."

Tormy picked up his blade ruefully. "I say, Buck old thing, d'ye think I'll ever be as jolly good as you are, wot?"

Buckler shrugged. "That's up to you, mate. Keep practising. Also, if I were you, I'd choose a lighter blade. You lack the paw power to wield a sabre. Try a long rapier."

The leveret cast a longing glance at Buckler's blade. "Like that blinkin' beauty of yours?"

The Blademaster cleaved air with his own special sword. It was a peculiar hybrid, longer than other rapiers, honed razor-sharp on both edges, with a cross-basketed hilt. The blade was thicker than that of a rapier but superbly tempered, to give it flexibility. Buckler winked good-naturedly at his pupil.

"There's not another sword anywhere like this un. I designed it myself, but he made it. Isn't that right, Brang?"

A flicker of annoyance showed in the Badger Lord's dark eyes. He beckoned Buckler to attend him.

Saluting the leverets with his blade, Buckler dismissed them. "That's enough for today, thank you."

They returned his salute with various weapons. A sabre, a cutlass, a claymore and a broadsword. Sloping his blade over one shoulder, Buckler wandered over to where the huge badger was seated.

"What's the matter? Have I done something wrong?"

Brang took the sword. He held it, feeling the balance. Bending the supple blade in an arc, he let it twang back, straight as a die.

"I had my doubts about forging this, but you were right—it's the perfect weapon for you. I'll tell you what you've done wrong, young un. Not showing your superiors the proper respect, that's what!"

Returning the sword, Brang turned his back on Buckler, staring fixedly out to sea. The young Blademaster sighed audibly as General Flackbuth continued where the badger had left off.

"It's the custom, laddie buck, to give title to those who've jolly well earned it, wot! How dare ye refer to the ruler of Salamandastron as Brang. 'Tis your duty to address him as m'Lord, or sah, d'ye hear me?"

Buckler stared coolly at the general. "Aye, I hear ye."

Flackbuth bellowed in his face, "I hear ye, General!"

Buckler shrugged, repeating slowly, "I hear ye . . . General."

Lord Brang turned back, his expression softening as he addressed the young hare. "Come up to the forge chamber with me, Buck. It's high time you and I had a talk."

Buckler gathered up his array of training swords. He piled them into the waiting paws of his trusty assistant, Subaltern Meliton Gubthorpe Digglethwaite, or Diggs, as he was more commonly known. He was the same age as Buckler, though marginally smaller and markedly tubby. They were lifelong friends, if poles apart in their views of mountain life and etiquette. Diggs nodded toward the retreating Badger Lord.

"What ho, Buck, are you in the stew again, wot? Has old Flackbuth slapped a blinkin' fizzer on you?"

Buckler winked at his friend. "No, it's just that the big fellow wants to give me another lecture. Put the blades away, Diggs. I'll catch up with you in the mess at supper."

The forge chamber was an airy room, carved from the living rock. It had all the equipment required by a Forgebeast. Weapons in various stages of construction hung everywhere. There was a low, wide window, facing the open sea, with a magnificent view of the western horizon. Lord Brang was proud of his elderflower and comfrey cordial. He poured two tankards, passing one to Buckler and indicating a seat on the window ledge.

Shaking his striped head wearily, the huge badger spoke. "Buckler Kordyne, what are we going to do with you, eh?"

A smile hovered about the young hare's lips. "I don't know. Tell me, what are you going to do with me?"

Danger flashed in the badger's eyes for one perilous moment. Then he burst out laughing, landing Buckler a hefty pat on the back, which almost sent him flying out of the window. Brang steadied him.

"Just like your grandsire—the same rebellious attitude, same carefree manner. Every time I look at you, I see him returned from beyond the silent valleys. Aye, you're the very model of Feryn Kordyne. You won't wear Long Patrol uniform, don't obey orders, always in trouble. You don't even speak like a Salamandastron hare. Why is that? What's the matter with you, eh?"

Buckler answered the enquiry with a question. "I never knew my grandpa, was he as good as me with a blade?"

Brang replied, as if loath to say the words, "Feryn was a great Blademaster, the best I ever set eyes upon . . . until you came along."

Embarrassed by the sudden compliment, Buckler quickly changed the subject. "Tell me again, how did he save your life?"

The sun was starting to drop beyond the horizon. Brang stared out at the crimson aisle it laid upon the calm sea. He never tired of relating the story of his escape from death.

"I was young in those seasons—your grandsire, too. We were about the same age as you are now. There was a plague of vermin sweeping the land. They were called the Ravagers. Aye, and a motley horde they were, murdering, burning, looting and torturing, right across Mossflower. Their leader was a silver sable, Armuk Rinn the Conqueror. Something had to be done to protect Redwall and all our woodland friends.

"I sent out Long Patrol Scouts to discover where he made his lair. They tracked Rinn and his Ravagers long and hard. They were located in an old quarry northeast of Redwall Abbey."

Brang stopped to refill their tankards. He tossed Buckler a rough-looking chunk of pastry, with nuts baked into it. The young hare felt quite privileged—hardly anybeast was allowed to share the Mountain Lord's scones, which he made himself on his forge. Brang watched him eating with pleasure.

"Nothing like Salamandastron Forge Scones. They'll put some iron into your muscles, young un. Now, let me see, where was I?"

Buckler reminded him. "The scouts had found the vermins' lair, you said."

Lord Brang took a sip from his tankard. "Aye, so they had. I ordered the full Long Patrol into battle order and marched on the villains. I must tell you, though, I was young and reckless then, wilder than you'd ever imagine. I take it you've heard of the thing they call Bloodwrath?"

Buckler nodded silently, allowing Brang to explain.

" 'Tis a terrible affliction, a sickness that drives a beast berserk. I had that Bloodwrath, the mad urge to fight, slay and slaughter. Nothing could stand in my way, one beast or a score. When my eyes went red with the rush of blood, I became unstoppable. I outpaced my own hares, charging into that quarry, straight into the foebeast. Fool that I was! The Ravagers had scouted our approach. They were waiting for us and had us heavily outnumbered. But I was out of control, roaring *Eulalia*s and laying waste to the vermin.

"By the blade and the hilt, I fought that day. Everything around me was one red mist, but I battled on. Those Ravagers pressed me hard—I still carry the wounds and scars they gave me. I became cut off from my hares, surrounded, so that I could scarcely move to swing my blade. Then I tripped and fell, the sword slipped from my bloodstained paws.

"That was when I saw him—Armuk Rinn, the great

sable. He was standing over me, swinging a battleaxe. I knew my fate was sealed, I was a deadbeast. But a miracle occurred. Your grandsire Feryn, my trusty right paw, came hurtling through the air, blade flashing, roaring his war cry. He struck like a thunderbolt, cleaving Armuk Rinn, helmet and head, right through his evil brain!"

Buckler's eyes were shining, even though he had heard the tale before. "And that's what settled the battle?"

Brang rose. Crossing to his forge, he leaned down heavily upon the bellows. A plume of golden flame and scarlet sparks shot up, illuminating the badger's powerful head, glinting in his fierce eyes. "Aye, young un, that was a battle to remember. Though it was my friend Feryn's brave act which carried the day. Those Ravagers who were still alive fled when they saw what happened to the mighty Armuk Rinn. Up until then, the vermin didn't believe he could be defeated."

Buckler laughed. "But my grandpa proved different! That's why you gave him the Coin."

The Badger Lord scowled. "Let me tell you about that thing, young un. It actually was a coin, a golden one, from someplace far beyond the sunset, long ago. When I was very young—I recall it was wintertide—I was walking the shoreline south of this mountain when I came across the wreck of an old vessel. It was buried deep by the seasons. There wasn't much to see, only a bit of old wood sticking out of the sand. Well, I started digging it up and choosing pieces, planning on taking them to old Corporal Cook Magirry. He was a real good old sort, often keeping a little plum duff in the oven for me. Actually it was Magirry who taught me to make Forge Scones."

Buckler sensed that Brang was going off into tales of his early seasons, so he interrupted. "But how did you come across the Coin?"

The badger came back to the point. "There was a hole in it, and a rusty iron spike fixing it to what looked like part of a mast." He smiled, winking at the young hare. "'Twas my secret treasure. I kept it, same as any young un would. That night I inspected the coin. It was a curious thing, worn smooth but quite heavy and bright. There were a few strange marks on one side—couldn't make out what they were— Er, hadn't you better run along now, Buck? They'll be serving supper in the mess."

Buckler, however, was intrigued by the tale. "Diggs'll save some for me. Tell me more about the Coin, please."

Lord Brang frowned, shaking his head. "'Twas never meant to be called the Coin. I wanted it to be a special medal for your grandsire. After the battle at the quarry, I polished all the marks from it and made some of my own. A picture of a paw holding aloft a sword, with the word *Blademaster* engraved beneath it. I wove a silken cord of scarlet and black, threaded it through the spikehole and there I had it, the Blademaster's Medal!"

Buckler shook his head. "I never heard it called that before. Everybeast calls it the Coin."

Brang gave the bellows a few more heaves. Bright flames shining upward on his huge, striped features gave him a fearsome appearance.

"Aye, well, that's your grandsire for you. Huh, the Coin, indeed! Just like you he was, a real young rip. Wouldn't accept proper regimental honours from me. Said he'd accept it as a gift, a keepsake, if y'please. The Coin, eh? Rebellious, disobedient rascal!"

Buckler grinned. "Just like me, I s'pose."

Lord Brang paused, then his attitude softened. "Aye, just like you."

The young hare stared out at the darkened seas. There was resentment in his tone. "Then why does my brother Clerun wear the Coin? He's no warrior, just a big, clumsy creature."

Brang shrugged. "Because he's the eldest Kordyne son. Your grandsire Feryn passed the Coin, and his broadsword, down to his firstborn son, your father, Adarin. Now it is the tradition to pass it on to the firstborn—that's Clerun. There's nought I can do about it."

Buckler protested. "But my father wasn't a warrior either. It's not fair!"

Brang watched the swift path of a comet crossing the night skies. "I sympathise with you, Buck, but your family traditions must be honoured. I know your father wasn't a warrior, nor skilled with a sword. But he was a very wise counsellor and served me well all of his life. Maybe if it had been up to me, I would have granted you both the Coin and the broadsword."

Buckler snorted derisively. "Huh, who needs a broadsword—great, hulking, clumsy things. But the Coin, that would've given me something to remember Grandpa Feryn by."

Draining his tankard, Brang slammed it down. "What's done is done, and neither you nor I can change it. We just have to accept things as they are."

The injustice of this stung Buckler. "But my brother Clerun doesn't even live at Salamandastron anymore. He got himself wed to Clarinna, Major Doughty's eldest daughter. They've both gone off to be farmers together. Hah, I'll wager she's wearing the Coin as an ornament now. Aye, and Clerun will be using the broadsword to chop firewood and cut weeds!"

Even though he did not show it, Brang felt sympathy for his young friend. "Well, everybeast to what they choose, I suppose. Clerun to farming, and you here at my mountain as Blademaster. It's not such a bad position."

Taking the sword from Buckler, Brang made a few swift passes. He was surprisingly light on his paws for such a big beast. Twirling the sword into the air, he caught it deftly. "A fine blade. I wouldn't mind making one for myself. Though I don't think I could repeat a weapon of this quality a second time."

He passed it back to Buckler, who bowed respectfully. "Nobeast but you could forge a sword like this, Lord."

Brang's dark eyes twinkled with pleasure. "I'm glad you respected my title, Buck. I think you'd get on much better with everybeast at Salamandastron if you tried to conform to our ways a bit more. If you know what I mean."

The young hare whipped his swordblade through the forge flames, as if trying to cut them up. He raised his voice bitterly. "Conform? You mean strut about in uniform, saluting and wot-wotting old chap! Playing at being warriors, and for what, eh? The days of battling vermin Ravagers are long gone. Now it's all parades, exercises, regimental balls and banquets. I'm a Blademaster, what's that supposed to be? A fool who passes his days teaching other fools how to play with swords!"

He was silenced by the heavy paw of Lord Brang landing on his shoulder. "Then what do you want—tell me, Buckler?"

The young hare was suddenly stuck for an answer. "I want . . . I want . . ."

He flung the sword. It flew across the forge chamber and stood quivering in the door as he shouted, "I don't blinkin' know what I bloomin' well want!"

The badger's eyes twinkled momentarily. "Let me suggest something. How about a bit of travel and adventure? Would that suit you?"

The young hare's ears twitched suspiciously. "Travel, adventure—what sort of adventure?"

Brang made a sweeping gesture at the outside world. "Travel is an adventure! When you go travelling, adventures happen along the way. So where would you like to travel to, eh?"

Buckler was totally unprepared for the question. "Travel, er, I don't know anyplace I could travel to."

Brang was ready with a suggestion. "It might be a nice idea to visit Clerun and Clarinna."

Buckler was uncertain. "But why?"

The Badger Lord explained patiently. "Well, 'tis quite a few seasons since they went. I think they'd be pleased to see you. Who knows, they've probably got a family now. There'll be young uns wanting to meet their uncle Buckler the Blademaster. I wager you'll enjoy being an uncle—has a good ring to it, Uncle Buck!"

Buckler scratched between his ears in bewilderment. "Whoa, slow down there, sir, me . . . an uncle?"

Brang retrieved the sword from the door, then tossed it to the young hare. "Don't stand there with your mouth open, laddie buck. There may be flies about."

Buckler did not know whether to smile or frown. "Forgive me. I'm just trying to get used to the idea. D'you really think I've become an uncle?"

Lord Brang closed the damper on his forge fire. "I don't see why not. A farmer and a farmer's wife are bound to raise a family. They'll need help about the place as they get older. Where exactly did they go to settle down, d'you know?"

Buckler nodded. "A small valley southeast of Redwall. Clerun said he spotted it when he was with the Long Patrol. I think he liked it at first sight."

The big badger brightened visibly. "Southeast of the Abbey, you say. Splendid! You can do an errand for me. Wait there."

Hurrying over to an elaborate oak chest, Brang opened it. Rummaging about, he produced two coils of rope. "Take these to Abbess Marjoram—she's a great friend of mine. Last time I was at Redwall, let me see, eight seasons back, Marjoram showed me around the place. I saw Matthias and Methuselah, the two Abbey bells, beautiful things, with wondrous tones. She allowed me to have a go at ringing them. Not such a good idea, as it turned out, me being so large and heavy-pawed. I pulled so hard that I snapped one of the bellropes. I felt so foolish, but the Abbess assured me that they were old ropes, long past their best. Brother Tollum, the Abbey Bellringer, repaired the broken rope. Before I left Redwall, I promised the Abbess that I would present her with two stout new bellropes. It took me all last winter, but I spliced these ropes myself. So, you will deliver these to Marjoram with my best wishes. I think they'll please her."

The young hare inspected Lord Brang's gifts. They were superbly made. Green and gold fibres had been plaited in an intricate weave. Each carried at their ends two pieces of weathered elmwood, cleverly carved and pierced to form tolling handles. Buckler ran his paw admiringly over them.

"Wonderfully made, sir. These should last a few hundred seasons, eh!"

Brang smiled broadly. "I take it you have decided to go travelling, then. Planning on going soon?"

Buckler felt the prickle of excitement running through him. He strove to keep his voice level. "Would tomorrow morning after breakfast suit you, Lord?" He winced as the badger shook his paw warmly.

"No better time, I'd say, my friend. Are you going alone? Mayhaps you'd do better to take a companion—always good to travel with a comrade. Might I suggest Subaltern Meliton Gubthorpe Digglethwaite?"

Buckler chuckled. "Of course, good old Diggs. Though I wonder, who's going to pull the cart?"

Lord Brang looked puzzled. "What cart?"

The young hare slotted his sword into the back scabbard he had designed so he could draw steel swiftly. The hilt showed over his left shoulder. "The cart we'll need to carry Diggs's vittles. Have you seen the amount of food that tubby rascal can shift?"

Diggs was waiting for his friend in the crowded Mess Hall. He pointed to a small heap of supper set out close to him. "Wot ho there, Buck! Just about saved you some scoff, wot. Y'have t'be nippy with this famine-faced mob about. Tuck in, old lad. You must be jolly hungry, wot wot!"

Buckler felt too exhilarated for food, but he kept calm,

nibbling some salad and cheese. "Hmm. No plum duff tonight. That's strange."

Diggs swiftly wiped crumbs from his tunic. "Er, there was only a smidgeon left, mis'rable little portion. Didn't know you were fond of the bloomin' duff, or I'd have jolly well saved you some, mate."

Buckler surveyed the empty bowls and platters lying about. "What happened to the apple crumble?"

Diggs patted his bulging waistline. "Measly bit left. Had to eat it before it went cold."

Buckler tasted a crumb from an empty dish. "And the mushroom and cauliflower bake?"

Diggs smiled guiltily. "Oh, that. No sense in lettin' the confounded stuff go t'waste. Had to polish it off, I'm afraid. Sorry about that, old stick!"

Buckler nodded as if in agreement with his gluttonous friend. "Hmm. Just as well, old chum. You'll need it to keep your strength up for tomorrow."

Diggs captured a slice of his companion's cheese. "Oh, y'don't say. Why, what's happenin' on the morrow?"

Buckler explained, "We're travelling southeast, to my brother's farm."

Diggs spotted a scone doing nothing; he snatched it. "What? Y'mean the Long Patrol are out on a march?"

Buckler tweaked his ear gently. "No, my old friend. Just you and I."

Diggs frowned as he demolished the scone. "Er, I'm no great shakes at all that trampin' an' marchin' stuff, Buck. P'raps I'd best stay home an' keep my blinkin' eye on things, don'cha know, wot?"

Buckler shook his head firmly. "Sorry, mate. It's a direct order from the great Lord Brang. You've got to accompany me all the way there and back, no excuses. Those were his very words to me."

Diggs stared miserably around. There was no more food to be had. He heaved a long-suffering sigh. "Ah, well, lackaday, poor young me. Who am I, a mere Diggs of the ranks, to argue with a Badger Lord? He must've known you'd need a cool head, some reliable chap like me, to keep you out of trouble. Well, don't worry, Buck m'laddo, I'll blinkin' well look after you!"

It was difficult for Buckler to keep a straight face. However, he managed to shake his friend's paw solemnly. "Lord Brang said I could rely on you. Thank you, my true and trusty comrade!"

3

On that shimmering summer noon, a traveller crossing the western plain toward Redwall might have viewed it as a haven of serenity. With Mossflower Wood's verdant foliage as a backdrop, the ancient sandstone Abbey towered over its surroundings. The Belltower stood silent, awaiting eventide chimes as the sloping roofs and timeworn buttresses, old dormitory windows and long, stained-glass panels reflected the sun's rays. Below, flower-bordered lawns and gardens spread from the huge main building, meandering round orchard and Abbey pool to the outer wall. Four high battlemented ramparts protected Redwall and its creatures. At the western threshold, stout oaken gates opened onto the path and ditch fronting the flatlands. Beyond those gates, the vision of tranquillity ground to a halt.

Seated at a long table on the front lawn, a group of elders tried to withstand the noise and chaos raging about them. That good mouse, Marjoram, Mother Abbess of Redwall, had to yell to make herself heard above the din. She cast a pleading glance at her friend Ruark Boldstream, Skipper of Otters.

"Please, can you not do something to stem this dreadful row, Skipper? I'm being driven out of my senses!"

The trusty otter saluted. "Leave it t'me, marm!"

Borrowing a hefty bung mallet from Cellarmole Gurjee, Skipper used the top of an empty October Ale barrel as a drum. *Boom! Boom! Buboom!*

The thunderous alarm stopped everybeast instantly. Fiddle-scraping hedgehogs, flute-twiddling squirrels, a choir of mousemaids, a group of moles twanging banjo-like instruments and numerous solo performers practising their singing. Every Redwaller involved ceased all activities. In the sudden silence that followed, Skipper dealt the barrel one more good whack. *Boom!* The brawny otter launched straight into his announcement.

"All rehearsals, an' all ructious rows, will stop forthwith. D'ye hear me? If'n the noise starts up agin, then Abbess Marj will cancel the contest for the Bard o' Redwall. Is that unnerstood? Now, sit down quietly, all of ye!"

The Redwallers obeyed dutifully, everybeast turning to glare at a little vole, who, by accident, plumped himself down on the inflated bag of a bagpipe, causing it to wail. He lowered his eyes, muttering a hasty apology. With echoes still ringing in her ears, the Abbess stood up to speak.

"Friends, we must get this event underway. So if you sit quietly, we'll call the first contestant. Er, Granvy, do you have the list, please?"

Granvy Shtuckle, an elderly hedgehog who served as Abbey Scribe and Recorder, began unrolling a long birchbark parchment. He coughed importantly.

"Ahem! Aye, marm, here 'tis. Right, it says here that Foremole Darbee will be first to sing!"

Darbee was not expecting to be called first. Burying his snout in his big digging claws, he retreated behind the other contestants, complaining in the quaint mole accent, "Burr nay, ho no, not oi, zurr. Oi never did be a wishen t'sing in ee furst place. Oi bee's too gurtly 'umble furr such ee thing, ho burr aye!"

Irately, Granvy scratched Foremole's name from the list.

"I just knew something like this'd happen! Well, who's going to perform first, eh? Speak up!"

Noisy uproar broke out afresh, until Skipper got order by whacking the ale barrel again. *Bubbooom!*

The Recorder consulted his list. "Sister Fumbril, please!"

The Dibbuns (a name bestowed on all Redwall babes) set up a rousing cheer, drowning out any objections. Fumbril, a big, jolly otter, Redwall's Infirmary nurse and Herbalist, was a huge favourite of all littlebeasts. As she tuned her small fiddle, the Dibbuns were already jigging about, shouting to her.

"Sing us a good un, Sis Fum—a dancey song!"

The good Sister happily obliged them. "Righto, me dearies. Here goes . . . one, two . . ."

She launched into the liveliest of ditties.

"When you an' me go out to tea,
oh, dear me, fiddle deedee,
we'll be the ones who scoff the scones,
an' slurp the soup with a whoopiddy doop.
We'll nibble the pies, surprise surprise,
sing pudden an' plum, rumbledy dum,
pastie an' pie, oh my, oh my.
We'll swig the cider an' chomp the cheese,
oh, give us more, you'll hear us roar,
such merry beasts are we, you see,
when we go out to tea!"

By popular Dibbun demand, she was obliged to play it again, this time at a quicker pace. The little dancers whooped and twirled joyfully. Even the elders clapped their paws in time with the music. Sister Fumbril did one more encore. She ended up flat on the lawn, mobbed by adoring Abbeybabes.

"Hurr, that'n bee's moi fayverrut, marm!" "Sing it again, Sista, more, more!"

Fumbril clasped the little ones to her affectionately. "No no, my dearies. 'Tis some other creature's turn now."

Granvy read a name out from the list. "It says here that Brother Tollum will sing."

Tollum, a fat, mournful-faced squirrel who was the official Abbey Bellringer, stepped forward.

Clearing his throat, he announced in sonorous tones, "Ahem, I will now give you a rendition from part two of *The Bellringer's Burial,* 'Oh, Lay Me Gentle and Deep.' "

A concerted groan arose from the Redwallers.

Several who had heard the song before were heard to comment, "Oh, no. That dirge can last half a day!"

"Huh, never heard anythin' so mis'rable in all me days!"

Skipper struck the barrel again. *Buboom!*

"Order there. Silence, if'n ye please, for Brother Tollum!"

At that moment, Foremole Darbee, having overcome his shyness, interrupted the proceedings. "Hurr hurr, if'n you'm doant moind, oi'll be a singen moi song naow!"

Brother Tollum looked aggrieved. "But ye didn't want to sing afore, so 'tis my turn!"

Guffy, a Dibbun molebabe, took umbrage at the Bellringer. "Yurr, zurr, doan't ee talk loik that to ee Foremole. Ee'm can sing, if'n ee'm 'aven a moind to!"

This sparked a dispute—Redwallers called out their opinions aloud.

"Tollum's right. Granvy said it was his turn." "Oh, let Foremole Darbee sing. Where's the harm?" "But it ain't right. He's already refused once!"

Brother Tollum sniffed sulkily. "Let the mole sing. It doesn't bother me!"

Foremole shook his velvety head. "Nay, zurr, you'm do ee singen. Oi don't feel loike et naow. Ee mood bee's gone offen oi some'ow!"

The molecrew set up a deep grumble of protest.

Boom! Boom! Bubooooom!

This time it was Abbess Marjoram who had struck the

barrel, with surprising force for one of her slight stature. She shouted at the noisy assembly in a stern voice, "Enough! Enough! I can put up with this no longer. The contest for Bard of Redwall is closed until you all decide to act in a proper manner! Granvy, I'll take charge of that list, please. You Redwallers, be about your business, now. I'm sure you all have chores and duties to occupy your time. Yes, what is it, Sister Fumbril?"

The jolly otter smiled winningly. "I'm sure you won't stop us dinin' in the orchard this evenin', Mother Abbess?"

Marjoram stowed both paws in her wide sleeves. "No, I suppose I won't, Sister. Providing, of course, that there are no more arguments."

There is an old saying in Mossflower Country: "There is no better food than Abbey food, and no better Abbey than Redwall to serve it." The trestle tables set up in the orchard attested to the truth of this. On the blossom-scented air of soft summer eventide, the tables were laid with clean linen, garlanded by flowers and greenery. Servers stood by, bearing jugs of pale cider, mint tea, fruit cordials and the good October Ale for which the Abbey was famed. From end to end the tables groaned under the array of fresh breads, salads, cheeses and pasties at the outer edges. Further in, there were platters of scones, tarts, cakes and pies, each with a different filling, most topped with whipped honey or meadowcream. The centrepiece was a magnificent flan of strawberries, plums and damsons set in red currant jelly on a shortcake base.

Heeding the warning from earlier that day, everybeast sat quietly. Nothing was touched until after the Abbess recited grace.

"All hail to wind, to sun and rain,
for offerings such as these,
and thanks to those who harvest them,
from soil, from bush, and trees.

We praise the skills of those good cooks,
commanded by our Friar,
who labour long in kitchen,
and toil by oven fire.
My final thanks to one and all,
who dwell in peace here at Redwall!"

The meal commenced with gusto, amidst much cheery banter from the diners. Skipper chuckled as he served the Abbess with bread and salad.

"I noticed that you said the last line o' grace with good, firm voice, marm."

A smile played around Marjoram's lips. "I merely reminded them that I'd brook no repeat of the afternoon's performance—all that ruction!"

Sister Fumbril poured cordial for her friend. "What, d'ye mean that liddle tiff? Why, marm, 'twas only a storm in a nutshell. Though I do confess, I was a bit surprised by Foremole's behaviour."

Granvy sliced himself a small wedge of soft white cheese. "Oh, Darbee doesn't mean any real harm. He's getting on in seasons now, so he's entitled to be a little grumpy at times. Age doesn't improve temper in somebeasts."

Cellarmole Gurjee gave a rumbling laugh. "Hurr hurr hurr! So oi've noticed, zurr, speshully when oi see'd you a-tryen to deal wi' yon list."

Granvy paused, the cheese halfway to his mouth. "Aye, and I've seen you the same, when somebeast disturbs your afternoon nap down in the wine cellar."

Gurjee nodded affably. "Burr aye, that bee's true enuff, zurr. Oi'm madder'n a toadybeast wot's been boiled, when moi arternoon slumber bee's asturbed!"

Skipper Ruark caught Marjoram's attention. "Marm, I think Friar Soogum would like a word with ye, if'n ye can spare him a moment."

The Abbess put aside both food and drink. "Why, of course. I'll spare him as long as he wishes. Push along there, so he can sit next t'me. Bring him here right away, please, Skipper."

It was not often that Soogum spent much time away from his beloved kitchens. The Friar was a huge, fat water vole, quite a shy beast, but a cook par excellence. Fumbling with his apron strings, he shuffled to the table. Sitting down next to Marjoram, he tugged one bushy eyebrow, the water vole equivalent of a bow. His voice was barely audible.

"Mother Abbess, is everythin' to yore likin'?"

She patted his paw fondly. "Soogum, my dear old friend, everything is perfect, doubly delicious. I don't know what our Abbey would do without your cooking skills. Now, how may I help you?"

The Friar avoided looking up. Staring fixedly at the tabletop, he replied, "Er, well, 'tis about the singin' contest. Will ye be carryin' on with it tomorrow, marm?"

Marjoram dropped her tone confidentially. "As a matter of fact, I probably will. But don't let the others know that yet. I'm keeping them stewing whilst they await my decision. Keeps them well behaved, you know. But why do you ask?"

The water vole played with some bread crumbs, lining them up in patterns, as he spoke hesitantly. "Well . . . well . . . y'see, it's just that I've got a lot on tomorrow, so I'll be too busy t'come, marm."

Skipper interrupted. "Take the day off, matey. Let yore crew do the work—you deserve a bit o' time off."

The Friar turned his shocked gaze upon the otter. "Nay, sir, I could never be doin' that, even though I have the best of assistants. There's certain things I wouldn't trust to anybeast. 'Twouldn't be right nor proper for a Redwall Friar, would it? That's why I wanted to speak with Mother Abbess."

Marjoram patted the water vole's paw again. "Have as many words as you like, Soogum. Don't be shy. You're amongst friends."

The Friar took a deep breath before letting it all out.

"Look, I know I never put my name on the list—nobeast expected me to. But here's the thing, I make up songs, y'see. Oh, yes, I invents 'em in my head an' sings 'em to meself whilst I'm workin'. Only yesterday I thought of a good song. I've been singin' it to meself ever since. So I'd like t'be considered for the contest."

Recorder Granvy topped up his mint tea. "Certainly. Every Redwaller's entitled to sing a song. But how will you sing if you can't attend, Friar?"

Soogum swept aside the bread crumbs decisively. "I'd like to sing my song here an' now, if y'please."

Granvy removed his tiny crystal spectacles and polished them furiously (always a sign that he was agitated). He shook his head several times.

"What, you mean right here and now, in the middle of a meal? Dearie me, I don't know what the rules state about that. I'll have to consult them!"

The Abbess dismissed him with a regal sweep of her paw. "Oh, confound the rules. I hereby change them. Friar Soogum, you have permission to sing where and whenever you so desire. Skipper Ruark, be so kind as to announce our Friar's song immediately."

The Otter Chieftain pounded the tabletop. "Ahoy, Redwallers! Attention, everybeast. Give good order for Friar Soogum. He's goin' to give us a song, which'll be entered into the contest. Friar!"

Mounting the table and straddling scones and pasties, Soogum beckoned. "Are ye ready, Drull? Don't make the key too high."

One of the kitchen staff, a small hogwife, began tuning a Hogalino. This is a stringed instrument, which hedgehogs hold upside down, plucking it with their headspikes by moving it back and forth.

After a short introduction, the Friar launched into his song. He had a good baritone voice and was able to quaver and warble readily.

"Pray hearken to this humble beast,
no warrior am I.
I crave no spear or sword to wield,
no arrow to let fly.
No foebeast have I ever slain,
my friend, I'll tell you why,
because I'm but a simple cook,
come try my apple pie!

"Let fighters from the battle rest,
victorious but sore,
they throng into my dining hall,
and what do they ask for?
More enemies to charge against,
no no, when war is through,
they'd trade their vict'ry medals,
for a bowl of my hot stew!
So look you on this humble beast,
and, pray, regard me well.
My paw has never swung a blade,
foul vermin for to fell.
My kitchen is no battlefield,
I'll shout no loud war cry.
Because I'm but a simple cook,
come try my apple pie!"

The Friar's ditty was so well received that Redwallers pounded the tables, cheering him to the echo. Some of the molecrew (who, it is common knowledge, can become quite emotional over the simplest things) wept openly into large, spotty kerchiefs.

"Boohurrhurr, oi do dearly loike songs about plain 'umble beasts. Will ee singen et agin, zurr?"

Abbess Marjoram addressed the assembly. "That was a fine ballad, and well sung, though there is no need for our friend to sing it again. I think he deserves far more applause for the delicious dishes he produces for us day in and day out. Friar Soogum, please take a bow!"

There was another round of wild cheering, but the good water vole was not there to acknowledge it. Being the timid beast he was, the Friar had fled back to his kitchens.

In the tree line, beyond the open sward at the Abbey's south wall, vermin lay watching and listening. A ferret named Raddi nudged her mate, eyeing Redwall enviously.

"Wot I wouldn't give ter be livin' in there, eh. A nice liddle pond, an orchard full o' fruit, an' woodlanders cookin' up all those good vittles!"

Her mate, Daclaw, nodded agreement. "Aye, they must have a big cookin' place in there. When the breeze was right, I could smell bread bakin', pies an' cakes, too. I 'ad to quit sniffin', t'stop me guts rumblin' an' growlin'. Redwall must be a rare ole place, mates."

A young stoat named Globby piped up. "Well, why don't we climb over the wall an' slay 'em all, exceptin' the cooks? They're only woodlanders, aren't they? We're Ravagers!"

A voice, low and menacing, silenced further talk. "Don't turn around. Keep looking straight ahead. I'm right behind you, carrying my sword."

It could be only one creature, their commander, Zwilt the Shade. How long had he been eavesdropping on them? Anybeast who had spoken swallowed nervously, hoping they had not condemned themselves with loose talk. Zwilt was merciless. There would be no running or hiding from him. Many vermin were of the opinion that it was not wise to even think the wrong thing in his presence.

Daclaw, the ferret who was group leader, ventured a reply. "Sire, we're just watchin' the place as ye ordered. Anybeast who steps outside those walls will be trapped an' captured by us. That was wot ye wanted, eh, Lord?"

Zwilt moved swift and silent. Raddi felt him standing alongside her; the hairs bristled upon her neck. She held her breath, not knowing what to expect.

The dead black eyes of Zwilt swept over the vermin band. He hissed scornfully, "Idiots, ye haven't the brain of a worm betwixt ye. Listen to me and learn. Redwall Abbey must never be touched. Ye don't have to understand that—just obey it. Leave the thinking to those with brains. Clear?"

Their heads bobbed in silent unison. Raddi was about to relax when she felt the broadsword at her neck.

Zwilt watched her throat pulsing against the blade's edge. He leaned close to the terror-stricken ferret, taunting her. "You, what have ye got to say for yourself?"

Raddi's voice was reduced to a fearful whimper. "Nu-nu-nothin', Lord."

It was one way of instilling obedience into others. Zwilt persisted with his torment of Raddi.

"Only deadbeasts have nothing to say. You're not a deadbeast, are ye?"

He uttered a low chuckle as he watched her striving to think of the right reply, but she had lost the power of speech. Keeping the broadsword at her neck, he turned his attention to Daclaw, knowing that he was Raddi's mate. "You tell me—is she a deadbeast?"

Daclaw knew what to say.

"Aye, she is, Sire, unless she lives only to serve you."

With eye-blurring speed, Zwilt swept the sword at Daclaw's head, stopping its point a hairsbreadth from his eyeball. The sable enjoyed seeing the fear of death in others. Daclaw was openmouthed, rigid with naked fright. Zwilt returned the weapon to his belt casually.

"A good answer, my friend, very good!"

He paced quietly backward until he was behind the group. None dared turn to see where he was. Again he spoke to Daclaw.

"If nobeast has left the Abbey by sunset, then split your force into four groups. You watch the front gates from the ditch on the west side. The others can take up positions where they can see the three small wallgates. Until then, stay here and keep your eyes on that building."

*

It was nearing sunset; none of the Ravagers had dared to move. Daclaw was shocked when the young stoat called Globby stood up and stretched himself.

Daclaw whispered hoarsely, "Wot are ye doin'? Get down, ye fool!"

Globby twitched his snout impudently. "Fool yoreself. Zwilt's long gone—take a look."

It was Raddi who ventured a peek. "Yore right, but how'd ye know Zwilt was gone?"

Globby shrugged. "He always does that. Whenever Zwilt tells ye to watch somethin', well, do it. Then count ten an' take a look behind ye. Hah, that's why they calls 'im the Shade—he's always gone."

Daclaw felt the need to regain his authority, so he pushed Globby roughly in the chest. "Think yore clever, eh? Well, you'll be dead clever afore long if'n ye carry on like that, smart mouth!"

The young stoat merely laughed. "Cummon, let's split up an' watch those liddle gates. Me'n Dinko'll take the back un. Let's go, mate."

Dinko, an equally forward young rat, bounded off after Globby, who was already on his way.

Daclaw called after them, "I never told youse t'go. Wait for my order—come back 'ere!"

Raddi waved a dismissive paw. "Ah, let 'em go. Those two are troublemakers—we're better off without 'em."

Daclaw took his mate's advice and set about picking watchers for the other gates. He winked at Raddi. "Yore right. Cummon, me'n'you'll watch the front gates together. We can take turns sleepin'."

Not far from the east wickergate at the back wall, the two young Ravagers had found a blackberry patch. Dinko sat in the loam, his lips dyed purple with juice.

"This is the life, mate— 'Ey, wot are ye doin' there? Git down outta that tree!"

Globby kept his eyes on a high branch as he climbed a

sycamore which grew reasonably close to the wall. "I can't get the smell o' that cookin' out me snout. Those scones, that bread, right out the oven, an' that cake. I've never tasted real cake afore!"

Dinko almost choked on a berry. "Git down, ye knot'ead, afore ye fall an' 'urt yoreself!"

Globby stopped to rest on a sturdy limb. "I'll be alright—don't you worry, cully. See that branch up there? If'n I climb along it, I'll bet I could jump an' reach the walltop. I'm a good climber."

Dinko was not so sure. "Ye'll get us both killed if'n Zwilt comes back. Don't chance it, Glob!"

Globby carried on climbing. "Yore like an ole frog wirra warty bum. Stop worryin'. Look, you stay 'ere—this won't take long. I'll be in an' out afore ye knows it. Tell yer wot, I'll bring ye a pie back, all for yoreself. How'd ye like that?"

Dinko spat out a sour blackberry. "Wot sorta pie?"

Globby, having reached the desired branch, looked down. "I dunno. Wot sort d'yer like? Apple or maybe plum? Suit yerself."

Dinko gave it some thought. "See if'n they got apple an' plum, an' damson, too, or strawberry."

Globby sniggered. "Wot, all in one pie?"

Dinko looked indignant. "Well, ye never know. Daclaw said they must 'ave a big cookin' place in there. I betcha they could cook all sorts o' pies."

Globby ventured out onto the branch, halting as it wobbled slightly. "Righto. I'll see wot I kin get!"

A moment later, he made his daring leap and was clinging to the battlements, hauling himself up, muttering, "Knowed I could do it. Now, where's the big cookin' place?"

4

The endless hiss of breaking waves was softened to a weary sigh by the ebbing tide. Gulls wheeled and soared over the dawn-lit sea. Clear skies and a rapidly blooming sun predicted another fine summer day. Leaving two sets of pawtracks in their wake, Buckler and Diggs travelled east from Salamandastron.

Buckler was packing one of the bellropes next to his long blade. He marched energetically, with a spring to his pawstep. Diggs, however, was already lagging behind, panting and blowing. He was burdened down by an overfull haversack, bulging with food. The bellrope he carried trailed the ground, constantly tripping him. Buckler halted, waiting for him to catch up.

"Pick those paws up, mate. It's a wonder you can walk at all. The size of that breakfast you scoffed would've staggered a regiment. Where'd you shove it all?"

The tubby Diggs hitched up his huge backpack. "Take my tip, old scout. A chap needs lots o' fodder t'keep himself goin', wot. Ever heard the sayin' that an army marches on its jolly old stomach?"

Hiding a smile, Buckler jollied him along. "I'll march on your jolly old stomach, if y'don't keep up. Hup two three,

Diggs—let's see you stepping out. I'd like to get to Redwall while I'm still young enough to enjoy the place."

Diggs caught up with an amazing burst of speed. "Red flippin' wall! Y'mean the blinkin' Abbey?"

Buckler nodded. "Must be. I've not heard of any other Abbeys called Redwall, have you?"

The revelation spurred Diggs to increase his pace further. "I say, simply spiffin', wot! All those wonderful vittles, the banquets an' whatnot, picnics an' super suppers. Hoho, I'll bet breakfast's a real treat. Wonder if they serve it t'you in bed, wot?"

He halted suddenly in a swirl of sand, rounding wrathfully upon his companion. "Just a tick . . . you cad! You flippin' rotter! You never said anything t'me about goin' to Redwall. I thought we were goin' to visit your bally brother. Oh, yah boo sucks t'you, Buckler blinkin' Kordyne. Some friend you jolly well turned out t'be, wot!"

Buckler had to double march to keep up with his indignant companion. "Sorry, mate. I must've forgotten to tell you we were going to Redwall first. But what d'you suppose these ropes are for?"

Diggs continued his rapid pace, waving his paws about in agitation. "How'm I supposed t'know, eh? You said your brother was a flippin' farmer. I thought ropes were things farmers used for . . . for tyin' up their confounded crops, or whatever. Alls I know is that this rope I'm carryin' is jolly heavy, heavier'n yours, I bet, wot!"

Buckler explained. "They're both the same weight, because they're bellropes. A gift from Lord Brang to Abbess Marjoram. He asked me to deliver them."

Diggs huffed. "Oh, very kind of him, t'be sure. Hah, you'd think a chap could deliver his own bloomin' bellropes instead o' weighin' a couple o' poor, weary young travellers down with the blighters, eh, wot!"

Leaving behind the shoreline, they cut off into the dunelands, digging their paws deep into the warm sand as they surmounted each hill. Diggs was immensely cheered by the prospect of a Redwall visit. However, he had still not completely forgiven Buckler for his loss of memory on the previous evening. So he spoke his mixed thoughts aloud.

"Hahahoho, Redwall, wot wot! Loads o' munchables, I'll be bound. I've heard the scoff there's second to none. Indeed, they prob'ly serve seconds all the time, eh! But you, y'scoundrel, wouldn't give a chap a single clue we were goin' to the place. Sneaky codwoofler! Er, I say, Buck old lad, it must be about time for lunch. What say we halt an' break out the old nosebag? All this trampin' about gets a chap confounded hungry."

His companion pointed up at the sun. "See, when that's in the centre of the sky, it'll be midday. That's the correct time to eat lunch. Until then, we keep going, alright?"

Diggs was a notorious creature at chunnering. He began dropping behind again, muttering darkly, "Huh, bally sun in the centre o' the bloomin' sky? Might be all season before that happens. A chap could starve t'death, shrivel up like a leaf an' be carted off by the blinkin' breeze. 'Tain't right, that's what 'tain't. Bet you won't shed a tear for me, though!"

To stem the tide of chunnering, Buckler made a suggestion. "How about striking up a cheery marchin' song, to help us along the way, eh?"

Diggs was not enchanted with the idea. "Yah, go'n' boil your beastly bottom! How can a chap skip along warblin' some jolly song when he's about to collapse from starvation? I'd die before we got much further. Oh, you'd like that, wouldn't you, wot? A grinnin' young skeleton whose last words were a line from some silly marchin' ditty. Indeed, 'tis a sad fact, my fiendish friend, that'd fit in with your wicked old plan. Then you could trot on alone to Redwall an' scoff all the tuck yourself. Well, you don't fool me for a ruddy moment. Shame on you, my one-time travellin' companion. Shame an' fie, I say!"

Buckler turned, glaring at his laggardly friend. "Are you goin' t'stop that bloomin' chunnerin', or do I have to kick your tail into the middle of next season to get a bit of peace!"

This threat did not bother Diggs, who carried on in full flow. "So, this is what it's come to, eh? Well, kick my tender young tail as much as y'please, sah. There's no law against a chap chunnering. I'll chunner as much as I bally well like—so there!"

Admitting defeat, Buckler dropped the haversack from his back. He sat down in the lee of a high sandhill, calling wearily to Diggs, "Righto, mate, let's have lunch, before you either starve or drive me insane with your chunnering!"

The plump complainer plopped down beside him, rubbing his paws and chortling gleefully. "Splendid day for a spot o' lunch, wot. Shall we dine from my rations or yours? Better make it yours, 'cos you've already got your haversack off. Heehee!"

Tearing open Buckler's supplies, he enthused happily, "Oh, I say, just the ticket, bread'n'cheese, an' a drop o' good old cider. What ho, Buck—nothin' like simple fare when a feller's famished. Hello, what's this? A jar of plums preserved in honey, what luck. That'll hit the jolly old spot, wot wot! Well, well, who'd have thought old Cooky would bung in some vegetable turnovers? Raspberry cordial, too, an' a hefty old fruitcake. It'll lighten your load once I've dealt with that. Hah, an' will you look at this—"

Buckler rapped his paw with the wooden bellrope end. "Hold up, there. This is only a light lunch, not a midsummer-eve banquet. Glutton, you'd wolf the lot if I let you!"

Diggs sucked his paw resentfully. "No need to break a chap's limb over a mouthful of tuck!"

Buckler shared out enough for a frugal repast. They dined on bread and cheese, a slice of fruitcake apiece and some cider. Diggs finished his in record time, then sat watching every mouthful his friend ate, licking his lips longingly.

When it became clear he was getting no more, he lay back upon the sun-warmed sand, complaining, "Hope we have afternoon tea at a respectable time. I'm still pretty hungry, y'know. Another cob o' that good cheese an' a pasty wouldn't go amiss, wot!"

Buckler ignored the irrepressible Diggs, who drew patterns in the sand, belched, excused himself, then lay back, closing his eyes.

Buckler snorted. "Y'great, idle lump, you're not going to nod off. We haven't made a half day's march yet!"

Diggs twitched his nose. " 'Sno good talkin' t'me, old lad. I'm asleep, y'see. Didn't sleep much last night, what with this bally journey hangin' over me, an' after all that fibbin' you did, not lettin' on about a visit to Redwall. Dearie me, it's depressin' my spirit so much I'll need a good few hours' shuteye before I even think about more pawsloggin' again."

Buckler decided he had taken just about enough. Shouldering his haversack, he rolled Diggs roughly over, relieving him of the bellrope and his backpack. He walked off, carrying the lot, without looking back.

Diggs sat bolt upright. "I say, where'n the name o' fiddlesticks d'you think you're goin?"

Without turning, Buckler shouted back, "I'm goin' it alone—don't need you. Report back to Lord Brang, see what he has to say!"

Suddenly Diggs was alongside him, claiming back his equipment. "Well, hoity-toity sirrah, who said I wasn't goin', wot? Just you try an' stop me. They don't call me old Determined Diggs for nothin', y'know. Step along lively now, laddie buck. I know, what about a good old marchin' song? Remember that one we made up when we were both leverets?"

Buckler suddenly found himself smiling. "I certainly do, mate. Go on, you lead off!"

Away they went at the double, often changing step and back kicking. It was more of a comic dance, which they had performed at mess parties as cadets. Sometimes they sang solo, though mostly together.

"They call me Diggs . . . an' my name's Buck,
If you draw a blade on us you're out o' luck!
I'm an expert with a sword!
I'm a champion with a spoon!
We'll fight or feast with anybeast
come mornin', night or noon.
So left right left right,
Wot ho, me pretty one!
Is your ma a good ole cook,
an' where do you come from?
Let's walk you home . . . don't go alone,
you charmin' little duck.
Then introduce your ma to us,
our names are Diggs an' Buck!
So left right left right,
are we nearly there?
Salute the Colonel's daughter,
parade around the square.
We're jolly brave an' handsome,
at war or scoffin' tuck,
we're perilously perfect 'cos . . .
they call us Diggs an' Buck!"

They sang it through again, trying to outdo each other with sidesteps and fancy twiddles. When they halted, both hares were panting and laughing.

Buckler adjusted his backpack. "It's been a few seasons since we sang that together."

Diggs flopped down on the warm sand. "Rather. Blinkin' wonder we still remember it, wot!"

Buckler noticed that the sandhills were getting smaller. "That's the worst of the dunes behind us, mate, though there's a tidy bit o' this heath an' scrubland still to go. Come on, matey, up y'come—there's plenty o' daylight left yet."

They pressed onward, with Diggs beginning to lag and chunner again.

"Blinkin' grasshoppers chirrupin'—it's enough t'drive a poor beast potty. Aye, an' those bees could pick better tunes to hum. Bloomin' monotonous buzzin', eh?"

Buckler suddenly held up a paw. "Hush—can you hear that noise?"

Diggs carried on until he bumped into his friend's back. "Noise? What confounded noise? A rowdy butterfly, d'ye think!"

Buckler clapped a paw around Diggs's mouth. "Give your jaws a rest an' listen. Sounds like somebeast in trouble t'me. Over there, behind that hill—d'ye hear it?"

Diggs cocked up his ears, removing Buckler's paw. "More'n one beast, I think. Shall we take a peep?"

Dropping their haversacks, the pair crouched low, then crept toward the source of the outcry.

A scrawny-looking fox and a hulking weasel had captured a young shrewmaid. They were trying to get a rope halter around her neck, threatening her with all manner of torments.

"Yew better 'old still, missy, or I'll knock yer snout outta joint, so 'elp me I will!"

However, the shrewmaid was a feisty little creature, giving back as good as she got. She swung the rope, striking the scrawny fox in one eye.

"Leggo a me, ye snot-bubblin' grubbers. Git yore filfy paws offa me!"

The hulking weasel drew a wicked-looking knife. "Grab 'er neck, mate. We'll see wot she 'as t'say when I carves 'er tongue out!"

Watching from the tall grass to one side of the hill, the two hares realised it was time to step in on the vermin. Buckler drew his long rapier, but Diggs stayed his paw.

"Allow me t'deal with this little fracas, old lad. I'll give you a hoot if I need you t'lend a jolly old paw, wot?"

Buckler watched as Diggs unwound his sling and loaded it with a sizeable rock.

"Go ahead, then, be my guest. But I don't think those vermin'll fall for that old trick."

Diggs winked confidently, as he swaggered toward the scene. "We'll bally well see what we shall see, matey!"

The tubby young hare called out in a commanding tone. (He could be rather good at commanding tones, when required.) "I say, you two, scraggy-bottom an' clod-head! Take your foul paws off that young creature this very instant! Refrain an' desist, sirrahs, an' pack it in!"

The weasel advanced on Diggs, wielding his blade. "Are you talkin' to us, rabbet?"

Diggs halted half a pace from the weasel. "Rabbet, is it? Have a care, barrelbottom—you happen to be addressing Subaltern Meliton Gubthorpe Digglethwaite. But let's not stand on ceremony. You can address me as sir. Now, unpaw that charmin' shrew."

The scraggy fox let the rope go. Joining the weasel, he sneered at the newcomer. "Or wot, eh?"

As he was saying this, the fox produced a wooden club.

The shrewmaid called out a warning. "Watch them—they're sly, dangerous vermin!"

Diggs chuckled nonchalantly, edging around until he was standing close to both his enemies. "Pish tush, m'dear, sly, dangerous?" He faced the weasel squarely, still twirling the loaded sling playfully. "Let me give you a demonstration of my prowess before you decide on attacking me, wot! D'ye see that skylark up there?"

The weasel stared up at the empty sky. "Where? Wot skylark—"

That was as far as he got. Diggs swung the heavily loaded sling up, thwacking it hard beneath the vermin's chin. He carried on with the blow, up and over. The rock-loaded sling made a distinctive *Bonk!* as it struck the scraggy fox between both ears.

The fox was out cold, but the weasel was sitting on the ground, making odd noises as he hugged his chin.

Buckler walked up, shaking his head. "When'll you ever learn, mate? You should've belted the fox under the chin first. The second hit would've put that weasel's spark out, if you'd have smacked him over the head."

Diggs consulted the half-stunned weasel. "You must have a flippin' granite jaw. Didn't that knock you out, old lad?"

The weasel looked dully up, nursing broken teeth and a bitten tongue. He said what sounded like, "Mmmmufffm!"

Diggs nodded sympathetically. "Sorry about that, old scout. Here, try this one!"

Whop! The sling bounced off the vermin's brutish head. He fell back, out to the world.

Diggs nodded to his friend. "I'll remember that next time—little un to the chin, big un right on the bonce, wot!"

The little shrewmaid was watching them both, giggling merrily. "Youse two are funny rabbets."

Diggs huffed as he proffered her a sweeping bow. "Hares, marm, Salamandastron hares of the Long Patrol. I'm Diggs, an' this is my friend Buck, wot! Pray, who have we the pleasure of addressing?"

The shrewmaid bobbed a quick curtsy. "Me name's Flibber, but youse kin call me Flib."

Buckler prodded the unconscious vermin with a footpaw.

"Pleased to meet ye, Flib. What did these two want with you?"

Flib shrugged. "Huh, I dunno. They jus' snucked up on me an' tried t'drag me off sumplace, dunno where!"

She took the knife from the weasel and the club from the scraggy fox, commenting grimly, "But they won't do it again—no blunkin' vermins will. Hah, jus' lerrem try, now that I've gorra few weppins meself!"

Diggs enquired, "What are you doin' out here on your own, missy? Where are you from, wot?"

She pointed the blade at him aggressively. "None of yer bizness, nosey!"

Diggs went off to get their supply haversacks, chunnering as usual. "Mind my own jolly business, indeed. There's flippin' gratitude for you. Lay two vermin low, save the wretch's life, an' that's all the bloomin' thanks one gets. If I hadn't made her my business, she'd be in a bally bad spot now, indeed she would, ungrateful liddle snip. Huh, young uns these days, wot!"

Buckler tried reasoning with Flib. "It wouldn't hurt to say where you hail from, Flib. What about your parents? I'll wager they're prob'ly quite worried about you."

It was all to no avail. She scowled at him. "Yore nosier'n yer pal, you are. Lissen, yew attend to yore bizness, an' I'll see t'mine, alright?"

Buckler turned away from her. "Suit y'self, miss."

Diggs, returning with their gear, was greatly cheered when his friend announced that they would camp there for the night. He promptly began setting up preparations for a meal. Flib feigned indifference, though she spoke to Diggs.

"Worra youse gonna do wid those two scum, eh?"

Diggs cast an eye over the two unconscious vermin. "Couldn't say, really. Er, what d'you suggest?"

The shrewmaid tested the edge of her knife blade. "Leave it t'me. I'll slay 'em wid this!"

Buckler swiftly wrested the weapon from her grasp. "You'll do no such thing! Vermin or not, they're helpless creatures, unable to defend themselves."

Not daunted, she grabbed her club and waved it. "Stan' outta me way, youse. They woulda slayed me!"

Buckler's long rapier sent the club flying. "You savage little murderer—keep away from them!"

Flib sucked her paw, scowling at him. "Yew two are daft.

Yer a right pair o' softies. Don't yer know that the only good vermin is a dead un? That's wot ole Jango sez!"

Diggs nodded as he chopped up a fruit salad. "I've heard that, too. Who's this Jango feller?"

She curled her lip contemptuously at him. "I've told yew once, mind yer own bizness, fatty!"

Buckler winked at Diggs. "If that's the way she wants things, mate, then let her be. She can sit apart from us and mind her own bloomin' business, for all I care!"

Diggs agreed stoutly. "Fair enough by me, old scout. She can sit alone in solitary blinkin' splendour, for all I care. Aye, an' she can shift for her bally self. I ain't givin' no supper to that ill-mannered little spitwhiskers, nor a drop t'drink, wot. I should jolly well think not, so there!"

Flib sat apart from them, her nose in the air. "I don't blinkin' well care!"

Diggs would not let it go. He retorted, "An' we don't jolly well care that you don't blinkin' well care, so yah boo sucks t'you, marm!"

The moment the two vermin began to stir and groan, Buckler took the rope halter to them. He bound the weasel and the fox back-to-back, tying both forepaws and footpaws tightly.

Pretending that she cared little, Flib commented, "Worra ye gonna do wid the scum now, eh?"

Buckler answered without looking at her. "Don't know, really. Haven't made up my mind yet."

Shades of evening were streaking the sky as Buckler joined his friend by their little fire. "So, young Diggs, what've we got here for supper?"

The tubby young hare was a very good cook. He announced the menu aloud. "Some summer fruit salad, toasted cheese on oatcakes, slab o' fruitcake an' a drop o' the jolly old dandelion cordial t'wash it down. How does that sound t'ye, young sir, wot?"

His friend rubbed paws together, pointedly ignoring the shrewmaid sitting by with her nose in the air. "Mmmm, just the stuff t'feed two Long Patrollers!" He bit into an oatcake, topped thickly with cooked cheese.

Diggs slurped down fruit salad as though he had lived through a famine season. Dipping fruitcake into the honeyed juice, he made loud sucking noises.

Flib suddenly slumped on the sand, allowing a strangled sob to escape.

Diggs looked up from his soggy cake. "I say, did you hear somethin'—sounded like a bloomin' toad bein' throttled, wot?"

Buckler replied conversationally, "Y'know, if I was a foolish little creature, a shrew, let's say, well, I wouldn't go about insulting those who helped me an' being an ill-mannered young grump. D'you know what I mean, Diggs?"

The tubby hare sucked juice from his paws. "Indeed, old top, I know exactly what y'mean. No excuse for bad behaviour, wot. I think I'd stop blubberin' an' beg chaps' pardons, show 'em I was civilized an' whatnot. Who knows, there might even be a spot o' supper left for the silly little swab!"

A moment went by, then Flib took the hint. Rubbing her eyes, she shuffled to the fire. Staring at her footpaws, she murmured, "M'sorry f'bein' rude."

Diggs began milking the situation, holding a paw to one ear and calling out like an irate old colonel, "Eh, what's that y'say? Speak up, young un, out with it!"

Buckler heard the shrewmaid's teeth gritting as she sang out lustily, "I said I'm sorry f'bein' rude. I 'pologise for me bad manners!"

Diggs kept up his aged-colonel act. "Hah, did ye hear the little maggot, Blademaster Buckler? I s'pose she thinks that entitles her to some of our bloomin' supper, wot?"

Buckler nudged his friend hard. "Right, that's enough, mate. Apologies accepted, Flib. Come and sit here. Diggs, serve our guest with supper, please."

She ate like a madbeast, cramming everything in with all the speed she could muster.

Diggs passed her a beaker of cordial. "Whoa, marm, slow down before ye go bang! Here, take a sip o' this, slowly now. Sufferin' stewpots, how long is it since you last had vittles, wot?"

Flib chewed hard, swallowed, then sighed. "Caw, nothin' like vikkles when yer 'ungry, eh? It's a couple o' days since I 'ad a feed."

Buckler refilled her beaker. "So now will you tell us what you're doing out here all on your own, bein' attacked by vermin?"

At that point, the scraggy fox, who was now wide awake, shouted angrily, "Untie us, I'm warnin' ye. Cut us loose right now!"

Buckler rose. Bowing to his supper companions, he drew his long rapier. "Pardon me a moment, please."

Crossing to where the vermin lay bound, he began assisting them to stand. "C'mon, up on your hunkers. That's the stuff, cullies!" Buckler the Blademaster circled them, swishing the air with his long, lethal blade.

"Cut ye loose, d'ye say? I'll cut you, ye hardfaced villains, though it mightn't be loose!"

The hulking weasel and the scrawny fox wailed in terror as he came at them with the whirring sword. *Whip! Snip! Whizz!* A few expert strokes shaved the whiskers from the petrified pair. Buckler chuckled grimly. "I'd hold very still if'n I was you. Don't want t'get in the way of my blade, now, do we?"

Keen steel slashed through the weasel's belt, causing his ragged pantaloons to fall round his footpaws. *Ting!* A brass earring was chopped neatly from the fox's earlobe. *Swish!* He lost a tail bracelet. *Thwup!* A shabby sleeve dropped from the weasel's dirty shirt. *Pingpingping!* This was the sound of three fancy bone buttons shooting off the fox's tawdry waistcoat.

Buckler surveyed his work, leaning on his sword hilt. "What d'ye think, Miz Flib. What next?"

The shrewmaid bellowed savagely, "Their ears, snouts-'n'tails, then their necks!"
The vermin collapsed on the sand, pleading pitifully.
"Aaarr no, sir, y'wouldn't do that, sir!"
"Don't kill us, yer Lordship. We've got families!"
"Aye liddle uns an' wives. Spare us fer their sakes!"
Buckler's eyes went cold; he kicked them both. "Get up, up, both of ye! Snake-tongued liars. If I believed ye, I'd finish both of ye right now just t'save any poor beast the misery an' shame of havin' the like of you as fathers. Now, which way am I pointin'?"
"North, sir, yer pointin' north," wailed the fox.
Buckler growled through clenched teeth, "Aye, north 'tis. Go now, an' don't stop for the next three sunsets, or I promise ye'll be flybait!"
A few stinging smacks from the narrow flat of his blade sent them scurrying awkwardly off. Still tied back-to-back and paw-to-paw, they stumbled and tripped off into the falling dusk.
To say that Flib was impressed was an understatement. She sat wide-eyed, whispering, "I never seen anybeast that good wirra blade, never!"
Diggs patted the shrewmaid's paw. "Indeed, an' you ain't likely to, missy. You've just witnessed a Salamandastron Blademaster, the best there is. But y'must remember, he was only toyin' with 'em, right, mate?"
Buckler speared a slice of apple from the fruit salad, flipped it up with his swordpoint and caught it in his mouth. He sat down, winking at Flib. "Right!"

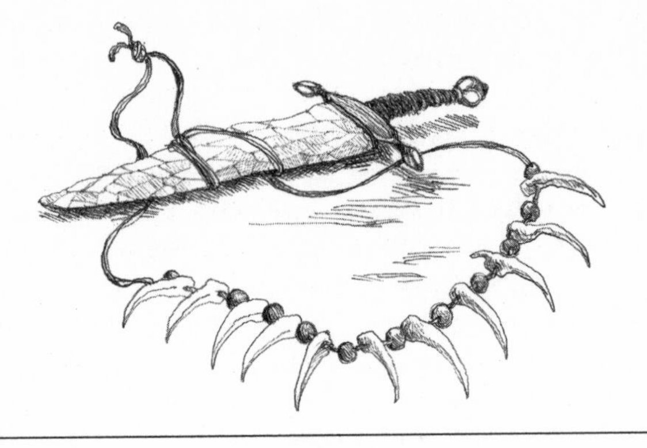

5

Zwilt the Shade waited until three of his Ravagers, with their two small captives, stopped to rest. Then he made a silent and unexpected appearance behind them. The leader of the vermin, a weasel called Grakk, spun around as the polecat tapped him lightly on the shoulder.

"Lord Zwilt, we were just—" Zwilt silenced him by raising a paw. "I know, Grakk. You were just stopping to rest before you carried on to Althier. Where did you capture the shrews?"

Grakk pointed with his spear. "By the south bend of the River Moss. Their tribe were camped there, Sire. These two had strayed off into the trees, so we took them."

Tugging gently on the halter about their necks, Zwilt drew the young ones closer. They were gagged and blindfolded; both looked exhausted.

The polecat nodded as he looked them over. "Good work, Grakk. You did well. The Sable Quean will be pleased when I tell her. I will take them to Althier."

The weasel saluted with his spear. "Lord!"

Zwilt wound the halter around one paw. "Go back and see if the shrewbeasts have any more little offerings for us."

Grakk and the other two Ravagers, both weasels, stole off into the woodlands.

Althier was the secret place. Only a chosen few of the Ravagers were allowed to be there. The main body of the vermin were camped half a league away in the depths of Mossflower Wood. In this way, there was no well-trampled pawpath, which would reveal the Sable Quean's location.

The two young shrews were stumbling with exhaustion as the Shade led them to the great oak. He tapped on the concealed door in its trunk. Two vermin guards admitted him, leading the new captives down a twisting tunnel into a large central chamber. The ceiling was formed by the arched roots of the mighty tree above. This was no vermin achievement—Althier had been constructed countless seasons before by far more noble beasts.

Prodding his little prisoners, Zwilt guided them to a side room. The Ravager standing guard stepped aside as Zwilt swept in with the shrews.

They blinked in the torch and lantern light as Zwilt flicked off their blindfolds with his swordtip. Both took a pace back at the scene which confronted them. Raised on two steps was a broad stone seat covered with soft mosses, dried grass and rugs made from the fur of beasts. Lounging gracefully upon it was a creature of barbaric beauty. Her fur was shining black and thick, with undertones of rich, dark brown. She was slender of limb, but lithe and strong. Her nosetip and ears were a dainty pink; her eyes, with a slight almond curve, glittered like two dark jewels. Beneath a fine silken cloak of regal purple, a necklace of snake fangs adorned her elegant neck.

The young shrews forgot their plight momentarily. They stared at her in awe. Crouched on the bottom step of the stone seat, an ancient rat clad in tattered raiment gave them a toothless smile.

"Is she not wonderful to look upon, my little dears? Bow your heads to Vilaya the Sable Quean!"

Her words seemed to break the spell. The younger of the shrews broke out sobbing. "Waaahaaah, I wanna go 'ome to Mammy!"

Vilaya bared a set of perfect sharp white teeth at him. "Be silent or I will eat you!"

The venom with which she spat out the words frightened the shrew into silence. She gestured to a guard. "Put them with the others!"

They were hustled swiftly off. From a distance, the sobs of the little shrew could be heard afresh.

Zwilt leaned on his sword hilt as he addressed Vilaya. "There are more where they came from. Shrews always have big broods. I told Grakk to go back and look for others. Though I think you already have enough."

Vilaya replied scathingly, "I will tell you when I have enough. Your job is to obey my commands, not to stand here giving opinions and bandying words with your Quean."

Zwilt knew how dangerous the Sable Quean could be. Avoiding further argument, he shrugged. "What would you have me do, then, Majesty?"

Vilaya let Dirva, the old rat, speak for her.

"There's been reports of river rats down on the Southstream—Grullba's crew, they say. Quean Vilaya thinks they would be a valuable addition to our Ravagers. She needs somebeast to challenge Grullba and defeat him. The river rats would follow one who could do it."

It was a rare thing for anybeast to see Zwilt the Shade smile, but smile he did. Drawing his broadsword, he cleaved the air in a deft pattern, making the wide blade thrum.

"Grullba Deathwind, eh? I've heard of his skill with the battleaxe. When I've slain him, I'll take off his head with his own weapon and bring them both here for you to see, Majesty."

Vilaya shook her head at the grisly prospect. "Forget the head of some oafish River Rat Chieftain. All I wish to hear is that you've added his crew to my army of Ravagers. Only that will please me."

Zwilt extended his sword at eye level, speaking as he peered down the length of its blade. "Then we will be strong enough in numbers to conquer Redwall Abbey. It will fall before us like an old dead tree!"

Vilaya stared at him for a moment, then turned away. As if ignoring Zwilt, she remarked to the old rat Dirva, "Does this fool never listen to the wisdom of his Quean?"

Stung by the slight, Zwilt looked up from his sword. "Victory and conquest are the only things that are wise!"

The Sable Quean closed her eyes and waved a languid paw at her ancient confidante. "This beast is beginning to tire me. Dirva, explain our plan to him again."

Chuckling at Zwilt's humiliation, Dirva outlined the plan briefly. "There is no need for warfare. Battles are a gamble in which one side must be defeated. Redwall Abbey has never suffered defeat. The conquering tyrants and vermin hordes who have been vanquished from that Abbey's walls are lost to memory. Their bones have long turned to dust. So, how do we achieve a victory over Redwall, and all the country of Mossflower?"

Zwilt's dead black eyes bored into the speaker. "Tell me."

The Sable Quean prowled down from her throne. Slowly circling the tall beast, she took up the explanation. "It's quite simple. We leave Redwall alone. They cannot fight what they do not see. The Abbey, and all this land, is inhabited mostly by woodlanders, would you agree? Good, honest, hardworking creatures, yes?"

Zwilt nodded, allowing her to continue.

"Woodlanders with families, relatives and friends. The young ones, their babes, their kindred, are the hope of the future, the very lifeblood of peaceful creatures. They would do anything to protect their brood, even fight. But how can they fight what is not there? The worry, the grief and sorrow at the loss of their dearest treasure. Where are their young ones? Are they alive or dead? No woodlander or Abbeydweller will know until I speak to them on my terms. Give me what I want, and your families will be allowed to live. They will, believe me, because the alternative would be too awful for them to imagine. That is my plan, Zwilt."

Returning the broadsword to his belt, the Shade nodded, then paused. "When will all this happen, Majesty?"

She moved close, whispering in his ear, "When I think the time is right. Once we have control, I will need Ravagers to enforce my will. I trust only you, my loyal commander, to help me in all things. Remember, the rewards will be great, and only we two shall share them. Now go and do as your Quean bids."

Zwilt bowed his head slightly. "Your wish is my command!"

Watching the tall figure striding away, Vilaya went back to her throne. Dirva waited until he had left the side chamber.

"I think he got your message, but I keep feeling that Zwilt the Shade would rather wage war on Redwall."

The Sable Quean produced a slim knife from the end of her snake fang necklace. "He would be dead and at Hellgates before he could shout charge. One scratch from my little toy would see to that."

Carefully, she withdrew the knife from its slender crystal sheath, watching the drops of adder venom collecting at its needle tip. She smiled. "On the day that Zwilt is no longer useful to me, he will learn the real power of Vilaya the Sable Quean."

With their bonds and gags removed, the two little shrews were thrust roughly into the holding chamber. This was the largest of the subterranean caverns. It had an oaken door, complete with a small grille aperture. As the guard bolted the door from outside, the younger shrew broke out crying again. "Waaaaah—I wan' my daddy'n'mamma . . . waaaah!"

The older of the pair, a little shrewmaid, hugged her brother, soothing him. "Hush now, Borti. Don't cry."

"Aye, tell Borti t'keep quiet, or we'll all suffer!"

Midda, the shrewmaid, looked around to see who had spoken.

The place was poorly lit by three guttering lanterns. She could see shapes of other creatures huddled around the walls in groups. The speaker was a young otter—he strode through the gloom to her side.

"I'm just warnin' ye, miss. Keep the liddle feller quiet. Thwip'll take the lanterns away, an' we'll all be left in the dark. If'n Borti makes a sound after that, we won't get any vittles. That scum's just lookin' for an excuse to punish us, so don't give 'im the chance."

Midda picked her little brother up, rocking him gently. "He'll drop off t'sleep soon—we're both very tired. My name's Midda. We're Guosim shrews. D'ye know what our name stands for?"

The otter nodded. "Aye. Guerilla Union of Shrews in Mossflower. My name's Flandor—ain't got no kin. I'm from the Eastlands. We've got a few shrews in here. Maybe ye might know some of 'em, Midda."

The shrewmaid peered into the shadowy interior. "Maybe I might, Flandor, but who's Thwip?"

A gaunt squirrelmaid appeared at her side. "Here, let me take the little un. Ye look about ready t'drop. Sit down here an' try to get some rest. I'm Tura."

Midda was grateful to Tura, who laid Borti down on a pile of rags and dry grass. They sat beside each other, with Flandor squatting before them. He kept his voice to a low murmur.

"You'll soon find out about Thwip. He's a wicked ole fox who's in charge of us. Him an' his mate, Binta—she carries a cane, an' he uses a whip. 'Spect that's how he got 'is name. Don't do anythin' to anger either of 'em. They enjoy bein' cruel an' tormentin' us. Best thing t'do is just be quiet an' do as they tell ye."

Midda leaned back against the rock wall. She felt bone weary. "I'll do as I'm told, but the first chance I get, me'n Borti are goin' to escape."

Tura grasped Midda's paw tightly. "That's foolish talk, friend. Have ye heard of the Ravagers, a big vermin mob? The one called Zwilt is their commander—nobeast can run from them. Huh, escape? D'ye know where you are? None of us do. Even if'n ye did get out o' here, where would you run to, eh?"

Midda roused herself indignantly. "I'm a Guosim, an' my father's Jango Bigboat. He's a Log a Log, Chieftain of all Mossflower shrews. So if'n me'n Borti are prisoners here, he'll find out. Hah, an' when he does, that Zwilt, aye, an' the one they call the Sable Quean, they'll be sorry, believe me!"

A gaunt-eyed bankvole nearby scoffed, "Huh, everybeast says somethin' like that when they first get here. Ferget about escapin'. Ye'll soon see it ain't no use, right, Flandor?"

The young otter gritted his teeth. "Maybe, maybe not. Someway, somehow, there's got t'be a way out to freedom. I'd sooner die now than spend the rest o' my days rottin' in here, mate. But we can't rush things. First we've got to make a proper plan. Another thing, we'll only tell those we can trust."

Midda was surprised. "Y'mean there's prisoners here who'd tell Thwip that we were escapin'?"

Tura nodded. "Aye, poor sillybeasts who'd do anythin' for an extra mouthful o' food. That's the way it gets some, after a while in here. Quiet now—here comes Thwip an' Binta!"

The door was opened. Two guards dragged a steaming cauldron in, followed by another two lugging a tub of water. Then the foxes swaggered in. Thwip was large and fat; he flourished a long whip, making it crack. Binta leaned on her yew cane, favouring a limp. Thwip folded his whiplash.

"Well, ain't yew lot the luckybeasts? A nice, dry roof over yore 'eads, comfy'n'warm. Good vittles an' drink aplenty—huh, ye don't 'ave t'do a thing to earn 'em. Just sit there nice an' quiet, eh, Binta?"

The vixen drew an imaginary line with her cane. "Line up single file an' be still. Anybeast pushin' or shovin' will get a taste o' this rod an' no vittles. Two pawfuls apiece, then line up over there for water."

As they hurried to get into line, Thwip pushed his whip stock under Midda's chin. He leered at her.

"New, are ye? Well, git t'the back o' the line, go on!"

Tura went with her, whispering, "You'll have to fetch Borti, or he'll get none."

Midda glanced at her baby brother sleeping peacefully. "Leave him there. He needs his rest. I'll try to get enough in my paws for both of us."

The gaunt squirrelmaid replied, "I'll see if I can manage to grab a bit extra, too."

It was the poorest of food, obviously the remains of their captors' meal mashed up with roots, leaves and a bit of wild oatmeal, all boiled in water to produce a pitiful gruel. There was also a single ladle of brackish water apiece for the young prisoners.

Borti woke briefly. He ate some of the mixture, which his sister and her squirrelfriend had saved for him, murmuring drowsily, "M'wanna go 'ome . . . go 'ome. . . ."

Midda picked him up and rocked him, singing a little song she had made up specially for him.

"Borti, Borti, my liddle Borti,
don't you weep an' don't be naughty.
If you promise to be good,
we will play in Mossflow'r Wood.
Sleep now, sleep now, close those eyes.

Midda's got a nice surprise.
When you waken up again,
I'll make you a daisy chain,
a daisy chain and y'know 'tis true,
my liddle Borti, I love you."

The baby shrew fell into a slumber, sucking his paw.

Midda watched him, trying to sleep herself. But the tears would not allow her to shut her eyes. So she sat staring into the gloom, quietly weeping for her mother and father, and the big logboat she called home.

6

Drull Hogwife was often up earlier than anybeast at Redwall. Being Friar Soogum's faithful assistant, she would go straight to the kitchens. Though he hated to admit it, the good Friar often slept a bit late, and who could deny him the privilege?

Being advanced in seasons, labouring hard and late into the night, Soogum slept on a little bed in his office, next door to the larder. Drull crept into the kitchens an hour before dawn, planning to start readying breakfast and wake her friend Soogum with a hot beaker of honeyed mint tea. It was a refreshment the Friar was always thankful for. Drull felt the warmth from the ovens as she took off her cloak and donned a rather flowery work apron. That was when she saw it!

Ruark, the Skipper of Otters, had taken to sleeping in the gatehouse of late. Granvy, the old hedgehog Recorder, always slept there, in his armchair, leaving the big, comfortable bed vacant. Ruark took full advantage of this. It was not yet daylight when urgent knocking roused him.

Granvy blinked drowsily from his armchair. "Eh, who's that? It's still dark out there!"

The big otter made a beeline for the door. "You stay there, mate. I'll see who 'tis."

He opened the door, to be confronted by an almost incoherent hogwife.

Drull kept covering her face with the flowery apron, gabbling nonstop. "Oh, corks a mercy me, wotever's 'appened—I never seen ought like it in all me borned days, so I never!"

Skipper pulled the hysterical creature inside and pushed her down into a chair, questioning her. "Wot haven't ye seen, marm? Slow down, now, what is it?"

Drull jumped up. Waving her paws, she bustled out of the gatehouse, still alarmingly talkative. "Come an' see, come an' see for yoreself, sir. Oh, corks'n'crabshells, y'ain't never seen nothin' like it. There's a vermin in the kitchens!"

Grabbing his javelin from behind the door, Skipper sped past her. "A vermin y'say, marm—stay away, an' keep everybeast out o' the kitchens!"

The young stoat, Globby, had indeed found the big cooking place, after a long, furtive search. Friar Soogum lay asleep in his office, unnoticed by the intruder. Globby had never seen so much food in one place. It was like paradise to the hungry young vermin. Trays of freshly baked scones, biscuits and breakfast bread were cooling on the shelves. The aroma almost sent him into ecstasy.

He was stuffing his face with a scone, a thin almond biscuit and a small crispy farl when he spotted the large earthenware jars with wooden ladles beside them. Honey, damson preserve, plum jam. In a moment, he was dripping with a combination of all three, his paws, chin, snout and cheeks literally plastered with the mixture. Then he discovered the flasks of pale cider, October Ale and elderberry wine. After a protracted period of sheer gluttony, gorging and swigging, Globby curled up on a ready floured table surface, nestling his head on a heap of unkneaded dough. He slumped into a satisfied sleep amidst the culinary wreckage he had created. Scones, bread, biscuits lay scattered in a soggy mess, with honey, preserves, spilled drink and an upset cauldron of cold oatmeal porridge.

Skipper Ruark spotted Globby as soon as he entered the kitchens. Knowing the slumbering vermin presented no immediate danger, the Otter Chieftain moved silently, searching the area for other foebeasts. He found Friar Soogum, who had just wakened. The old water vole yawned, rubbed his eyes and smiled.

'G'mornin', Skip. I'll get breakfast goin' right away."

Skipper placed a paw to his lips. "Nay, sir. You stay there until I call ye. Don't come out!"

Word had swiftly gone around the early risers. Abbess Marjoram, Foremole Darbee, several of his crew and Cellarmole Gurjee crowded the doorway as Skipper roused Globby into consciousness.

The young stoat blinked, stared at the otter for a moment, then bounded from the table with the mound of dough still stuck to the side of his face. The brawny Skipper seized him by the tail, slamming him back onto the table. Grabbing a breadknife, he put the point against Globby's nosetip.

"If'n ye value yore mizzrubble life, mudface, ye'll start talkin' fast. Wot are ye doin' here, eh?"

The young Ravager had expected to be slain on the spot. Finding himself still alive, his natural insolence came to the fore. He grinned cheekily. "I was 'ungry, so I thought ye wouldn't mind me borrowin' a bite o' vikkles an' a drop t'drink."

Abbess Marjoram came to the table, staring at him coldly. "And tell us, pray, how did you get into this Abbey?"

Globby wrinkled his jam-smeared snout at her. "That's my liddle secret, missis. I ain't tellin' yer!"

That was when Skipper's temper got the better of him. Throwing aside the breadknife, he grabbed a wooden oven paddle. Roughly flopping Globby over on his stomach, he proceeded spanking away with the paddle.

Thwack! Splat! Thwack! Splat! Thwack! Splat!

Skipper roared over the Ravager's squeals and screeches. "Who d'ye think ye are, talkin' to the Mother Abbess o' Redwall like that, ye hardfaced liddle whelp!"

Marjoram stayed the big otter's paw in midspank. "You'd best stop before you injure him seriously!"

Skipper released Globby, who immediately fell to the floor holding his rear end as he wriggled about in a horizontal dance.

"Waaaahwaaaah! Eeeeeyowwww! Hoohoohoowaaaah!"

Foremole Darbee shook a hefty digging claw at him. "Hurrhurr, may'aps ee'll keepen a siverful tongue in you'm 'ead, moi bold vurrmint. Naow, you'm answer ee h'Abbess, noice an' perloit loike!"

Kicking his footpaws frenziedly, Globby continued his agonised howls. Skipper grabbed the scruff of his neck, hauling him back over the table.

"I don't reckon he 'eard ye, sir. I'll just carry on 'til his manners improves."

Globby wailed brokenly, "Waaaahaaah—don't 'it me no more. I'll tell ye. I climbed over the back wall!"

Marjoram continued her interrogation of the stoat. "The back wall? You mean our eastern rampart? How in the name of seasons did you manage that?"

One glance at Skipper's stern face convinced Globby to reply truthfully. "Climbed uppa big tree an' went along a branch near the wall. I jumped it."

Skipper clapped a paw to his brow. "We've forgotten to trim back the branches for three seasons now. They must've grown good'n'long!"

Marjoram reassured him. "It's my fault, friend. There's been peace for so long that there's been no need of tree trimming. So, let's remedy the situation today!"

Skipper Ruark saluted. "Leave it t'me, marm. Gurjee, bring any axes, saws or cuttin' tools up from yore cellars. Brother Tollum, gather the best climbin' squirrels t'gether. Foremole, take yore crews up to the walltops.

Drull, marm, tell the Friar we'll need packed lunches for the workers, if'n ye please."

The hogwife fidgeted anxiously with her apron strings. "But nobeast's 'ad brekkist yet, sir."

The Abbess interrupted. "I'm sure the branch trimming is far more important, Drull. Besides, breakfast is already ruined, and it'll take time to clear up the mess, no thanks to this scruffy savage!"

Friar Soogum emerged from his makeshift bedroom. The old water vole shook his head in disbelief. "You mean t'tell me one vermin did all this to my kitchen? Drull, you see to the packed lunches. You, what's your name?"

The young stoat avoided the Friar's icy stare. "Globby."

Soogum rolled up his habit sleeves in a businesslike manner. "Well, listen to me, Globby. You're goin' to clean this kitchen from top t'bottom. What are you goin' t'do?"

Globby saw the Friar pick up the oven paddle and give the air a few experimental whacks.

"Er, leave it t'me, sir. I'll 'ave the ole place shinin' like a new pin afore ye knows it!"

Dawn was streaking the skies with pale light as Dinko dropped into the ditch beside Daclaw and Raddi. His arrival wakened Daclaw, who had been catching a nap. He glared sourly at the young rat.

'Wot are yew doin' 'ere? Yore supposed t'be watchin' the back gate with yer mate."

Dinko told his group leader what had taken place. "Well, it's like this, y'see. When we was round there last night, Globby kept on about the nice vittles wot must be inside. So 'e climbed a big tree, crawled along an 'igh branch an' jumped onto the top of the wall. Said 'e was goin' t'look for stuff to eat. Any'ow, he went in, an' I ain't seen 'ide nor 'air of 'im since, Chief. So I thought I'd better tell ye."

Daclaw paced up and down the ditchbed irately. "Went into Redwall, did 'e? Jelly-brained idjit! Young Globby's dead either way. If'n those inside don't slay 'im, Zwilt the Shade will fer disobeyin' orders. Frogskins an' 'ells teeth, wot am I goin' t'do now, eh?"

Raddi came to his help. "Git the others round 'ere, where we can keep an eye on 'em. We'll carry on watchin' this front gate for a while."

Dinko shrugged. "Wot good'll that do?"

Daclaw cuffed him across the ears before speaking. "Aye, wot good'll that do, eh?"

Raddi explained, "Well, if'n they've slayed Globby, they'll throw 'is carcass out 'ere in this ditch, mebbe. Then we can tell Zwilt wot 'appened. It'll show 'im that at least we was carryin' out orders properly. Don't stand there gawpin', young Dinko. Get the others an' bring 'em round 'ere, go on!"

Granvy unbolted the small east wickergate, peering out at the verdant woodland. "It looks peaceful enough to me."

Skipper strode out ahead of Brother Tollum and some squirrels, all of whom were carrying woodcutting tools. He paced the tree line closest to the wall. Looking up, he noted several long limbs and branches, some of them almost touching the battlements.

"Brother Tollum, start with yonder sycamore, then take that beech next to it. Oh, an' there's an oak further along. Tell yore crew t'chop 'em well back, all those long branches."

The gaunt Bellringer nodded solemnly. "Right y'are, Skip. We'll get right to it!"

The Otter Chieftain made for the east wallsteps, where he met a group of Dibbuns about to go up.

"Ahoy, mateys! Where do ye think yore off to?"

Guffy the molebabe was waving a table fork, which he deemed a very useful implement. "Ho, doan't ee fret about us'n's, zurr. We'm a-goin' up thurr to 'elp out, hurr aye!"

The big otter smiled. "Well, thankee, mates, but you

ain't allowed on the walltops until you've growed a bit. I'm afraid 'tis a bit dangerous for Dibbuns. Run off an' play, now, there's good liddle beasts."

Foremole Darbee and his crew were on the ramparts. Though not greatly fond of heights, the moles worked industriously. Tollum's squirrels would tie ropes to the chosen branches, throwing them across to the moles. Tugging hard on the ropes, the molecrew stopped the branches springing and bouncing. It was a lot easier to cut the wood once it was held steady. Whenever one was sawn or chopped through, Skipper would yell, "Ahoy, mates, heave 'er away!"

Some hefty limbs were hauled onto the walltops. They were dropped down to the Abbey lawns, where other Redwallers would cut them into small lengths, either for Friar Soogum's firewood store or for Cellarmole Gurjee's workshop. Good timber was never wasted.

The Ravager group were crouching in the ditch by the west wall, when Daclaw held up a paw for silence. He listened intently.

"Where's all that noise comin' from?"

"Shall I go an' see, Chief?" Dinko volunteered.

Daclaw ignored him, pointing to a fat weasel. "Slopgut, you go. See wot it is an' report straight back."

Dinko did not like being left out. He was curious. "Wot d'ye think it is, Chief?"

Daclaw stamped on the young rat's tail. "We'll get t'know when Slopgut gits back. Why d'ye think I sent 'im, thick'ead? Now, shut yer trap!"

The work was going well on the east side. Stout branches of sycamore, beech, oak and hornbeam were being sawn into manageable sections by Sister Fumbril and a big hedgehog named Bartij, who besides being the Infirmary Sister's aide, was also Redwall's orchard gardener. Together they worked a double-pawed logsaw, keeping up a steady rhythm.

Brother Tollum called out to Skipper, "There goes the last branch, Skip, a nice piece o' spruce!"

Darbee Foremole waved to his crew. "Haul 'er in, moi beauties. Ee job bee's well dunn!"

Granvy clapped his paws cheerfully. "Aye, an' just in time, here comes lunch!"

Hogwife Drull and her kitchen helpers hove into view. They were wheeling two trolleys piled high with good things to eat. Abbess Marjoram was with them. Molebabe Guffy and his friend, a squirrel Dibbun called Tassy, took the Abbess by her paws.

"Yurr, marm, cumm an' see all ee wudd we'm choppered up furr ee—b'ain't that roight, Tassy?"

Marjoram chuckled. "Is that little Miss Tassy under all that sawdust and woodchips?"

The tiny squirrelmaid piped up, "I been very, very bizzy wivva natchet, chop chop!"

The Abbess dusted bark chips from Tassy's ears. "Then you should be ready for some mushroom and leek soup and vegetable pasties. Then we've got apple and black currant crumble with arrowroot sauce."

Everybeast surged forward at the mention of the treats to come. They were halted by Skipper's shout.

"Sit down where y'are, all of ye, or there'll be no lunch!"

He bowed gallantly to Drull and the Abbess. "Serve away, marms. Feed these savage beasts, if ye please!"

Guffy scowled darkly as he plumped down on the lawn. "Samwidge beast you'm self, zurr!"

Slopgut had watched the tree-lopping exercise. He scurried back and reported to Daclaw.

Furtively the group leader took his Ravagers around to the east wall—the wickergate was open. Bidding the rest to wait in the shrubbery, Daclaw and his mate, Raddi, peeped carefully through the gateway. Raddi watched the Redwallers lunching. She could smell the soup and the other food. The ferret licked her lips.

"I don't blame young Globby wantin' vittles like that. Makes ye wish y'was a woodlander yerself, don't it?"

Daclaw glared at her. "Don't talk like that, mate. If'n Zwilt the Shade hears ye, it's sure death!"

Raddi pulled him back from the gateway suddenly.

"Wot did ye do that for?" Daclaw protested indignantly.

She clamped a paw around his mouth, whispering fiercely, "Didn't ye see? There's two young uns comin' this way. The others haven't noticed 'em. I think they're takin' their vittles out into the woods, mebbe to 'ave a picnic. Lissen, mate, we'll grab the pair of 'em, gag their mouths an' clear out of 'ere fast before they're missed. Are ye ready?"

Daclaw whipped off his tattered shirt, tearing it into two makeshift gags. He passed one to Raddi.

"Ready as I'll ever be, mate. Ssshh, I can 'ear 'em!"

Back inside on the Abbey lawn, everybeast relaxed after the work, lying about in the sun as they enjoyed a well-earned lunch.

Sister Fumbril made certain the Abbess was sure to hear her as she called out her request. "Perhaps some kind an' beautiful creature'll give us permission to carry on with the Redwall Bard Contest. Round about teatime this afternoon, in front of the gatehouse—that's a quiet, sunny place."

Granvy wiped soup from his whiskers, commenting, "Sunny it may be, but quiet? Not with this lot scrapin' fiddles, bangin' drums an' caterwaulin' away. What d'ye think, Mother Abbess?"

Marjoram chuckled. "Then you'd best plug your ears up, my friend, because the kind, beautiful creature has just given her permission for the contest to carry on."

Brother Tollum waited until the cheering had died down

before he asserted his claim. "Er, I think it was my turn to sing next, right, Granvy?" The hedgehog Recorder sighed. "So be it, Brother. But please don't sing any mournful dirges with a hundred verses."

Skipper smiled mischievously. "Oh, I dunno. I think ole Tollum's songs are nice an' restful. How's about 'The Burial Lament for the Flattened Frog's Granpa'?"

Tollum brightened up slightly. "I know that one!"

There were yells of dismay and groans of mock despair. The Redwallers shouted impassioned protests, plus some rather impudent insults. They carried on eating lunch and joking about various singers.

Nobeast had noticed the absence of two little Dibbuns, who had been trapped, gagged and carried off by a band of vermin Ravagers.

7

It was a pleasant enough stream, running from the woodlands out onto the flatlands. However, this was where Oakheart Witherspyk ran the raft aground. The big, florid hedgehog had dozed off at the tiller, causing his craft to bump over some rocks which lurked in the shallows. The *Streamlass* was a fine old craft, with a blockhouse of logs at its centre. It had ornate wooden rails and a single mast, from which hung strings of washing and a square canvas sail. The faded sign painted on this sail announced "The Witherspyk Performing Players." (Though the sign painter had made a spelling error—the word *Performing* read "Preforming.")

The shock of the raft bumping roughly aground caused chaos on board. Oakheart's mother, Crumfiss, and his wife, Dymphnia, clutching baby Dubdub to her, came stampeding onto the streambank. These were followed by the rest of his family, four other hedgehogs, a mole, a squirrel, and two bankvoles. (The latter four creatures he and his wife had adopted.) Everybeast was waving paws in alarm and crying out, either in panic or anger.

Dymphnia bellowed at her husband, "Oakie, you dozed off again, you great bumbler!"

Rising from his armchair, which was nailed to the deck alongside the tiller, Oakheart pointed at himself, booming out dramatically, "Dozed? Did I hear you say dozed, marm? Nay, alas, 'twas a cunning twist of devious water current which cast us ashore thus. I never doze whilst navigating, never!"

A young hogmaid held a drooping paw to her brow, declaiming, "Oh, Papa, I thought we were all to be drowned, lost sadly 'neath the raging waters!"

Dymphnia wiped the babe's snout on her shawl, casting a jaundiced eye on her daughter. "Do be quiet, Trajidia. Don't interrupt your father. Well, Oakie, are we stuck here?"

Removing a flop-brimmed hat and sweeping aside his timeworn cloak, Oakheart stared glumly over the rail at a number of rocks beneath the surface.

"Aye, m'dear. Fickle fortune has swept us hard upon the strand. Rikkle, can you see if anything can be done to relieve our position? There's a good chap!"

One of the bankvoles hurled himself into the water and vanished beneath the raft. After a brief moment, Trajidia, who never missed the opportunity to be dramatic, clasped her paws, staring wide-eyed at the place where Rikkle had submerged.

"Oh, oh, 'tis so hard to bear, one of such tender seasons, gone to a watery grave!"

One of her brothers, Rambuculus, smiled wickedly. "It's plum duff for supper. If he doesn't come up, can I have his share, Ma?"

Dymphnia clouted him over the ear with her free paw. "Ye hard-hearted young blight!"

Baby Dubdub, who was learning to speak by repeating the last words of his elders, shook a tiny paw at his brother. "Young blight!"

Rikkle climbed back aboard shaking himself, treating those nearby to a free shower. "Ain't no good, Pa. We're jammed tight, unless we can find somethin' to lever 'er off with."

Oakheart was not in the levering mood; he sniffed. "Leave it 'til the morrow. Perchance the stream may run at flood and float our *Streamlass* off."

Wading into the shallows, he held forth a paw to assist his wife and their babe onto dry land.

"Right, Company, all paws ashore, if ye please!"

Dubdub shouted in his mother's ear, "Paws ashore, please!"

They were grounded in the area where the trees thinned out onto the heathland. Oakheart rummaged through a pile of effects on the bank, coming up with a funnel fashioned from bark. This he held to his mouth and began calling aloud for the benefit of anybeast within hearing distance.

"Hear ye, hear ye, one and all!
All goodbeasts now, hark to me,
see here upon this very spot,
the Performing Witherspyk Company!
What'll you see here when we start?
Why, tales to delight the rustic heart,
plays enacted on nature's stage,
dramas of avarice, war and rage.
Stories of love to make you sigh,
tragedies bringing a tear to the eye.
Mayhaps a comedy we'll make,
You'll feel your ribs with laughter ache.
Yet what seek we as our reward?
Merely to share your supper board.
A drop to drink, a crust, perchance.
We act, we sing, recite or dance.
Aye, food would aid our noble cause,
though mainly we feed upon applause.
You'll not regret a visit to see,
The Performing Witherspyk Companeeeeeeeee!"

Oakheart's mother, Crumfiss, a venerable greyspiked hog, prodded him none too gently with her walking stick. "Oh, give your face a rest, Oakie. This is the back of nowhere. There's nobeast around for leagues!"

Rambuculus sniggered wickedly. "Poke him again, Granma. Go on—good'n'hard!"

Crumfiss brandished the stick at him. "I'll poke you, ye impudent young snickchops! Do somethin' useful. Go on, gather firewood for your ma!"

Oakheart rounded on them, paw upraised. "Hist, voices, d'ye hear?"

From not too far off, a voice sounded, getting louder. "I say, there. Are you chaps callin' to us, wot? Hold on a tick, we'll be right with you!"

Two hares and a shrewmaid approached through the woodland fringe. It was Buckler, Diggs and Flib. Oakheart beamed a welcoming smile.

"Over here, friends. Over here!"

Flib wiggled a paw in one ear, wincing. "Do ye have ter yell through that thing?"

The florid hog lowered his megaphone. "Ah, forgive me, my dainty miss—force of habit, y'know."

Flib scowled at him. "Ye can cut that out right now. I ain't nobeast's dainty miss—I'm Flib the Guosim, see!"

Buckler rapped her paw lightly with the bellrope. "Mind your manners. He's just trying t'be friendly."

Oakheart did not seem to take offence. He continued holding forth merrily. "Ah, a Guosim shrew, no less. Stout creatures. Perhaps you know one who is an acquaintance of mine, Jango Bigboat by name, something of a chieftain amongst his kind, I believe."

Flib seemed flustered by the mention of Jango Bigboat. She dropped back, standing behind Diggs, murmuring, "No, I ain't 'eard o' that un, sir."

After introductions had been made all round, Buckler strode down to the streambank, where he viewed the grounded raft.

"Mister Oakheart, perhaps we could help you to refloat your craft. It's a wonderful thing—I've never seen one like it."

Dymphnia took over from her spouse. "Oh, just call him Oakie, Mister Buckler. Everybeast does. Maybe you'd like to come aboard the *Streamlass* and share supper with us, such as it is. We can always refloat our raft tomorrow."

Buckler bowed gallantly. "A pleasure, marm. But call us Buck, Diggs and Flib. We have supplies we could share with you. Oakie tells me you are actors."

Diggs unhitched the haversack from his back. "Jolly types, actors. We've had visits from them once or twice at Salamandastron, doncha know."

Granma Crumfiss leaned on Diggs's paw as they went aboard. "Salamandastron, ye say? I played there when I was nought but a young hogmaid. A fine young badger was the Lord. Brang, as I remember. Is he still there?"

It was a memorable evening. The raft's log cabin was comfortable, if slightly crowded. The two hares contributed food from their packs. Dymphnia served them with bowls of plum duff, ladling her special pear and hazelnut sauce thickly over it. Oakheart broke out a cask of his own brew, which he had named Witherspyk Waterporter. It was slightly sweet, very dark and nourishing.

As they ate, Trajidia fluttered her eyelashes at Diggs, enquiring, "Pray, to where are you warriors of the wilderness bound?"

Crumfiss spoke sternly. "Don't be so nosey, miss. 'Tis none o' yore concern where these goodbeasts are goin'!"

Buckler smiled. "Oh, it's no secret. We're bound for Redwall, with a gift for the Abbess."

Oakheart banged his tankard down in surprise. " 'Pon my liver spikes'n'paws! Why, that's also our destination, friend Buck. Perhaps when we float our vessel into navigable waters on the morrow, you'd wish to accompany us to that hallowed establishment?"

Buckler winked at Diggs, allowing him to answer. "Wot, oh, I say, wouldn't we just jolly well love to, Oakie, old lad. Super wheeze, wot wot?"

Baby Dubdub, who was being fed by his mother, pushed away the spoon. "Wheeze, wot wot!"

Everybeast laughed, and Trajidia fluttered her eyelashes even harder. "Oh, how brave and gallant, Papa. We'll have valiant hares to guard us from any vermin foes!"

Oakheart refilled his tankard. "Indeed we will, m'dear! Eat hearty now, my trusty protectors, and thank ye kindly for offering your skills to us."

Buckler returned the compliment. "No sir, thank you for offering us such a wonderful way to travel. It's Diggs an' I who are grateful to you."

Diggs winked roguishly at Trajidia. "Rather! An' in such bally charmin' company, wot! Never travelled with actors before. Wouldn't mind havin' a go at the jolly old actin' m'self."

Rambuculus did not hold out much hope for Diggs. "Hmmph, bein' a warrior, you might come in useful for fights an' battle scenes. There's more to actin' than ye think. You've got to be a singer, a dancer, an—"

Diggs cut in on him. "Dancin'? Listen t'me, laddie buck. I can twiddle as neat a flippin' paw as anybeast. Ask Miggy M'ginnerty, our drill sergeant's daughter. She'n'I were the bloomin' toast of the Mess Ball when we tootled round the floor t'gether. Twinklepaws Diggsy, they called me, ain't that right, Buck?"

Buckler nodded. "That's correct, mate, an' you were a good warbler, too, as I recall. Go on, give us a song!"

His chubby companion needed no second bidding. Bounding from his seat, he threw his paws wide and launched into his favourite ditty.

"Oh, I hail from Salamandastron,
that old mountain in the west,
with a pack upon me shoulder,

an' a smartly buttoned vest.
My ears stand to attention,
an' gels cry out, Look there,
he's a member of the Long Patrol,
a handsome gallant hare!

"What ho what ho, 'tis true y'know,
no creature can compare,
to a dashin' singin' harum-scarum,
Salamandastron hare . . . wot wot!

"I'll whack a score o' weasels,
or marmalise a stoat,
there's many a ferret shiverin',
when I've torn off his coat.
I'm vicious with all vermin,
but show to me a maid,
I'll kiss her paw an' shout haw haw!
Pray, marm, don't be afraid.

"What ho what ho, I tell ye so,
ye gentle gels so fair,
I'm a high-fulorum cockle-a-dorum,
Salamandastron hare . . . wot wot!"

As Diggs finished his song, he made an elegant bow. The Witherspyk Company applauded him heartily, even young Rambuculus. Oakheart was impressed.

" 'Pon me snout'n'spikes, young Diggs, ye have the makin's of a fine performer. There's a position in me troupe for you, should you ever wish to take it! But an actor's life can be hard, y'know, and hungry, too. Some seasons ye can see more suppertimes than suppers. Well, what d'ye say, friend Diggs, eh?"

The young hare's ears seemed to wilt. "Er, I think I'll stick to the jolly old warrior's path, sir. It's prob'ly better in the long run."

Trajidia looked disappointed. "You're not afraid of acting, are you?"

Buckler answered for his friend. "Diggs ain't afraid of anything, miss, except starvin'."

Diggs pouted a little. "Well, a chap needs his scoff, y'know. I wouldn't look so jolly han'some if I was thin."

Dymphnia patted his paw. "We understand. Now, tomorrow we'll follow the stream overland, going south and a point east. That should take us over some flatlands, then back into the trees. When we spy the rock ledges, it's not far from there to the Abbey. Right, time for sleep, my dears. Early call at dawn, I think. The *Streamlass* will need to be worked on, so that we can free her."

The twins, Jiddle and Jinty, went to fetch their blankets. "Mamma, Mamma, can we sleep out on the bank?"

Dymphnia raised her headspikes indignantly. "Certainly not. Who knows what goes on out there at night? You've got perfectly good bunks onboard!"

The twin hedgehogs complained bitterly.

"But Granma Crumfiss snores somethin' dreadful!"

"An' Trajidia keeps talkin' in her sleep, recitin' lines from the plays!"

Dymphnia remained obdurate, until Flib interceded. "Let 'em sleep outdoors, marm. I'll go with the twins an' keep an eye on 'em. Oh, go on—it's a warm night."

Oakheart sighed. "Aye, let them sleep on shore, m'dear. 'Twill stop 'em gettin' up for drinks o' water all night."

Wearing their blankets like cloaks, Jiddle and Jinty dashed from the cabin, whooping and squealing.

As Flib followed them, Buckler cautioned her, "Remember now, missy, keep a sharp eye on them!"

The shrewmaid replied icily, "No need t'remind me. I knows wot I'm doin'!"

Diggs caught hold of her paw. "You jolly well take heed of what he says, m'gel, wot!"

She broke his hold roughly, snarling, "An' yew mind yer

own bizness, fatty. Keep an eye on yoreself in case ye go bang after all that scoff!"

To ease the tense moment, Crumfiss turned to her son. "Oakie, why don't ye sing us a nice little comic ditty before we turn in. Buck an' Diggs have never heard you performin'."

Oakheart Witherspyk was never a beast to miss a chance of displaying his talents. Holding that most peculiar of instruments, the Hogalino, over his head, he strummed it across his top spikes and burst into song.

" 'Twas a snowy morn one summer,
an' the moon was shining bright,
when my dear ma kissed me a fond good-bye.
So I asked where I was going,
as she shoved me out the door.
She blew her snout and then began to cry.
'Oh, don't run off to sea, my son,
you'll break your mother's heart.
I've reared you since you were an ugly pup!'
But I didn't want to go,
and I tried to tell her so,
but she locked the door and nailed the windows up.
Off I went to sail the main,
as cabin hog aboard the *Scruffy Dog*.
The Skipper wore no vest, and tattooed upon his chest,
was a picture of a flea lost in the fog.
Well, it turned out that old Captain,
was a hog named Gusty Snout,
my long-lost daddy that I'd never seen.
So me and that old tar, sailed right back home to Ma,
who saw us coming and let out a scream.
She cried, 'Alas alack, are you two villains back?'
And beat us soundly with a knotty log.
And as she wouldn't stop it, well, we both had to hoppit,
now we're back aboard the good old *Scruffy Dog*!"

Sometime later that night all paws on the raft were fast asleep. The woodlands were still, and the ground was warm from the summer day, with not even a whisper of breeze to stir either grass or leaves.

Grakk and two other weasels had not taken any more captives. On returning to the River Moss, they had been unable to locate the Guosim shrews. Following a sidestream south, Grakk and his cohorts met up with two other Ravagers. It was the small, scrawny fox and the burly weasel who had been in trouble with Buckler and Diggs.

All five vermin were at that moment lying low in the woodland fringes, watching the three young creatures who were sleeping not far from the streambank. The small fox looked around nervously.

Grakk crawled up alongside him. "Wot are yew lookin' so jumpy about, eh?"

The fox pointed to Flib, who was curled up amidst the moss and fallen leaves. "See that un? She's a shrew—we met up with 'er afore. I know 'tis the same beast, 'cos I kin see a knife an' a club wot she stole off us."

Grakk's whisper oozed scorn. "Yer let a shrewmaid take yore weppins, huh, an' you two calls yerselves Ravagers?"

The burly weasel defended himself and the fox. " 'Twas a trap, see. We was tricked by 'er—she 'ad two others lyin' in wait fer us. Aye, two o' those big fightin' rabbets, an' they weren't short o' weppins, big swords an' loaded slings, daggers, too, an' prob'ly a couple o' spears. I tell ye, Grakk, ye wouldn't like t'meet up wid that pair. Killers they were, champeen warriors!"

Grakk stared hard at the fox. "So, wot 'appened? Why wasn't ye killed by 'em, eh?"

The small fox glared right back at him, lying earnestly. " 'Cos we escaped from them. We 'ad to run fer it, an' we lost our weppins in the scramble. They chased us fer over a day an' night, but we outran them."

"Hah, youse two ran faster'n two big rabbets? Ye must be jokin'!"

The burly weasel butted in belligerently. "Well, we ain't, an' if'n you 'ad two big fightin' rabbets chasin' ye with long swords, you'd 'ave run, too, fer yore life. 'Cos ye don't stop t'mess about wid beasts like them, see!"

Not wanting to continue the dispute, Grakk held up a paw. "Keep yer voice down, mate. I believe ye. So, if'n ye can't see the big rabbets anyplace around, let's grab those three young uns an' get movin' fast, while the goin's good."

Flib had been knocked out cold by a blow from the club, which had once belonged to the vermin. The small fox kicked her spitefully.

"I should kill ye right now for wot ye did to us!"

Grakk slammed his spearpoint into the ground beside the fox. "Ye can cut that kinda talk, or ye'll answer to Zwilt the Shade. You'n'yore mate, lash 'er paws t'gether an' sling 'er on the spearpole. Are those two young 'ogs ready t'go?"

Jinty and Jiddle sat terrified, with their mouths gagged. A weasel bound their forepaws, dragging them upright.

Grakk blindfolded them and tapped both their snouts with his dagger point as he hissed savagely, "One wrong move an' we'll roast ye for dinner. If'n ye want t'live, then do as yore told, got it?"

Not waiting for them to nod, he shoved the young hogs roughly. "Now, git goin'—move yerselves."

The Ravagers sped off into the night, prodding their captives forward.

Flib was still unconscious, hanging from the spearhaft as the burly weasel and the small fox hurried to keep up with the others.

The early noontide peace was shattered as Redwall's twin bells, Matthias and Methuselah, tolled out a brazen alarm.

Casting dignity to one side, Abbess Marjoram hurried about, yelling, "Everybeast to the east wallgate. There's two Dibbuns missing. Has anyone seen Guffy and little Tassy?"

She was intercepted by Granvy. The old hedgehog scribe tried to calm her down. "Mother Abbess, we don't know if they're lost out in the woodlands. They may still be within the Abbey. Who can explain what Dibbuns get up to? Listen, now, you go inside, take Friar Soogum and whatever kitchen helpers he has to spare. Search inside the Abbey from attics to wine cellars. Guffy and Tassy may be hiding, or perhaps merely taking a nap."

Marjoram managed a smile. "Yes, you could be right, my friend. If they're in there, I'll find the scamps. But where are you going?"

The Recorder tapped the side of his snout knowingly. "I've got an idea. You know I just said, 'Who can explain what Dibbuns get up to?' Well, I think I know the answer. Other Dibbuns! When I began looking for Guffy and Tassy, I saw the Dab gang over by the gatehouse, playing near the steps. I'll ask them."

Marjoram looked puzzled. "The Dab gang?"

Granvy chuckled. "Haven't you heard of the Dab? Dibbuns Against Bedtime, that's their initials."

The Abbess nodded. "Of course. I'd just forgotten about it. Right, you go and see them, and I'll search the Abbey building. Good luck!"

By teatime that afternoon, there was still no sign of the missing Dibbuns. It was a worried gathering of Redwallers who sat upon the main Abbey steps. Friar Soogum passed around with food and drink, doling it out to everybeast.

"C'mon, now, eat somethin' for seasons' sakes. It won't do any good if'n ye make yoreselves ill with hunger. Oh, there's a thought, Skipper. I'll wager those two liddle rascals will show up once they get empty tummies!"

The Otter Chieftain sighed. "Ye could be right, Friar, but

they already 'ad vittles at lunchtime, so they won't be 'ungered just yet. Wot luck did you 'ave, Granvy?"

The hedgehog Recorder scratched his untidy beard. "Well, I should've expected not to get much sense out of Dibbuns. One small wretch said that he actually saw Guffy and Tassy fly up in the air, when I asked him where they went—he said right up over a moon! I quote him literally. Another fanciful little miss said that the big butterfly had eaten them, and some other tiny fibber said Friar Soogum had made them into soup. Though most just spread their paws and said 'Gone!' Just as babes will, no explanation but 'Gone!' So, that's the sum total of my information."

Skipper sipped a beaker of cold mint tea. "Well, me an' some others searched outside the east wall. We had no real luck, though. Most of the ground an' foliage was well trampled by the tree trimmin'. Creatures goin' to an' fro there, haulin' branches. That's all the tracks I could make out. We'll have to range further into the woodlands if'n we're searchin' for pawtracks."

The Abbess enquired hesitantly, "Will it be very difficult to find the prints of two little ones, Skipper?"

The big otter's brow furrowed. "It always is with babes, marm, but they ain't the tracks I'd be lookin' for."

Tollum Bellringer nodded toward the woodlands. "You mean vermin tracks, Skip—is that wot yore thinkin'?"

To save upsetting everybeast further, Friar Soogum spoke. "Well, now, me'n' the Abbess an' our party, we still got plenty o' searchin' yet t'do. We scoured the cellars, Great Hall, an' Cavern Hole, too. We're up t'the dormitories so far. But there's still the attics. Though why anybeast in their right mind would want t'go wanderin' up in those dusty ole chambers is beyond me. You scouted out yore Infirmary yet, Sister?"

Fumbril replied promptly. "First thing I did, Friar. Everythin' is as it should be, no sign o' Dibbuns!" The otter paused, tapping her rudder thoughtfully. "Er, Friar, I just thought o' somethin'. That stoat vermin we caught in yore kitchens—it might be worth talkin' to him about our Dibbuns. 'Tis worth a try, eh?"

Skipper clenched his paws. "Yore right, Sister. Don't fret, if that un's got anythin' t'say, I'll learn the truth, one way or another, trust me. Where's the wretch now, Friar?"

"When we went off t'search the cellars, I tied him to the leg o' my heavy ole worktable, good'n'tight."

The young stoat, Globby, was watching them from an upper dormitory window. He saw the Friar making paw movements, telling Skipper how he had bound his captive to the table leg.

Globby chewed on an oat farl which he had stuffed with cheese, smiling over his easy escape. Hah, that stupid old fool had only tied him by the footpaws. The Friar was in too much of a hurry to join in the search for the precious little ones.

They had left him alone—everybeast from the kitchens went along with the Friar, and the mouse they called Mother Abbess. Idiots! He had watched Soogum cut the length of cord to tie him with. Unbelievable! The old duffer had left his knife on the table and dashed off. Globby cut himself loose, tucked the knife into his belt, helped himself to a few vittles and sneaked out of the kitchens.

The moment he put his head outside the Abbey door, though, the young Ravager saw that it was not going to be so simple escaping from Redwall. The grounds were being combed by Redwallers, both singly and in small groups. Globby retreated from the door as he heard some moles passing by.

"Yurr, Gurrfa, us'n's bee's best lukkin' round unner ee windows—they'm moight 'ave leaved tracks!"

Flattening himself against one of the sandstone columns in Great Hall, the stoat saw Drull Hogwife passing, holding two Dibbuns' paws.

"You lend me some 'elp, my dears, an' don't go strayin'

off, now. Two Dibbuns is enough loss for one day. Let's take a look round by the tapestry."

When they had gone, Globby ventured out. He avoided going downstairs, knowing the cellars were being searched. Upstairs, that was the place to hide, and he had heard one of the kitchen helpers saying that the dormitories were upstairs. Not knowing what a dormitory was, Globby hurried up the stairs. Opening the first door he came to, he was confronted by neat rows of little truckle beds.

So, dormitories were bedrooms. He was learning all the time. Hearing voices approaching, he nipped inside. Partially closing the door, he peeped through the crack.

Sister Fumbril and a squirrelmaid Infirmary helper bustled by, talking animatedly.

"We'll search that sickbay again from top to bottom!"
"I'll check all the big linen cupboards, shall I, Sister?"

"Good idea, Twissle. That's always a favourite Dibbun hidin' place."

They went up a short, curving flight of stairs to the left.

Globby waited a moment before leaving the dormitory. He took a flight of stairs off to the right. It led to another dormitory, one with fewer, larger beds, obviously for the older Redwallers. That was where he watched from the window, and saw the big otter and the Friar heading indoors. The young stoat sat on a bed, reviewing his position.

Where to go? How to avoid the searchers?

8

Out in the woodlands, beneath the roots of the giant oak in the system of chambers and caves known as Althier, new captives were arriving constantly. Vilaya the Sable Quean stared down at three tiny squirrels, huddled piteously on the bare floor below her throne seat.

Thwip and Binta, the two foxes who were her jailers, scowled at the new inmates. Binta pointed at them with her cane. "Majesty, they're very young."

The old rat Dirva, sitting on the steps close to Vilaya, shrugged. "The younger, the better. Their kinbeasts will worry more about them."

Thwip coiled his lash. Circling them, he shook his head. "These look too young, I don't give much for their chances. They got nobeast to look after 'em."

The Sable Quean's dark almond eyes glittered as she fixed the fox with her riveting stare. "Is that what you think, Thwip? Then let me tell you what I think. I don't give much for your chances, or your vixen, Binta, if anything happens to these three. If I were you, I'd look after them very carefully. Do I make myself clear?"

Thwip's stomach was so large that he grunted as he bowed low. "I hear an' I obey, Majesty."

Vilaya's expression changed. Ignoring the foxes, she spoke almost teasingly to Dirva. "I'm so glad. It pleases me when my servants obey me. Does it please you, my friend?"

The old rat rested her chin fawningly upon her Quean's footpaw. "Makes little difference what pleases me, Majesty. Though it does please me to see what happens to anybeast that'd displease you, eh?"

The ghost of a cruel smile crossed the Sable Quean's face. "You always give the right answers, my ugly old friend. Thwip, Binta, take these cringing little things out of my sight, and remember, treat them with care."

Thwip peered around the dungeon chamber. All the young prisoners shrank against the rough rock walls, cowed by the presence of their cruel jailer. His gaze rested a moment upon Midda and her little brother, Borti, then shifted to Tura.

Unfurling his whiplash, he cracked it, pointing at her. "You, squirrel, come 'ere. Move yerself!"

The young squirrelmaid stood shaking in front of him. "Sir?"

He pushed the three squirrelbabes forward with his footpaw. "Yore a squirrel, ain't yer? Well, look after these three. Take good care of 'em, or I'll 'ave the hide off'n yer with this lash, see."

Binta stood alongside Thwip, brandishing her rod. "You lot, when the vittles arrive, stay back 'til they've been served, or ye'll feel this cane!"

The two foxes stalked out, leaving the young captives in the guttering half-light amidst the shadows.

Tura took a ragged cloth and some dried grass. Making a rough resting place, she laid the three squirrelbabes down on it.

Flandor the otter took off his rough tabard and covered them with it. "Strange they ain't cryin' an' weepin', eh, Midda?"

The Guosim shrew looked them over sadly. "They're in shock. Wait'll they wake up, poor little mites. Tura, wot's goin' to become of us?"

The squirrelmaid lay close to the babes, shielding them with her body. "I'm too afraid to think, Midda."

Being a chieftain who headed fivescore savage river rats, Grullba Deathwind feared nobeast. He ruled by strength and his skill with the double-headed battleaxe—he was a real barbarian fighter. Even his own crew knew that he could, single-pawed, defeat any three of them. He was not a beast to challenge idly.

When the newcomer appeared unannounced in the midst of his camp, Grullba eyed him up and down curiously. Neither he, nor any of his river rats, had ever encountered a sable. Zwilt the Shade seemed to materialise out of the campfire smoke. He stood impassive, the long, dull-purple cloak draped lazily about his tall body. River rats surrounded him, brandishing an array of weapons. Zwilt ignored them, staring with his dead black eyes at Grullba.

The chieftain returned his gaze, instinctively checking that the battleaxe was within easy reach. His guttural accent split the air like a blade. "Oo arr ya, beast, worra yew do 'ere? Come ta die?"

Zwilt replied with a question. "Are ye the one they call Grullba Deathwind, leader of this crew?"

Some of the rats guffawed but fell silent at a glance from their chieftain. Grullba, his eyes locked on Zwilt, nodded. "Yarr dat's me. Worra dey call yew?"

The tall sable appeared unconcerned as he made his demand. "I am Zwilt the Shade, Commander of all Ravagers. From this day forth, you and your beasts will serve under me."

Immediately the air was filled with danger. A deathly silence fell over the assembly awaiting their murderous chieftain's next move.

Grullba threw back his head and laughed aloud. "Yarrharrharr! We serve 'im? Lizzen to der deadbeast!"

Zwilt was moving even as Grullba leapt forward swinging his axe. Like magic, the broadsword was in Zwilt's paws as he circled away from his opponent.

The river rats gathered in a big ring, eager to see their chief slay the upstart.

Grullba's weapon made a loud swishing noise. This was because of the pattern of holes forged through the axehead, giving confirmation of his title, Deathwind. However, he struck only empty air.

Zwilt had swayed a mere hairsbreadth to one side, causing his opponent to stagger off balance with the force of the strike.

Grullba recovered swiftly, this time swinging his weapon horizontally, as if to cut the sable in half.

Zwilt took a pace backward, watching the momentum turn Grullba round full circle. The Rat Chieftain gave a roar, charging his foe head-on. Zwilt's cloak swirled; he sidestepped neatly, tripping Grullba as he thundered by. The river rats, who had been cheering their chieftain on, fell silent.

Grullba Deathwind had never even come close to being defeated. Now he was being made to look foolish by the tall, lean stranger. His face smeared with soil and torn-up grass, Grullba arose, breathing heavily.

"Yarr, stan' an' fight, cowwid!"

Zwilt attacked like lightning. The broadsword clanged, sending the battleaxe flying from Grullba's grasp and pinning him through his right shoulder. The river rat screeched in pain as Zwilt ripped his blade free.

A savage kick to the rat's stomach drove Grullba to his knees, head bent as he gasped for air. Zwilt slammed his broadsword into the earth. Picking up the fallen battleaxe, he hefted it, staring at the bowed head of his adversary. Zwilt spat out the word scornfully. "Deathwind!"

The last sound Grullba heard was the battleaxe singing his deathsong with one whistling swish.

Zwilt tossed the axe aside, retrieving his broadsword. He turned slowly, his cold eyes taking in the faces of the stunned river rats.

"I am Zwilt the Shade, hearken if ye wish to live. From now until you die, you'll serve as Ravagers under the Sable Quean. I am her Commander, you'll obey me. So challenge me now, if you wish to dispute my word."

They stood dumbstruck, not daring to answer. Anybeast who could defeat Grullba Deathwind so easily merited all their fear and respect.

Zwilt pointed his sword at a burly vermin, who was armed with a long pike. "You, speak your name!"

Avoiding the dead black eyes, the river rat replied, "Kodra."

The sable turned his back on them, calling as he strode off, "Stick that fool's head on your pike, Kodra. You'll bring up the rear. The rest of you, follow me. And remember, anybeast stupid enough to desert will be found. I'll hunt him down myself, chop off his footpaws and make him follow me on the stumps. You will receive further orders soon, but for now, march!"

They went without question, with Kodra trudging stolidly along at the rear of the bunch, holding up his pike with the grisly object spiked upon it. The eyes of Grullba Deathwind stared sightlessly over the backs of his former command. There was not a single thought in his head.

Consternation reigned on the streambank where the Witherspyk raft was still stuck in the shallows. Though it was not that which was causing the hullabaloo, but the fact that Jiddle, Jinty and Flib were missing. As troupe leader, Oakheart did his best to avoid panic amongst the family. He reasoned, "No use getting upset, my friends. This isn't the first time those two young scamps have wandered off.

Calm down, I beg you. Let's partake of breakfast before we take any drastic action. Agreed?"

His wife, Dymphnia, hugged baby Dubdub to her. The loss of any family member, whether trivial or temporary, was always of concern to her. She glared at her husband.

"How can you think of sitting there stuffing down food, when our dear little twins are lost? Shame on you, Oakie!"

"Shame a you Oakie!" Dudbdub echoed.

Buckler interrupted. "No, marm, the shame is on us, Diggs an' I. We should never have allowed a young shrew like Flib to guard your young uns. Leave it to us, eh, mate?"

Diggs declared stoutly, "Indeed, we're the very chaps for the blinkin' job, m'dear. We'll find your infants without delay. Aye, an' that Flib, too, wot, wot! There's a young madam that's in for a severe tail kickin' when we jolly well catch up with her!"

A gruff cry rang out from the stream. "Ahoy the raft, mateys. Guosim comin' aboard!"

They poured out of the blockhouse to see a half-dozen shrew logboats heaving to the rail. Each was crewed by ten Guosim, small spiky-furred shrews wearing kilts, broad-buckled belts, short rapiers and multicoloured headbands. From the largest of the vessels, a grey-whiskered but fit-looking shrew hopped aboard the raft.

Making his boat fast with a headrope, he thrust his paw at the troupe leader. "Well, burst me britches if'n it ain't ole Witherspyk. How are ye, Oakie? Fat an' well, I 'ope?"

Oakheart shook the proffered paw. "Log a Log Jango Bigboat, as I live'n'breathe. What are you doing in these waters, sirrah?"

Jango got right to the point. "Searchin' for three lost young uns. Ye haven't come across any lost Guosim, have ye?"

Dymphnia interrupted, "Indeed we haven't—we're looking for three of our own!"

Diggs corrected her. "Two actually, marm. Young Flib was with Buck an' I, wot?"

Jango set his jaw grimly. "Flib, is she a shrewmaid?"

Buckler answered, "Aye, sir, that she is."

The Shrew Chieftain nodded. "Well, let me tell ye, 'er name ain't Flib—she made that up. She was named Petunia Rosebud by me'n' her ma."

Diggs stifled a snigger. "Petunia Rosebud? No wonder she bally well changed it, wot."

Jango shot him an icy stare. "Been nothin' but trouble since the day she was born, that un. Well, now she's gone missin'. Aye, an' so has her younger sister Midda an' the babe, Borti. He's only a liddle mite, ain't 'e, Furm?"

Jango's wife, Furm, wiped an eye on the back of her paw. "Ain't seen two seasons o' daylight yet, pore tiny sprig! But at least Borti's with Midda—she's got a grain o' sense about 'er. Not like that other rascal wot calls 'erself Flib. Huh, Flibberty Jibbet's wot I'd call 'er!"

Dymphnia Oakheart passed Furm a handkerchief from her sleeve. "Dry those eyes now, dearie. That won't get our young uns found. You come inside with me an' we'll share a pot o' hot mint tea. As for searchin' after the missin' ones, wot d'ye suggest, Mister Buckler?"

The young hare bowed gallantly. "I think we'd be best joinin' forces, marm. That way we can cover more ground. That's if Log a Log Jango is agreeable to the idea."

The Shrew Chieftain hitched up his wide belt. "Aye, 'tis a good plan. We'll scour the banks from offshore—you concentrate on the last place the young hogs were seen. We'll meet up back 'ere at midday. Be sure to sound an alarm if'n ye find anythin'."

Rambuculus shot into the blockhouse, then reappeared brandishing a battered old bugle. "Right y'are, Loggo. Would ye like me to give ye a blast now, just t'see how it sounds?"

Oakheart seized his son firmly by the ear. "I'll give you a blast ye won't soon forget, if you start blowin' on that confounded instrument. Right, form up, troupe, and let's get to work. Buckler, would you and Diggs take the lead?"

It was midmorning when Buckler led the Witherspyk group out of the trees onto the streambank some fair distance down from the stranded raft. Diggs checked upstream.

"I say, Buck, here comes the jolly old shrew fleet, wot."

Jango and his logboats came drifting slowly down on the unhurried current. He halted his craft by holding on to the branch of an overhanging willow.

"We've had no luck up that ways, have ye found anythin' yet—a sign of either shrews or hogs?"

Buckler explained, "We found tracks leading away from where they slept. Couldn't be sure, though, might've been rats an' other vermin. Pawprints o' the little uns had been trampled over, an' no sign of Flib. We trailed 'em to here, but they fade out on the bankside."

One of Jango's scouts examined the faint prints. The Shrew Chieftain watched him closely. "Wot d'ye think, Sniffy?"

Sniffy the Tracker made his report. "Buckler's right, Chief. Somebeast's been here. Hard to tell, though—they've covered their trail well. They've gone into the water, stickin' close t'the shallows, as far as I kin see."

Diggs tossed a pebble into the stream. "Point is, which flippin' way have the blighters gone? Prob'ly downstream, but they might've gone upstream just to fool any pursuers, wot!"

Jango scratched his grey whiskers. "Couldn't have gone upstream or we'd have spotted 'em before we got to the raft. I think downstream's the best bet. Wot's yore verdic', Oakie?"

Oakheart stared downstream to where the water ran out into open country before it looped back into woodland. "A plausible thought, sirrah. Actually, that's the route we were planning on taking today. Bound for Redwall, y'see. Er, that's before we had a turn of ill fortune and went aground. Purely through no fault of my own, I assure you, *Streamlass* is jammed tight on the rocks."

Jango signalled his logboats to dock on the bank. "Hmm, I'm havin' a few thoughts on this situation. Tell ye wot. Jump aboard an' let's git back to yore raft, Oakie. I'll have a word with the wives. But lissen, all of ye—don't make any mention of vermin tracks in front of the ladies. Y'know 'ow that sort o' thing upsets 'em. Leave the rest t'me."

Furm and Dymphnia were questioning them even before they had boarded the raft.

"Was there any sign o' my liddle twins—did ye see them?"

"Did ye pick up Midda an' Borti's trail? Wot about Flib?"

Diggs was at his courteous best. "Patience, ladies. There was no sign of any young uns, but that's all t'the bloomin' good, really. Now, Log a Log Jango has a proposition to discuss with you. By the way, marms, is there any chance of a jolly old bite or two? We'll eat on the bank while the Guosim crew refloat your craft, wot, wot?"

Whilst the shrews made the raft streamworthy again, the rest sat on the bank lunching on mushroom pasties and celery soup.

Jango explained his scheme. "Now, we don't know if the little uns are lost or just roamed off someplace, like young uns do now'n'then. Any lost creatures in this neighbourhood always ends up at the same place, Redwall Abbey, right?"

Furm agreed. "Aye, that's right enough. The Abbey always welcomes lostbeasts, especially young uns. But suppose they're not there, wot then?"

Oakheart spoke encouragingly. "Then what better place to enquire than Redwall? Have they not got more knowledge of this area than anybeast? Why, 'pon me spikes, I'll wager Abbess Marjoram will be ready and more than willing to assist us!"

Buckler took the initiative, silencing any doubts by declaring stoutly, "Then there's no more t'be said, friends. Next stop Redwall, I say. Agreed?"

Everybeast raised a shout of assent, except Diggs, who had a mouthful of pasty—he nodded furiously.

The Guosim lashed their logboats to the sides of the raft. With their combined paddling and a light breeze to swell the sail, *Streamlass* got underway in brisk style. To assure himself that there were no long faces and to avoid speculation about the young uns' fate, Jango gave the order for his Guosim to give a shanty. This had the added virtue of keeping the paddle strokes in unison. To the tapping of small drums and some fancy headspike work on Oakheart's Hogalino, the shrews sang out lustily.

"A rum tum tum, a rum tum tum
Oh, pass me a paddle, matey!

"I'll be sailin' all me days,
along these good ole waterways,
there's nothin' like a gentle breeze,
an' bein' alive on days like these.

"A rum tum tum, a rum tum tum,
Oh, pass me a paddle, matey!

"Through woodland thick our logboats ply,
that's how I loves to see the sky,
a-driftin' by in sun an' shade,
round willowy bank an' leafy glade.

"A rum tum tum, a rum tum tum,
Oh, pass me a paddle, matey!

"Now, I could never understand,
why somebeasts spend a life on land,
an' never hearken to the call,
of rapids wild or waterfall.

"A rum tum tum, a rum tum tum,
Oh, pass me a paddle, matey!

"An' when my stream of life runs out,
don't weep for me or mope about,
just lay me in some ole logboat,
an' to the sea of dreams I'll float.

"A rum tum tum, a rum tum tum,
Oh, pass me a paddle, matey!"

The logboats emerged from the woodland fringe onto the heathlands. Buckler and Diggs leaned on the rail of the raft. Several times they had volunteered to wield paddles alongside the shrews. Their attempts elicited some fruity rebuffs from the Guosim, who were convinced nobeast was their equal at paddling.

One wag called out, "Ye wouldn't need paddles—you two could do the job wid those long ears o' yores!"

Log a Log Jango rebuked the caller sternly. "Mind yore manners, Fligl, or I'll take that paddle to yore tail!"

Diggs munched on a pasty he had rescued at lunch. "This is the life, old scout. Hah, I'll wager General Flackbuth'd go spare if he could see us now, wot!"

Buckler sighed. It was indeed a pleasant interlude, just leaning on the rail taking in the scenery. Bees buzzed around the red clover growing in clumps on the heath. Clouded yellow butterflies winged gaily in and out of the harebells and scarlet poppies. Dragonflies patrolled the stream edges on iridescent wings, guarding their territory from caddis fly and alderfly.

Young Rambuculus joined the hares, pointing to the distant tree fringe off to their left. "We'll be there by eventide. See the way this stream takes a broad curve? Prob'ly arrive at Redwall some time afore tomorrow evenin'."

Buckler nodded. "Does this stream flow right to the Abbey?"

Rainbow, the Witherspyks' resident mole, joined them. "Nay, zurr, she'm stream bee's a-runnen some ways off. Us'll 'ave to walk to ee h'Abbey frum thurr."

Rambuculus explained further, "There's a liddle dead-end cut-off backstream. That'll be the closest to Redwall we can get. It's a good place to stow the raft an' the shrew-boats, too. Not too far a walk from there, mates."

Diggs brushed pasty crumbs from his tunic. "By the left an' the centre, Buck. These chaps have certainly got it worked out, wot! Paddle an' sail wherever you jolly well can, an' march as little as bloomin' possible. Y'know, I think Salamandastron could do with some sailin' craft, have a sort of navy of its own, wot! That'd be just the flippin' ticket for me. Think I'll suggest it to Lord Brang. Admiral Diggs, that could be me!"

Buckler chuckled. "What do you know about sailin', you great fat fraud?"

Diggs replied indignantly, "Huh, as much as you or any other beast knows. I've been lissenin', y'know. Aye, an' I've learnt a blinkin' thing or three—I know all the sayin's an' commands!"

A shrew who had been eavesdropping from the logboat closest to them called out, "Go on then, rabbet—show us wot ye know!"

Diggs waggled his ears scornfully at the Guosim. "Rab-bet, y'self, spikebonce. Right—listen t'this."

Cupping both paws around his mouth, Diggs called out in what he imagined was true nautical style, "Lower yore tillers, me hearties. Take 'er about an' swell me scuppers, make fast yore rowlocks an' forard yore stern, then unfurl yore mastheads—ahoy, mateys, an' so on. Well, how was that for an old riverdog, eh?"

Log a Log Jango gave him a scornful wink. "That's enough t'sink any vessel an' drive the crew mad."

As predicted, they made the woodlands by midevening, sailing on in search of a likely place to spend the night. The trees were tall, ancient and sombre, blocking out daylight completely—a far different atmosphere from the sunny, open expanse of heathland. Silence shrouded everything, making the surroundings rather eerie. The Guosim lit lanterns, which reflected the gloomy green light of the overhead leaf canopy. Oakheart drove a spiked timber into the shallows, mooring *Streamlass* so she would not run foul of underwater obstacles and get stuck again.

Once everybeast was ashore, things began to jolly up a bit. A long-dead fallen pine upon the bank soon provided a big, cheerful fire. Guosim cooks took over, and from the pooled provisions of themselves, the two hares and the Witherspyk troupe, they provided the travellers with a supper which would have passed muster in most places.

Buckler was concerned about the size of the fire. "Jango, d'you think this blaze could spread?"

The Guosim Log a Log waved a paw at the massive trees surrounding them. Some of their trunks were of great girth and coated in moss.

"These things are so big'n'old an' damp that ye could light a fire at their bases, an' it wouldn't harm 'em. C'mon, sit ye down, Buck. No need to worry over things like that. The beer's brewed an' the bread's baked."

Guosim vittles were good; shrewbread had various fillings baked into it, some sweet, others savoury. The nettle beer had been towed along behind the logboats all day. It was cold and bitter, but very refreshing.

Everybeast was enjoying supper when Sniffy, the Guosim scout, began twitching his snout. He sidled over to sit beside Jango and Buckler.

The young hare watched as the scout whispered something to his Log a Log. They held a brief conversation together, then Sniffy beckoned some other shrews. Slowly, casually, they retreated from the camp, vanishing into the surrounding woodland.

Realising something of importance had taken place, Buckler kept his voice low. "Jango, what's going on? Anything wrong?"

The Shrew Chieftain's lips barely moved as he murmured, "Keep yore wits about ye, mate. We might 'ave a chance t'see how good ye are wid that long blade o' yores. Now, don't make any sudden moves, Buck, but sniff the air—not too deep, though."

Buckler did as he was bade. "Hmm, strange smell, sort of musty an' sweet. Smoky, too, but I don't think it's coming from our fire. What is it?"

Jango stirred the ashes at the fire's edge with his rapier as he explained. "It's a vermin tribe called the Flitcheye. They're split into two bunches, one lot out o'sight in the trees. The rest are right here inside our camp."

Buckler knew enough not to make a move. He kept his tone low and level. "I don't doubt your word, friend, but I can't see any Flitcheye loiterin' about here."

Jango replied with a quick flick of his rapier point. "Over there, in the loam, t'the left o' those ferns, I saw the dead leaves stir a bit. Flitcheye are experts at camouflage an' hidin' theirselves. That smoke ye can smell—sooner or later, it'll send ye fast asleep. Oh, they ain't in a hurry. They'll just wait 'til we're all settled down for the night afore they comes out o' cover to murder us."

Buckler touched the long blade at his side, where he had laid it. "So, I want to wake up in the mornin'. What's your plan?"

Jango stroked his grey whiskers, smiling thinly. " 'Tis already in operation, Buck. Just wait for my shout."

Buckler noticed that the Guosim seated around the fire had pulled their headbands down about their mouths to avoid breathing in the knockout smoke. Feeling about, he gathered a pawful of damp moss to protect himself. Already, Oakheart and several members of the Witherspyk troupe were yawning and settling down, ignorant of the danger.

Buckler nudged Diggs, whose eyes were drooping. He muttered to his companion, "Hush, Diggs, don't say a word, just listen to me—"

The tubby young hare blurted out, "I haven't said a blinkin' word yet, an' what do I get for it? A bloomin' sharp nudge in the ribs, that's what, wot!"

He got no further, because at that moment Jango bellowed, "Logalogalogaloooooggg! Guosim chaaaaaarge!"

Then pandemonium reigned. Roars from Sniffy's party, mingled with enraged screeches, rang out from beyond the camp. The shrews around the fire sprang up, wielding their short rapiers as the very ground around them seemed to erupt. Ragged, tattered figures burst forth from hiding.

They made a hideous sight in the dancing shadows and firelight, waving primitive weapons as they chanted eerily, "We d'Flitcheye Flitcheye! Haaaayeeee!"

To further confuse the situation, the Witherspyks stumbled to their paws, with Oakheart declaiming, " 'Tis a foul ambush—save the ladies an' babes!"

A ragged, shadowy figure seized Trajidia, who warbled dramatically, even in that grave situation, "Murder and abduction has befallen us! Help, oh, help!"

Buckler felled the creature with a swift blow from his sword hilt, echoing Diggs's war cry as he threw himself into the fray. "Eulaliiiiiaaaa! Give 'em blood'n'vinegar!"

9

Abbess Marjoram stood close to the big tapestry in Great Hall, staring up at the image of Martin the Warrior, the long-dead founder of Redwall Abbey. The figure woven into the fabric of the wonderful picture was that of a heroic mouse, armoured and resting upon his fabulous sword. Above the tapestry the actual sword was mounted on two silver wallpins. It had been forged from a fragment of meteor in the long-distant past by a Badger Lord at Salamandastron. Marjoram gazed into Martin's eyes—they were strong, the eyes of a true warrior, but with humour and compassion dwelling in them. The Abbess spoke.

"I know it seems trivial, after all the wars and tribulations Redwall has undergone, but I can't help worrying about our two Dibbuns, poor little things. Martin, who knows, maybe they'll turn up and my fears will have been for nothing. But suppose something bad has befallen them, what shall I do?"

No answer seemed forthcoming. However, Marjoram sat on the worn stone floor, still staring up at the face of Martin the Warrior. Sometimes it seemed to move slightly in the flickering candle and lantern light which surrounded the tapestry, but that could have been a stray draught moving the material. She continued her vigil, hoping against hope for a response.

Then somebeast was shaking her gently. "Mother Abbess, are you alright?"

Marjoram found herself looking up into the kindly face of her friend Sister Fumbril. The Infirmary Keeper helped her to stand upright, explaining, "I saw you lying there and thought you had fainted away."

Marjoram could tell by the evening light from the stained-glass windows that some time had elapsed since she came down to the tapestry. She blinked.

"Er, I'm fine, Sister—don't know what happened to me, really. I must've dozed off. Huh, I must be getting old."

The jolly otter smiled as she led her to the kitchen. "We all have t'get old at some time, Marj, though I don't think you've quite reached those seasons yet. I thought you'd be someplace searchin' for Guffy an' Tassy. What were you doin', takin' an evenin' nap?"

They sat down at Friar Soogum's kitchen table, helping themselves to beakers of hot mint tea, which was often left steaming on the oven plate.

Marjoram sipped gratefully. "Oh, that tastes good, Fumbril. Actually, I went to the tapestry to see Martin the Warrior. I hoped I might get some hint about our missing Dibbuns."

Sister Fumbril topped up her beaker. "And did you?"

The mouse Abbess shook her head. "I'm afraid not. Maybe we've neglected our Abbey's guiding spirit. Perhaps he doesn't speak anymore."

Fumbril patted her friend's paw. "Surely not. Martin's being is in these very stones that surround us—he's part o' Redwall. Think now, is there anything in your mind, anything?"

Marjoram shrugged. "Only Corim Althier. My goodness! Where did that come from?"

Fumbril looked up from her tea. "Corim Althier? Did

Martin put that in your mind? What's it supposed to mean?"

The Abbess was really perplexed. "Martin must have spoken while I was asleep. Corim Althier . . . I haven't the foggiest notion of its meaning. Have you any ideas, Sister?"

Fumbril stirred honey into her mint tea. "How should I know, Marj? I ain't a riddle solver, or a wise ole scholar. Granvy the Recorder, I think he'd be the one to ask."

They were about to set off for Granvy's usual habitat, the gatehouse, when Cellarmole Gurjee came trundling through Great Hall, calling to Marjoram, "Yurr, marm, cumm ee farst, naow. Ee rarscally vurmint bee's spotted!"

They followed him out onto the side lawn, where a dozen or more Redwallers stood at the orchard entrance, all looking up at the Abbey, pointing and calling out.

"There, up above the dormitories—he's in the attics!"

Marjoram peered up at the high, tiny windowspaces. "How d'you know? Has anybeast seen him?"

Bribby, a little Dibbun mousemaid, piped up. "H'I see'd 'im Muvver Marj, stannin' by dat winder!"

The Abbess lifted the babe up. "Show me where."

Following the line of Bribby's pointing paw, the Redwallers stared up at the window she was indicating.

Bartij, the big hedgehog Gardener, sighted Globby, the escaped young stoat. "Aye—did ye see? He jus' popped his head out but pulled it back in quicklike when he saw us all lookin' up there. That's the rascally stoat, alright!"

The Abbess clenched her paws decisively. "Then he must be caught. That stoat may have information about our little ones. Fumbril, you stay here and watch the Dibbuns. Bartij, Brother Tollum, will you come with me? Where's Skipper?"

Friar Soogum answered, "Prob'ly still in the woodlands searchin' for the liddle uns, marm."

Accompanied by Bartij and Tollum, Marjoram headed

indoors. "As soon as Skipper gets back, send him to us—we'll be up in the attics."

It was plain to Globby he had been spotted. He knew they would be coming up after him, so trying to get past them was out of the question. Dusk was falling—he had no lantern or torch with him. He was scared of venturing higher on the dark, winding stairs, and he could not go down.

So he did the only thing he could think of. Barring the door of the little attic room, he crouched in a dusty corner, grasping the knife he had stolen from the kitchen. He had no more to eat or drink and did not know what to do next. The young stoat could see a single star through the small open window. Without comrades around him, all pretence of being a vermin Ravager dropped away. He sobbed quietly, cursing his ill-fated trespass into Redwall Abbey.

Carrying lanterns, the three searchers made their way upstairs. They had four flights to climb, two of dormitories and sickbay, and two of deserted attics, where nobeast had set paw for many seasons.

When they reached the long, gloomy passage, Brother Tollum placed a paw to his mouth. "Hush now—we may yet surprise the villain."

Taking the doors on the right side of the corridor, they opened them, one by one. The first three creaked on ancient hinges, revealing nothing more exciting than broken furniture shrouded in dust, with the odd bird feather here and there.

On trying the fourth door along, the Abbess turned to her companions, silently mouthing, "Locked."

Brother Tollum took over. He rapped the door sharply, his sepulchral voice booming out, "Come on out—we know you're in there, vermin!"

There was no reply, so Bartij tried. The big hedgehog had a naturally gruff voice: "The longer ye keep us waitin', the worse 'tis goin' t'be for ye, so git yoreself out 'ere, ye scallywag!"

There was a sob in Globby's voice as he shouted back, "Come out, an' wot for? So ye can drag me down t'that cookin' place an' beat me wid one o' those long paddles. Lissen, youse, I gotta big knife 'ere, an' I'll gut the first un who comes in 'ere. So go 'way an' leave me alone. Go on, clear off!"

This time the Abbess tried, speaking in a soothing tone. "Globby—it is Globby, isn't it? I promise you won't get beaten. Come out. We just want to talk."

The young stoat's reply was scornful. "Lissen, I ain't comin' out fer you or nobeast . . ."

Brother Tollum whispered to Marjoram, "Keep him talkin'. I've got an idea."

He crept off along the passage, leaving the Abbess to continue reasoning with Globby.

"You'll have to come out sooner or later. Don't be silly, friend. Unlock the door—you've got my word that you won't be hurt."

Globby laughed bitterly. "Hah, so you say. But when we talk, if'n I don't give ye the answers yore after, then ye'll turn me over t'dat big riverdog wid the paddle, an' he'll belt the daylights out o' me tail. Yew lot must think I'm stoopid!"

Meanwhile Tollum had raced downstairs and grabbed a coil of rope. The tall, thin Bellringer was still in his middle seasons, sound in wind and limb. Carrying the rope, he made the speedy ascent back upstairs, passing the floor in question, and sprinting up to the floor above it. Counting the rooms, he entered the fourth one, then knotted one end of the rope over a crossbeam, paying it out of the window. Tollum did all this with silent efficiency, not wanting to give away the element of surprise.

With squirrellike agility, he vaulted through the window, holding the rope out with both paws. Kicking hard against the wall, he bounded out from the Abbey into space. Tollum swung hard at the open window, unable to see his quarry in the darkness.

Globby had run to the door to hurl more insults at his tormentors. He heard the sudden whoosh of displaced air and turned, grasping the knife, thrusting it forward.

It was ill fortune for both creatures. The knife sank deep into the squirrel's midriff, but his outstretched footpaws, rigid with shock, smashed into Globby's narrow chest just below the throat. Fatally injured, both beasts slumped to the floor.

The pair outside the door heard the crash and the thud of bodies falling to the floorboards.

Abbess Marjoram pounded on the door. "What is it—what's going on in there?"

"Step aside, Marm. We'll soon see!"

It was Skipper, returning from the woodlands. "Righto, Bartij, mate, both together . . . one, two . . ."

On the word *three,* they charged the door together. There was a splintering snap of the wooden bar which held the room locked, then the door burst open.

Skipper was at Brother Tollum's side instantly. The Abbey Bellringer was sitting with his back to the wall, staring at the knife plunged deep into him.

The otter cradled his head as he slumped to one side. "Tollum, can ye hear me, mate? It's Skipper!"

The normally saturnine squirrel smiled oddly. "Who's sounding the bells? I can hear my bells being tolled. They sound . . . so beautiful. . . ."

Abbess Marjoram knelt at Tollum's side, clasping his paw. "Hurry, Skip—run and get Sister Fumbril. Tell her to bring herbs, dressings, salve, anything!"

Prying the Abbess's grip loose, the brawny otter lifted Brother Tollum bodily. "Too late, marm. This goodbeast's gone."

Marjoram looked suddenly lost. She stared blankly at the Otter Chieftain. "Brother Tollum dead? It's not possible. I'll go and get Sister Fumbril myself!"

Bartij stopped her hurrying from the attic room. Taking Marjoram's face in both paws, the big hedgehog assured her softly, "Take Skipper's word, marm. Pore Tollum's already gone to the quiet meadows. Let's take a look at the other one. We need to get some information out of him, even if'n 'e is hurted."

Marjoram pulled herself together resolutely. "Yes, you're right. I'd best see what we can do for him. I need to talk with that one."

Globby was lying in a crumpled heap, footpaws twitching, forepaws clasped tight to his chest. The Abbess turned him over carefully, calling to Bartij, "Go and bring something for him to drink."

She lifted the young stoat's head. He coughed, a harsh, rattling noise from his blood-flecked lips.

Marjoram came right to the point. "Globby, what's happened to our two young ones, a squirrelbabe and a tiny mole? Where are they, d'you know? Have they been taken?"

Globby peered up at the Abbess; his eyes were drooping. His lips moved slightly, but no sound came out.

Something told Marjoram that the stoat's life was ebbing fast. She continued more urgently, "You must tell me—where have the little ones gone? Say something, Globby, speak!"

The Ravager stared at her. He shook his head weakly.

Martin's words flashed through Marjoram's mind. She leaned close to Globby, whispering desperately, "Corim, Althier—does that mean anything to you? Think! Corim . . . Althier?"

The young stoat seemed to recover momentarily. He moved as if trying to sit up straight, his eyes wide as he pointed a shaking paw toward the open window. "Althier . . . Althier . . . Sable Quean!"

Then he gave one last bubbling sigh as the life fled from his broken body.

Accompanied by Bartij, Sister Fumbril hurried in. She took a flask from her satchel of medications, but Marjoram shook her head.

"He's gone, just like Brother Tollum."

Fumbril nodded sadly. "I passed Skipper on the landing—he was carryin' Tollum downstairs. An awful thing, Mother Abbess, dreadful! I know 'tis not the time t'be askin' questions, but did the vermin give ye anythin' to go on about our missin' Dibbuns?"

Marjoram relinquished the limp form of Globby. "He never said anything about them. Then I asked him if he knew what Corim Althier meant."

Fumbril covered the young stoat with a blanket. "Oh, an' did he?"

The Abbess answered, "Well, he didn't seem to know anything about the word *Corim,* but it seemed he was trying to tell me something—he looked frightened, pointed to the outside through the window. 'Althier, Althier, Sable Quean!' That was all he managed to say. Then he slipped away before I could ask him anything more."

Sister Fumbril shouldered her bag. "More reason to speak with our Recorder. Let's go and find Granvy."

Vilaya the Sable Quean stared distastefully at the head of Grullba Deathwind fixed onto the pike point. She turned her attention to Kodra, the river rat who was bearing it.

"Who told you to bring that thing into my chambers?"

The big dull rat looked up at the head, as if expecting it to reply. He spoke haltingly. "Er, Lord Zwilt brought me 'ere, said to show Grullba ter yew. Er, 'e'll be 'ere soon."

A moment later, Zwilt the Shade appeared, dragging a laden sack behind him. Signalling to the sentries, he snapped curtly, "Give these to Thwip and Binta. Have them put with the others when they waken!"

Zwilt's manner changed completely as he turned to Vilaya. A rare triumphant smile lit up his sinister features. "Majesty, did I not say that I would bring you the head of Grullba Deathwind? Well, here it is, along with every beast he commanded—they are with our Ravagers, at the camp in the woodlands."

The old rat Dirva wrinkled her nose in disgust, pointing to the pike bearer. "An' who is that big clod, eh?"

Zwilt directed his reply at Vilaya. "That's Kodra. He's going to be one of my captains."

The Sable Quean's glittering dark eyes turned to the big stolid river rat; her voice was like silk over ice. "Put that dirty thing down and come here, Captain Kodra."

Laying the pike and its grisly burden down, Kodra approached. He stood stiffly to attention in front of Vilaya. She exchanged a sly smile with Dirva, then beckoned Kodra closer. "Now, kneel and bow your head before me, then repeat these words: 'I will serve you until I die.' "

The river rat obeyed Vilaya, kneeling and repeating the oath. He flinched slightly as she patted the exposed back of his neck. Dirva sniggered, but fell silent at a glance from her Sable Quean, who issued further orders.

"Go outside now, find a stream in the woodlands, and wait until you hear my call, Captain Kodra."

The river rat marched off with a proud smile on his oafish features. Zwilt was curious.

"I've never seen you do that before, Majesty . . . ?"

Vilaya showed her small, sharp teeth angrily. "That's because you've never brought strange vermin to Althier. How many more of your new recruits have you told about this place? Fool!"

Zwilt was unused to being addressed in this manner. He knew how dangerous his position might become. So he answered courteously. "None of the others know about Althier. Don't worry—I'll have a word with Kodra. He'll keep his mouth shut, I'm certain."

Dirva sniggered again, and Vilaya shook her head slowly at Zwilt's ignorance. When she spoke again, her voice was a savage hiss. "Oh, Kodra will keep his mouth shut forever—I've made sure of that. He won't be talking to anybeast!"

Zwilt was puzzled. "Majesty?"

The Sable Quean held up her paw, the one that had

patted Kodra's neck. Lying flat upon it was her small dagger tipped with the poisonous adder venom. She returned it to the crystal sheath, which was filled with the deadly fluid. Vilaya exchanged another meaningful glance with the old rat, Dirva.

"Well, he did promise to serve me until his death. How long do you think that'll be?"

Dirva cackled. "Not long, my Quean, not long at all!"

Vilaya turned to two of her Ravager guards. "Pick up Kodra's trail. When he's dead, push him into the stream, 'twill save burying the idiot. Take that head with you and throw it in after him. Go!"

As they hurried off, she turned her attention back to Zwilt. Obviously flustered by events, he shrugged lamely. "Majesty, accept my apologies. I didn't think—"

The Sable Quean leaned forward, claws bared, clutching the sides of her throne, eyes blazing and fur bristling. "Althier is my own secret place, d'you hear? If you ever bring ragtag newcomers here, then I vow you'll be following them to wait by the stream. Nobeast must know of Althier—all my plans hinge upon it!"

Zwilt the Shade bowed his head in acknowledgement.

Dirva waited for him to look up again before speaking. "What was in the sack you brought? More young uns?"

The tall sable looked to his Quean for approval. "Two hares, very young creatures."

Vilaya toyed with her necklace of snake fangs. "I did not know there were hares in this area."

Zwilt made his report. "As I was bringing the river rats back, I came across what looked like a small farm. These were the babes of the two hares who were working the land there. I slew the father and wounded the mother, but left her alive to tell the tale."

Vilaya's manner changed, her voice became silky. "You did well, my faithful Zwilt. I see you are carrying a new blade. Show me—and the medallion, too."

Zwilt swept aside his cloak. "Majesty, there is nothing I

could hide from one so keen as you." He took the medallion from his neck, passing it over by the scarlet and black woven cord.

The Sable Quean inspected it, reading the engraved word, *Blademaster,* noting the picture of a paw holding a sword aloft. " 'Tis of little use to me. Blademaster, eh? Do you consider yourself a Blademaster, Zwilt?"

The Shade drew the broadsword. He twirled it, allowing the lantern light to reflect along its length. "I was always the best with a broadsword, Majesty. Though only now do I truly feel like a Blademaster. My former weapon was nought but a crude lump of metal compared to this wonderful blade. Whoever forged this sword was an expert with steel. Look at the quality of it, the balance, the edge, the length. Truly wonderful!"

Vilaya placed the cord over Zwilt's blade, letting the medallion slide back down to him. "Keep the trinket. How will you use your new sword?"

Zwilt saluted skilfully with the blade. "Only in the service of Vilaya, my Sable Quean!"

She nodded. "Well spoke, Zwilt. You may go, but I will soon use you and the sword when I make my move."

BOOK TWO

Go Find the Babes!

10

One thing was certain, the Flitcheye had never faced two battle-crazed Salamandastron hares before. It soon became clear that the furtive vermin had bitten off far more than they could chew. The Guosim shrews, headed by Jango Bigboat, were fearless. They waded into the ragged, prancing enemy with rage and vigour, yodelling, "Logaloga-logaloooooog!"

Not to be outdone, Oakheart Witherspyk seized a blazing log from the fire, laying about him like a madbeast, whilst being joined by the rest of his troupe. What they lacked in warrior's skill they made up for in energy and enthusiasm—they invented their own war cries.

"Haharr, strewth an' have at ye, stinky vermin!"

"Zounds an' batter pudden, ye rascally snivellers!"

"Raxilly snivvers!" (That was baby Dubdub's contribution.)

Diggs got to the truth of the matter when he walloped a loaded sling over a Flitcheye head. He shook his quarry like a rag doll, until all the trailing weeds, clinging vines, leaves and a barkcloth mask fell from the beast, exposing it for what it really was.

Diggs shouted, "What'n the name o' raggedy trousers is

this? I say, you chaps, these cads are nought but runty little weasels. You impudent rogues, c'mere, tatty bum!"

In a remarkably short time, the Flitcheye found themselves being soundly trounced by hares, shrews and hedgehogs. None of their assailants seemed the least scared of them. Even Trajidia found herself throttling one of them and declaiming, "For shame, you dreadful scruffy midget—trying to pass yourself off as an ambushing warrior, eh? Take that, you snotnosed impostor, and that, an' that'n'that'n'that! Now, are you ready for another walloping?"

Caught twixt the blazing campfire and the stream, the would-be ambushers found themselves severely punished. Their numbers were swelled when Sniffy and his band drove in the Flitcheye from the woodlands. These were the beasts who had been creating the noxious smoke.

The travellers had battled so wildly that all the fight had been knocked out of their enemies. Surrender was total.

The defeated vermin fell down, grovelling for mercy amidst agonised sobs.

"Yowwwooooow! Spare us, kind gennelbeasts!"

"Ye wouldn't 'ave me kil't, would ye, sirs? I gotta pore mother an' ten liddle uns ter look arter!"

Young Rambuculus pointed the pleader out to his sister. "Hah, ye could take lessons from that rascal, Trajidia!"

Buckler restored order, bawling out in fine parade-ground manner, "Silence, you horrible lot! Next beast to make a sound gets slain forthwith. Now shut up!"

This had the desired effect. The Flitcheye fell quiet, apart from the odd groan, sob or sniffle.

Dymphnia Witherspyk glanced fearfully at Buckler. "What do you plan on doing with these unfortunate wretches?"

Baby Dubdub echoed her—"Affortunate wrenches!"—and went back to sucking his paw.

Diggs twirled his loaded sling nonchalantly. "Aye, thought up any blinkin' dreadful fate yet, old lad?"

Jango Bigboat interrupted, with the age-old solution: "Wipe 'em all out, mate. They'd have murdered us—aye, an' not swiftly either. I've 'eard tales o' Flitcheye deeds that don't bear thinkin' about. Right, Sniffy?"

The Guosim scout tested the point of his rapier. "Right, Chief. The only good vermin's a dead un!"

Oakheart protested, " 'Pon me spikes, sirrah, you don't mean that we should slaughter them all? It's unthinkable!"

Oakheart's mother, Crumfiss, a shrewd old hedgehog, looked to Buckler, who was obviously in command. "What's your opinion, Longblade?"

The young hare stared at the quivering, prostrate vermin. "I'm with Oakheart. It's one thing slaying a foebeast in the heat of battle, but defeating 'em then killing the survivors isn't right. That'd make us murderers, an' no better than the Flitcheye. Where I come from, that sort o' thing just ain't done. It's against any true warrior's code."

Jango nodded. "Ye may have a point there, Buck. But wot are ye goin' t'do, eh? We can't just turn 'em loose."

A sudden idea came to Buckler. "Give the Flitcheye a taste of their own medicine."

Rainbow, the only mole in the Witherspyk troupe, chuckled gruffly. "Ahurrhurr, you'm mean to make ee vurrmints sniffen they'm own narsty smoke, zurr?"

Diggs backed his friend up to the hilt. "I say, what a super wheeze, Buck. Send the filthy blighters off for a jolly long snooze, wot. That'll teach the little rotters. Hawhawhaw!"

The plan seemed to catch the approval of everybeast, even Jango and Sniffy. Buckler set the scheme into action, calling out orders. "Take all their weapons and chuck 'em in the stream. Get them all out of those scary rags an' face masks—burn the lot! Sniffy, scout along the streambank. See if you can spot a couple of willows near the edge. Jango, Oakie, get all their supplies of those herbs they use to create the knockout fumes!"

It took a while, but finally everything was in position. Stripped of all their barbarous apparel, the Flitcheye were exposed for what they really were, a pathetic, primitive tribe of stunted weasels. They stood in sullen silence as Guosim logboat crewbeasts bound them securely, neck to neck, tail to tail and paw to paw.

Both hares and the Witherspyks escorted the hobbling gang along the bank. Sniffy had chosen well. Three big weeping willows growing side by side spread their leafy canopy down to touch the stream current. To both sides and the rear of the willows, Jango and his Guosim were piling up mounds of dried brush, dead leaves and damp loam.

The Flitcheye wailed and moaned as they were bound to the trunks and branches of the willows.

"Ayaaaaah! No, no, please, sirs. Mercy!"

Diggs wrinkled his nose at them. "Oh, stop blubberin'. A few days' sleep an' a bloomin' big headache when ye wake should do you rotters the flippin' world o' good, wot, wot. Cheer up now, chaps!"

The entire supply of the dreaded herbs was spread on the mounds. Jango was allowed the privilege of setting light to the fires. The Guosim Log a Log was in jovial spirits as he tossed lighted brands onto the heaps of combustibles, grinning from ear to ear.

"Sweet dreams, ye stinkin' villains! C'mon, now, all together, breathe deeply. . . . In an' hold, an' slowly out! There, that's the style, an' I hope ye'll wake with a headache that'll last ye a half season, ye scurvy vermin. Now, how does that feel, mateys?"

Standing clear of the fumes, everybeast waded into the shallows to watch what would happen. The overhanging willows acted like an enveloping canopy, catching the smoke and holding it as it grew more dense. Dimly, they could see the Flitcheye being punished for their misdeeds. With eyes streaming, the vermin stood bound to the willows, some trying to hold their breath, others weeping and moaning as they slumped into a nightmarish pit of dreams.

Buckler shouldered his blade. "Justice done, eh, Jango?"

The Shrew Chieftain clasped his paw warmly. "Aye, done, an' seen t'be done, matey!"

Diggs winked at Sniffy. "Y'see, old scout, there's more ways to skinnin' a frog than feedin' it 'til it bursts, wot. Come on, let's go, but quietly, please—don't want to disturb those chaps from their snooze!"

The rest of the night passed uneventfully. They took a quick breakfast in the dawnlight and set off upstream with the flotilla of logboats and the raft. The woodlands were still enclosed in the gloomy green-tinged half-light as they turned off down the sidestream.

The water was foul and stagnant, because it terminated, further up, in a dead end. Much to the relief of everybeast, the tree foliage thinned out, exposing blue sky and sunlight overhead.

Log a Log Jango called a halt, whilst one of the Guosim produced an earthenware jar full of an evil-smelling unction.

Diggs sniffed it and gagged. "Phwaw, what a bloomin' pong! Is it some sort of secret weapon for chuckin' at the blinkin' enemy?"

Taking a pawful, Sniffy began smearing it on his face. "This is shrewgoo, mate. Ain't you ever 'eard of it? Lissen, we're goin' t'be sailin' through all sorts of stingy insecks soon. Wasps'n'ornets, zingers'n'biters. The blighters'll eat ye alive if'n you ain't got shrewgoo on yore face."

Jango began daubing the stuff on his head. "Sniffy's right. Those insecks don't like the ole shrewgoo—they won't bother ye if'n ye smear some on."

Taking the Guosims' advice, all the travellers applied the anti-insect unction to their faces, though not with any great relish.

Trajidia wailed pitifully, "Alas, this fair maid will never

again smell like a dawn-dewed rose. Creatures will run a mile from me!"

Auroria, Oakheart's other daughter, leaned over the rail of the raft. "Whooohoops! I think I'm going t'be sick, dreadful pongy shrewgoo!"

"Shooey pongroo!" was baby Dubdub's comment.

Diggs watched in horror as Buckler smeared his face. "Good grief, Buck! You ain't actually puttin' that confounded stuff on your han'some young fizzgog, wot? Keep it well away from me, chaps. I'd sooner put up with the jolly old zingers. Hah, I ain't smellin' like a mouldy old toad's midden on a rainy day. Not me!"

Jango's wife, Furm, shook her head at Diggs. "We'll see, my friend. We'll see!"

Though the trees had thinned out, the reeds, bulrushes and waterweed thickened up drastically. Travelling in single file, the logboats had to force a passage through for *Streamlass.*

Then the insects struck. The still, hot air buzzed and thrummed as they attacked in myriads. Clouds of winged tormentors rose from the disturbed waters of the sidestream.

Dymphnia, carrying baby Dubdub, urged her daughters, Furm, Crumfiss and the other ladies into the blockhouse on the raft. They slammed the door and let down the shutters. It worked rather well, so they lit a smoky fire, which poured out of the little chimney, giving some relief to the paddlers. Diggs was in a pitiful condition, his whole head, from eartips to throat, covered in angry swellings.

Buckler assisted Jango to push him into the blockhouse, even though Diggs was protesting.

"Ab aw bwight, chabs—lee me balone!"

Jango hustled him roughly inside, calling to the ladies, "Take care o' this young idjit. His mouth is so badly stung he can't even talk proper!"

It was midnoon before they lost the insects, owing to the tall trees closing in on them again.

Buckler sat down on the raft deck, sighing with relief as he stared up into the green-tinged gloom. "I'd sooner face a vermin horde than have t'go through that again. We'd best go an' see how our wounded warrior's doing, eh, Oakie?"

The irrepressible Diggs was surrounded by females dabbing him with soothing salves of dockleaf, sanicle and foxglove. He gave them a lumpy smile, winking one swollen eyelid as he supped up warm vegetable soup through a hollow reed.

"Hewwo, chapth. I bee alwight thoon, woth woth!"

A shudder shook the raft as Jango called from outside, "That's as far as we goes. Make fast all vessels, fore an' aft. Sniffy, see everythin' is well covered with branches'n'bush. Form up on the bankside. We'll be movin' out soon!"

They sat on the banks of the cul-de-sac making their last meal that day. Buckler thanked Dymphnia and her daughters as he tucked into vegetable soup, a hazelnut bake and some cold plum duff.

Trajidia fluttered her eyelashes furiously as she giggled. "Think nothing of it, sir. 'Tis the least we could do after the way you steered us through that pestilence!"

Dymphnia chided her daughter. "Stop that outrageous flirting and get busy serving vittles to these hungry beasts!"

"Vikkles to 'ungry beaks!" Dubdub echoed.

Packing all they needed, the travellers set off at a leisurely pace into the woodlands. Jango walked up front with Buckler.

"I don't reckon we'll make Redwall Abbey tonight. Still, no hurry—we'll take brekkist in the Abbey tomorrow mornin', if'n we gets an early start. Then we'll talk to Abbess Marjoram an' her elders about the problem of our young uns. I'm sure she'll be able to 'elp us."

Buckler ducked an overhanging yew branch. "You seem to have confidence in Redwall an' its creatures, Jango."

The Guosim Chieftain smiled. "Aye, an' so would you, if you'd ever visited the Abbey afore, mate."

They trudged steadily onward. In his mind, Buckler was going over all that had happened to him and Diggs since they had left Salamandastron. Lord Brang was right, travel was an adventure, and there was more to come!

Much more.

11

The two fox jailers, Thwip and Binta, usually struck fear into the hearts of their little prisoners at Althier. Wielding whip and rod, they would swagger about, snarling and threatening the young creatures, reducing them to quivering wrecks.

However, this was not the case with the shrewmaid, Petunia Rosebud—or Flib, as she had named herself. The instant she was unbound from the spearhaft she had been carried on, she flew at her captors, attacking them savagely.

"Ya scrinjee-gobbed babe robbers, git yer filfy paws off a me or I'll rip yore 'eads off!"

Thwip cracked his lash. "Hoho, a tough un, eh?"

Binta came at Flib, swishing her cane. "Get in there with the others afore I beat the hide from yore back. . . . Eeeyah, she bit me!"

The shrewmaid had her teeth into Binta's ear. She hung on, growling like a wild beast. Thwip could not use his whip for fear of striking Binta. He grabbed Flib, trying to pry her loose from the other fox's ear.

"Right, I'm goin' to teach ye a lesson yer won't forget missy . . . gnnarrrrgh!"

Two well-aimed kicks from Flib smashed into his mouth.

"Yeeeh yeeh! Guards! 'Elp us . . . 'eeeeelp!"

It took four other Ravagers to subdue Flib. Swiftly binding her paws, they managed to fling her into the gloomy holding cavern.

Thwip held three broken teeth out to the guards. "Look wot she did ter me! That un's crazy mad, I tell yer!"

One of the guards passed Binta a pawful of dried moss. "Git that on yore lug, afore ye bleeds t'death."

The vixen could taste her own blood—it was running down the side of her muzzle. She spat out spitefully, "No vittles or drink for two days—that goes for 'em all! Maybe that'll calm 'er down, when the others see it's 'er fault they ain't gettin' fed!"

One of the guards, a stern-faced ferret, spoke. "That ain't fer you t'say, Binta. Our orders come from the Sable Quean, not from you. Now go an' get their grub ready."

Flib stared at her younger brother and sister in the badly lit cave. "Midda, Borti, wot are youse two doin' in 'ere?"

Borti began crying. Midda covered his mouth. "Shush, baby—look, it's our big sister!"

Flib was simmering with rage. She gnawed at the cord binding her paws, snapping at her younger sister, "Why'd ye let 'em capture Borti, eh?"

Midda snapped back at her, "If I'd run off an' left Borti, I might have got away. You were on yore own—why did you let 'em capture you?"

Flib never answered. She bit away madly at her bonds, staring around at the pitiful groups of young beasts who cowered in the wall shadows. As she did, her temper became more unreasonable. She snarled at them, "Wot are yew lot starin' at? Why don't ye all try to escape, instead of jus' mopin' round?"

Flandor, the young male otter, gave her the answer. "Right, we charge the vermin without a weapon twixt us. A pile of young uns, some who can just about toddle, an' some with little uns to look after, like yore sister. Have ye got any more bright ideas, shrew?"

Flib finished chewing through her bonds. She flung the cord away angrily. "No, riverdog—have yew?"

Flandor dropped his voice. "I'm rackin' my brain for a way out of here, but it ain't that simple. Most of 'em in here are too hungry t'think of plans. They're more worried about where their next meal is comin' from an' if it's goin' to be enough t'live on."

Tura the squirrelmaid sided with Flandor. "Aye, we heard the way you fought Thwip an' Binta out there. Very brave of ye, I'm sure. But think about this—they'll prob'ly stop our vittles as a punishment."

Even Midda was in agreement with Flandor and Tura. "Us older ones can stand a few days' hunger, but what about these poor babes? There's not just Borti. Infant mice, squirrels, hedgehogs, moles, even two little hares arrived just afore you did. How long d'ye think any of those can last without vittles?"

Flib was in no mood to be reasonable. She carried on rebelliously. "They can't stop the vittles. Let's all tell 'em so. C'mon, all of ye shout, We want vittles! Right, all together, now. One, two . . . we want vittles!"

At first there was only Flib shouting. She began seizing others and shaking them. "Shout out, will ye? We want vittles. Shout! Shout!"

For some unknown reason, everybeast obeyed. Not only did they cry out, but they repeated, louder and louder, "We want vittles! We want vittles!"

The stern-faced ferret guard bellowed back at them, "Alright, stop that noise. The vittles are on their way!"

Flib felt triumphant. Her mood changed to one of optimism. She grinned at Flandor.

"See? I told ye so. If'n ye shout loud enough, they gotta do somethin' about it. Ahoy, wot's that you've got?"

Flandor held up a small wooden spoon. "It's my spoon. I had it with me when I was captured."

Flib took the spoon. She inspected it carefully before putting out a general question to all the prisoners. "Who else has a spoon, or anythin' like one?"

Several creatures had spoons, but the one who caught the shrewmaid's eye was a young mole. She had what looked like an old broken knife made of iron. "Et wurr moi ole granfer's, but et bee'd broked, so ee give'd et to oi."

Flib took it, along with several other spoons that were strongly made and a fork carved from some type of thick bone.

Midda cautioned her sister, "Hide 'em. The foxes are here with our vittles!"

Thwip had armed himself with a spear. He waved it at Flib. "Keep yer distance, shrew. I ain't servin' yer. Wot's left in the cauldron after they've all been served will do fer you!"

Flib silently joined the back of the line. When it was her turn, she scraped out the remains of the meagre meal. Plopping it on the piece of slate which Midda used as a plate, Flib said gruffly, "I don't want any o' that bilge. Give it t' Borti."

When the meal was over, the foxes removed the cauldron and the water tub, leaving the captives alone in the gloomy cavern.

Flib posted Jinty and Jiddle Witherspyk at the entrance. "Youse two, keep yer eyes peeled an' yer ears open. If'n ye hear anybeast comin', let us know, sharpish! Flandor, fetch me those tools—the knife'n'fork an' those spoons I picked out."

Tura the squirrelmaid watched Flib going to the rear of the cavern. "What are you goin' to do?"

The Guosim shrewmaid stared at the walls speculatively. "I was keepin' me eyes open when they carried me 'ere hangin' from that spearpole. I think this whole place is built underneath an ole giant of an oaktree. Look up. Can ye see the great thick roots runnin' all ways above us? My guess is right, eh?"

Flandor passed over the eating implements. "Maybe so, but wot does that prove?"

Flib explained, "No tree as big as an oak could grow on solid rock. Trees need earth, soil to grow in. Now, you there, molemaid, wot's yore name?"

The molemaid who had donated the broken iron knife curtsied, introducing herself. "Oi'm Gurchen, marm."

Flib could not help smiling. "Well then, Gurchen, yore a mole—take a look round this place an' tell me, where's the softest spot t'start diggin'?"

"Hurr, oi'd say roight yurr whurr oi be a settin'." It was Guffy, the Redwall Dibbun.

Gurchen toddled over. She scratched the caveside where Guffy sat. "Burr aye, ee'm coorect, 'tis gurtly soily!"

Flib dug the broken knife in. It went easily, right up to the hilt. She chuckled happily.

"Good enough! This is where I starts diggin' the tunnel. Seein' as we can't fight our way out o' the front entrance, we'll dig our way outta the back!"

This news caused shouts of joy. Tura waved her paws frantically at the young ones.

"Hush! Be quiet all of ye, we don't want the vermin to know. Flib, we're all with ye, friend. Now, what can we do to help?"

The shrewmaid was in full charge; she began issuing her orders. "The two liddle moles kin 'elp me. Flandor, I want you to make a cover. Use moss, beddin', anythin' that we can disguise the hole with. Tura, get some o' the others to 'elp ye. When the soil comes out, it'll need spreadin' over the floor, so it ain't noticed."

Midda approached; she was hugging Borti, who was weeping softly for his mother. "Petunia . . . sorry, I mean Flib, wot can I do to help ye?"

Flib smiled as she stroked little Borti's head. "Just keep the babe from cryin' for his ma. Much more o' that, an' I'll be weepin' meself!"

Tassy the Redwall Dibbun smiled prettily at Flib. "Fank yoo for 'elpin' us all, nice shrew!"

Flib wiped a paw roughly across her eyes. "Don't thank me yet, darlin'. Not 'til we're outta this mouldy ole place."

Tura murmured to Flandor, "I don't think anybeast'd snitch to the vermin to get extra vittles, d'you?"

The young otter wagged his rudder. "Certainly not. Look at 'em—you can see hope in their eyes. Hope, at the chance o' freedom!"

Subaltern Meliton Gubthorpe Digglethwaite was consumed by a longing to be at Redwall Abbey as soon as possible. By that token, so were his travelling companions. Accordingly, they were all awake and on the march long before dawn. The prospect of breakfast at the Abbey lent a spring to their steps.

Young Auroria Witherspyk began singing—she was noted in the troupe for her sweet voice. It was not a particularly rousing marching song, but the beauty of it soon took effect. Everybeast felt lightpawed, dreamy almost, as the hogmaid's clear tones rose to the softly dawning day.

"When gentle dawn bedecks the land,
through woodlands green I roam,
where friendly trees stirred by the breeze,
shed deep their leafy loam.
Small birds sing sweetly to the sky,
'Pray turn dark night to day.'
By copse and hill, o'er brook and rill,
I wend my happy way.

"For there 'mid joyous scenes like these,
a heart finds rest and ease.

"Where moss and fern and forest flow'rs,
of every rainbow hue,

play host to bee and butterfly,
all bathed in early dew.
Whilst hawthorn, oak and sycamore
in every quiet glade
do please the eye of passersby,
with dappling sun and shade.

"For there 'mid joyous scenes like these,
my heart finds rest and ease."

The last tremulous notes of the lovely melody had scarce died in the pale dawnlight when Diggs roared out, "There 'tis, there 'tis! Wot ho, chaps, Redwall Abbey! The very place, wot!"

He was pointing through a break in the trees at a dim, distant shape.

Log a Log Jango confirmed the sighting. "Aye, that's the Abbey rooftops ye can see. When we gets closer, ye'll see the belltower alongside it."

Old Crumfiss shook her greyspike head. "I doubt we'll be in time for brekkist. 'Tis too far off yet. These paws o' mine can't go any faster. Unless ye all want to run along an' I'll follow."

Oakheart Witherspyk would hear of no such thing. "We all go together, Mother dear, even if I have to carry you on my back!"

Buckler drew his long blade. "There's no need for that, Oakie. Here, you Guosim, let's see if we can't make a litter. Let's lop some good branches off that fallen hazel!"

The combined swords of Buckler and four shrews had soon hewed six useful branches. These were bound, two to either side, with the remaining two spaced crossways to form a stretcher. Oakheart volunteered his tattered cloak as a seat.

They pressed on, with Crumfiss perched comfortably. Diggs, Buckler, Oakheart and Jango, with the assistance of several stout Guosim, shouldered the old hogwife. Not missing an opportunity, Dymphnia passed the hogbabe Dubdub over to Crumfiss.

They bobbed along, with Dubdub repeating the end of his grandmother's sentences.

"My my, this is comfy!"

"Comfee comfee!"

"It'll rest my ole paws, indeed it will!"

"Deed 'twill, deed 'twill!"

The going was good, with other volunteers taking the bearers' places. They trotted at a fair rate. Buckler was striding along in the van when he discerned a figure upon the walls, which had grown much closer.

"Look, there's somebeast pacing the walltops yonder!"

Oakheart stood on tippaw, peering keenly. "Hah, 'pon me spikes, there's only one as tall as that at Redwall, as I recall. I'll hail him, eh?"

Being a member of the acting profession, Oakheart prided himself upon his vocal powers. He winked at Buckler. "Projection, sirrah—that's what 'tis all about!"

Drawing forth his funnel-shaped bark hailer, the portly troupe leader boomed majestically forth, "Ahoy, there! Is that a rascally riverdog a-beatin' the bounds? Somebeast name o' Skipper?"

When put to the test, the Otter Chieftain was no slouch at the bellowing game. Leaping up on a battlement, he waved vigorously and gave voice. "Haharrharr! Is that an ole pincushion rollin' this way? Why, salt me rudder, 'tis Oakie Witherspyk 'imself. I'll tell 'em to hold brekkist for ye!"

He vanished with a backward leap. Diggs waggled his ears admiringly at the hedgehog. "You have my thanks, sir. Anybeast who can delay breakfast 'til I jolly well get there is an absolute star amongst creatures, wot!"

Word had spread around the Abbey like wildfire: a travelling troupe, Guosim visitors and two strange hares. Skipper guarded the open north wall wickergate with good-natured banter for the press of Redwallers who had gathered there.

"Give 'em a chance to get in, mates. Move back there, Granvy. Here they come, now—stand back. Let the Abbess greet 'er guests!"

Abbess Marjoram took Oakheart's paws warmly, knowing it was not always wise to embrace large hedgehogs.

"May I be the first to welcome old friends, the Witherspyk troupe and our stout Guosim allies!"

Sweeping off his floppy hat, Oakheart bowed low. "Faith, ye can indeed, but let's not stand on ceremony. I'm still Oakie, if you're still Marjy!"

Dubdub piped up, "Still Marjy, still Marjy!"

Amidst the laughter which followed, the Abbess took the hogbabe from Crumfiss's lap. "Well, good morning, little nutnose—and what's your name?"

The infant pointed a chubby paw at himself. "I Dubdub!"

Log a Log Jango nodded to Skipper. "Sorry t'say this, mate, but we're here on business. Bad business—some of our young uns are missin'."

Abbess Marjoram left off tickling Dubdub. "Aye, we've got the same problem. Two of our Dibbuns ain't nowheres t'be found."

Marjoram waved her paws for silence. "Please, friends, the day is still young. There's time aplenty for bad news later. But for now let's all go to breakfast together, be introduced to those we haven't met and mayhaps hear a bit of good news. Follow me to the orchard—it's all set out there."

Picnic mats had been arranged on the grass, laden with food to suit every taste.

Diggs was almost incoherent at the sight. "I say! Burn me blinkin' scut an' rip me old auntie's pinnyfore! It's . . . it's . . . oh, corks!"

Skipper checked the tubby glutton from diving in headfirst. "Ahoy, young feller, let the Abbess say the grace afore ye start vittlin'."

Marjoram spoke quietly in the silence.

"All hail upon this summer morn,
thrice welcome to ye all,
who visit us in friendship here,
good comrades of Redwall!"

Skipper chuckled. "That's what I like—short'n'sweet!"

He released Diggs, who, at a sharp nudge from Buckler, sat down sedately on the grass and passed a beaker of dandelion and burdock cordial to Trajidia. That done, he fell like a famine-stricken wolf on the food.

Buckler introduced them both to the Abbess. "He's Subaltern Digglethwaite, an' I'm Blademaster Buckler Kordyne, from Salamandastron, marm. Call us Diggs'n'Buck, everybeast does."

The Abbess smiled fondly. "Ah, Salamandastron! Tell me, Buck, how is my old friend Lord Brang?"

Buckler loosed his long blade, setting it beside him. "Lord Brang is as mighty as he ever was, marm. He sends his compliments an' good wishes to ye. Oh, an' a pair of new bellropes woven by his own paws. He said they are to replace the old uns. Diggs, pass me that rope."

Diggs was too far gone sampling the delights of mushroom, spring onion and gravy pasties. So his companion had to retrieve the rope from him.

Marjoram ran her paws slowly across both ropes. She produced a kerchief and wiped her eyes. "Poor Brother Tollum would have appreciated these fine gifts. I'll tell you more about that later. Big Bartij, our Gardener and Infirmary aide, has taken over as Bellringer to the Abbey now. Bartij, what d'you think of Lord Brang's present to us—look!"

The sturdy hog inspected the ropes admiringly. "What a pair o' beauties, Mother! Just look it the weave o' these ropes, all gold'n'green, too. With fine carved elmwood handles on 'em. Hoho, these'll make ole Methuselah an' Matthias sound out o'er our Abbey like honeyed thunder. I'll fix 'em up right after brekkist. Thank ye, Buck, thank ye kindly!"

Several Dibbuns had gathered around to watch the gluttonous Diggs foddering up. They gazed wide-eyed at the tubby hare, who winked roguishly at them.

A tiny molemaid threw her frilly apron over her face. "Boi 'okey, whurr bee's ee a putten et all?"

Diggs relinquished a hefty fruitcake for a brief moment. "Hollow legs, little beauty—least that's what our regimental cooks says I've bloomin' well got."

Jango's wife, Furm, looked up from her mint tea. "Aye, an' hollow stummick, tail, ears an' head. Invite an 'arebeast t'dinner an' ye'll regret it all yore days. That's wot my ole ma used t'say."

Sister Fumbril was feeding Dubdub his second bowl of arrowroot cream pudding. She grinned. "Land sakes—it looks like this liddle rascal's about t'catch Mister Diggs up, ain't ye, young master?"

The hogbabe echoed her dutifully, "Younger masta!"

The morning was almost half gone when the guests sat back, replete and sighing. Even Diggs was heard to remark, "Hope they hold off with the bally lunch for a while, wot!"

Abbess Marjoram called for their attention. "Now, let's address our problems. Oakie, who have you lost from your family?"

Oakheart sighed. "Two, alas—our lovely little twins, Jiddle an' Jinty, scarce four seasons old. There's another, too, a young shrewmaid, calls herself Flib."

Log a Log Jango made his report. "We lost three, if'n ye count the one Oakie just mentioned. She's a daughter o' mine, y'see."

Furm, the mother of all three shrews, sobbed, "Petunia Rosebud, the one who calls 'erself Flib, is the eldest o' the three. She's always wanderin' off an' gettin' into scrapes. Flib can take care of 'erself, but the other two, Midda an' Borti, ain't never gone off afore. My Midda's very young, but she always looks after Borti, pore liddle mite—'e's only a babe. Oh, I 'ope my Borti ain't come to any 'arm!"

Furm broke down weeping; Jango could only stand awkwardly by. Guosim Log a Logs are not supposed to cry, though he did wipe a paw roughly across his eyes.

"Now, now, me ole darlin', don't worry, we'll find 'em sooner or later. You say you lost young uns, marm?"

Marjoram placed a comforting paw around Furm. "A little squirrelmaid called Tassy and a molebabe, Guffy. They've been gone half a day and a night now."

Buckler commented, "Hmm, seven young uns in all just vanished into thin air. There's got to be an explanation. Mother Abbess. Has anything unusual happened round Redwall lately? Have ye spotted any strangebeasts lurkin' about?"

Skipper spoke. "Aye, we caught a vermin, a young stoat, early yesterday. Sittin' as pretty as ye please, stuffin' 'imself with vittles in Friar Soogum's kitchens."

The good Friar piped up, "Huh, typical vermin, made a right old mess—food scattered everywhere. Skipper caught the villain, though. Gave 'im a right ole pastin' with an oven paddle an' made him clean it all up!"

Diggs heaved himself upright, stifling a belch. "Just as the blighter deserved, wot. Do ye still have the rogue? Me'n Buck should have a word with the blighter."

Marjoram explained, "Alas, no. The Dibbuns went missing, so we all went off to search for them. The stoat escaped and hid himself up in the attics. He was seen, and we went up there to get him. That was when the tragedy occurred. Poor Brother Tollum and the wretched stoat were killed in the attempt to recapture him."

Buckler paced up and down, deliberating. "The vermin

must've had an accomplice outside the walls. Whoever it was is the one who took your babes!"

Foremole Darbee nodded his velvety head sagely. "Hurr, wee'm figgered that owt already, zurr. But wot do us'ns doos abowt et?"

Abbess Marjoram interrupted. "May I say something? Coming from Salamandastron, no doubt you've heard of our Abbey founder, Martin the Warrior. Now, I know this is hard for you to grasp, Buck, but Martin spoke to me in a dream."

The young hare shrugged. "Nothing new, Mother Abbess. Our Badger Lords have been known to have many visions that can't be explained. What did Martin say?"

Marjoram repeated the words carefully. "Corim Althier—just those two words. I don't know what they mean. However, just before the stoat died, I repeated the words to him. He didn't seem at all familiar with the first word, Corim. But when I mentioned Althier, he looked very frightened. Globby—that was the stoat's name—sat up and pointed to the open attic window. Then he said, 'Althier . . . Sable Quean!' That was all. He went limp and died. So that's what we know. Corim, Althier, Sable Quean. What d'you make of it, Buck?"

Buckler stopped pacing. He remained silent awhile, thinking hard. Then he gave his verdict. "Well, I don't know what either Corim or Althier means. You say the vermin looked frightened when you said Althier, then he said Sable Quean. To my mind, Sable Quean must be the title for some vermin ruler. So it follows that she has others in her service. Many others, that's why she's a Quean. The young ones were stolen from three different areas. So for some reason unknown to us, she's stealing small woodlanders. Hedgehogs, shrews, a mole and a squirrelmaid. Right?"

A sudden thought occurred to Diggs. "Right you are, old scout. D'ye recall when we first met young Flib she was being attacked by those two vermin bullies? They had a rope round her—the cads were tryin' to jolly well haul her off!"

Buckler picked up his sword. "So they were. You see? That proves there's a whole band of vermin roamin' the countryside, taking young prisoners!"

Granvy the Recorder scratched his chin. "So what can we do, except lock our gates, an' keep close watch on our Dibbuns?"

Skipper thumped his rudder down with such force that he startled the old scribe. "Well, we couldn't do much afore now, but we've got an army o' Guosim an' two warrior hares alongside us. We'll form a band o' fightin' searchers!"

Buckler was in total agreement with the Otter Chieftain. "Aye, that's the right move. We'll leave Redwall during the night, in secret. Then we'll hunt through Mossflower woodlands until we meet up with some o' these vermin. We'll ambush the scum and take some prisoners of our own. I'm sure if we ask 'em nicely, they'll tell us all about Althier and this Sable Quean!"

Diggs fondled his loaded sling lovingly. "Oh, I'll ask the blinkin' bounders nicely, you can jolly well rely on that!"

Oakheart Witherspyk declared stoutly, "Well said, sirrah. Me an' my gallant troupe are with ye!"

Log a Log Jango shook his head. "Sorry, Oakie. Yore lot are actors, not fighters. Ye'd just be in the way out there. Best thing you can do is stay 'ere an' defend Redwall."

Abbess Marjoram noted the crestfallen look on her old friend's face, so she seized his paw anxiously. "Please say you will, Oakie. I can't abide the thought of my Abbey lying undefended!"

Oakheart Witherspyk gave her paw a squeeze. "Fear not, gentle Marjy. My troupe and I will guard Redwall with our very lives. To defend this wondrous place will be my honour and privilege!"

Baby Dubdub tried, but got the words muddled. "Oppener rivilege!"

Under cover of darkness that night, the party headed out into the woodlands by the small east wickergate. Skipper and Buckler headed the column, with Sniffy a way out front, scouting the land. Diggs and Jango brought up the rear.

Everybeast was on the alert as they stole through the silent fastness of the woodland depths. A pale half-moon rode the scudding clouds over the breeze-swayed treetops. Behind them, the twin bells of the Abbey boomed the midnight hour.

Diggs could not resist smirking a bit as he nudged Jango. "D'ye hear that, old lad? A marvellous sound, ain't it? Couldn't have been done without the new bellropes y'know. I carried 'em all the way from Salamandastron on me own. Indeed I did! Lord Brang entrusted 'em to me, of course. 'Diggs,' he said, 'Diggs, you make sure that these bellropes reach Redwall safely. You're the only one I can bally well trust with 'em!' "

Jango hissed in the garrulous hare's ear, "An' did yore Lord Brang tell ye to get me killed when we're out huntin' vermin, by chunnerin' on aloud all the time?"

The tubby hare replied huffily, "No, he didn't, actually!"

Jango nudged him sharply in the ribs. "Then shut up, or I'll shut ye up!"

They had been on the go for quite some time when Sniffy came stealing back through a fern bed. He cautioned the leaders, "Somebeast ahead blunderin' about in a stream. I think there's only one, but I can't be sure. Couldn't get close enough without bein' seen."

Buckler's long rapier swished as he drew it from across his shoulder. "Right, Skip. Let's take whoever it is."

12

Thwip the fox jailer leaned against the door which separated him from the young prisoners in the cavern. Trailing the tip of his whip in the dust, he gnawed at a grimy claw.

His partner, the vixen Binta, saw his furrowed brow. "Wotsa matter with ye? Yer look like you lost a goose an' found a wren. Wot's up? C'mon, tell me."

Thwip nodded at the prison cavern. "Somethin's brewin' in there, I'm sure of it, Binta."

The vixen shrugged. "They seem all right t'me. Huh, always 'ungry or cryin' for their mothers. Same thing as usual. Hah, yore worryin' over nothin', mate!"

The brutal fox shook his head. "No I ain't. There's somethin' goin' on in there, an' I just can't put me paw on it. Look, I'll show ye."

Drawing Binta close to the door, he whispered, "Ye can always hear those liddle nuisances in there, movin' about, whimperin' an singin' daft songs about their homes an' families. Lissen close—there's not a sound comin' from in there . . . right?"

The vixen took her ear from the door. "Right, but wot does that mean? They're prob'ly sleepin'. Captives ain't got much else t'do."

Thwip lifted the lock bar silently, carefully. "Now, watch this!"

He flung the door open wide, almost knocking two small hedgehogs flat. He glared at Jinty and Jiddle, the Witherspyk twins.

"Wot are yew two doin' stannin' there like that, eh?"

Jinty was a good actress. She rubbed her stomach sadly. "We was on'y waitin' for ye t'bring us vittles, sir. Will ye bring us some, please? We're all 'ungry!"

Binta took a practised glance around the interior. All she saw was huddled groups of young ones lying about on the floor and the low ledges at the rear of the badly lit cavern. She drew Thwip to one side, muttering out the side of her mouth at him, "Y'see? I told yer there was nothin' wrong. They all look sleepy an' down'earted. Must be through all the time they've spent in this gloomy 'ole. Huh, you'd be the same if'n ye was one of 'em. Bein' short o' vittles, too, I'll wager that breaks down any spirit they once 'ad. C'mon, let's get outta this dungeon, afore it starts t'get us down, too!"

Thwip took a moment to peer about at the captives. "I don't see nothin' o' that fierce liddle shrew, d'you? P'raps we'd best take a count of 'em, eh?"

Binta was beginning to lose patience with her mate. "If'n that mad shrew's gone off in a corner an' died, well, who's bothered? Less trouble fer us, I say. An' as fer takin' a count, d'yer know 'ow many are in 'ere?"

Thwip coiled his whip up reluctantly. "No. Do yew?"

Binta gave an exasperated sigh. "No, I don't, an' I ain't about t'start countin' 'em. Wot's the matter wid yew, are ye goin' soft?"

Shoving Jinty and Jiddle to one side, Thwip stalked out, turning on his mate as she barred the door. "Lissen, smart-mouth—don't yew start talkin' t'me like that in front of the prisoners. I'm not 'avin' it, so there. Just keep yer clever remarks to yoreself!"

Binta was in no mood to continue the argument. "Alright, keep yer brush on. Cummon, we'd better go an' get the vittles. That lot's gotta be fed, ain't they?"

Back inside the cavern, Flandor, the young otter, hurried to the shield of grass, mud and woven twigs which disguised the tunnel entrance. Calla and Urfa, the two little leverets, were sitting with their backs against it.

Lifting the two baby hares out of his way, Flandor removed the shield and called into the hole, "You can come out now—they've gone!"

The Dibbun Guffy and his friend the molemaid Gurchen scrambled out, rubbing soil from their faces.

Guffy spat out a fragment of wood. "Zurr, ee Flimbeast bee's stuck unner a gurt root in thurr, we'm bee's a-tryen t'pull hurr owt!"

The young otter thumped his rudderlike tail impatiently. "Not again. That's the fifth time she's gotten herself jammed by roots!"

Gurchen was a well-mannered molebabe. She curtsied prettily before replying. "Burr, thurr bee's more rooters than ee cudd shake a stick at en thurr. Et b'aint gunner be no h'easy job, oi tells ee, zurr h'otter!"

Flandor wriggled into the tunnel entrance, muttering, "I'm gettin' a bit fed up o' pullin' little missy trouble out o' roots. Ah, well, here goes!"

Tura and Midda stood by, giggling as they heard Flib being hauled out backward by Flandor.

"Yaargh! Ya great clod'oppin' riverdog—yer rippin' me tail out by the blinkin' roots. Leggo!"

"Oh, go an' boil yore head, shrew. If'n ye tried pushin' harder, I wouldn't 'ave to tug like this. Stop moanin', I'll have ye out soon!"

"Well, 'urry up, planktail, afore I suffercate!"

They tumbled out together just as Jiddle called from the door, "Here comes the vittles. I can 'ear the foxes outside!"

There was no time for Flandor and Flib to clean themselves up, so to cover their dishevelled state, they staged a fight in the middle of the floor. Actually, they were so mad at each other that there was little need for play acting. Thwip rolled the cauldron in on its trolley, followed by Binta with the water tub.

The vixen grinned, pointing at the pair tussling in the dust. "There's yore mad shrew, tryin' to slay that otter!"

Thwip curled his lip. "Hah, leave 'em an' let's 'ope they kills one another! Come on, yew lot. Line up 'ere if'n ye wants to eat!"

Binta broke off serving water and set about the fighters with her water ladle, beating them hard. "Break it up, now. Stop this fightin', d'er 'ear me?"

Thwip sighed ruefully. "Yore right, mate. If'n anythin' 'appens to 'em, 'tis us that gets it in the neck from the Sable Quean. You, shrew, any more trouble an' ye don't get vittles or water. Is that clear?"

Flib snarled at her jailer, "No vittles, eh? Lissen, foxy-face, yew try that an' I'll stuff that whip down yer gullet an' make yer eat it!"

Thwip cracked the whip, making Flib jump back. "Ye can wait'll the last t'get served fer that!"

Zwilt the Shade sensed that there was something in the wind when Vilaya sent for him. Standing in her presence, he knew it was not bad news for him, or a reprimand. The Sable Quean invited him to eat with her.

Two plump, freshly grilled rudd lay on a bed of dandelion leaves in front of her. The aroma of the cooked fish was mouthwatering. Allowing her servant Dirva to pour out goblets of pale cider, she smilingly beckoned Zwilt to sit at her side.

"Ah, my faithful commander, I have things to tell you. Come, eat with me and enjoy!"

Vilaya uttered a low, melodious chuckle, as the other sable looked hesitantly at the two fish. "Dirva, eat a small bit from each of these rudd, just to assure my brave friend that they are not poisoned. Take a sip from both goblets also."

The ancient rat sampled the fish, washing the fragments down with a sip from each drink. She cackled, showing the stumps of her gnarled teeth. Zwilt drew back as she clutched the hem of his cloak.

"Heehee, still not sure, noble warrior? I'll take your portion, if you so wish."

The Sable Quean smiled, dismissing Dirva. "Enough. See my cooks and get one for yourself."

Using a dainty rosewood spike, she speared a piece of fish, then swallowed it gracefully.

"Now comes my time of triumph. Zwilt, you have served me well, but there is yet more to be done."

The fish was delicious. Zwilt cleared his mouth with a draught of the fine pale cider. "More, Majesty?"

Vilaya's glittering eyes held him entranced. "My army is ready now. We have a sufficient number of Ravagers but not to fight with—war is a fool's game."

The Shade did not share his Quean's view of things, but he nodded, eager to hear more. "Majesty, what do you intend doing with all these warriors at your command? They are trained and seasoned fighters."

Vilaya's small pointed teeth showed; she leaned forward. "I know you trained them well, Zwilt. Nothing escapes the eyes of your Sable Quean. Listen now—go to the Ravagers' camp. Make them ready to march tomorrow morn. Be sure they are well armed, as my personal bodyguard should be. It will be a display of my power and ferocity."

Zwilt bowed his head. "I hear and obey, Majesty. But why are you doing this?"

Vilaya spat out a fishbone. She held it up, inspecting it. "Because tomorrow we go to the Abbey of Redwall." Ignoring Zwilt, she turned to her servant, Dirva. "Go and select three of my young prisoners. They will accompany me."

The old rat hobbled off, cackling hoarsely, "So now the game begins!"

Silent as night shadows, the Otter Chieftain and the Salamandastron Blademaster crept through the darkened woodlands. Skipper halted, keeping in the shelter of a small pine grove. He pointed with his javelin.

"Stream ahead. Can ye see anythin', Buck?"

The young hare nodded. "Aye, there's a bit o' movement by those bushes skirtin' the bank."

Any further discussion was cut short by an agonised groan and the sound of somebeast falling heavily into the shallows. They hurried forward, weapons ready and all their senses on the alert. Whilst Buckler guarded his companion's back, Skipper waded into the water. A moment later, he was hauling something up onto the bank, calling hoarsely, "Ahoy, Buck, lend a paw, will ye? It's a hare!"

Between them, they heaved the limp form onto dry land. Buckler identified her immediately.

"It's Clarinna, my brother Clerun's wife!"

Jango came hurrying up with his Guosim warriors—he was mystified. "I thought all the other hares were back at yore badger mountain. Wot's she doin' here, mate?"

Jango's wife, Furm, made a quick inspection of the unconscious Clarinna. "She's been wounded in two places, through the left shoulder an' at the back of 'er skull. Looks as if she was like this for quite a while afore she finally passed out. If'n I was you, Buck, I'd get this pore beast back to Redwall an' take 'er to Sister Fumbril."

Skipper agreed with Furm. "That's good advice, marm. Jango, you'll have t'go on alone with the search. Buck, me'n you'll get Clarinna back to the Abbey."

Buckler began chopping down two sapling sycamores. "A stretcher's what we need. Diggs, you carry on with the Guosim. No need for you to go back to Redwall."

"Right y'are, old scout. I'd best take flippin' charge around here, wot!"

Jango thrust out his chin belligerently. "I'm Log a Log round 'ere. Now get in line an' cut out the chatter. Move!"

Diggs was about to make an outraged riposte, but Buckler gave him a hard stare. "Best do as he says, chum. See you when ye get back."

It was not yet dawn when Granvy came out of the gatehouse to open the main entrance for them. He grabbed a lantern and escorted them across to the main building. Abbess Marjoram, Drull Hogwife and Sister Fumbril rushed Clarinna up to the Infirmary.

As the good Sister attended to her patient, Buckler explained the situation. "My brother Clerun and his wife, Clarinna, left Salamandastron some while back. I think they set up a small farm somewhere east of here. Neither of them were cut out to be warriors. They just wanted the quiet life, tending the soil an' growin' crops."

Marjoram rubbed Clarinna's paw as she showed signs of reviving. "We didn't know they were out in the woodlands. They'd have both been very welcome to visit Redwall at any time."

Buckler heaved a sigh of frustration. "Well, that's my brother Clerun for ye, stubborn an' stolid. She's the same. That's what prob'ly attracted 'em to one another. A real pair of loners. Abbess, you'll have to pardon me, but I think I'd better get back on the trail an' find this farm of theirs. I'll need to see Clerun!"

Skipper placed a paw about Buckler's shoulder. "Ye'd be better waitin' a bit, matey. See, she'll soon be conscious—mayhap she'll have a tale to tell. Then ye can decide for yoreself before dashin' off."

Having bandaged and poulticed as much as she could, Sister Fumbril revived Clarinna with a few drops of old elderberry wine, which she kept for medicinal purposes. The harewife sat up, coughing and weeping.

Marjoram spoke soothingly to her. "There, there. You're

safe amongst friends now, at the Abbey of Redwall, and look who's here. Buckler!"

Clarinna clasped Buckler's paw tightly. "Oh, Buck, they slew Clerun and took our babes!"

There was shock and disbelief in Buckler's voice. "Slew Clerun? Who was it? Tell me, tell me!"

Drull Hogwife patted the young hare's back. "Easy, now. Don't frighten 'er, sir. Tell us more about wot 'appened, Miz Clarinny."

Then the whole story came out. Though she was greatly distressed, Clarinna gave them chapter and verse.

"Clerun and I were tending some apple seedlings; our babes, Calla and Urfa, were in a basket lined with moss taking their nap. Clerun was going to make them two little cradles from a nice pine log he had found. But now he'll never make it or see our little ones grow up. . . ."

She broke off, weeping bitterly.

Buckler waited for her tears to subside, then spoke softly. "Clarinna, tell us exactly what took place. Was it vermin that attacked you?"

Her eyes went wide with horror at the recollection. "They came out of nowhere—we were surrounded. A big gang of rats led by a tall, dark-furred beast. One of them carried a rat's head stuck on a pike. The tall, dark one, he drew a broadsword, taunting Clerun until he was forced to draw his own blade. Then this strangebeast said that he would fight Clerun. I'll remember his words for the rest of my life. He said, 'Defeat me and your mate, the brats and yourself will go free. But nobeast has ever bested Zwilt the Shade, so you'll die!'

"Poor Clerun, he didn't stand a chance, though he tried his best. The one called Zwilt toyed with him, wounding and taunting before he cut Clerun down. Then he took the medal, which Clerun had given me, from my neck. He gave his sword to one of the rats and took Clerun's blade. He said it was far superior to his own. Then he used it to wound my shoulder and strike me over the back of my head. I went down. He must have thought he had slain me, too. I heard him say to the others that he had struck a blow for his Ravagers and the Sable Quean. I must have passed out then.

"When I woke, it was late evening. Our babes were gone, Clerun was lying there dead, and the little home we had built together was in ruins, robbed and plundered. I staggered off into the woodlands, calling out for my little ones. After that, I don't recall anything else, until I woke up here. Oh, Buckler!" She broke down grieving again.

Buckler was rigid with sorrow and rage. He loosed his paw from Clarinna's, gritting out through clenched teeth, "Ravagers, eh! And there's that name again, Sable Quean! Hah, now we have another one to add to the list. Zwilt the Shade, carrying my family's broadsword and the Coin!"

Clarinna fell back upon the pillow, wailing, "My babies. What would anybeast want, stealing two tiny leverets, little helpless things!"

Buckler's long rapier swished as he drew steel. Dry-eyed and stone-faced, he kissed the blade. "I swear that Zwilt the Shade and his Ravagers—aye, and the one they call the Sable Quean—will die by my paw. Nor will I rest until the babes are safely back with their mother, the wife of my brother Clerun. I will wear the Coin of the Blademaster and pass on my brother's broadsword to his son. I take this oath upon the honour of the Kordyne family. This is my word!"

The high, bright sun was up and dawn well broken when Log a Log Jango led his Guosim in by the main gates. Buckler and Skipper took breakfast on the west walltop, watching them troop in.

The Otter Chieftain called out, "Ahoy, Jango—did ye have any luck out there?"

The shrew shook his grizzled head. "Nary a vermin

whisker in sight, but don't worry. Soon as we're rested, we'll set out agin, matey. Oh, how's the hare lady farin'?"

Buckler replied, "She's not too good, mate. Bring your breakfast up here an' I'll tell ye the whole tale. Er, where's Diggs? I don't see him with your lot."

Jango came striding up the wallsteps. "I chased him off. Don't know where the nuisance is."

Buckler nodded. "I might've known that'd happen. Ole Diggs takes some gettin' used to. Was he chunnerin' again? Nothin' can silence that fat rogue."

Jango stamped a footpaw on the ramparts. "Chunnerin', is that wot ye calls it? The rascal never stops—he's like a babblin' brook, goin' on an' on. I kept warnin' Diggs to shut up, but he wouldn't. I told 'im he was endangerin' us all with the noise he was makin'. Enny'ow, one thing led to another, an' I told 'im to get lost. I think yore Diggs took my advice, 'cos we haven't seen 'im since."

An unmistakable sound, that of the chubby subaltern, rent the morning air. "Halloooo! I say there, you rotters, are you goin' to open this bloomin' gate an' let us in, wot?"

The shouts were coming from beyond the east wall.

Skipper and Buckler ran around there by way of the walltops. There was Diggs, looking up at the battlements, grinning like a demented frog. He had with him a ferret, whom he whacked with his loaded sling every time the vermin made a move.

Skipper smiled down at him. "Ahoy, young Diggs. Who's that scallywag ye have in tow?"

The tubby hare kicked the prisoner's tail end cheerfully. "C'mon, don't stand there like last season's leftover pudden. Tell the nice chap your flippin' name—smartly now, laddie buck!"

"Gripchun, sir, me name's Gripchun!" the unhappy captive shouted.

Two Guosim unlocked the east wickergate, and Diggs swaggered in, kicking the ferret before him.

Jango glared at the garrulous hare. "Where did ye get that un?"

Diggs waggled his ears at the Shrew Chieftain. "Oh, nowhere, really, old Log a Thing. I just came across the blighter prowlin' round the shrubbery, so I surrounded him an' chunnered him into submission, wot!"

Jango glared at him sourly and stalked off.

Buckler clapped his friend on the back. "Good old Diggs! A captive, eh? I'll make him talk!"

Diggs threw a headlock on the wretched ferret. "Rather y'didn't, Buck. Leave old Gripchun t'me. I'll soon have the blighter talkin' faster'n me." He applied the headlock tighter. "Ain't that right, my stinky old friend? Dastardly Diggs the Terrible Torturer, that's what they call me!"

Assisted by Fumbril and Marjoram, Clarinna was escorted into Great Hall, where Diggs had bound Gripchun to a sandstone column.

Buckler pointed to the ferret. "Was this one of the vermin who attacked you, Clarinna?"

She shook her head. "No. They were all large rats, except for the dark-furred one, Zwilt. He's not one of them, I'm sure."

Diggs made a great show of rolling up his tunic sleeves. "Right ho, then, Gripchun, me foul old vermin. Let's find out a little bit about you, wot! Now, there's no sense in beatin' round the jolly old bush, so we'll get right to it. Can some kind creature please bring me a large sharp axe, the larger'n'sharper, the better? Oh, an' some boilin' water, about a cauldron full. Hmm, I suppose we'd better have a few iron pokers an' stuff to light a good roarin' fire. That'll do for now, wot. No good interrogatin' victims without the proper stuff!"

Abbess Marjoram was horrified. "Mister Diggs! Surely you're not planning on torturing this beast inside my Abbey?"

Diggs saluted cheerily. "Pardon me, marm. I'll take the

scoundrel outside, if the noise bothers you, wot. These rascals do screech an' wail a bit, y'know!"

Turning his back on the ferret, Buckler tipped Marjoram a huge, mischievous wink. "You leave it to Diggs, marm. I've never known a vermin that wouldn't talk after a session with him!"

Marjoram knew then that it was all a ruse to loosen Gripchun's tongue. She kept up the pretence. "Well, take him outside, over to the west wall steps. I'm not having this Abbey messed up with the result of axes, pokers, boiling water and fires!"

Diggs bowed, making an elegant leg. "My thanks t'ye, marm. It shouldn't take too long."

Skipper chuckled. "Oh, I think it will—ole Gripchun's just fainted clear away with fright. Look at him!"

They carried the ferret out to lay him on the wallsteps, then waited until he stirred.

Buckler watched him closely, remarking to Diggs, "I think he should sing like a skylark now. Leave this to me—you go and find something to eat, mate."

The tubby hare needed no second invitation. At the mere mention of food, he scooted off kitchenward.

Buckler borrowed a beaker of water from the gatehouse. He sprinkled it on Gripchun until the ferret was awake once more. Wide eyed, he lay there, not daring to move.

"That fat rabbet, Diggs, 'as 'e gone, sir?"

Buckler nodded. "Aye, but I can bring him back if ye so wish—"

The ferret let out a wail. "Noooooo! Don't let 'im near me, sir, please. I'll tell yer wot ye wants ter know, on me 'onner I will!"

Buckler patted his tear-stained muzzle. "That's the stuff—but trust me, I'll know if you're lying. So I want straight answers. Now, who is this creature they call the Sable Quean, and what is she doing here in Mossflower?"

Gripchun swallowed hard. "I've never seen 'er, sir, on me life I ain't. I'm just one of the Ravagers. Zwilt gives all the orders, an' we just carries 'em out."

Buckler nodded. "So this Sable Quean prob'ly gives Zwilt his orders, and he passes 'em on to you?"

The ferret's head nodded vigourously. "That's right, yer 'onner. There must be about tenscore of us Ravagers by now. Zwilt brought in a mob o' new beasts, river rats, they are."

Buckler exchanged glances with Skipper, who was sitting on a higher step, taking it all in. He put his next question to the prisoner.

"An' what exactly are your orders?"

Gripchun replied obediently, "To take any youngbeasts we comes across, liddle woodlanders. We catches 'em an' passes 'em over to Zwilt. I don't know where 'e takes 'em though, I swear!"

Buckler leaned closer, staring hard at the ferret. "Don't you have any idea where the young ones go to?"

For answer, Gripchun spat on his pawpad, then dabbed it on either eartip—a vermin habit to show that he was speaking truly. "If'n I knowed, I'd tell ye, sir."

The young hare tried another tack. "Tell me more about this beast, Zwilt the Shade. Who is he? Where did he come from? How did he choose you to become a Ravager?"

The vermin became more animated with his reply. "I ain't seen nothin' like Zwilt, sir. 'E's tall an' slim but real strong, very fierce, too. Ye never knows where Zwilt's goin' to turn up. Some says 'e's magic, appearin' an' vanishin' jus' like that! But I tells yer, Zwilt'd slay ye soon as look at ye. I never seen one so quick wid a blade as Zwilt is with that big sword 'e carries under 'is cloak—pure murder, 'e is!"

Skipper interrupted. "So how did ye meet up with him?"

Gripchun shrugged. "I used t'roam far north o' Mossflower wid a gang o' weasels, stoats an' ferrets like meself. Our chief was Gadra the Spear, a real warrior, expert killer 'e was. Then one night, Zwilt jus' turns up at our camp an' tells Gadra that we're all gonna be Ravagers an' that 'e's the new chief."

Skipper raised an eyebrow. "I'll wager ole Gadra didn't like the sound o' that, eh?"

Gripchun continued, "Gadra challenged Zwilt to a fight, right off. Huh, pore Gadra, Zwilt made 'im look like a fool—'twasn't nice ter watch. Zwilt tore Gadra t'bits with the big sword, laughin' an' tormentin' 'im like a snake wid a worm. Once 'e finished with Gadra, we was left wid no choice but ter follow Zwilt the Shade. So, that's 'ow I came t'be a Ravager, sir."

Skipper murmured to Buckler, "Zwilt the Shade sounds like a reg'lar terror t'me." A dangerous look entered the hare's eye. "We'll see how much of a terror Zwilt is when he meets a warrior who can fight back!"

Oakheart Witherspyk had been patrolling the walltops, a part of his duties as protector of Redwall. He marched grandly down the wallsteps. "Well, well, 'pon me spikes an' snout, what have we here? A fiendish vermin, eh!"

Buckler felt that he wanted to talk over the information he had gleaned with Skipper. So he delegated charge of the prisoner to the portly hog. "I know he doesn't deserve it, Oakie, but I want you to take this rascal over to the kitchens an' see that he's fed'n'watered. Keep an eye on him, though!"

The big hedgehog took his responsibilities seriously. Gripchun found himself seized tightly by ear and tail. Oakheart frogmarched him off, admonishing the vermin sternly, "Zounds, one rascally move out o' ye, sirrah, an' I'll belt ye from here to suppertime an' back!"

Buckler called out, as the unhappy ferret was hauled off, "If that villain gives you any trouble, just turn him over to Diggs—he'll know what t'do!"

Shaking his head, Skipper expressed an opinion to Buckler. "If'n that Sable Quean an' Zwilt have a crew of over tenscore vermin, I think we'll have to secure the Abbey. Armed guards patrollin' all walls, an' others watchin' all four gates. You an' Diggs should be able t'help there. We need warriors like ye, mate, Salamandastron trained."

Buckler strode to the walltop. Leaning on a battlement, he stared out over the western plain. "Oh, we'll do the best we can for ye, Skip. But what bothers me is the stolen little uns. What d'ye think this Sable Quean intends on doin' with 'em?"

The Otter Chieftain shrugged. "That I don't know, Buck. It's a puzzle, ain't it? Pore young things, it don't bear thinkin' about, wot a crowd o' vermin scum could do to them."

Even though it made him shudder at the thought, Buckler tried to address the problem logically. "Hmm, one thing we can be sure of, the Sable Quean isn't stealin' the young uns just to slay 'em."

Skipper agreed. "Aye, mate. I'll wager me rudder they're all alive someplace. . . . But where?"

His companion smote a paw on the battlement. "Somewhere out there in Mossflower, this Zwilt rascal is hidin' 'em. Right, let's see if we can squeeze some more information out of that ferret who Diggs nabbed. Vermin usually know more'n they'll tell you."

The Otter Chieftain clenched his strong paws. "I think we'd best git him up 'ere on the walltop. We don't want to upset any gentlebeasts. Squeeze him, d'ye say? I'll squeeze the blaggard until he sings like a brace o' nightingales!"

Gripchun was feeling much better since he had been taken to the kitchens and given good Redwall fare. The absence of Diggs added to his well-being; he felt his natural vermin insolence returning. It came as an unpleasant shock when Skipper strode in and seized him by the scruff of his neck.

Gripchun tried to wriggle free, snarling, "Git yer paws off a me, riverdog. Who d'ye think ye are?"

The brawny otter pinned him to the wall with one hefty paw. He began clouting the ferret's ears with the other.

Skipper explained who he was, accentuating each word with a stinging smack.

"I'll tell ye who I am, Dibbun robber! I'm the beast who's goin' to knock yore head off if'n ye tell any lies, or give me any more of yore lip!"

Gripchun began sobbing relentlessly. "Please, sir, don't 'it me no more. I've told ye all I know, I can't tell ye no more, honest I can't!"

Diggs ambled in, munching on an oversized vegetable pasty. "Oh, hello, Skip old scout. What's that rascal been up to, wot? I say, d'ye mind holdin' my pasty whilst I give him a few smacks? I feel sort of responsible for the scoundrel, havin' captured him an' all that!"

Skipper left off cuffing Gripchun's ears long enough to explain, "Me'n'Buckler thinks this un knows more'n he's sayin'. I'm takin' him back up to the walltop so we can question him without upsettin' everybeast."

Diggs brushed pasty crumbs from his chubby cheeks. "Good idea. I'll lend a blinkin' paw—you take one ear an' I'll take the other, wot!"

They went off with Gripchun hobbling tippawed between them and wailing pitifully, "Owowow—leggo, you'll pull me lugs off!"

Oakheart joined them as they left the kitchen. " 'Pon my word, does that wretch never stop bleating?"

Halfway across the lawn, they met Granvy, who enquired where they were taking the captive. On being told, he decided to tag along.

Gripchun cowered against the battlemented wall, nervously licking dry lips as he looked from one to the other of his interrogators.

Diggs was finishing off his pasty; Skipper was flexing his paws. Oakheart had taken the liberty of bringing along a wooden oven paddle, which he was tapping on the rampart stones. Granvy had sat down, taking from his belt pouch a piece of bark parchment and a thin charcoal stick. He smiled at the ferret.

"Just to take down anything you tell us."

However, it was Buckler who was causing the captive some real apprehension. The young Blademaster was honing his long rapier blade on a whetstone. Without looking at Gripchun, he spoke, testing the keen edge against his paws: "I want you to think very carefully. I must have an answer to every question I ask."

A lump appeared in Gripchun's throat as he swallowed hard. He nodded furiously.

Buckler continued in a level tone, "Are the young uns alive and well?"

The ferret kept nodding as he found his voice. "They're all still livin', as far as I knows, sir."

Log a Log Jango Bigboat came bounding up the wallsteps. "I heard a kitchen helper sayin' you was tryin' t'make this scum talk. Has he said anythin' yet?"

Granvy looked up from his writing. "He says the little uns are all still alive, as far as he knows."

The Shrew Chieftain's blade was out in a flash, its point a hairsbreadth from the vermin's throat. Jango's voice was shaking with rage. "As far as ye know? I'm the father o'three of those youngsters! So ye'll have to do a bit better'n thinkin' ye know. If'n they're alive, yore chief must be keepin' 'em hid somewhere. . . ."

Jango's voice rose with his rage. He drew back the short Guosim rapier, readying it for a thrust. "I'm right, ain't I? My liddle uns are bein' held prisoners. Where? Tell me where, ye useless cob o' flotsam. Tell me or die!"

Gripchun gave a hoarse screech as Jango swung the blade. Fortunately, it was knocked to one side as Buckler deflected it with a deft flick of his long rapier.

The ferret threw himself flat on the walkway, sobbing hysterically. "I keeps tellin' ye, I don't know nothin'. All I does is carries out Zwilt's orders. I ain't got a clue where Althier is, on me oath I ain't!"

Oakheart bounded forward. Heaving the vermin upright, he shook him like a rag, bellowing into his face, "Althier, what d'ye mean, Althier?"

Gripchun rattled on like a babbling brook. "I 'eard Zwilt sayin' it, an' I didn't think nothin' of it at the time, honest I didn't, sirs. But just now the name came into me mind. Althier, I think that's the name of the place where they keeps yore little uns!"

Oakheart dropped the hapless vermin. "Well, well. What d'ye make o' that, friends?"

Granvy ceased writing. He whispered to Skipper, "I believe him, but let's not frighten him into telling lies to save his skin. Leave this to me. Maybe I can persuade a bit more out of him."

Diggs gave the Recorder a broad wink. "Aye, but first allow me to jolly well scare the blighter a bit more. Then you can come in, all blinkin' kind'n'gentle, eh, wot!"

Diggs dived at the ferret, hauling him up once again and bellowing aggressively, "So then, you mouldy rotter, you were fibbing when y'said you'd told me every bloomin' thing. Hah, an' I was tryin' to be nice to you. Right, that's it! No more good old Uncle Diggs for you, m'laddo, c'mere!"

Even though he was tubby, Diggs was a hare of some strength. With a grunt, he swung Gripchun over his head and held him above the battlements.

"One thing a chap can't abide, an' that's a fibber! So it's over the wall for you, mudface. You're free t'go—though it's a bit of a way down from the top o' these flippin' walls. Hah, your pals will prob'ly need three sacks an' a spade to shovel you up an' carry you off, wot!"

The vermin screeched despairingly, "No, noooo, mercy, sir, I begs ye! Owoooo 'elp!"

That was when Granvy interceded. He pulled Diggs back, managing to take possession of the prisoner. "Mister Diggs, sir, there's no need for all this violence. I'm sure this creature would sooner talk to me, right?"

The ferret began kissing Granvy's footpaws. "Right, sir, yore right. I'll talk to ye, fair'n'square, honest I will, sir. Just keep that fat rabbet off me!"

Diggs was about to fetch him a good clout for his insolence when the old Recorder held up a calming paw.

"Please, friends, go away. Let me take charge of this beast."

Buckler nodded. "He's right, mates. Let's go and take tea in the gatehouse. Just shout if y'need us, Granvy."

The Recorder smiled meekly. "Thank you so much."

They went off down the wallsteps, with Diggs chunnering indignantly. "Bloomin' nerve o' the blighter. Fat rabbet is it, wot? One more word out of that scoundrel an' I'll fat rabbet him. Squashed ferret, that's what he'll jolly well be. I say, you chaps, if we're havin' tea, I'll just nip off t'the blinkin' kitchens an' see if I can't conjure up a few scones, or a spot o' piecrust!"

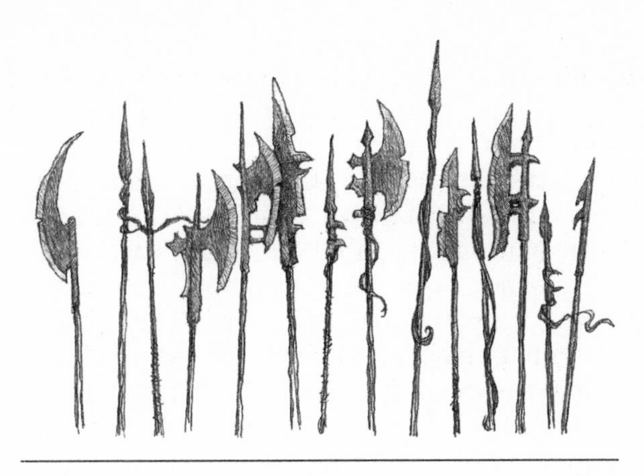

13

It was a terrifying moment for the young prisoners in the gloomy cave, and it happened swiftly. One moment they were lying about listlessly, wondering how long it was until their next meal, some dozing, others just gazing blankly into space. Then the door to the dungeon slammed open. Thwip, Binta and Dirva swept in with an escort of guards, all carrying lighted torches.

There was an immediate hubbub, with the little captives shielding their eyes against the sudden invasion of flaring lights. Dirva pointed to the closest three creatures. "They'll do—take 'em!"

Flandor the young otter grabbed a stoat who was shoving the Dibbun squirrelmaid, Tassy, into a big sack. "Leave her alone, you dirty villain!" He dealt the stoat a good punch to the right eye.

That was where the resistance ended. Flandor was set upon by guards and beaten senseless with spearbutts. Thwip was cracking his lash, snarling, "Get back! Back, I say, all of ye!"

Screams and cries of young creatures echoed round the dungeon walls as the raiders speedily retreated with their victims. As quickly as it had started, the incident was over. The door slammed and was bolted tight, leaving the prisoners blinking in the sudden darkness. Everybeast was wailing and sobbing at the sudden violence of the raid.

Flib came tumbling out of the escape tunnel, followed by her two small mole assistants. The Guosim shrewmaid spat dust, wiping the back of a grimy paw across her eyes. "Wot'n the name o' bludd'n'boulders is goin' on?"

Midda grasped her sister Flib's paw. "They took three of us, jus' barged in an' took 'em!"

Flib wiggled a paw in a dust-filled ear, shouting, "Will ya shut that noise, all of youse! I can't 'ear meself thinkin' for all the weepin' an' wailin'. Now, shut up, d'ye hear me? Be quiet!"

The din subsided into faint moans and sniffles.

The young squirrel, Tura, spoke out. "I think they've killed Flandor—look!"

Flib ran to the fallen otter's side and turned him over. He groaned softly. Midda managed to unhook one of the dim lanterns from the prison wall. She held it over Flandor as Flib inspected him.

"Flandor ain't dead. Anybeast got a drop o' water t'spare?"

A small quantity of the precious fluid was donated. Midda tore off a strip of her kilt, soaking it and bathing away blood from a cut on the otter's brow. She forced the remainder of the water between Flandor's lips. He spluttered, trying to sit up, but Flib pressed him back down.

"Stay put awhile 'til yer feel stronger, mate. Now, who was it did all this?"

Tura answered, "The two foxes an' that ole scrinjy rat. They burst in with a load of guards carryin' torches an' weapons. Shoved three little uns into sacks an' took 'em away. Wasn't much we could do, it all happened so sudden. Y'can see wot they did to pore Flandor, beat him terrible, they did!"

Flib nodded grimly. "So, who did the cowardly scum take?"

Midda replied, "One was the Redwall squirrel, Tassy."

Jiddle the Witherspyk hog sobbed, "They stole my sister Jinty, put her in a sack!"

Flib patted his head gently. "There, there. No good cryin', mate, at least they never took you. Who else?"

Gurchen the molemaid had been taking a look around. "Burr, oi think they'm tukken ee likkle hurr babbie, ee wun called Urfa. She'm gone frum 'er bruther."

A mousebabe began wailing, "Wahaaah, they're goin' to eat them, we'll be next. Wahaaaah!"

Flib tugged the mouse's tail, silencing him. "Don't talk stoopid. If'n they was goin' to eat us they woulda done it long ago, while we was all still fat an' 'ealthy."

Midda picked up Borti, who had been wakened by the mousebabe's cries. She rocked him to and fro. "Then what d'you suppose they plan on doin' to 'em?"

Flib raised her voice bad-temperedly. "Well 'ow am I s'posed to know, eh? They took 'em, an' that's all there is to it, see? We'd better be ready to fight 'em off if'n they comes back t'take more of us."

Tura shrugged. "An' how are we supposed to do that?"

Her enquiry seemed to throw Flib into a greater rage. She waved her paws about wildly. "Look, I ain't in charge 'ere. Can't yer think for yoreselves, instead o' sittin' there scrinjin' an' moanin'? At least I'm doin' somethin'—I'm tryin' to dig a tunnel out of 'ere. In fact, that's wot I think I'll do now, carry on diggin'. Cummon, youse two!"

A moment later, she and her two mole helpers had vanished into the tunnel, leaving the rest to their own devices.

Tura took up the wet rag and began wiping Flandor's wound, her jaw set tightly. "Huh, not much good askin' yore sister for help, is it?"

Midda saw that Borti had gone back to sleep. She placed him carefully down on a bed of old dried grass. "That's not very fair, Tura. Flib's doing her best to dig that tunnel so we can all escape. I know she can get a bit moody at times, but she's always been that way. Take my word for it, Flib has a good heart. She'll help us in her own way, you'll see."

Flandor sat upright, nursing his head. "Aye, Tura, she's right—hush, did ye hear that? Somebeast's unlockin' the door. Get them all back against the walls. Be ready to fight this time!"

The light of fear banished the dullness from young eyes as everybeast put their backs to the wall and waited with bated breath.

The door opened to reveal Thwip, Binta and two guards with the prisoner's food. Flandor recognised the guards as part of the group who had beaten him with their spear-butts. Despite his injuries, the young otter charged at them with teeth bared.

"Dirty cowards! Only two of ye this time. Well, let's see how brave ye are without yore gang!"

Thwip pushed the cauldron of gruel forward and backed off, cracking his whip. He called to the others, "Binta, leave the water. Let's get out of this place. Leave 'em to feed themselves. That streamdog's gone mad!"

The four vermin hurried from the scene, slamming the door and peering through the grating. The other captives, urged on by Flandor's example, hurled themselves at the locked door, banging on it, shouting insults and threats at their jailers.

"Yah, dirty rotten stinky cowards!"

"Give us back our three friends."

"Yore too scared t'come back in here an' face us!"

"Burr, you'm muthers shudd be unshamed of ee!"

Avoiding a pawful of soil which rattled through the grating, Thwip laughed harshly. "Eat hearty, me liddle friends. That's the last vittles ye'll get off us. We'll see how brave ye are after a few days without food'n'water!"

Any further threats from the fox were cut off by a loud rumbling noise from inside the dungeon. It was from the vent of Flib's escape tunnel. With a boom and a crash, a big boulder shot out like a cannonball. This was followed by a shooting slide of debris, soil, pebbles, pieces of tree root and thick sandy dust.

Binta fell back, coughing and spitting as the dust came through the grille. "Wot'n the name . . . wot's 'appenin' in there?"

One of the guards, who had wisely stood aside, missing the choking debris, commented ironically, "Go an' see, if'n ye wants to. I'm gettin' outta here afore the roof caves in on me!" He took off in a hurry, with the other three following him.

Flandor waded paw-deep through the mess which had enveloped half of the cavern. "Tura, Midda, are ye alright? Get the little uns up on that side ledge—make sure they're all safe!"

Anybeast who was unhurt came to help the shrewmaid and the young squirrel. It took a while for the dust to settle and for the few lanterns to be set right. Fortunately, no life had been lost, and nobeast was seriously injured. Once the babes were made safe on the ledge and the remainder of their food and water had been salvaged, Flandor took a look around.

The tunnel had vanished completely. There was only a sloping hill of debris where it had once been. Midda immediately threw herself upon it, digging furiously with her bare paws. "Flib's in there. Help me—she might be injured!"

Flandor overpowered her, pulling her clear of the wreckage. "Come away, mate. Nobeast could've lived through that. There's been some massive kind o' collapse, maybe an earthshift of some kind. You won't do any good tryin' t'dig through that lot."

Midda struggled in the young otter's grasp, then gave up. She sat on the hill of rubble weeping. "Oh, Flib, poor Flib! What a way to die, crushed under all that rock and earth. Oh, my poor sister!"

Tura shook her head sadly. "Aye an' those two moles who were with Flib, they'll be dead, too."

The Witherspyk hog, Jiddle, wiped dust from his eyes. "They'd be the lucky ones, goin' quick like that. Look at us trapped in here, an' they ain't comin' back to feed us, I wager. We've been left here t'die slow."

Jango Bigboat was not a beast to sit about in the gatehouse drinking hot mint tea and nibbling scones spread with damson preserve. Diggs appropriated the Guosim Log a Log's share as he watched Jango leave the table.

"Hah, jolly bad form, leavin' scones t'go stale like that. Where are you off to, old lad?"

The Shrew Chieftain gestured upward. "Goin' to take a look up there, see if ole Granvy's gettin' any information out o' that vermin. You comin'?"

The irrepressible Diggs waggled his ears. "Oh, by an' by, m'friend, by an' by. Soon as I've nourished me tender young body. You run along like a good chap. We'll be up presently, wot!"

Oakheart Witherspyk shared Jango's scones with Diggs. The big hedgehog really enjoyed his food. "Rather toothsome, this Redwall cuisine, y'know. One could develop a real taste for it."

Diggs watched him devour the last scone. He gazed mournfully at the empty tray. "Oh, really? Y'don't say!"

They were distracted by Jango yelling from the walltop, "Ahoy, mates, come up 'ere an' take a look at this lot!"

Buckler, Skipper and Oakheart were up on the ramparts in the twinkling of an eye.

Jango was pointing to a vermin horde arrayed on the west flatlands in front of the Abbey. It was the full complement of Ravagers, everybeast armed to the teeth, headed by the Sable Quean and Zwilt the Shade.

Buckler muttered quietly to Granvy, "Get back down to the Abbey quick. Tell the Abbess to send every able-bodied Redwaller up here an' make sure they look as if they're armed. Go!"

Trying to put a bold face on things, Diggs turned his

back upon the vermin throng, commenting lightly, "Hmm, looks like we've got visitors, chaps. What d'you suppose that mangy mob want, wot?"

Skipper played along casually. "Well, they ain't come to swap scone recipes an' take tea on the lawn. What d'ye think, Oakie?"

The big Witherspyk hog sniffed disdainfully. "I think they should assemble downwind from us, sirrah. 'Pon my word, the smell's enough t'make a dead frog sick!"

Zwilt and Vilaya stood motionless, as if awaiting some reaction from the walltop. However, the creatures on the ramparts continued ignoring them and chatting coolly amongst themselves.

Jango placed a footpaw on Gripchun, who was sitting out of sight with his back against the wall. Pressing the ferret firmly in place, the Guosim Chieftain murmured to him, "If'n ye want to stay alive an' healthy, mate, stay where ye are an' don't move. Unnerstand?"

The vermin nodded vigorously. One look at the shrew's fierce eyes, and he understood.

Without warning, the twin Abbey bells began booming out the alarm. Redwallers, Guosim and Witherspyks came hastening up the wallsteps and onto the battlements. Buckler sighed ruefully as Granvy saluted him.

"They're all here, just as you asked."

The young hare returned the salute, adding, "There was no need for alarm bells. It could've been done without all the fuss, just t'show the vermin we're not anxious or concerned."

Abbess Marjoram spoke. "Don't blame Granvy. 'Twas my decision to sound the bells. I'm sorry if I did the wrong thing. But we've never had a situation like this to my knowledge. My apologies to you, Buck."

Buckler bowed gallantly. "Accepted, Mother Abbess. Now, if you aren't used to facing vermin hordes, then perhaps you'll leave this to me?"

Marjoram touched his paw. "Willingly, my friend."

Buckler gave orders quietly. "Log a Log Jango, would you split your force? Take half the Guosim to the southwest gable and send the rest to the northwest corner, please."

Jango nodded to Sniffy the Tracker. "You take half our tribe an' cover the nor'west end. I'll take the rest and stand at the sou'west corner."

They moved off promptly as Buckler continued with his strategy. "Diggs, Skipper, stay with me at the centre threshold. Oakie, Foremole, spread everybeast the length of this west wall, but send six to watch the other walltops. Two to the east, two to the south and two to the north. They can give the warning if the vermin start sending beasts round the walls. Wait, now—before you go, listen to what I say."

He looked at the Abbeybeasts and woodlanders, who, apart from the well-armed Guosim, were carrying a variety of makeshift weaponry—spades, digging forks, hoes, window poles, wood axes and kitchen knives. "All of you, stay in clear view holdin' your weapons so they can be seen. But don't do anything until we give the order. Above all, stand silent. Don't start threatening and shouting war cries. Right, go to it!"

There was an air of tension pervading the warm summer noon as both sides faced each other in complete silence. All that could be heard was a few larks on high over the western flatlands beyond the walls.

Buckler used an old unsettling tactic, addressing a Ravager at random. Pointing to one at the left flank, he enquired, "You, what d'ye want here?"

As the dumbfounded vermin stared up at him, Zwilt stood out, answering sharply, "If you have anything to say, you'll speak to me!"

Buckler leaned on a battlement, replying casually, "I've got nothin' t'say at the moment, except for what I asked that other clod. What d'ye want here, an' who are ye, eh?"

Zwilt stiffened, his paw seeking the longsword beneath his flowing cloak. "I am Zwilt the Shade, Commander of the Ravagers, and I wish to speak with your leader, the one who rules this place!"

Buckler twitched his ears, smiling easily. "Well, ain't that a pity? You'll just have to speak t'me. Buckler Kordyne at y'service, Blademaster of Salamandastron."

Zwilt looked about to speak, when Buckler halted him with an upraised paw. "Zwilt the Shade, eh? I've heard of you. Aren't you the one who sneaks around the countryside stealin' babes from their mammas' paws? A real brave warrior!"

A loud snigger from Diggs was heard clearly as Buckler continued. "I don't think I want to bandy words with a coward like you. No, I'll speak with her, Vilaya the Sable Quean, who lives at Althier."

The young hare could tell by the look which passed betwixt Zwilt and Vilaya that his remark had hit home. How did he know of Althier?

Vilaya answered him, "I did not come here to play guessing games and exchange insults. No doubt you are wondering what has become of your young ones?"

Abbess Marjoram could hold herself back no longer. She leapt forward, shaking a clenched paw. "You filthy Dibbun thief—it was you!"

Before they could be stopped, Oakheart's wife, Dymphnia, and Jango's wife, Furm, were yelling at the Sable Quean.

"What've ye done with our babes, you wicked scum?"

"Give us our little uns back. How could ye do such a bad thing?"

Whilst he felt sorry for both mothers, Granvy rounded on the pair, muttering fiercely, "Shuttup, both of ye. It's not doing any good, insulting a vermin Quean like that. You'll only bring more trouble on the little ones. Leave it to Buckler—he knows what he's doing!"

They fell back and were comforted into silence by Sister Fumbril and some molewives. Buckler felt that the vermin had got the better of that exchange. This set him to try another tactic. He called out challengingly, "How do we know you've got the young uns. Where's yore proof?"

The Ravagers brought forward three large sacks which, on a signal from Vilaya, they turned out. The little Witherspyk hogmaid Jinty, Tassy the Redwall squirrelmaid and Urfa the baby leveret tumbled forth, blinking in the sunlight.

Skipper ground his teeth, whispering to Sister Fumbril, "Keep their mothers out o' sight. Don't let 'em see the little uns, I beg ye, marm!"

Diggs moved swiftly up alongside Buckler. "Let's find out what the rotters do when they see we've got one of their crew, wot?"

It was a standoff. Buckler realised he would have to take the gamble. He nodded. "There's nothin' else we can do. Try it, mate!"

Grabbing Gripchun roughly, Diggs hauled him up onto the battlements.

Buckler shouted, "This is one of yours—Gripchun, I believe. Harm any one of those babes, and he'll pay!"

Zwilt whispered to one of the Ravagers, who passed the word on to some others. The tall sable called to the prisoner on the walltop, "Gripchun, friend, how would you like me to free you from those creatures?"

The ferret's head bobbed rapidly. "Aye, sir, I'd like that!"

Zwilt was smiling as he raised his paw, then let it drop suddenly.

There was a buzzing noise, like several angry hornets, as three arrows zipped out from the horde. One went wide, but the other two found Gripchun. He gave a startled gurgle, then went limp. Falling from Diggs's grasp, he hurtled from the battlements to the path in front of the main gate.

The three little captives were swiftly returned to their sacks. On the walltops, most of the defenders were ducking below the parapet, fearing further arrows would follow. But none came.

Zwilt had a brief whispered conference with Vilaya,

then drew his broadsword, signalling a retreat. "We will be back here before too long. Do not try to follow or discover where Althier lies. It would be very sad for your young ones if ye did!"

Buckler tore down the wallstairs and unbarred the main gate, calling to Diggs, who had followed him, "Bar the gate behind me, stay in here—that's an order, Subaltern!"

Drawing his long rapier, he crossed the path. Taking the ditch in a single leap, he roared, "Eulaliiiaaaaa!"

Marching at the front of the Ravagers, Zwilt and Vilaya both heard the hare's war cry. She nodded to the tall sable.

"Go back and warn that fool off—and don't get into a fight with him. He could be a dangerous beast."

Buckler was waiting as Zwilt came striding over the flatland, brandishing the broadsword. "I've been given orders not to slay you, longears. What is it that you want? Speak!"

Buckler did his best to provoke Zwilt to fight. "You rotten, stinkin', murderin' coward! That sword you hold is my brother's blade. How did ye kill him, yellow guts? By stabbin' him in the back?"

Buckler drew his long rapier; Zwilt took a pace backward. He opened his cloak to reveal the medal hanging about his neck. Showing his teeth in a malevolent smile, he replied, "Your brother, was he? Stupid, clodhoppin' soil plougher! No need to stab that one in the back—I cut him to ribbons with one paw behind my back. I took his pretty medal, too. D'ye like it, longears?"

The young hare's steel made the still air thrum as he came at the tall sable.

"Put up that blade or the young ones die!" Vilaya had dropped to the rear of her Ravagers. Her eyes glittered with menace as she hissed, "I warn ye, do you want their blood on your head?"

Buckler sheathed the rapier back over his shoulder.

The Sable Quean called to her commander, "Leave him, Zwilt. Don't waste your time with the fool. Come on."

Buckler was quivering from ears to tailscut. He had trouble keeping his voice level. "We'll meet again, vermin, and when we do, 'twill be your death day. I swear on my oath!"

Zwilt sneered. "Big words for a rabbet with a skinny blade. When we meet again, I'll do to you what I did for your big clumsy brother, but I'll do it slower so you'll suffer longer. Now, run back and hide behind those walls with your friends." Turning his back upon the hare warrior, Zwilt strode off to join the horde.

Filled with an incandescent rage, Buckler took a pace toward Zwilt as the world turned red in front of his eyes. What he would have done next he would never know. Vilaya's voice stopped him short.

"Do as he says, or you will die before the young ones do. Look, fool, and obey me!"

As his vision cleared, Buckler saw what she meant. He was facing six vermin archers with shafts drawn fullstretch on their curving bows. There was nothing more he could do.

Turning, he began walking slowly back to the Abbey, where the defenders were watching him from the walltops. Suddenly an arrow skidded by his neck, furrowing a shallow wound. He heard mocking laughter from behind him and Zwilt calling, "Faster, rabbet, or we won't get the chance to meet again—they'll kill you!"

Shafts were zipping all around Buckler. He felt one cut sharply into his footpaw, and he fell. Picking himself swiftly up, he staggered and stumbled in a zigzag path until he reached the Abbey.

Diggs and Skipper flung the gate open, hauling him inside. Log a Log Jango shouted from the walltop, "The treacherous blaggards! Guosim, string yore bows!"

Buckler roared back at the Shrew Chieftain, "No! No! Don't fire at them. They'll kill our young uns. Don't do anything!"

Reluctantly, Jango gave his archers orders to stand

down. Everybeast flocked about the young hare. Dymphnia Witherspyk and her daughter Trajidia supported him to the Abbey building where Sister Fumbril took over.

"Bring him to the Infirmary. Those vermin arrows may be tipped with poison—hurry now!"

Trajidia looked aghast. "Poison! Oh, the foul fiends, and you were so brave out there, Mister Buckler, so valorous! Facing all those foebeast single-pawed. Alas, only to be fatally pierced by poison weapons!"

A swift kick in the tail from her grandmother caused her to yelp indignantly. Crumfiss pushed her onward.

"Don't let him go, missy. Keep tight hold or he'll fall. An' ye can stop all the drama. Save yore moanin' and wailin' for the proper time!"

Skipper watched the ladies escorting Buckler upstairs, commenting to Oakheart, "Ye won't get near Buck, not with that lot. He's in more danger of bein' nursed, cared for an' fed t'death than he is from bein' slayed by vermin. See!"

Drull Hogwife and the Abbess hurried by, bearing a tray of food and drink as they followed the others.

Diggs sat down on the bottom stair, chunnering. "Huh, I should've gone with old Buck. Blinkin' chap could starve t'death round here if he's not been jolly well wounded, wot!"

Jango turned to Granvy. "Bad luck, losin' yore vermin prisoner like that. Ye won't get no more out o' him."

Granvy looked over the top of his rock-crystal glasses, nodding sagely. "Oh, really, d'ye think so? Well, let me tell you, my friend, I learned enough from Gripchun to put a few things together myself. You don't get to be a Recorder of Redwall by letting your brain go idle."

The others were immediately intrigued by this statement.

Skipper thumped his rudder excitedly. "Things? Wot sort o' things, matey?"

Oakheart whispered confidentially, "No secrets here, sirrah—you can tell us."

The old scribe chuckled. "Later, perhaps, when Buckler gets back from the clutches of Sister Fumbril. I'm afraid I don't know everything yet, so I may need a bit of help and some quick-witted ideas."

Diggs brightened up slightly. "Chap t'help with quick-witted ideas, d'ye say? Hah, you're lookin' at the very fellow, old lad. My quick-wittedness is legendary at Salamandastron, wot wot!"

Jango chuckled. "I'll wager it is—tryin' to work out how t'get more vittles than the rest, figurin' how ye can pinch pies from the cookhouse an' so on."

Diggs wrinkled his ears at the shrew. "Steady on, there—that's a jolly hurtful thing t'say about a chap, y'know. Still, I wish I knew where I could pinch a bloomin' pie or two right now. Most unusual for me, but I do feel a bit bloomin' peckish."

Granvy smiled. "Right, then, shall we say after supper let's all meet in the gatehouse?"

Diggs nodded. "Supper, a capital idea!"

Abbess Marjoram pushed the tray of untouched food toward Buckler as Sister Fumbril tended to his wounds. He hardly glanced at it.

She chided him jokingly, "Tuck in, young sir. Even warriors have to eat, you know."

Buckler did not even flinch as Fumbril washed his neck wound with hot water and herbal cleanser. He sat on a sickbay bed, gazing bleakly at the wall.

Dymphnia Witherspyk looked up at him as she began bathing his footpaw. His dark mood was plain to see. "Don't take it to heart so much, Buck. You did all you could have done. 'Twas very brave of you."

There was a bitter edge to the young hare's voice. "Did all I could've done? Huh, I had to run away like a frightened babe. Very brave, I'm sure!"

Log a Log's wife, Furm, passed him a bowl of hot summer vegetable soup, commenting, "Oh, I see, you'd 'ave much sooner stood yore ground and gotten shot full of arrows. That would've made ye feel better, eh?"

Buckler's eyes, still hot with seething anger, swept the ladies. "That Zwilt . . . that piece of filth! He was wearing my dead brother's medallion—aye, an' wielding his sword, too. That tiny leveret, the one they had in a sack, I've never set eyes on it before, but I'll take my oath that the babe's my nephew. Where else would they get a little hare around here?"

Trajidia clasped her paws, declaiming dramatically, "Oh, the agonies you must have suffered, sirrah, standing there helpless in front of your tormentors!"

Catching her mother's icy glance, she trailed off into silence. Sister Fumbril bound a neat light dressing of sanicle and dockleaf to Buckler's footpaw.

"There, you're as good as new, matey. How d'ye feel?"

Buckler touched his neck, which was smeared with a healing unguent. He stood up, testing his weight upon the paw. "Better, thanks. I don't have to stay here, do I?"

Abbess Marjoram moved the tray out of his way. "Not if you don't want to. Could I tempt you to take a little food before you leave?"

She spoke as Diggs entered the room. The tubby Subaltern beamed, thinking the remark was addressed to him. "You certainly can, Mother Abbess, marm!"

Plonking himself on the bed, he pulled the tray to him. "What ho, Buck, you look jolly chipper. Still, I was just sayin' to old Log a Thing, takes more'n a couple of mis'rable vermin arrows t'stop a Salamandastron chap, wot!" He swigged off the soup and wiped his lips. When he looked up, his companion had gone.

"Well, now, didn't stop to chat, did he? My word, what'n the name o' fur'n'feathers ails him?"

Furm shook her head. "Huh, warriors. No tellin' wot goes on in their minds. I should know, I'm married to one!"

Diggs bit into a plum turnover. "Say no more, dear lady. Know exactly what y'mean. Us warriors are a jolly odd lot, wot, wot!"

Supper was a very subdued affair. Everybeast was mulling over what had taken place that day. Most Redwallers were feeling apprehensive following the appearance of a vermin horde at their very gates. They ate in silence, keeping their feelings to themselves.

Skipper finished eating quickly, then nodded to Buckler. "D'ye fancy a stroll over t' the gatehouse with some of us? Ole Granvy reckons he's onto somethin' that might help with our problem."

Buckler had hardly touched food; he stood promptly. "Lead on, Skip. Anythin's better than sittin' round wondering what t'do next."

The Abbey Recorder looked about at the assembly in the little cottage. Skipper, Buckler, Diggs, Jango, Oakheart and the Abbess. He tapped his quill pen on a stack of yellowed scrolls, obviously ancient writings. "Listen now, friends, I've been trying to piece together a few things which might reveal the location of where the Dibbuns are being kept."

Oakheart scratched his headspikes. "Aye, sir, but will it do any good? You may be bringing disaster on our young uns heads. D'ye recall what that scoundrel Zwilt said? If we try to follow them, or find the babes, then they'll harm our little ones."

The sound of Jango's teeth grinding together was clear—the Guosim Chieftain practically spat out his words. "So wot d'we do, eh? Sit about twiddlin' our paws, an' let those scum have all their own way? Never trust wot a vermin says, Oakie."

Skipper's rudder thwacked the floor. "Aye, yore right there, matey. We should be doin' all we can to free the little uns, an' quick about it, too!"

Buckler had hardly spoken thus far, but now he came

to the fore, firm and decisive. "Are we all agreed, then—action must be taken?" They called out as one, "Aye!"

The Blademaster nodded. "Good! So, then, Mister Granvy, what've ye got to tell us?"

The Recorder adjusted the little spectacles on his snout. "Right. First things first: I don't think that the Dibbuns are being held more than a day's march from here. Why should the vermin keep them any great distance away? It doesn't make sense. Agreed?"

Abbess Marjoram nodded. "Agreed, that's my feelings. Also he said that they would return to our Abbey before too long, so they can't be far away."

Granvy acknowledged Marjoram. "Thank you, Mother Abbess. Now, this word, *Althier,* is a strange name, not one we'd know around Mossflower. I kept repeating it to myself—*Althier.* You may say that I have a quirky mind, and so I do, friends. So I wrote the name down and tried to decipher it. D'you know, I think it's actually made up from two words. The first one would be probably a word we use all the time—*the! The* pond, *the* Abbey, *the* orchard, *the* kitchen. And it's definitely there. So, take away the word *the,* and what are we left with? Four letters. *A . . . L . . . I . . . R.* What does that suggest to you?"

After a moment's thought, Oakheart spoke out. *"Rail!"*

Granvy shook his head. "What word might we associate with most vermin, eh?"

Diggs shouted out, *"Liar,* that's the word. Hah, didn't Jango say that only a moment ago? Never trust a vermin, an' why? 'Cos they're all liars, flippin' liars!"

The solution dawned on Buckler. *"Lair.* Vermin hide in lairs, that's what Althier means . . . the Lair!"

Granvy patted the young hare's back. "Well done, Buck. The Lair. So, what are we seeking?"

Oakheart sounded excited. "A vermin lair within a good march from Redwall!"

Diggs began chunnering. "Dearie me, it must be a jolly

big lair. Somewhere large enough to take all those bally ravagin' rascals, plus the young uns. Anywhere that bloomin' size you could spot from a flippin' league away. Sounds like a pile of balderdash to me chaps, wot!"

Granvy shook his head. "No, no, you're wrong. Didn't Gripchun say that he didn't know where Althier was? That suggests Zwilt and the Sable creature keep the main body of their army well away from it. There's lots of places in Mossflower where you could set up a camp for a mob of vermin. Doesn't have to be particularly secret—nobeast is going to attack that number of armed vermin. But Althier, now, that's the secret hideout, where only the chosen few are allowed to be. The Quean, Zwilt, some guards and jailers and, of course, the captives."

Jango scratched at his scrubby beard. "You got a point there, scribe, but where is it, where do we start lookin'?"

Skipper tried reasoning. "Well, those Ravager vermin ain't been seen hereabouts until lately. So maybe they ain't had time to build Althier. P'raps they just found it, an' the Quean made it their lair."

Abbess Marjoram was in agreement. "It sounds feasible to me. So, what natural hideouts do we know of around Mossflower Country? Who has a working knowledge of the area? Abbeybeasts mainly stay here at Redwall—we're not travellers. Jango, maybe you could suggest someplace?"

The Guosim Chieftain pondered. "Hmm, lemme see. I've spent all me life on Mossflower's waterways. Hah, wot about the old quarry? That's full o' caves!"

Granvy pointed a paw at Jango. "You could be right. I read in the records that the quarry was where they took the stone from to build Redwall. That's how it became a quarry. It was said to be a breeding place for serpents, though, poisonteeth adders. D'you think they'd choose that? I'm not so sure, friends."

"Corim, the place of Corim!"

The words had come from the Abbess, but the voice did

not sound like hers. Granvy stared at Marjoram. "What was that you said? Corim?"

Abbess Marjoram shook her head and rubbed her eyes, as if just waking from a nap. She blinked at Granvy. "I don't know. What did I say?"

Oakheart held out his paw theatrically. "As I heard it, marm, you said, 'Corim, the place of Corim!' I never forget my lines, you see, and neither should you, Mother Abbess. Corim, the place of Corim. Heard it m'self, distinctly—though I recall, your voice sounded rather different."

Granvy spoke in hushed tones. "That's because it was the voice of Martin the Warrior! It isn't the first time he's spoken through some other creature. Martin's sending us a message."

Jango carried on with his former idea. "I think the ole quarry'd be a likely place—"

"Silence, please!"

Granvy had both his eyes shut tight, his paws clenched. The old Recorder was concentrating hard.

Jango went quiet; they all stared at Granvy. Now he was rocking back and forth, muttering, "Corim, Corim, the place of Corim . . . Corim, where have I heard that name before? Corim, a word from long ago . . ."

He suddenly leapt up in a fever of elation. "Hahah! Of course! Now I know, 'twas here all the time, here right under our snouts!"

Skipper could stand it no longer. The big otter picked Granvy up and stood him on the gatehouse table. "Corim here? Granvy, me ole mate, will ye stop jumpin' about an' talkin' in riddles? Wot's right under our snouts? Now, calm down an' speak plain!"

Granvy sat down on the edge of the table. He took a deep breath, then polished his glasses slowly. "Er, forgive my little outburst—not quite the thing for an Abbey Recorder. However 'twas not without reason. Buckler, d'ye see that bookshelf on the far wall? I'd like you to find me a volume there. I'm not quite certain of the title, though."

Diggs chunnered. "Not quite certain, eh? That's jolly useful, wot. Confounded great load o' books on those shelves, an' the blinkin' chap doesn't know the flippin' name o' the one he wants. Hah!"

Buckler's paw gagged his voluble friend's mouth as Granvy continued, "I know it's a weighty book, huge, thick thing, probably with a green cover. Or was it red? Something about a journal of somebeast or other. Name began with a *G*."

Now it was Marjoram's turn to get excited. *"The Journal of Abbess Germaine!"*

The glasses slipped down Granvy's nose. "How did you know that?"

Marjoram explained, "Because when I was made Abbess of Redwall I borrowed it from you to learn how other Abbesses ruled here!"

Granvy scratched his ears. "Did you, really? Dearie me, I must be getting old. I don't remember. Tell me more, please."

Marjoram did just that. "You were right. It's a thick old green volume, but you won't find it in here. I kept it in my study, you see. 'Twas very wrong of me, because I've never found the time to read it, though I keep promising myself that I will sometime. Shall we go and take a peep at it?"

As they crossed the moonlit lawns, Diggs saw the dormitory lights going out one by one. He yawned. "Only one thing I like better'n' scoffin', an' that's snoozin'. In a snug little bunk with a soft pillow, wot!"

Granvy blinked; Skipper caught him as he stumbled.

"Are you tired, too, me ole mate?"

The hedgehog Recorder shook himself briskly. "Not at all. Lead on, my friend!"

The Abbess breathed in deeply. "Ah, just smell that summer night air. So warm and soft. I love the different scents, fennel, marigold, dandelion and gentian, so delicate, faint almost."

Jango growled, "Let's get on an' look at this book instead o' yafflin' about goin' to bed an' sniffin' the flowers!"

Oakheart chuckled quietly. "Ah, a true lover of nature and its many wonders."

The study was a neat room. Marjoram could not abide untidiness. The friends began sorting through her books, but she rapped sharply on her writing desk.

"Touch nothing, please. I know exactly where everything is. See, here is the book!"

Granvy immediately opened it, flicking through the yellowed barkpaper leaves.

It was a huge green-bound volume. The Recorder muttered to himself as he leafed through it. "Must've taken Abbess Germaine many seasons to write all this. A good deal is about the time before our Abbey was even built. Goodness knows when that was!"

Abbess Marjoram hovered about the old squirrel anxiously. "Please be careful with the book. It's so old, and very precious. Take care you don't damage it!"

Granvy, however, was paying little attention to her. Knowing what he sought, he riffled speedily through. "Hmm, wildcats, vermin, Martin, Gonff, Bella of Brockhall . . . Ah, here it is!"

Buckler leaned over his shoulder. "Here's what? Have you found something valuable?"

The Recorder raised a small spurt of dust as he slammed his paw down on the open page. "The answer to our problem, friends. Now I know what Corim means, and Althier, too. This has to be it!"

14

There are those in Mossflower who would deny the existence of a Warrior mole. None of these doubters had ever met Axtel Sturnclaw. There was not the slightest doubt that Axtel was a warrior. He was also a loner—bigger, stronger and fiercer than any of his species. In his broad belt, Axtel carried a war hammer, which he mainly used for breaking stones when he was tunnelling. Other than that, the big fellow needed no fancy weaponry. Just one glance at his massive digging claws was enough to warn anybeast. Axtel Sturnclaw was not a mole to be messed with. He led a solitary life, wandering the woodlands, furrowing his own workings and, for the most part, shunning the company of others.

Vermin had never bothered him. The few who had tried never lived to tell the tale. He left their carcasses up in the branches of trees for carrion to dispose of. It was Axtel's view that he would not sully good soil by burying vermin in it.

In short, Axtel Sturnclaw was a warrior mole who lived quietly but by his own principles. He was a stranger to the Mossflower woodlands, so he was exploring.

This particular day, he was tunnelling near a gigantic old oak, hoping to find a cave beneath the roots. Having dug all day with not much success, Axtel was about to finish and go back up to the woodland surface when something unexpected occurred.

His tunnel collapsed. Not on his head but beneath him. Without warning, he shot downward and was only stopped from falling further by his own prompt action. Feeling the floor going out from under him, the powerful mole grabbed a thick root and hung on. As suddenly as it had started, the subsidence ceased. Axtel hung there in darkness for a moment, puzzled by the turn of events. Then something grabbed him by the footpaw.

The stolid warrior mole did not panic; he was more overcome with curiosity than anything. Reaching down, he grabbed the creature who was clutching him and hauled it up. It was a little molemaid holding a lantern. With a single heave, Axtel lobbed her up into his own tunnel.

Spitting out debris, she nodded. "Hurr, thankee, zurr!"

Axtel eyed her suspiciously. "Yurr, missy, wot bee's you'm doin' daown thurr?"

Gurchen, for it was she, dispensed with long-winded explanations, informing him, "Us'ns got curlapsed in, thurr bee's two uthers a-buried asoide oi. Wudd ee be so koind as to diggen 'em owt, big zurr?"

Axtel took the lantern, hanging it on the oak root. He shook a large digging claw at the molemaid. "You'm stay put, yurr—oi'll gerrum!"

Gurchen leaned over the tunnel edge, shielding her eyes as he shot into the loose soil, like a furry cannonball. Everything was still for a short time, then the ground erupted where Axtel had gone down. Gurchen was forced to move aside as he tossed the limp form of Flib up into the tunnel.

Axtel blew soil from his snout. "Did ee say thurr wurr two?"

A nod sent him burrowing back down. Loose earth moved this way and that, then he emerged with little Guffy clinging to his neck for dear life.

Seizing the root, Axtel passed Gurchen the lantern. He clambered back up into the tunnel. Guffy sprang into Gurchen's paws, weeping with fright after his underground ordeal. The big mole slung Flib across his back, gesturing upward.

"Goo on with ee, back into ee fresh h'air!"

It was dark night in the woodlands. Gurchen and Guffy breathed deeply, overjoyed even though they were moles to be free of the underground, no longer imprisoned in the cave. They both began to chatter, explaining their plight to their huge new friend, but he silenced them with a snort.

"You'm 'ushed naow, whoilst oi see's iffen this young un bee's still aloive!"

Retrieving the gear he had left above ground, Axtel cleared debris from Flib's mouth and nostrils. He poured water between her open lips, until she gurgled and jerked, vomiting sludge and fine root tendrils onto the grass. Axtel sat her up.

"Burr, she'm soon bee's roighter'n'rain!"

Leading them off a small distance, he sat the escaped prisoners in a dry gully. Lighting a small smokeless fire from the lantern flame, Axtel dug food from his pack. "You uns must be furr 'ungered'n'thursty."

Guffy threw his paws around his saviour's neck. "Hurrhurrhurr, thankee muchly, zurr. You'm a guddbeast!"

The Warrior mole had never been around young ones, nor had he ever witnessed a display of genuine affection. He allowed himself to be hugged awhile, then sitting Guffy down with Flib and Gurchen, Axtel covered his shyness, mumbling gruffly as he busied himself.

"Yurr, naow, you'm likkle uns set thurr whoilst oi gets ee summat t'be eaten."

Flib, still spitting up bits of rubble, was unable to eat, though she did drink some of the big mole's excellent dandelion cordial. The two little moles tucked gratefully into acorn and chestnut scones. They had no sooner finished eating and drinking than both Dibbuns fell instantly to sleep.

Axtel dug an old cloak out of his gear and covered them both. He turned his attention to Flib. "Naow, mizzy, may'aps ee can tell oi abowt 'ow ee cummed to be daown thurr unnergrounds."

The Guosim maid told her story, recounting from the time of her capture up to the tunnel collapse. She described in detail her vermin captors and their regime over the young prisoners, the darkness of the gloomy dungeon, the meagre rations and harsh treatment. Flib mentioned that she had a younger sister and a brother, a mere babe, still held in captivity with the rest. She also told of Thwip and Binta, the cruel fox jailers.

When she had finished her report, Flib watched Axtel Sturnclaw closely. The Warrior mole sat silent, his eyes flickering savagely in the firelight. He picked up a thick dead root end, wrenching it from the earth with one paw. His formidable digging claws snapped the root with a quick swat. Throwing the wood on the fire, he turned his gaze on the sleeping Dibbuns.

"You'm a sayin' ee vurmints gotten gurt numbers o' likkle uns locked away daown thurr, miz?"

Flib nodded. "About a score of 'em. Most been stolen from their families, some babes scarce two seasons old, pore liddle mites."

She fell quiet, afraid to say more. Axtel's teeth were grinding audibly; his eyes had taken on a fearful glaze. Taking the war hammer from his belt, he shook it right under Flib's nose, growling, "Gurt brave vurmints, eh? A-locken up babbies an' keepin' 'em 'ungered! Et b'aint roight, no, miz, et b'aint. They'm villuns got t'be punishered! Hurr, bo aye, an' oi bee's ee one who'll do ee punishen, take moi wurd fur et!"

Out in Mossflower woodlands, Zwilt dismissed the main force of Ravagers, sending them back to their camp. Joining Vilaya and Dirva, he accompanied them, his chosen cave guards and the three small hostages back to Althier.

Even before they reached the entrance in the old oak tree trunk, Dirva began twitching oddly.

The Sable Quean eyed her coldly. "Why all the shaking and hopping about?"

Dirva replied darkly, "I feels it in my bones'n'fur, Majesty—there's somethin' amiss. Althier isn't the same as when we left it!"

Vilaya knew enough to trust her aide's feelings. She commanded Zwilt, "Leave two guards here with the prisoners. Go ahead swiftly—find out what has gone on in my absence. We'll follow on."

When the Sable Quean eventually reached Althier, Zwilt was standing inside the entrance. His Ravagers were holding guards, two of the four who had remained behind with Thwip and Binta.

The tall sable shoved both vermin forward, snarling at them, "Report to your Quean, tell her what happened here!"

The elder of the two swallowed hard. "It was a collapse, Majesty, inside the prisoners' cell. We heard the noise and saw soil comin' out o' the door gratin'."

Both guards quailed under Vilaya's piercing eyes. She pointed to the younger vermin. "Did you see it? Were any of the captives hurt?"

He told her, constantly looking at his companion for reassurance. "Majesty, we didn't see it. We only heard the noise, but we went quickly t'see wot it was. The dungeon door was jammed, with rubble piled up agin it."

The older guard nodded, as if his life depended upon it (which it did). "Aye, Majesty. The foxes saw it. They was there, just outside, all the time."

The younger one added, "Those other two guards, the ones you left with us to mind the prisoners, they was with the foxes. They must've saw it 'appen!"

The Quean held up a paw, silencing them. "Then send them to me, immediately!"

Zwilt interrupted, "Majesty, they are gone, deserted—Thwip, Binta and the two sentries."

Vilaya's nostrils flared with wrath. "Find them. Hunt them down and bring them back here to me!"

Zwilt the Shade bowed low. This was work he enjoyed. "Leave it to me, my Quean!" He indicated four guards. "Bring ropes to bind them. Hurry, I must go before the trail runs cold."

After the hunters departed, Vilaya had a seat set up close to the dungeon, where she could direct operations. There was no way of pushing open the dungeon door, with all the debris behind it. She watched awhile as a half-dozen guards tried to force an entrance, then sighed in irritation.

"Break the hinges and pull it down."

Spearpoints hacked at the woodwork until the old iron hinges were exposed. The rusty metal creaked as the guards' spearhafts levered them loose. With a joint heave, the vermin pulled the battered door down. A guard held up a lantern, peering inside through the settling dust.

"There's still many in there, sitting on the ledges mainly. I can't see clearly yet, but there's quite a number of them."

Vilaya sounded irate. "Then get them out before they become buried by another collapse. Guards!"

Shortly thereafter, the young creatures, dusty and bedraggled, were seated on the floor gazing up at their captors. Vilaya questioned the guard who had first sighted them.

"Are they all here, or are any missing?"

The vermin's voice trembled as he answered, "I dunno, yore Majesty. 'Twasn't my job to count 'em."

The Sable Quean swept the other guards with an icy glare. "One of ye must know. Speak up—how many prisoners were there?"

The old rat Dirva tugged at Vilaya's cloak. "None of these know, Mighty One. Only those foxes, Thwip an'

Binta, knew, but they're gone. Allow me to try. I'll soon find out."

She confronted the young ones in a calm manner. "Tell me, do ye have any sisters, brothers or friends missin'? Was anybeast lost when the collapse happened?"

Young Jiddle Witherspyk held up a paw. "My sister Jinty's gone, an' Tassy, an' a liddle hare, too. Those vermin put 'em in sacks an' took 'em away. They're bad, wicked villuns!"

Dirva nodded, as if in agreement. She smiled at the small hog. "I'll trade ye, if'n I get 'em back. Will ye tell me who's missin' then, eh?"

Flandor spoke out boldly. "None of us are sayin' a word 'til we sees 'em safe back!"

The Sable Quean signalled a guard. "Bring them here!"

Three Ravagers carried the sacks in. They emptied the little trio out roughly.

Tura carried Urfa to her brother, reuniting the leverets.

Tassy, the Redwall Dibbun, ran to Midda, calling, "Where's Guffy, my likkle molefriend?"

Jinty scurried to Jiddle; they hugged each other tightly.

Midda put a paw about the little squirrelmaid. "There's been no sign of Guffy, or Gurchen an' Flib, not since the collapse."

Tears popped out onto Tassy's cheeks. She blurted out without thinking, "Did the tunnel fall in on them?"

Like a whirlwind, Vilaya was amongst them. She seized Midda, shrieking as she shook the shrewmaid savagely. "Tunnel, what tunnel? Tell me or I'll rip ye apart!"

Flandor charged to Midda's aid. Leaping on the sable's back, he battered at her with clenched paws, roaring, "Git yore paws off'n her, ye slimy bully. Let her go!"

Vilaya almost went down under the young otter's attack. She was saved by her guards. They hauled Flandor off her forcibly. As they dragged him away, he lashed out with his rudder, catching the Sable Quean a smashing blow in her left eye.

They crowded in on the brave young creature then, subduing him by main force. Vilaya turned on him. Leaping forward, she struck him in the throat. Flandor clapped a paw to his neck and fell. The sable stood over him, covering her injured eye.

She returned the tiny poisoned dagger to its crystal sheath, hissing viciously, "You dare to strike a Quean? Fool, you will never again raise a paw to anybeast!"

Midda was instantly at Flandor's side, holding up his head. The courageous otter smiled dreamily up at her, his eyes starting to droop.

"I'm thirsty, mate . . . thirsty. . . ."

He shuddered, then slumped to one side and lay still. The shrewmaid shook her friend's limp form. "I'll get water for ye, Flandor. Flandor?"

Tura realised what had happened. The squirrelmaid ran at Vilaya, shouting, "You've murdered him, you rotten scum!"

The Sable Quean retreated several paces, allowing the guards to intercept Tura, who struggled in their grip.

"You dirty, stinkin' vermin, Flandor was worth ten of you!"

Holding the bunched hem of her cloak over her injured eye, Vilaya stood quivering with rage and pain. She screamed, "Get them out of my sight, all of them! Throw them in a cave where they can't dig their way out. Lock them in there and double the guard!"

The captives were herded off at spearpoint. Midda, Tura and some of the older creatures scrambled to pick up the babes. Frightened and bewildered, the little ones began weeping piteously. Dirva attempted to place a poultice over her mistress's eye; it was swollen and discoloured.

"Hold still, Majesty. This will help with the pain."

Vilaya flung the poultice from her, snarling, "Keep that foul rubbish away from me. Go and stop those brats wailing or I'll take a blade and do it myself!"

*

Like most Guosim shrews, Log a Log Jango was no scholar, nor was he gifted with patience. He curled his lip sourly at the Recorder.

"Well, come on—spit it out, matey. Are ye goin' to sit there starin' at yon book like a stuffed frog? When d'ye think ye'll get round to tellin' us where our young uns are bein' held, eh?"

Granvy did not like being hurried or ordered about by gruff beasts. He looked slowly up from the thick, open volume, blinking over the rim of his spectacles. "All in good time, sir. Being rude won't speed me up."

Abbess Marjoram judged by the look in Jango's eye that Granvy had said the wrong thing, so she took charge of the situation without delay. "Friend Granvy, I think that the good time you speak of should be right now. Kindly tell us what you know."

The Recorder was about to speak when the door to the Abbess's room opened. The late Clerun Kordyne's mate, Clarinna, staggered in. The harewife was wearing a flowing nightgown. Her head was in bandages, her paw in a sling and she looked totally distracted.

Making a beeline for Buckler, she seized his tunic, tugging on it as she implored him tearfully, "Where are my poor babes, Calla and Urfa? What have those vermin done, where have they taken them? Oh, Buck, bring them back to me, I know you can! Say you will—oh, my little ones. Help me, please!"

Buckler had never been in such a situation; he was really embarrassed. Clarinna was clinging so hard to him, he could not loosen her grip without hurting her. He felt all eyes in the room on him as he managed to stammer, "Er, yes of course I will, Clarinna, but shouldn't you be resting in the sickbay, after what you've been through?"

Sister Fumbril came hurrying in. The big otter herbalist was carrying a small beaker of medicine. Abbess Marjoram exchanged glances with her as Fumbril held up the beaker.

"I only popped into the next room for a moment to make this up. When I got back, there she was . . . gone! Pore creature, she ain't well at all. Keeps goin' on about her liddle uns, an' what beast could blame her? I'd be just the same in her position."

The good Sister's voice dropped to a whisper. "She'll fall into a deep sleep if'n I can get this down her."

Surprisingly, Diggs took charge of the medicine. "Beggin' y'pardon, allow me, marm!"

Almost casually, he pried Clarinna loose from Buckler, chatting amiably to her. "Retrieve your little uns—I should say so, marm. Why, old Buck an' I were about to dash off posthaste an' do that very thing. Indeed, we'll jolly well have the little blighters back here before y'can say Salamandastron, ain't that right, Buck, wot?"

Clarinna instantly attached herself to Diggs's sleeve. "Oh, thank you, Subaltern Digglethwaite, and you, too, Buckler. Are you going to get them right now?"

Diggs nodded affably. "This very instant, dear lady—but 'fraid we can't leave until you've taken this stuff. Mmmm, smells rather nice, wot, may I taste it?"

Sister Fumbril caught on promptly to the tubby hare's ruse. "Mister Diggs, sir, you give that beaker to Miz Clarinna right away. T'aint for you. She'll need all her strength to care for those babbies once they're back at Redwall."

Clarinna released Diggs. "Yes, I will, won't I? Calla and Urfa can be very lively, y'know. I'd best be ready." Taking the beaker, she drained it to the last drop.

Sister Fumbril put a supporting paw around the harewife, nodding to Skipper, who did likewise as Fumbril coaxed her along. "A nice, soft bed an' a quiet room are the best things for ye, dearie. You come with us now."

Log a Log Jango turned to the Recorder after Clarinna

had left. "Don't let me stop ye, old un. Carry on with what ye was about to tell us."

Granvy tapped the open page of the volume he had been studying. "Thank the seasons for ancient records. Funny how places and events get forgotten after a while—"

Abbess Marjoram cut him off sharply. "Granvy, will you stop dithering and get on with it? What's the matter—don't you want to tell us what you found?"

The old Recorder sighed. "Of course I do, but I blame myself for not studying our Abbey's history. I've always been too busy doing other things."

Marjoram nodded. "I, too, friend—so part of the blame rests with me. Tell us now and all's forgiven."

Granvy looked directly at Jango. "Why are your tribe called the Guosim?"

The Log a Log shrugged. "We've always been known as Guosim. 'Tis a word made from the first letters of wot we're about: Guerilla Union of Shrews in Mossflower. But why d'ye ask? Everybeast knows that."

"Aye, but now I know what *Corim* means—that's made up of first letters, too: Council of Resistance in Mossflower. Bear with me whilst I explain. In the long-distant past, there was no Abbey of Redwall, just a castle named Kotir. It was ruled by a wildcat, Queen Tsarmina. She commanded a vermin horde, which enslaved the whole country. Well, to cut a long story short, the woodlanders, led by Martin the Warrior, waged war against Kotir and its evil beasts."

Diggs nodded stoutly. "Well, good for them, say I. Must've been jolly excitin'. Did they win?"

Buckler nudged his friend. "Stow the gab and listen."

Granvy paused, then picked up the thread of his narrative. "Martin and his friends had to have somewhere to live, a base to operate from. Fortunately, there was an ancestral badger home, place called Brockhall. A brave badger lived there, Bella of Brockhall. She offered them her home, even fought alongside them. As I've said, it's a very long story. But they were victorious in the end, the

Corim—that's what they called themselves. Without those gallant creatures, there would have never been a Redwall Abbey. There you have it."

Oakheart Witherspyk stroked his headspikes reflectively. "Hmm, so 'tis possible that Althier an' Brockhall are one and the same place. D'ye have any ideas as to where we might find it, sirrah?"

The Recorder shut the big volume ruefully. "Alas, no. It's so long ago, shrouded in the mists of countless seasons, I'm afraid."

Buckler took over. "Well, let's see what we've got so far. This Sable Quean creature is obviously using it as a hideout. But she doesn't keep her main force, the Ravagers, there. Now, the young uns are probably imprisoned at Althier, and as we've established, it ain't more than a day's march from here. Remember what she said, she's returning here soon. At a rough guess, that's a day for her to get back there, a day's rest, then back here the day after, right?"

Jango nodded. "Aye, an' d'ye recall wot that vermin prisoner said? Most of the Ravager force don't know where Althier is—they're kept away from there by Zwilt the Shade. If'n tenscore vermin were camped at Althier, it'd be pretty easy to track 'em, eh, Sniffy?"

The Guosim Tracker agreed. "That's right, Chief!"

Diggs, who had been taking it all in, gave his opinion. "Indeed, old lad. The dreadful old Sable Quean must have just a bodyguard an' some jailers at her hideaway. That leaves the rest o' the blighters camped out in the blinkin' woodlands somewhere. Any ideas, chaps?"

Skipper had returned; he was standing in the doorway. "Here's an idea for ye. Wherever the Ravagers' camp is, it can't be far from the Quean's hidin' place. Find 'em an' the young uns will be locked up not far away."

Foremole Darbee rapped his digging claws on the volume. "Hurrhurr, roight clever thinkun', zurr. Ee mole cuddent not've dun better, boi 'okey!"

Diggs brightened up considerably. "Then alls we've got t'do is find the bloomin' place, wot?"

Buckler shook his head. "Wrong. You've forgotten two important things, mate. First, those vermin aren't stupid, especially the two sables. They threatened to harm the young uns if we were spotted tryin' to follow 'em. Second thing is Redwall itself. We'd be fools to leave it undefended with tenscore armed Ravagers in the neighbourhood. I think we're in a bit of a cleft stick."

Oakheart placed a big paw on the young hare's shoulder. "You're right, sirrah, on both counts. But what's t'be done about our little uns? We can't just leave them at the mercy of those scurvy vermin."

It was a pretty subdued group of friends who were gathered in the Abbess's room, pondering the results of the meeting. Unable to stop himself, Diggs emitted a cavernous yawn. He recovered his composure. "Oops, pardon me, chaps!"

Marjoram looked around the group. "It's late. Without proper sleep, we won't be good for anything. Consider this—the young ones aren't in any immediate danger. The Sable Quean knows they're far too valuable to her alive. She won't be returning here until the day after tomorrow, so this gives us a bit of time to think things out. Agreed?"

Buckler bowed to the Abbess. "Agreed, marm, what you say makes sense. We'd do well to sleep on it for the moment. A rest might refresh our minds."

They broke up then. The Abbess left, followed by Oakheart. Buckler intercepted the others before they could leave. Jango winked at him.

"Yore goin' after 'em, aren't ye?"

The young hare nodded grimly. "Aye, I'm leaving right now. Diggs, will you see to the defence of the Abbey? I'm puttin' you an' Oakie in charge."

The tubby hare made an elegant leg. "At y'service, sah, leave it t'me. I'll shake this lot into some sort o' Salamandastron shape, by the left I will!"

Jango pulled a face. "I ain't havin' that chunnerin' fat bucket givin' me orders. I'm comin' with you, Buck."

Buckler allowed himself a smile. "I was hopin' you'd say that, mate. We'll need Sniffy, your Tracker, along with us. Are you comin', Skip?"

The brawny otter clasped Buckler's paw. "You try an' stop me, culley. I'll just get me javelin."

Before the Abbey bells had tolled the midnight hour, they slipped away by the east wallgate—Buckler, Jango, Sniffy, Skipper and Big Bartij, the Gardener and Infirmary assistant. They were dressed in muted green cloaks made from old Redwall habits, and armed.

Diggs bolted the east wickergate behind them, whispering, "Good luck, you chaps, an' if ye come across any vermin, give 'em blood'n'vinegar, wot!"

15

Flib lay alongside Guffy and Gurchen in the dry woodland gully where the Warrior mole Axtel Sturnclaw made his temporary camp. Axtel had gently tucked his old cloak about Guffy and Gurchen, his dark eyes moist as he stroked their heads. The two little moles were sleeping deeply, but despite all she had been through, the Guosim shrewmaid could not rest; Flib was pretending to be asleep. Then she opened one eye and saw the big mole watching her. He grunted quietly.

"Shudden't you'm be asleepen, miz? Ee needs yore rest."

Flib sat up. "I've tried, but it ain't much good. I suppose I'm not in a sleepin' mood."

Axtel covered the dead embers of their fire with soil. "Hurr, then you'm can be keepen watch round yurr."

Flib agreed readily. "Righto, I don't mind keepin' guard if'n ye want a spot o' shuteye."

Axtel thrust the war hammer into his belt. "Shutten eyes b'aint furr oi—you'm watch o'er ee likkle uns whoilst oi bee's gone."

Flib was filled with curiosity. "Where are ye goin'?"

Standing upright, the Warrior mole stretched his huge paws. "Back daown yon tunnel, to 'elp yore friends, miz."

The shrewmaid leapt up. "I'll come along with ye—"

She sat down hard as Axtel nudged her with his paw. He stood over her, wagging a thick digging claw under her nose. "Ho, no you'm b'aint, moi deary. Oi sayed stay yurr an' watch ee likklebeasts, an' oi means et, boi 'okey!"

The look in his eyes, and the set of his powerful body, told Flib that it would be unwise to argue the point.

She tried to appear nonchalant. "Do as ye please. 'Tain't none o' my business. When'll ye be back?"

Axtel crouched down in front of her. He smiled and ruffled her ears. "Oi'm gurtly sorry you'm can't cumm, Miz Flib, but this bee's wurk oi does best alone. Naow, thurr's vikkles an' drinks in moi pack, if'n ee gets 'ungered. Oi gives ee moi wurd, oi'll cumm back yurr soon as oi can."

Flib nodded. "Fair enough, mate, but have ye got a weapon t'leave with me, just in case . . . ?"

Axtel went and rummaged in his pack. He chuckled. "Yurr—oi tukken this frum a vermint, he'm won't be a-needin' et no more."

He passed her a long dagger, a typical vermin weapon. It was a stiletto, both edges sharp, with a keen point.

She wielded it, feeling the balance. "Huh, heavy enough t'do a bit o' damage with, eh?"

The mole produced a walking staff and a length of cord. "Ee'd do well t'make a spear of et, miz."

The Guosim maid applied herself to the job. When she looked up, Axtel Sturnclaw had gone.

Flib lashed the cord tightly, securing the dagger by its handle to the pole. Hiding it under some dead leaves within easy reach, she lay down, murmuring to herself, "Hah, any vermin out there plannin' on payin' us a visit, just come on, that's all I've got t'say. Just come on!"

Back down inside Althier, the captives found themselves in a different cavern. It was smaller and had a narrow entrance but no door to keep them locked in. However, there were four guards posted there, tough-looking rats, two armed with crude swords, the other two with spears. After a while, as the prisoners were fed and watered, Midda sat with Tura, feeding the babies as they discussed their position.

Midda spooned warm cornmeal to Borti, commenting, "At least the food's better than it was. There's a bit more of it, too, and the water looks fresher."

Tura was trying to feed the two harebabes at once. They fought greedily for each mouthful. The young squirrelmaid nodded toward the guards. "They seem better, too, not cruel like those two foxes."

Jinty, the Witherspyk hogmaid, sitting nearby, huffed, "Better, are they? Well, just you try gettin' by them an' escapin' from here. Huh, you'll see how much better they are!"

Midda cleaned little Borti's face up with a damp rag. "Don't talk about escape anymore, Jinty. Not with Flib and Flandor both dead."

Jinty's twin brother, Jiddle, picked up a pebble and hurled it angrily at the wall. "Well, what are we supposed to do? Just sit down here 'til we die like a pack of silly frogs?"

The pebble he had thrown bounced off the rock wall. It ricocheted, narrowly missing one of the guards, who strode across to Jiddle and jabbed him none too gently with a spearbutt.

"Did yew chuck that stone just now, eh?"

Midda put Borti down. She stood up, facing the rat aggressively. "He never chucked any stone—I did!"

The rat, whose name was Gilfis, was slightly taken aback. "Er, well, don't throw any more stones, see!"

Midda imitated her sister Flib, acting tough. "An' wot'll yew do if'n I don't, eh?"

One of the other rat guards had heard the exchange. He swaggered over, paw on sword hilt. "I'll tell ye wot we'll do, cheekyface. We'll give yer a good hidin', that's wot we'll do!"

Tura was tugging Midda's sleeve to make her be quiet. However, the shrewmaid was not to be silenced. She thrust her chin out belligerently. "Why don't ye call yore two mates, eh? Between the four of ye, it shouldn't be hard. I'll bet yore good at beatin' up helpless prisoners. Big brave vermin!"

The one called Gilfis pulled his friend away. "Leave it, Fidra. If'n we lay a paw on 'er an' the Quean gets t'find out, we'll both be in the soup!"

They retired to the cave entrance, with Midda calling after them insultingly, "Go on, quick, afore yore scummy vermin Quean finds out. Lissen, rats, I'm a Guosim shrew from a real warrior clan. One Guosim's worth ten of yew scringe-tailed cowards!"

Tura managed to gag Midda's mouth with her paw. "What are you acting like this for, friend? Be quiet!"

Midda pulled her friend's paw away. She chuckled. "I'm enjoying it—my sister Flib was like that. She was a real tough one. I could be just like her, you know."

One of the captives, a mouse of about four seasons, upbraided Midda. "Aye, an' get yourself killed like your sister. Wot'll happen to your baby brother then?"

Midda subsided and clasped Tura's paw. "I'm sorry. I really spoke out of turn there. I won't do it again, promise. It only puts us all in danger, making enemies of the guards."

Tura smiled at her friend. "I'm glad you realise that." Suddenly the squirrelmaid began to chuckle. She had to cover her mouth to hide the merriment as she spoke. "Did you see that vermin's face, though? He didn't know what to do when you challenged him!"

Jiddle was good at impressions; he aped the guard. "Er, well, don't throw stones anymore, see!"

His impersonation was so good that all the captives began laughing. One of the guards called from the entrance, "Belt up in there an' stop that silly laughin'!"

Jiddle shouted back, repeating the words exactly like the rat guard. Helpless laughter broke out amongst the young captives; even the babies joined in. The one called Fidra stormed in, waving his sword.

"Shuttup, all of ye! Silence, or there'll be no more vittles for ye, not a single bite, d'ye hear?"

Midda was rocking back and forth with baby Borti in her paws. They were both giggling hysterically.

Then Jinty yelled back at the guard, "Go on then—starve us t'death, wot do we care? But I wouldn't like to be you if'n yore Quean finds out. She'll have ye roasted alive, then slain!"

This time there was no reply from the vermin. Tura commented bleakly, "I think they got your warning. But wot's the use of it all? There's no more chance of escape. They can do exactly wot they like with us down here. We might never get out of this place."

Little Tassy sobbed brokenly. "Never see the sun again, or the woodlands, or Redwall Abbey. I couldn't bear it—I'd sooner just die!"

Midda glared at the squirrelmaid. "Thanks for that, Tura. You've really cheered pore Tassy up. Listen, if'n ye can't say anythin' good, then keep yore mouth closed, that's my advice!"

Tura felt immediately sorry; she hugged the tiny Redwall squirrel to her. "Hush now, Tassy, don't cry. Why, I'll bet there's all sorts of search parties from your Abbey scouring Mossflower to find us at this very moment. Right, Midda?"

The Guosim maid nodded confidently. "No question about it, mate. Aye, an' wot about my dad, Jango Bigboat? He's a Log a Log Chieftain. Hah, he'll have the woodlands teemin' with Guosim warriors just searchin' for us. They'll find us sooner or later, I'm certain. Come on, dry yore eyes, little un."

Tassy managed a damp smile, snuffling. "I 'ope it's sooner an' not later!"

*

For some of them, it really would be sooner. Axtel Sturnclaw was at that moment burrowing his way back into Althier. For an expert digger of his strength, it did not pose any problems. He soon found the place where his tunnel had collapsed under him. Hefty digging claws ripped into the earth, making soil, roots and clay fly out behind him.

Stopping for a moment, he sniffed his surroundings, probed around, then muttered to himself, "Hurr, this'n bee's whurr they'm was a-maken thurr excape."

Straight down he dug, right into Flib's partially excavated tunnel. The rest was pretty much easy going. Axtel widened the tunnel, leaving plenty of room for his departure. Encountering a large boulder blocking his path, he dug around it. Finding a thick section of oak root, he jammed it alongside the boulder to hold it still. Tying a length of cord to the root, he tossed it behind himself, where it could be recovered easily. That done, the Warrior mole pressed on.

Reaching the now-abandoned dungeon, he exercised extreme care. Moving slowly, Axtel inched out over the pile of rubble to the broken door, which lay on top of the heap. The passage running from left to right was illuminated with lanterns and torches. Pulling a torch from its holder, he snuffed it out against the floor. Huddling down, the big mole lay against the wall, hidden in the patch of darkness provided by the missing torch. To any vermin who happened by he would look like a heap of debris, without shape or form.

That was exactly what the weasel Ravager guard who was coming down the passage thought—nothing but a pile of rubble. As he passed it, Axtel sprang up, gagging the weasel's mouth with one big paw whilst pinning him to the passage wall with the other.

The Warrior mole did not waste time. He growled straight into the guard's petrified face, "Whurr you'm keepin' ee young uns?"

The weasel managed a strangled grunt. Axtel bore forward, shutting his mouth even tighter. "Just point ee way!"

The Ravager pointed to the right. Axtel nodded. "Thankee!"

He slew the vermin guard with a single blow to the neck.

Hurrying silently along the passage, he halted at the sound of voices in low conversation. The four guards at the narrow cave entrance were taken by surprise. Axtel swung his war hammer, braining the one called Fidra. Bulling the other three in front of him, he thrust them into the cavern, roaring, "Cumm ee with oi, quick loik!"

As he shouted, Axtel lashed out, felling another guard and knocking the rat Gilfis flat. With his outstretched paws, he grabbed little Borti and Tassy both.

Gilfis struck with his spear, almost pinning the mole's footpaw to the ground.

The remaining guard slipped past the wounded rescuer. Dashing out into the passage, he screeched, his voice echoing off the walls, "Heeeelp! Attack! The prisoners are escapin'!"

Still holding the two Dibbuns, Axtel limped out after him with the spear stuck clean through his footpaw. He stumbled and the spearhaft struck the wall, breaking off but leaving him still transfixed by the point. Gritting his teeth, he hung on to Tassy and Borti, shuffling down the passage, calling to the captives, "Cumm ee naow, follow oi!"

Midda and Tura quickly urged the others out.

"Hurry up, please—oh, do be quick!"

The very young ones were frightened. Some of them sat where they were, setting up a wailing.

Vermin were charging in from all sides. Vilaya and Dirva could be heard screeching, "Stop them! Guards, block all exits off right now!"

Tura had the two baby hares with her, practically dragging them along, with Midda pushing the rest in her wake. They never even made it out into the passage, as the narrow entrance was blocked by guards wielding weapons.

"Get back or we'll slay ye! Back! Back!"

Tura retreated, yelling at Midda, "Back in before they kill us all!"

Axtel made it to the deserted dungeon, where he threw the two little ones in onto the rubble. Turning, he wielded the fearsome war hammer, felling the first three Ravagers to reach him. Limping back, he charged them with a loud war cry.

"Yooohurrrr! Cumm an' meet Sturnclaw! Yoooohurrrr!"

Nobeast wanted to be the next to die. They ran back from the berserk Warrior mole. Taking advantage of this, he scrambled back. Clambering over the fallen door, he gave a loud roar and lifted it up into its former position.

With several mighty shoves, Axtel managed to ram the door at an angle into its former frame. It made grating sounds as the splintered woodwork lodged itself into the rock. Holding it there with the strength of his broad back, he nodded at the two Dibbuns. "H'up ye go into yon tunnel. Oi'll foller arter ee!"

Borti was not much use at climbing, being only a toddler, but Tassy helped him up into the hole.

"Cummon, likkle Borti, take my paws—good baby, good!"

A spearpoint came right through the shattered door timbers, narrowly missing Axtel's neck. He could feel the door shuddering as the Ravagers threw themselves at it. Vilaya was yelling at them.

"Push, you spineless idiots! Knock it down!"

Axtel abandoned the door then. Trundling awkwardly over the pile of debris, he scrambled into the tunnel entrance. Pushing the two little ones in front of him, he went upward.

The door fell. With the Sable Quean behind them, the

Ravagers held up lanterns and torches. Dirva pointed to the tunnel in the far wall.

"They've gone in there—after them! They can't get far!"

The vermin had to enter single file, with Vilaya at the tunnel entrance, kicking and beating them with the flat of a sword.

"Move yourselves, they mustn't escape. Move!"

Axtel shepherded Borti and Tassy around the boulder. He could hear the grunts of vermin behind him. Seizing the rope, he gave it a sharp tug, pulling the piece of oak root loose. The big rock made a dull thud as it fell into the shaft behind the escapers, completely blocking it and crushing one of the Ravagers in the process. The Warrior mole gritted his teeth, fighting against the pain of the spearhead embedded in his footpaw.

He inched his way upward, pushing the two Dibbuns in front of him, encouraging them to move forward. "You'm keep a-goin', moi gudd likklebeasts. Oi'm roight ahind ee!"

Tassy kept tight hold of Borti, who was whimpering with fright, rubbing soil from his eyes. "Waaah, want my mamma!"

The young Redwall squirrelmaid pulled him along with her. "C'mon, it's not far now. Soon see y'mamma."

Axtel gave them both a final shove, heaving them out into the nightdark woodland. He crawled out after them, giving an anguished grunt as the spearhead struck a stone, gouging at his wounded footpaw. The Warrior mole lost consciousness then, falling senseless on the grass.

Tassy cleaned the soil from Borti's face. "There now, likkle un, that much a-better, eh!" She turned to Axtel. "Thankee for gettin' us out, sir."

He lay inert. Tassy shook him, but he did not move.

"Wakey up, sir, wakey up, please. . . ."

The squirrelmaid patted Axtel's forepaws, tweaked his snout and forced one of his eyes open. It fell back shut.

She began shouting in his ear, "Don't be asleep. Wakey up now, please, please!"

Little Borti had recovered from his ordeal. He giggled, imitating Tassy as he chafed the unconscious mole's paw, calling out, "Wakey h'up, wakey h'up, zurr!"

The mole Warrior was still not moving, even though Borti clambered up onto him. Tassy pulled the little shrew off Axtel's still form. She began to cry then, rocking the shrewbabe back and forth as she clutched him to her.

"Oh, Borti, wot we goin' to do?"

16

Flib was obeying Axtel's orders, watching over Guffy and Gurchen, guarding the little camp whilst the young ones slept. However, just sitting and doing nothing could become tiresome and at times a little disconcerting.

Constantly peering into the surrounding woodland, the Guosim maid started to imagine all manner of things. The trees seemed to close in on her, conjuring up fearsome visions. These turned out to be nothing but a light breeze, stirring the leafy foliage amidst moonshadows. Flib mentally reprimanded herself for being so foolish, remembering that Guosim shrews were made of sterner stuff.

To buoy up her spirits, she began to sing. It was a jolly old Guosim nonsense ditty, which always caused much merriment when sung at a streamfeast or a watermeadow gathering. Flib sang, but not too loud, for fear of waking up the mole Dibbuns.

"A Guosim maid sat by the fire,
a-reading a letter one day,
with a flea in her ear, and a tear in her eye,
at what the sad note had to say, ay aaaaay!
Yore granny is deeply drownded,

inna river so wild an' rough, rough rough rough!
She should 'ave sailed off in a logboat,
but instead she left home in a huff, huff huff huff.
She might have gone off in a temper,
but she'd lost that long ago, long long agooooo!
If she'd left in a rush or an 'urry,
we'd have all been sure to know.
So I leave you with this lesson,
if you must leave home, my dear,
'twill break my heart if you take the cart,
an' the wheels will fall off, I fear."

There was another verse, and possibly a chorus, but Flib had forgotten it. She sat there trying to recall the silly little ditty, remembering some of the happy times she had spent with her tribe—the high-summer days, with good food and peaceful surroundings. It all seemed so long ago now, somehow. Her head slowly began to droop, then her eyelids closed. Sleep was finally getting the better of her.

It was a rude awakening when her ear was grabbed roughly and a voice snarled, "Well, lookit wot we got here, our liddle shrewmate!"

A whip cracked in front of Flib's face. She looked up and found herself staring into the cruel eyes of Thwip, her former fox jailer.

His mate, Binta, was nearby. She prodded at the two sleeping mole Dibbuns, snarling nastily, "Aye, an' here's 'er two liddle pals. Chubby young things, ain't they?"

Instead of fear, the Guosim maid was instantly filled with a red rage against herself, for napping whilst on guard, and deep hatred for her former tormentors.

Throwing herself forward, she twisted her ear from the fox's grasp, falling flat in the carpet of dead leaves. Swift as lightning, Flib seized the makeshift spear. Thwip was halfway through swinging the lash at her when Flib lunged with the spear. The whip fell unheeded on the ground.

Thwip looked puzzled as he stared down at the spear protruding from his midriff. He turned his gaze to Binta. There was a note of complaint in his last words.

"She's killed me!"

He fell backward, his paws grasping the spear pole, as if he was holding it there. Binta gave an angry sobbing wail. She ran at Flib, swinging her long willow cane. The shrewmaid tried to pull the spear from Thwip, but it was locked in the fox's death grip.

A stinging rain of strokes hit her—the vixen swung her cane madly, shouting aloud, "You've slain my Thwip! I'll flog ye to death for that!"

The willow slashed down mercilessly at Flib. She huddled on the grass in a futile attempt to protect herself. Then, quite by accident, her paw fell upon the dead fox's whip.

Roaring with pain, Flib leapt up, wielding the lash. It cracked and snaked viciously as the tables turned and the beater became the beaten. The shrewmaid became an avenging fury, belabouring her enemy ruthlessly.

Dropping the cane, Binta ran off into the night, wailing.

The din had wakened the two mole Dibbuns. Gurchen trundled across to Flib, exclaiming, "Boi 'okey, marm, ee surrpintly gived ee foxers ole billyoh! Yurr, bee's you'm 'urted?"

Flib shook her head. "Not so much as 'urted—more 'urting than anythin'. I never used a blinkin' whip afore. I hit meself a few times by mistake. It stings more'n that cane. No serious damage though, just welts an' bruises."

Guffy had found Thwip's body. He tried unsuccessfully to pull the spear loose. The little mole shook his head admiringly. "Hurr, miz, you'm gurtly slayed this yurr vermint. Ee'm b'aint a-cummen back furr more!"

The pain from her beating, plus the realisation that she had killed another creature, sent Flib into shock. She sat down abruptly, her whole body shivering as she rocked back and forth, whimpering and moaning.

Guffy stared solemnly at her. "Burr, wot bee's ailin' ee, Miz F'ib?"

Gurchen went rummaging through Axtel's pack. "Oi thinks she'm bee'd a-sickened with summat. Yurr!" Opening a small flask, the molemaid sniffed it. "Smells loike summ blacker-bee woine, gurtly strong!"

Wrapping Flib in the cloak they had used as a blanket, the sensible little molemaid forced the flask between her patient's lips, administering the blackberry wine. "Yurr, Guff, see if'n ee can make sum foire t'keep this un warm."

This was an absolute joy to Guffy, who as a Dibbun, had been prohibited by Redwall elders from ever playing with fire. He found flint and an old knifeblade in the pack. Chuckling to himself, he set about his task, piling up dried leaves and grass.

"Hurrhurr, oi'll make Miz F'ib a gudd ole blaze!"

True to his word, Guffy soon had a big fire burning.

Gurchen stopped him from piling on more fuel. "Yurr, you'm rarscal. Oi never asked ee to set all ee wuddlands ablaze. Oi only wants a likkle foire, enuff to keep Flib warmed."

When they had a respectably sized campfire, all three sat by it, the moles either side of Flib. The Guosim maid still seemed very distant, rocking slightly as she stared fixedly into the flames. Gurchen tried to elicit some response by chatting to her.

"You'm gudd'n warm noaw, marm. Hurr, oi 'spec ee gurt Wurrier mole bee's a-comen back soonly."

Guffy began thrusting a twig into the fire. He liked playing with the flames. Gurchen warned him, "Play with foire an' ee'll burn yoreself!"

Almost as she said it, the burning twig broke, dropping a glowing red fragment onto the little mole's paw. He yelped, hopping about and beating at himself.

"Ah, sure, the young uns never listen, do they? I was the same at his age, thought I knew it all, so I did!"

None of the trio had noticed the water vole. She had appeared from nowhere and was seated by the fire, warming her paws. Grabbing Guffy, she dabbed his paw with some damp moss, nattering away conversationally. "There now, ye liddle scallywag. That'll teach ye t'play with fire. Wot's wrong wid yer friend the shrew, there? Is she in some kind of an ould trance?"

Gurchen answered the question by asking one of her own. "Burr, marm, who moight you'm be, an' whurr did ee cummed frum?"

The water vole was an amiable-looking beast with thick, glossy fur, a chubby face and a blunt snout. She wore an old tattered shawl pulled about her ears like a hood. Leaning forward on a knobbly hawthorn stick, she introduced herself.

"Ah, sure, I'm nobeast of any importance at all, at all. Mumzillia O'Chubbacutch is me given title, though I wouldn't consider meself offended if'n ye called me Mumzy. Now, me darlin', wot do they call you?"

Gurchen rose, performing a small curtsy. "Oi bee's Gurchen. Ee'm likkle rarscal bee's Guffy, an' hurr's Flib. We'm waiten furr our gudd friend to cumm back yurr. He'm ee mole Wurrier, marm."

Mumzy waved her stick at the carcass of Thwip. "An' which one of you bold creatures slayed that un?"

Guffy pointed a grimy paw at Flib. "Et wurr Miz F'ib, marm. She'm vurry brave."

Mumzy rose with a groan. "Sure, me ould back isn't wot it used t'be. Gettin' old is a tribulation, as me fat uncle Shaym used t'say."

She began extinguishing the fire by kicking soil on it. "C'mon now, up off yore tails, me darlin's—let's go!"

Gurchen protested. "But us'ns must wait fur ee h'Axtel!"

Mumzy got Flib standing upright. The shrewmaid did not resist. The water vole beckoned Guffy. "Lend a paw here, me liddle sir. Ye can't wait here, not with vermin roamin' the woods. Ye'd end up as dead meat if'n they claps eyes on the likes of ye. I'd be correct in sayin' that yore on the run from them?"

Gurchen just nodded, willing to fall in line with their new friend's advice.

Mumzy prodded Axtel's pack with her stick. "Right, then, bring that along with ye. Me'n' the liddle feller'll help Flib. 'Tis best ye stay out o' sight at my place. 'Tisn't far, only a hop'n'skip over yonder."

They followed her on a zigzag route under bushes, through a fern bed and across some rocks to a streambank. There was a rocky outcrop with an entrance beneath it—this was hidden behind a curtain of knotweed, sundew and watercress. Pushing it to one side, the water vole led them in.

"This is Mumzy's Mansions, such as it is. Nothin' fancy, but 'tis good'n'safe, t'be sure. Sit ye down now, an' take a beaker of me own special brew whilst I tell ye of wot I've seen."

The brew was delicious, a hot cordial of coltsfoot, dandelion and pennycress. They sat in the little cave, which was lighted by a small fire. It was very cosy, with moss-and-dried-grass-padded ledges, which could serve as seats or beds.

Mumzy bustled about, tidying up as she informed them, "Those ravagin' villains are about in Mossflower tonight. Earlier on, I spotted five o' the dreadful scum, four weasels led by the big boyo, the one they calls Zwilt, tall sable beast, wears a long cloak and carries a big sword. As if that wasn't enough, they'd no sooner got out o' sight, when I see tracks, two rats an' two foxes. The tracks split—rats went one way, foxes t'other. So I follows the foxes' tracks. That's when I found you three. There's no sense in sittin' on yore tails out in the woodlands with that lot roamin' abroad. You bide 'ere with ould Mumzy 'til the coast clears, eh?"

Gurchen looked worried. "But wot abowt Axtel, marm?"

The water vole set about pulling hot food from a clay oven at the back of her fire. "If'n Axtel's a warrior, as ye say he is, well, he should be well able o' takin' care of hisself. I'll find him for ye when things quietens down out there. Here, now, have ye ever tasted whortleberry an' chestnut flan? 'Tis a fine ould recipe I got from me good uncle Shaym, an' he was after bein' a top champeen cook, so he was!"

The flan was exceedingly tasty but rather hot.

Flib did not seem to want either food or drink.

Mumzy sat in front of her, staring into the shrewmaid's blank gaze. "Hmm, an' ye say she's a shrew, one o' those Guosim, I'll wager. I spent a few o' me salad seasons with 'em. Sure, they were a grand lot, those beasts. Maybe I can snap Flib out of her mood. Let's try an ould Guosim lullaby. Reach me that there vole o'lin, young Guff."

Guffy passed Mumzy the instrument. It was a tiny three-stringed fiddle, which she played by bowing it with a dried water-violet stalk. The water vole had such a pleasant, soothing voice that Guffy dropped off to sleep on a moss-covered ledge.

Gurchen politely stayed awake, though Flib's eyelids began drooping as Mumzy sang the Guosim lullaby.

"When the warm sun sinks gently from out of the sky,
hear the tired old breeze sigh a yawn,
and the bees cease a-humming, now dark night is
coming,
to blanket the earth until dawn.

"Then the logboat of dreams drifts away o'er the
streams,
as we sail on it, baby and me,
past meadow and vale, without paddle or sail,
we both slumber on down to the sea.

"Where birds circle silently, winging on high,
deep waters run silent and calm,
'neath the soft gentle bloom of a honeydew moon,
with no wind or wave to cause harm.

"Then the logboat of dreams will grant wishes it
seems,
all a little one's heart could require
'til rainbow-hued dawn turns to fresh summer morn,
and a world full of hope and desire."

No sooner had the last strains of the quaint vole o'lin faded than Flib blinked, as though waking from a dream. "My ma used t'sing that un. I never bothered learnin' it, but me sister Midda did. She sings it t'Borti—he's our liddle brother."

Mumzy busied herself, chatting away to Flib with no mention of the shrewmaid's former state. "Ah, 'tis a grand ould song, sure enough. C'mon now, darlin'. Try a drop o' me hot cordial an' a piece o' me good flan."

Flib sat up straight. "Thankee, marm, that'd be nice. By the way, my name's Flib. Wot's yores?"

The water vole served Flib. "Ah, sure, ye can just call me Mumzy. There now, Flib, ye'll enjoy that!"

As Flib concentrated her attention on the food, Gurchen whispered to Mumzy, "Yurr, marm, she'm lukkin' ee lot betterer."

The water vole kept her voice low. "That's 'cos she's blanked out the slayin' o' that ould fox. I've seen such things happen afore. But ye must never mention that she killed the fox. Don't want her t'go all funny agin, do we now?"

Mumzy paused a moment, then warned her guests, holding a paw to her mouth, "Husha now—somebeast's outside!"

They sat with bated breath. The water vole murmured, "You stay here, now, I'll go an' take a peek."

Flib was right at her side. "I'm comin' with ye—don't argue, it'll do ye no good!"

Zwilt the Shade stood on top of the rocky streambank. He watched his four Ravager guards climb down to the water. They drank from the cold, clear-running stream, then, seeing the abundant watercress, began stuffing mouthfuls. The tall sable allowed them only a moment before he gave orders.

"Enough of that. Get back up here whilst the trail is still fresh. I intend to catch those runaway deserters today. Come on, move yourselves!" The vermin guards knew better than to disobey. They scrambled hastily up, trotting after their leader, who was already marching swiftly off into the woodlands.

Two heads popped over the banktop—Mumzy and Flib.

The water vole rubbed a paw on the grass. "Ah, sure, that was close. I don't know fer the life o' me how they managed not t'see us. That last eejit trod right on me paw. Are you alright, Flib darlin'?"

The shrewmaid smiled grimly. "Oh, I'm fine, but wait'll ole Zwilt sees that fox. Hah, that's one piece o' scum won't be goin' back with him!"

Mumzy stared at her companion. "Ye remember wot happened to the fox, do ye?"

Flib narrowed her eyes fiercely. "Of course I do. It was him or us. That lousy vermin woulda murdered me an' the two liddle moles without blinkin' an' eye. So I got in first an' killed him. An' I ain't sorry I did, so there. I'd do it agin if'n I had to!"

Mumzy chuckled. "An' here was meself, tryin' to spare yore feelin's. Sure, a real ould killer you've turned out t'be, Missy Flib!"

The shrewmaid stared after the retreating vermin. "That's 'cos I'm from a line o' Guosim warriors—nothin' can change that!"

*

Dawn broke pale over the eastern treetops as Buckler and his friends made their way cautiously through the woodlands. They could not move at a fast pace, because of the Guosim Tracker, Sniffy, scouting the ground ahead of them. On fording a small streamlet, they saw him on the other side, seated on a fallen alder trunk, waiting for them.

They sat down with him—it had been a long trek through the Mossflower night, avoiding obstacles, skirting swampland and other such hazards. Sharing a flask of October Ale, they broke their fast with oat farls and cheese. As they ate, Sniffy made his report.

"I cut four sets o' tracks up yonder—two vermin, a weasel an' a stoat, runnin' alongside two foxes, one of them a vixen. Then they split in different directions, vermin headin' nor'east, an' the foxes travellin' more southerly."

Buckler questioned him further. "No sign o' that tall sable, Zwilt?"

Sniffy took a pull from the flask. "None. Just the weasel, the stoat an' the foxes."

Skipper consulted the young hare. "Wot d'ye say, Buck? Shall we split up an' follow 'em?"

Buckler took a flat piece of shale. Spitting on one side, he tossed it in the air. "Your call, Jango—wet or dry?"

The Guosim Log a Log called, "I say dry."

Buckler looked at the fallen stone. "Dry it is, mate. What do ye want t'do?"

Jango looked at Sniffy. "Which of 'em'll be the hardest to track?"

Sniffy replied after a moment's hesitation. "Foxes I reckon, Chief. They seems t'know the ins an' outs of most places—allus been slybeasts, those foxes."

Skipper cut in. "Then me'n Buck'll trail the foxes."

Jango shrugged. "Suit yoreselves, but ye best take Sniffy. No fox could give him the slip. I'll take Big Bartij. We'll go after the other two, right?"

Buckler nodded. "Right, mate. Later on we can either meet back here or pick up each other's trail."

After putting Jango and Bartij on the vermin trail, Sniffy set off with Skipper and Buckler on the track left by Thwip and Binta.

Axtel Sturnclaw, the Warrior mole, had regained his senses. He woke to the sound of Tassy and Borti weeping. The pain in Axtel's footpaw was agonising; it had swollen with the spearhead still impaling it. However, his first thoughts were not for himself, but for the two babes.

Tassy was hugging little Borti, trying to comfort him, even though she herself was in tears. It was a pitiable sight.

Axtel beckoned to them. "Cumm yurr, likkle uns. 'Ush you'm weepin'—oi'll take gudd care of ee."

They sat close to him, leaning against his velvety fur. With an effort, Tassy got her sniffling under control. The Redwall squirrel Dibbun winced at the sight of the big mole's wound.

"Yore paw is very hurted sir. 'Ow you goin' t'fix it?"

Axtel sat up slowly, leaning forward to inspect the impaled limb. "Furst thing we'm got to do, likkle mizzy, is to be getten you spearpoint owt. Yurr, foind oi a gudd stone—that un o'er thurr."

Tassy had to struggle a bit, but she fetched the chunk of limestone over to him.

Axtel smiled at her. "Gudd! Naow, put et unner moi futtpaw, so 'tis restin' agin' ee spearpoint."

The squirrelbabe did as she was bidden. Axtel took a deep breath, readying himself. "You'm stan' clear, naow, an' moind ee babby sh'ew."

Tassy obeyed without question. The mole took out his war hammer and set the haft between his teeth. He took hold of the stump of spear pole. Squinching his eyes tight shut, he shoved the spearpoint hard against the stone whilst at the same time giving the stump a swift, strong heave. Axtel roared. "Hoooouuuurrrr! Hoooaaaargggh!"

He went backward, lying flat out, with the freed spearpoint grasped in his forepaws.

Carrying Borti, Tassy hurried to his side. "It's out—you did it! But it' bleedin' blood!"

The big mole prised his jaws loose from the war hammer. "Hurr, so 'tis. Oi'll needs to bandage et upp!"

Tassy placed Borti at her friend's side. "You mind Borti. I know how t'make dressin's—Sista Fumb'l teached me. Jus' wait here, sir. I don't be long." She dashed off to find what she needed.

Seeing her go, Borti began wailing again. "Waaah, want my mamma!"

Axtel sat the little fellow on his chest, chuckling. "Hurr, an' so do oi, zurr, but b'ain't no use a-howlin' fur hurr. Coom on, naow. Make ee gurt smile fur oi!" He tickled the shrewbabe with his snout.

Borti was very susceptible to tickles. He was soon wriggling and giggling through his tears.

Tassy returned with an apronful of stuff. She took over like a proper little Infirmary nurse. "Now, you lie still an' I fix a paw up!"

Axtel adopted a look of serious obedience.

"Yuss, marm, oi'll do azzakerly loike ee says!"

He watched in pleasurable wonder as the Redwall squirrelmaid worked on the injured footpaw. Wiping the wound clean with crushed sanicle flowers, poulticing the bleeding with soft moss, she dressed it with dockleaves and sainfoin, tying the whole thing off with chickweed stems, which she knotted neatly.

"There, now. 'Ow doo's that feel?"

Axtel winked at Borti. "Yurr, she'm a vurry clever creetur, b'ain't 'er?"

Tassy declared proudly, "I gonna work inna 'firmary wiv Sista Fumb'l when I growed h'up!"

The Warrior mole chuckled. "Oi'm shure ee will, miz!"

A sound of approaching creatures alerted Axtel. "You'm hoide in ee bushers, naow. 'Urry—sumbeast bee's a-comen!"

They ran for the bushes, practically bumping into Sniffy. He swept Borti up in his paws joyfully.

"Seasons o' streams, lookit wot I found. 'Tis Jango an' Furm's babe. Borti, ain't it?"

Tassy gave a delighted squeal. She ran right up Skipper, as if scaling a tree. "Yeeeheee! Skippa, it me, Tassy!"

The Otter Chieftain hugged her happily. "Well, burn me rudder if it ain't. Where's the other little uns, Tass?"

Axtel saw that the newcomers were friendly. He tried to stand upright. "They'm mostly apprisoned, zurr, tho' oi manarged t'get they two owt. Hurr aye, an' three more who bee's at moi camp!"

Buckler strode up to the mole and shook his paw warmly. "We're grateful to ye, sir. Are you badly hurt?"

Favouring the wounded paw, Axtel leaned against the hare. "Oi was, zurr, but oi'm gurtly attended to boi likkle Mizzy Tass, thankee."

Buckler drew his sword, tossing it to Sniffy. "See if'n ye can cut this bravebeast a crutch, mate."

Skipper fed them from his pack. The big mole was enjoying October Ale with cheese and onion pasty so much that Buckler had to wait before asking him, "Have you noticed two foxes hereabouts of late?"

Axtel held out his beaker to be refilled. "Two foxers? Nay, zurr, nary a sightin' of 'em."

Sniffy, who was hacking at a forked hazel limb, snorted with displeasure. "We've lost the rascals. Told ye foxes were slybeasts, didn't I? We'll 'ave to backtrack, sorry."

Buckler broke a pasty, sharing it between the young ones. "I only asked about the foxes out of curiosity—they're not important now. The main thing is that we've found the little uns or, should I say, our molefriend has."

The Warrior mole tugged his snout politely. "Axtel Sturnclaw at you'm survice, zurrs!"

Whilst Buckler introduced himself and his companions, Sniffy passed Axtel the crutch he had hewed from the hazel.

"There y'are. That should serve ye well enough." He went chasing off after little Borti, who was toddling away on his own into the trees. "Gotcha, ye liddle rogue. You stick close by ole Uncle Sniffy, now, d'ye hear . . . ahah, wot's this?"

Dropping on all fours, the Tracker inspected the ground. "Ahoy, mates, I never lost the foxes—here's their trail, I've picked it up agin. Aye, this is it, one dogfox an' one vixen, headed over that way."

Axtel followed the direction Sniffy's paw was pointing. "Yurr, moi camp's o'er thurr, with ee uther three likkle uns. They'm foxers bee's sure t'foind et!"

Buckler issued swift orders. "Skip, you follow with Axtel and the young uns. Sniffy, lead the way, mate. We'll have t'move fast if the other three babes are alone in that camp!"

Shortly thereafter, the Guosim Tracker and the hare arrived at Axtel's camp. They found it deserted, except for the presence of Thwip's grisly carcass. Sniffy wrenched the spear from the dead fox's midriff, passing it to Buckler.

"I dunno wot went on round 'ere, but it looks like we're only trackin' one fox now, the vixen. You stand still there, Buck. Let me cast around for more tracks."

Whilst Sniffy was engaged in his task, Skipper and the others arrived.

Buckler held up the homemade spear. "Stay back. Sniffy's lookin' for fresh tracks. There was nobeast here—just this fox, he was slain with this."

Axtel took the spear. "Hurr, that'll be ee likkle sh'ewmaid, Flib. She'm a boldbeast, oi kin tell ee!"

Buckler relaxed slightly. "Aye, she is that. Flib can take care of herself, but what about the other two?"

Axtel shook his large velvety head. "H'only babbies, two likkle molers, cuddn't 'arm anybeast."

Skipper, who was carrying Borti on his shoulders, enquired, "Any trace of 'em, Sniff?"

The Tracker scratched his head. "There's trails goin' everyplace, mate. Here's the foxes, two arrivin' an' only one leavin', alone. The vixen didn't take the molebabes—some otherbeast did. Whether 'twas friend or foebeast, I dunno. Thick tail, long fuzzy prints, big 'airy paws, prob'ly."

Buckler grasped his long rapier hilt. "Which way has it gone—can ye make out the little moleprints?"

Sniffy had his nose practically stuck to the ground. "Little uns that size don't leave much trail t'follow. They don't weigh much, y'see. Now, as for this otherbeast, a female, I think, an' she really knows 'er way round this neck o' the woods, I can tell ye. Nah, this is a creature wot won't be found by any if'n she don't want 'em to. Still, let's see if'n I can't pick up the track."

The going was slow and hard, with many a false trail. Mumzy had spent a lifetime avoiding pursuers in Mossflower. Sniffy commented on this as they crawled on their stomachs beneath widespread thick bush and shrubbery. "Like tryin' to track a fish unnerwater, this is!"

They pressed on laboriously, unaware that they were being watched by evil eyes.

BOOK THREE

Escape from Althier!

17

Back at Redwall Abbey, there was some slight disagreement about who was responsible for guarding the walls. Diggs and Oakheart Witherspyk were not seeing eye-to-eye on the business of guard duties. Moreover, an officious shrew named Divvery had decided that the Guosim were not going to take orders from anybeast who was not of their tribe.

Diggs had selected all the able-bodied creatures he could find, regardless of who they were. The tubby young hare split his command into two shifts, one for daytime, the other for night. It was a good and fair system: Moles, Abbeybeasts, Guosim and Witherspyks found themselves standing together on the ramparts.

Those not on guard were employed at making weapons. Bows, arrows, slings and spears were being constructed down in Cellarmole Gurjee's cellars. The whole scheme worked fine for a day. Then things started to go awry.

Friar Soogum forgot to send lunch up to the walltops, so Divvery took the shrews off to the kitchens. Instead of taking their food back up to the walltops, they went into the orchard to eat. Oakheart was not too pleased at being left lunchless on sentry duty. The large, florid hedgehog was halfway down the wallsteps when he ran into Diggs, who blocked his path.

"Tut, tut, Oakie, wot's this? Desertin' your bloomin' post? Back up t'the jolly old walltops, this instant!"

Oakheart pushed past him indignantly. "Back up y'self, sirrah. There's only my goodself and a mere scattering of guards up there. Those shrew chappies have taken themselves off to lunch, if y'please!"

Diggs was taken aback. "Gone off to lunch? Deserted, just to feed their blinkin' faces! Right, leave this t'me. One thing I will not tolerate is rank disobedience. An' as for you, laddie me hog, back up on duty, before I put you on a bloomin' fizzer. On the double!"

Oakheart's stomach began rumbling. This made him take umbrage against Diggs. "Pish tush, laddie. I'm senior to you, both in season an' rank, and I intend to take lunch forthwith. You stop me at your peril, I warn ye!"

Trajidia came hurrying down the wallsteps. "Oh, Father, pray, do not strike him down!"

Foremole Darbee came trundling along the ramparts. "Yurr, thur'll be no strikin' h'inside ee Abbey!"

Oakheart held up his paws. "Who said I was goin' to strike him?"

Drull Hogwife pointed a paw at Trajidia. "She did!"

Young Rambuculus Witherspyk sniggered. "Can I come to lunch with ye, Pa? I'll help ye to strike him!"

Oakheart was incensed at his son's insolence. "One more word out of you an' I'll tan your hide!"

"What's all this about beasts being struck within my walls? The very idea of it!"

Everybeast fell silent at the sudden appearance of Abbess Marjoram. Oakheart faltered lamely. "But we've had no lunch. . . ."

Marjoram faced him squarely, her voice stern. "Is that any reason for argument and talk of striking?"

Trajidia uttered a dramatic sob. "My dear father is

the gentlest of creatures. He would never strike another beast!"

Drull Hogwife spoke out. "Then why did ye say he would?"

Rambuculus chortled. "She's always sayin' things like that."

Marjoram had heard Rambuculus volunteering to help his father strike Diggs. She fixed both young hogs with a severe stare. "You two are relieved of wall duty. Go and see Gurjee. Tell him that you're on cellar-sweeping duty for the next two days."

She turned to Drull for further information. "Now, how did all this disagreement start?"

Drull explained, "All the shrews marched off to lunch."

Diggs spoke. "Leavin' the walls only half defended, marm."

Oakheart could not resist adding, "Aye, and us only half fed!"

The Abbess relieved the situation. "I'll have Friar Soogum send up lunch for you all. Stay by your posts—it'll be here shortly. Diggs, Mister Oakheart, stay up here in joint command. As for the shrews, leave them to me."

Divvery and the other Guosim were enjoying a post-lunch nap in the orchard when the Mother Abbess, backed up by Sister Fumbril, marched in on them. Marjoram did not hesitate.

"Excuse me, are we disturbing anything?"

Divvery did not even bother rising. "No, you ain't. We're havin' our lunch, marm."

Marjoram nodded. "So I see. And what about guarding the walltops? Doesn't that interest you?"

Divvery shrugged. "Ain't no lunch up there. We came down to get somethin' to eat. Got a right to vittles, ain't we?"

The Abbess kept her voice level, betraying nothing. "Yes, of course you have. But now you're finished, perhaps you'd better resume guard duties."

The other shrews looked to their self-appointed leader. Divvery had not stirred, so they stayed put.

Marjoram turned, as if to walk away. "Log a Log Jango will be pleased to hear of your conduct when he returns."

They leapt up immediately and began hurrying off. No Guosim wanted to face his Log a Log for disobedience.

The Abbess called Divvery back. "Not you. I've got a different job I need taking care of."

Sister Fumbril, who was much bigger and stronger than the shrew, tripped him and neatly relieved him of his short rapier. She held him firmly as he blustered, "Wot d'ye think yore doin'? Git yer paws offa me!"

Fumbril smiled sweetly, retaining her strong hold. "I will, young sir, as soon as yore down in the cellars with a sweepin' broom in yore paws. Come along now!"

Granvy had been watching the incident from a distance. He approached Marjoram. Together they watched the rebellious shrew being hauled off to the cellars.

The Recorder commented, "Was he troubling you, Mother Abbess?"

Marjoram settled both paws in her wide sleeves. "Not at all, my friend. The only thing troubling me is those missing Dibbuns. I can't help thinking about them, wondering if they're still alive and well."

In the caverns beneath Althier or—to give the place its real title—Brockhall, the remaining young ones were alive. However, they were not well. Confinement, rough treatment and poor food were taking their toll. Slack-limbed, and dull-eyed, Tura and Midda wandered amongst the youngest creatures, trying to comfort them by telling them to sleep. Mostly the young ones wept, either for their mothers or for food. Calla and Urfa, the leverets, were the youngest of all, mere babes who could hardly talk. Tura and Midda nursed the little hares, rocking them gently, murmuring softly to them.

"There, now, get some dinner soon, sleep now, hush."

A mousebabe tugged Midda's sleeve. His name was Diggla, and he was at that age when young ones feel compelled to question everything. "Why d'we got t'go asleep?"

Midda pushed him gently down, tucking in his tattered smock. "Because it's time t'go to sleep."

Diggla persisted. "But wot time's sleep time?"

Midda explained patiently, "Nighttime is sleep time. Now, close your eyes."

However, Diggla was not about to comply. "Is it nighttime now?"

Midda pondered the question briefly, then spoke to Tura. "D'you know, I can't tell whether 'tis night or daytime down here, can you?"

The squirrelmaid yawned, lying back wearily. "It's got t'be nighttime 'cos I feel sleepy."

Midda snuggled down next to Diggla. "I suppose you're right. Let's all get some rest. If they bring vittles, those guards'll soon wake us."

Diggla tugged her sleeve again. "Singa warmer teddo song f'me."

Tura opened one eye. "Warmer teddo, what's that?"

Midda sighed. "He means the watermeadow song."

A molebabe piped up gruffly, "Hoi loikes that un. You'm can sing et furr uz."

The Guosim maid chuckled wearily. "How can I refuse? But don't blame me if'n I falls asleep before I finishes it."

Diggla giggled. "Silly, y'can't sing y'self to sleep."

Midda answered wryly, "Huh, can't I, though!" She began singing the beautiful watermeadow ballad, beloved of all creatures who used streams and waterways.

"Hear that hum in the lazy noontide,
that's a bee who'll rest a day or so,
all around the summer watermeadow,
creatures come and go.
Damselflies on gossamer wings,

water beetles, funny little things,
caddis, stone and mayfly, too,
skim and hover all round you.
Let your paw trail in the greeny water.
Paddle in the shallows, wade around,
where the bleak and tiny minnows quiver,
chub rise up with ne'er a sound.
Mid the bulrush and the reed,
sundew cleavers and brookweed,
toothwort, comfrey, watercress,
waterlilies calmly rest.
Watermeadow, rainbow-flow'red, spreading far and
wide,
shimmering 'neath golden sun, 'til shades of eventide."

The final line trailed off as Midda fell into a doze, which soon deepened into sleep. It was not cold in the captives' cavern, merely gloomy and depressing to the spirit. Everybeast lay slumbering in the feeble glow of two small lanterns. All except Diggla the mousebabe.

The little fellow had decided that sleep was not for him—he felt active and restless. Crawling out from beneath the limp restraint of the shrewmaid's paw, Diggla toddled off to explore his surroundings, free and unhampered.

Sometime later, the guards hauled food and water in for the prisoners. They were roused by a stoat banging a ladle on the side of the meal cauldron, shouting with heavy-pawed humour, "Sooner sleep than eat, would ye? An' us 'ere with the best o' vittles to tempt ye. Wot a fine life youse lucky lot leads, eh? Nothin' t'do but eat, sleep'n play. Well, if'n yer ain't in line afore I counts three, we'll take this feast out an' toss it in the stream. One . . ."

The captives hurried into line, some little ones still half asleep, rubbing paws into eyes as they tottered about.

Midda kept hold of Calla and Urfa, the harebabes, whilst Tura tended to some others. Having been served with the thin gruel of leftovers and edible roots, they collected their water ration and sat down to eat.

Tura was feeding a molebabe when she noticed one of their charges was missing. She turned to Midda. "Where's the mousebabe, wotsisname, Diggla?"

The Guosim maid cast a searching glance about. "I don't know. Wasn't he with you?"

Tura shook her head, questioning the others, "Jiddle, have you or Jinty seen little Diggla? Has anybeast caught sight of that rascal? Where in the name o' seasons has the mousebabe gone?" Her voice rose in concern. "We'd best ask the guards. He might've wandered past them when they went to fetch the vittles."

Midda silenced her friend. "Sshh! You'll have them back here upsettin' us all. Jinty, sneak up to the entrance and see if ye can spot Diggla anywhere." The Witherspyk hogmaid was not gone long. She scurried back, whispering, "No sign of him out there—those guards are all sitting round nappin'. Must be time for 'em t'sleep."

Midda nodded. "Give 'em a few moments t'drop off, then you an' Jiddle have a good search about this cave. If Diggla ain't out there, he's got t'be in here."

Tura was in agreement. "Aye, hiding someplace, I shouldn't wonder, an' he's missed his dinner. When he's found, I'm goin' to have a word or two with little Master Diggla!"

After the required time, Jinty went to check on the guards. On her return she reported to Midda and Tura, "They're snorin' up a gale, 'specially that big fat stoat. I peeked out into the passage. The two guards at both ends are still awake."

Midda rose slowly. "Right, you'n'Jiddle search to the left. Me an' Tura will take the right. Do it quietly, though, or we'll have the guards in here yellin' an' shoutin'. They'll be in trouble if'n their Quean knows one of us is missin'."

There was not much to look at—one dusty ledge, a few

crannies. It was a fairly basic old cave. Midda checked the little ones again on the off chance that Diggla had crept back and mingled in with the rest. She shook her head, baffled at the turn of events.

"If he'd wandered outside, those guards would have him by now. Where in the world has that infant vanished to?"

Jinty came hurrying back—she was all agog. "Found him, the blinkin' liddle rogue!"

Tura and Midda followed her to the far left wall at the back of the cave. Tura glared impatiently at the young hog.

"Well, I don't see him! Where is he?"

Jiddle materialised, as if by magic, out of the solid rock and earth face. "Fast asleep behind here—come'n'see!"

Stepping to one side, he disappeared. It was like some sort of optical illusion. They hurried forward to investigate.

There was a slim space twixt an outcrop of rock and the wall of hard-packed earth and root formation—Jiddle's spikes were almost flattened in the narrow aperture. He pointed down to Diggla, who was lying asleep.

Midda humphed in exasperation. "Get him out o' there, this instant!"

Diggla was wakened as Jiddle tried to lift him. "Waaa-haaah! Ya hurtin' me—I stucked!"

Tura stepped forward, calling advice to the young hedgehog. "Go easy with him, Jiddle, he's only a babe. Here, come out, I'll get him!"

Jiddle lifted the complaining mousebabe with a last effort. "No, it's alright, Tura, I've got him—yowch!"

Diggla had retaliated at the rough treatment he was being dealt by biting Jiddle's snout. The young hedgehog tripped, falling backward. He shot out a paw to save himself. It went right through the earth wall, collapsing a portion of it. All that could be seen was Diggla's tail and Jiddle's footpaws, kicking in the narrow space.

Midda grabbed one of the lanterns and thrust it into the gap. "Jiddle, are you alright? Is Diggla hurt?"

The young Witherspyk hog's voice boomed hollowly

back. "We're both alright. There's some sort of passage in here, but it's terrible dark!"

The little ones gathered round clamouring. "A passage—Jiddle found a passage!"

Midda whirled on them fiercely. "Shut up! Not another word from you!"

Such was the ferocity of her voice that they fell instantly silent. It took a little while, but with a deal of gentle exertion, Midda and Tura got Jiddle and Diggla out of their predicament and back into the cavern.

Tura was having trouble keeping herself calm at the possibilities of their new find. She took the lantern from Midda, her voice low and urgent. "Act as if nothin' happened, mate. Take these little uns an' settle 'em down, sing to 'em, anything! Jinty, you keep an eye on the guards. Let's hope they sleep good an' sound. I'm goin' back through that crack—it could be a way out o' this place for us. Wish me luck!"

Midda grasped her friend's paw tight. "Luck an' good fortune go with ye, Tura!"

A moment later, the squirrelmaid had vanished behind the narrow rock screen and through the wall opening.

18

Zwilt the Shade was not having the best of luck with tracking the four vermin who had deserted from Althier. He had trailed them through the woodlands accurately. Then he came to the spot where the four had parted company, the stoat and weasel going one way, whilst the foxes went the other. Zwilt chose to keep on the trail of Thwip and Binta, wanting to catch them and teach both a long, painful and ultimately fatal lesson.

But as Sniffy, the Guosim Tracker, had observed, foxes were tricky beasts to follow. Accordingly, it was not long before the trail went cold and the sable and his four Ravagers were lost. Zwilt had never been a great tracker—he was used to employing otherbeasts to do the job. He carried on stubbornly for a while before turning to one of his escort, a thin, one-eyed ferret.

"You, what's your name?"

The ferret saluted with his spear. "Aggrim, Sire."

Zwilt's cold, dead gaze assessed him. "Can ye track?"

Aggrim nodded. "I ain't too bad at follerin' a trail, Sire."

The tall sable sat on a fallen alder. "Take one of these with ye. Cast wide until you come across any prints, foxes or not. Then stay where those tracks are and send the other guard back here to me with the information. Do ye understand that?"

Aggrim saluted again. "Aye, Sire. Feril, you come with me."

Feril, a younger ferret, trotted off behind him.

Zwilt took out his long broadsword and honed its double edges on a smooth stone. The two guards did their best not to look nervous. Nobeast could tell what was on the sable's mind. However, he ignored them, concentrating almost lovingly on caressing his blade with the stone slowly, evenly. Listening to the soft hiss of rock upon steel, planning a suitable fate for the two foxes who had deserted their post.

Far sooner than he expected, Feril came loping furtively back. His voice sounded low and eager. "Sire, Aggrim's not only found tracks, but he's spotted somebeasts, not too far from here!"

Zwilt's impassive face never changed expression. "Where?"

Feril pointed. "Over that ways, Sire. There's two little uns wot must've escaped from Althier, a big mole, one o' those riverdogs, a shrew"—he halted, smiling, as he had saved the best for last—"an' ye recall that big rabbet ye met at the Redwall place? Well, him, too!"

The smile that dawned over the sable's features was one of pure evil. He murmured softly to his guards, "You three, along with Aggrim, can take care of the riverdog, mole and shrew. Slay the little uns, too. They're more trouble than they're worth. But not a word to Quean Vilaya, or you'll answer to me. As for the rabbet, he's mine. Leave him to me. Understood?"

As they nodded, Zwilt beckoned to Feril. "Lead on."

Buckler and his friends were taken completely by surprise. Following Sniffy, who was leading them through a thick bed of tall ferns, they did not see the enemy until the vermin were almost upon them. They were ambushed from both sides.

Skipper heard a movement to his left. He turned, calling out, "Wot the—"

A spearhaft thudded into his jaw, and he fell. Then chaos broke loose. Axtel threw himself across Tassy and Borti, protecting them with his body as he lashed out with his crutch, slaying Feril with a mighty blow to the throat.

Sniffy yelled as he saw Zwilt rise up at Buckler's back. "Buck, behind ye!"

A spear took the Guosim Tracker through the shoulder. He held on to it, drawing his short rapier and fending off his attacker.

Buckler wheeled about swiftly, his own long rapier out and ready as Zwilt's heavier broadsword crashed down against it. The young hare's paws went numb from the shock, but he knew he was fighting for his life, so he parried the stroke.

Zwilt turned to one side, anticipating a lunge, which did not come—Buckler knew the sable's tactic, to slash down as he went by. Dropping back, he made his assailant come to him.

Zwilt was forced to move forward. Caught upon the wrong footpaw, he stumbled. Buckler's long blade came up at him in a blur of small circles. It caught the broadsword in a whirl of lightning motion, twisting it from Zwilt's grasp.

With his paws still stinging from Zwilt's first blow, Buckler glimpsed Aggrim thrusting his spearpoint down at Skipper, who was still half stunned. To distract the ferret, Buckler yelled the Long Patrol war cry.

"Eulaaaaaliiiaaa!"

He flung himself through the air, blade outstretched. Aggrim paused long enough to seal his own fate. He fell with the blade through him and Buckler on top of it.

Now Skipper was up. He threw his lance, which pierced

another Ravager at the exact moment that Axtel's war hammer snuffed out the foebeast's life.

Tassy wriggled free of the Warrior mole. Grabbing a stone, she hurled it at the fallen vermin. "Ooh, ye naughty wicked beast, take that!"

Axtel winked at the little Redwaller. "Thankee, likkle marm, but oi a'ready fixed 'im!"

Buckler scrambled upright. Retrieving his blade, he turned to reenter the fray, but it was all over. The four vermin guard were slain. And Zwilt the Shade had vanished—he was gone!

"Ahoy, mates, we're comin'! Logalogalogalooooog!" Crashing through the ferns, Jango and Big Bartij came charging in. The Shrew Chieftain was disappointed.

"Yah, mudlumps, we've missed the battle!"

Sniffy staunched his shoulder wound with a clump of moss. "Aye, Chief, so ye did. Wot 'appened with the stoat'n'weasel?"

Jango slashed at the ferns with his rapier—he was not happy. "Hah, my one got away. Greasy-livered swab, I never knew stoats could run that fast. Took off like a duck with its bum afire, prob'ly still runnin'."

Skipper chuckled. "An' the other one, the weasel?"

Bartij was a simple soul. Toting a hefty oak limb, he explained apologetically, "He was tryin' to run me through with a spear, so I had t'stop him. Didn't think I hit him that hard, really." His homely face broke out in a smile as he spotted Tassy. "Hoho, lookit wot we got here—a Redwall Dibbun!"

Jango had found his little son, Borti. The pair of them were laughing and weeping, hugging each other fiercely.

Buckler smiled. "There's a happy sight for ye!"

Mumzy suddenly bustled in from the shrubbery. "A grand ould sight I'm sure, but 'twill look much better when ye clear them durty varmint carcasses away!"

Hiding his surprise, Buckler bowed. "Sorry about that, marm. We'll get right to it."

The water vole folded her paws firmly. "Sure, there'll not be a bite o' vittles for ye 'til this lot is floatin' downstream. Now, would I be wrong in sayin' that yore lookin' for more missin' babbies?"

Buckler touched his lips to her paw. "You'd be correct, m'dear. Pray, where might we find 'em?"

Mumzy smiled at Buckler, giving him a playful push, which almost sent him sprawling. "Ah, will ye lissen t'the silver tongue on that un? There's a creature wid manners for ye. Come on, then. Foller Mumzy an' we'll get ye fed an' acquainted wid the liddle mites."

Skipper gave her an elegant rudder salute. "We'd be forever in yore debt, me darlin'."

Mumzy dug an elbow into Jango's side, winding him. "Sure, an' there's another one born with his tongue in the honeypot. Well, flatter away, me fine friends, compliments are scarce these days fer an ould volewife like meself!"

They followed her tortuous route, which twisted and turned until Sniffy scratched his head, declaring, " 'Tis a bloomin' wonder she doesn't git 'erself lost. I never seen a better-covered trail than this un, mates!"

On reaching the water vole's dwelling, they entered through the curtain of vegetation which masked it.

Guffy immediately hugged Skipper's rudder. "Oi knowed ee'd cumm furr us'n's, zurr. Oi wuz surrtin!"

Flib jibed the molebabe cheerfully, "Hah, that ain't wot yew was sayin' when we was locked up in that cave!"

Jango tried to hide his surprise at the sight of his daughter. "Petunia Rosebud, is that you?"

The rebellious Guosim maid stuck out her chin. "No, it ain't. It's Flib, see, me name's Flib!"

The Shrew Chieftain was equally stubborn. "Well, me an' yore ma named ye Petunia Rosebud. Huh, Flib sounds like some kind o' fish. 'Tain't a proper name for the daughter of a Log a Log."

Flib stood face-to-face with her father, eyes blazing. "Well, 'tis the name I gave meself, an' I like it, see!"

Jango was shaking from paw to tail. "Ye . . . ye . . . hard-faced young—"

Skipper stepped between them. "Ahoy, mates, wot's all this? A fine pair you two are, bickerin' an arguin' like enemies. Wot's the matter with ye, eh? Jango, ain't you glad t'see yore daughter alive an' well? Flib, ye should be happy that yore pa came searchin' an' found ye!"

Mumzy chipped in. "Sure, ain't it the truth? Huh, ye should be ashamed o' yerselves, carryin' on like two starlin's over a worm. An' wot for, pray? Does it matter whether she's called Peculiar Nosebud, Flibbity Jib, or Wifflesplotch? Get some sense into yore thick 'eads. Come here!"

Grabbing both shrews, the water vole thrust them together. "Flib, he's yore da an' yore his daughter. Jango, she's yore blood kin, so act like a proper father t'the maid. Now, give each other a big kiss, or ye'll both feel the back o' me paw. Go on!"

Jango was still carrying Borti, who got squeezed between them both and uttered his first full word. "Gerroff!"

Father and daughter started laughing at the ridiculous situation. Jango kissed her, then tweaked her snout.

"Righto, Flib it is, then, ye disobedient wretch!"

Wiping tears from her eyes, Flib pinched Jango's cheek hard. "Log a Log Jango Bigboat, ye grumpy ole Guosim!"

The exchange seemed to clear the air, but no food was forthcoming until Skipper and Big Bartij disposed of the slain vermin in the fast-flowing stream. Whilst they were away, Mumzy, who was well versed in most things, treated the wounded with her own homemade remedies.

"Now then, Sniffy, me ould tater, grit yore teeth an' be brave. Aye, an' you, too, big molebeast, though I can't see you cryin' out in pain, warrior that ye are."

Axtel held up his footpaw. "Ee likkle Tassymaid fixed et up, marm, but if'n it bein' not to yore loikin' then doo's wot ee must!"

Mumzy made two evil-smelling poultices, which she

laid on bark and moss. The water vole placed them over the fire until they were steaming, then applied them to the wounds of each creature. Passing Tassy some woven grass strands, she patted her back.

"Bind 'em up now, missy, like a grand ould healer!" When they were treated and Skipper returned with Bartij, Mumzy served them with huge bowls of what she termed Streamabye Stew. It went down well with chestnut bread and pear'n'apple cordial.

As they supped, Buckler said the words they were waiting to hear. "Right, friends. It's a Council of War!" He went straight to Axtel. "This place that you rescued the young uns from, could you find it again, sir?"

The Warrior mole left no room for doubt. "Burr, h'oi surrpintly cudd, zurr. 'Tis unner a gurt ole h'oaky tree—"

Skipper interrupted. "A massive, big thing? Maybe fourtopped, would ye say?"

Axtel nodded. "Aye, that ud be et. 'Tis filled wi' tunnels an' caves unnerneath. They'm gotten ee likkle uns thurr."

Skipper's powerful rudder slapped the ground hard. "I've seen it afore, I'm sure of it. Aye, an' I reckon I could find it agin, Buck!"

Jango turned to his daughter. "How many vermin have they got down there, Flib?"

The shrewmaid put aside her drink. "There's quite a few. I've counted a score or more different ones, rats, ferrets, weasels. I s'pose they come an' go. But there's two that's always there, a nasty liddle ole rat an' the one called Sable Quean. She's real evil an' scary. I was frightened of 'er."

Buckler nodded. "From what I've seen of her, I can understand ye bein' fearful. Did ye see any other beasts down there? Think."

Flib nodded. "Aye, I saw the tall one who carries the big sword. Zwilt, that's his name. I think he's some sort o' chief, though the Quean is the mighty one. I 'eard the liddle rat callin' her that."

Buckler looked pensive. "Hmm, so there's a score or

more Ravagers down there—say about thirty—an' you say y'could find the place, Skip?"

The Otter Chieftain pawed at his javelin. "Pretty sure I could, matey. Are ye plannin' a move on the vermin, some sort o' lightnin' strike?"

The young hare smiled grimly. " 'Tis a nice thought, but there's only six of us. Well, four an' two wounded. Goin' up against thirty of 'em, I think we'd be on a loser."

Jango growled, "I know you've got some kind o' plan, Buck—come on, out with it."

Buckler looked at the eager faces of his friends. "Think about this. If'n there's thirty down there, well, they've got another hundred an' seventy to call upon. You saw them when they came to Redwall. There was at least tenscore, an' they all seemed like seasoned fightin' vermin."

Bartij scratched his headspikes. "So yore tellin' us it can't be done, Buck?"

The Blademaster held up his paws. "I never said that, but how's this for a plan of action: Axtel, could you dig a way back into Althier?"

The big mole replied without hesitation. "Ho aye, zurr. Oi cuddent be a-diggen too farst wi' this paw oi moine, but oi cudd do et."

Buckler patted Axtel's huge paw, then turned to Jango. "An' how many fightin' Guosim have ye got to paw?"

The Log a Log slapped his rapier hilt. "Threescore, mate, an' every one a proper battler, ready an' willin' at my command!"

Mumzy dished out more of her tasty Streamabye Stew, serving Buckler an extra-large portion. "Sure, an' aren't you the canny beast? I likes the sound of yore plan. Carry on, Bucko!"

Buckler smiled. "Thankee, marm. Now, the first thing is to get these young uns back to the Abbey. Once they're safe, we can move fast, 'cos that'll be the plan. Like you said, Skip, a lightning strike, quick'n'hard!"

Mumzy interrupted. "Quick'n'hard, is it? Well, ye won't

be so swift wid two ould wounded beasts in tow. I'll look after Sniffy an' Axtel 'til ye get back in full force." She cast a glance at the Dibbuns. "Ah, 'tis a pity they'll be goin' with ye. I likes the liddle babbies. Don't suppose there's any chance one of 'em could stay here with an ould volewife? It'd be grand fun, an' I'd feed the mite well."

Skipper gave Mumzy a hug. "It ain't possible, marm, but when this is all over, ye can come an' live at our Abbey. There's enough babes t'keep anybeast busy for ten seasons! Right then, mates, shall we get movin'?"

They were soon underway, with Skipper in the lead. Mumzy pressed small parcels of goodies upon the young ones. "Here now, me darlin's, there's a few slices of me grandest plum cake. That'll keep ye goin' 'til ye get back home. I'll see ye agin when I comes to yore fine Abbey t'live!"

Jango sat baby Borti on his shoulders, and Buckler slung Guffy up on his back.

Flib muttered to Buckler as they jogged through the woodlands, "I'll be comin' back with ye for this lightnin' raid. I ain't sittin' round Redwall with a pile of babes an' gossipin' mothers."

Jango had overheard his daughter. "So, you'll be takin' part in the attack, will ye?" Flib stared bleakly at her father. She seemed several seasons older all of a sudden. "Aye, I will!"

Jango nodded. "Then I suppose ye will!"

There was no way that Midda could keep the other captives totally quiet. Most of them were chattering away, all agog with what might lie behind the crack at the rear of the cave wall. One or two even ventured to the entrance of the rift, trying to peer in and maybe catch a glimpse of Tura. Midda drew the smallest babes close to her. She hummed tunes softly, rocking back and forth, hoping they would drop off.

Jiddle and Jinty began calling into the rocky fissure, in what they imagined were furtive undertones.

"Tura, can ye hear us? What's it like in there?"

"Aye, ye can tell us—have y'found a way out?"

A harsh vermin voice made them jump with fright. "Wot's goin' on in 'ere? Wot's all the shoutin' about?"

The fat stoat guard, who had wakened, eyed them blearily. Jiddle and Jinty approached him, trying to look innocent.

"We were only playin', sir."

"Aye, 'cos we couldn't sleep, sir."

The stoat glared at them. He was not in a good mood. "Oh, playin' were ye, 'cos ye couldn't sleep? Well, I can sleep, see. I'm bone tired, an' it was yore playin' wot woke me up. Now, any more noise outta youse two, an' we'll play a little game called Beat the Hogs!" He waved his spearhaft at the young Witherspyk hedgehogs. "So just wake me agin, ye spiky brats, just one peep outta any of youse, an' I'll bring ye out in blood blisters!"

Midda watched the stoat lumbering off. She was about to give a sigh of relief when he turned, looking around suspiciously.

"Why's it so dark in 'ere? Where's the other lantern? There should be two of 'em in 'ere."

Midda tried to keep the panic out of her voice. She babbled nervously, knowing that Tura had taken the other lantern with her. "Er, haha, it's always dark in here, sir. I always thought we had only the one lantern—ain't that right, Diggla?"

"No, we got two lanter's. Too'a squiggle got one."

Midda groaned inwardly, until Tura startled the fat stoat by looming up out of the darkness with the extinguished lantern in her paw.

"The little un's right, sir. We have got two lanterns. Here's the other one, but it's gone out."

The vermin guard grabbed it roughly from the squirrelmaid. "Gone out, eh? Wait there!"

He stumped off, returning a moment later with a lighted lantern, which he passed to Midda. "Here's a new un. Yore in charge of it. Don't let these liddle brats play with it an' it'll stay lit, unnerstand?"

There was genuine relief in the shrewmaid's voice. "Aye, sir. I'll look after it, thankee sir!"

The stoat stared sourly at her. "Never mind thankee sir. Yew just keep this lot quiet an' let me get a bit o' sleep . . . or else!"

He went off back to the guardpost, where within a short time, his slobbering snores were audible.

Tura sat down next to Midda. They began conversing in hushed whispers.

"Whew, you just made it back in time, Tura. Well, what did ye find in there?"

Tura glanced at Jinty, Jiddle and some of the others who had gathered around to listen. "Now, hold yore silence or we'll have that stoat back in here. There's a tunnel behind that back wall!"

Midda's paw shot out, gagging Jiddle, who was about to squeak aloud happily. The young hog mumbled, "Mm surry," allowing Tura to continue.

"Aye, a long dark tunnel. It goes both ways, t'the left an' right. I took a look both ways but couldn't stay long enough. I had t'come back when I heard you two young thick'eads yellin'. D'ye realise that yore voices echo all round behind that wall?"

Tura issued them both with a stern look before she carried on. "I don't know, but I had a feelin' that the tunnel t'the left was the one I fancied."

Midda clasped her friend's paw. "You did well, mate, an' if ye want to go left down the tunnel, then left it is!" She turned as Jinty's paw tapped her back. "What is it? Keep yore voice down."

The Witherspyk hogmaid asked timidly, "Two things, really. Are we all goin'? And when?"

Tura chuckled quietly. "Of course we're all goin'. If we're goin' to escape, then nobeast gets left behind."

Midda stroked little Diggla's head; he was dropping off. "Right, but when'll be the best time to go?"

Jiddle was not in any doubt. "There'll never be a better time than now, while the guards are asleep!"

Tura nodded. "He's right, Midda, but we'll have to move fast. Once they find we've gone, that Sable Quean'll have the whole lot of 'em right on our tails!"

"Unless . . . !"

She looked questioningly at Jiddle. "Unless what?"

The young hog gave a sly smile. "Unless we block the openin'—sort of disguise it so they can't tell where we've gone to."

Tura tweaked his snout. "That's a great idea. How d'ye think we should go about it?"

Jiddle cast swift glances around the cavern, his ingenuity coming to the fore as he outlined his scheme.

Jinty went first. Once she was through the crack, she held up a lantern and guided the youngest ones through. When only Midda, Tura and Jiddle were left, they scoured the cave for any loose rock and rubble. There were some quite sizeable lumps of stone, large clumps of earth made up of dead roots and clay-based soil and some single pieces of thicker root limbs. Working swiftly and noiselessly, they passed the material through to Jinty, who piled it up. "That should be enough, mates. Come on through now."

Once on the other side, Jinty and her brother led the little ones off down the left of the tunnel, holding up a lantern to guide their way. With the aid of the remaining lantern, Tura and Midda commenced blocking up the escape hole. They jammed the rocks, earth clumps and root limbs into the narrow aperture, ramming it hard with their footpaws. They completed the task, panting with the force of their efforts.

Midda gave the jammed mass a final pat. "There, I think that should do it. D'you think it'll fool 'em?"

Tura shrugged. "Well, if'n it doesn't, let's just hope it buys us enough time to get clear away."

They hurried off to join the others, the lantern casting a pool of light around the rough-hewn tunnel as they went.

The passage took a sharp bend after a while. That was where they came upon Jiddle and Jinty sitting in a huddle with the little ones.

Tura reproved the Witherspyk hogs. "Wot'n the name o' fur'n'fancies are ye thinkin' of, sittin' about like moles at a meetin'? We're supposed t'be bloomin' well escapin'!"

Jinty indicated the babes, some of whom were curled up slumbering soundly. "It ain't our fault. It's these little uns—they're tired. Some can't go any further without rest."

Tura lifted the mousebabe Diggla up onto her back. "Well, we can't stop here. We'll just have to carry 'em. You two take one apiece. Me'n Midda will take another two. The rest look fit enough to go on."

Midda heaved one of the harebabes onto her shoulders, jollying the rest along with a cheery comment. "Haha, you lot are all bigbeasts now—y'don't need carryin', do ye!"

The remaining babes all voiced their various opinions.

"Gurr, oi'm turrible 'ungry!"

"An I be thirsty, too—gimme a drink, Midda!"

A volebabe set them all off with her impassioned wails. "Waaahaahhaah! I want my mammy!"

Immediately, the tunnel echoed to the cries of homesick babes wanting mothers, fathers and grandkin.

Midda decided the only way to be kind was to take a firm stand and suffer no nonsense. Holding up her lantern, she set off down the tunnel with the harebabe Urfa on her back, calling to the others, "You'd best follow me, then, 'cos ye won't get mammies, daddies, vittles or drinks by sittin' there cryin'. Ain't that right, Tura?"

The squirrelmaid set off after her, assuring the babes, "Aye, that's right enough. You come with us an' soon you'll get everythin'—vittles, kinbeasts, the lot!"

Once Jiddle had picked up the remaining lantern and followed Midda, the rest scrambled to join them. Nobeast wanted to be left alone in a darkened tunnel. However, it did not take long before the questions started, little ones being what they were. Both Midda and Tura did their best to answer.

"When do I sees my mammy?"

"Oh, t'won't be long now. Just keep goin'."

"Wot sort o' vikkles bees us'n's agoin' t'get?"

"Er, nice vittles, I imagine, only the best."

"Do we gets h'apple pudden?"

"Aye, lots of apple pudden."

"Wiv hunny on, an' meddycream?"

"As much as ye like and arrowroot sauce, nice'n'hot."

"Yikk, I not like harry'oot sauce, not nice."

"Then you don't have to have it. Catch up, now."

"Yurr, wot we'm bee's a-drinken, marm?"

Tura stifled an anguished groan. "What d'ye like to drink, eh?"

Mousebabe Diggla, from his perch on the squirrelmaid's back, shouted aloud into her ear, "Straw'bee fizz, dat's wot us likes!"

Tura clapped a paw to her ear. "Right, strawberry fizz it is!"

The babes set up a rousing cheer. Apparently strawberry fizz was a firm favourite with little ones.

They carried on along the tunnel until Tura suddenly halted. Midda bumped into her.

"What's up, mate? Why've ye stopped?"

The splashing was audible underpaw. Both lanterns were held up, revealing a flooded expanse lying ahead of them.

19

It was the fat stoat who discovered the loss of the captives. Fearful of the consequences, he searched the deserted cave in silence. His lantern revealed nothing but shadows. Realising that this would mean an instant death sentence from the ruthless Sable Quean, he kept quiet. Strolling out, he hung up his lantern at the entrance, then spoke casually to the other three vermin who were posted outside.

"All quiet in there. They won't wake 'til they're called fer vittles. We'll let the relief guard do that."

When the next four vermin marched up, the fat stoat reassured them in a routine manner. "The brats are still takin' their shuteye. No rush to feed 'em yet. They'll let ye know when they wakes up, 'ungry, noisy liddle nuisances!"

The fat stoat hurried off, satisfied with his pretence. He would not be the one to take the blame if questions were asked—his fellow guards would back him up, anything to avoid the wrath of Vilaya.

It was only when the guards wheeled the cauldrons of food and water in that they became aware something was wrong.

An older ferret called into the gloomy interior, "Wot's 'appened to the lanterns? It's dark in 'ere!"

A lanky rat, who had not been paying attention, banged

a ladle on the side of the cauldron. "Cumm an' gerrit! 'Ere's yer vi—oof!"

The ferret had whacked him in the stomach with his spearbutt. He grabbed the ladle and flung it at the rat.

"Idjit, can't yer see there's nobeast 'ere?"

Another rat, who was in charge of the water, blurted out, "Wotjer mean, not 'ere? Where've they gone?"

There was panic in the ferret's voice as he shouted, "I dunno, do you? Look, see fer yerself!"

The lanky rat staggered up off the floor, yelling, "Escape! Escape! The prisoners've escaped!"

Vilaya and Dirva arrived hurriedly, with an armed guard of Ravagers which included the four who had been on duty previously. Lanterns flooded into the cavern, illuminating it brightly.

Dirva set about the closest vermin with a stick. "Search this place. Find 'em. Now!"

"No. Everybeast stand still—stay where you are!"

They froze at the high-pitched, imperious tone of the Sable Quean, who stood where they could all see her.

Many of the vermin were bigger than she, brawnier, more hefty, but they all feared Vilaya. Even Dirva, her aged soothsayer, could sense the foreboding in the air. The sable's bright eyes glittered. Her small, sharp teeth showed as she hissed softly. Every eye was riveted on the sleek barbaric figure with her silken purple cloak and her necklace of snake fangs. Vilaya was every inch a ruler who had to be obeyed under pain of death.

She spoke slowly and distinctively. "Who are the guards on duty here?"

The older ferret stood forward, accompanied by the lanky rat and two others, both rats.

Vilaya nodded to the ferret. "Make your report to me."

The ferret swallowed several times before he found his voice. "Majesty, we had just taken over from the last guards. We went in with the vittles, but they was all gone—the lanterns was gone, too, it was dark."

The Sable Quean allowed an agonising moment to pass before she spoke. "Before you went in, could you hear the prisoners talking or moving around?"

The four shook their heads, with the ferret answering for them. "There wasn't any sound at all from in there, Majesty. We thought they was all asleep. The others we took over from said they was afore they went off duty."

Vilaya toyed with the crystal vial hanging about her neck. "Bring them here to me."

Dirva had the previous guard line up quickly—the fat stoat, a pair of weasels and a rat. They stood quaking, with their eyes fixed on the ground, not even daring to look at each other.

The silence became almost deafening as Vilaya gazed from one to the other. She spoke suddenly and sharply, snapping the words out. "Who was the last beast to see the prisoners?"

They were too frightened to reply, but she noticed that three of them shot a swift glance at the stoat. She beckoned him to her with one claw, continuing the movement until he was so close that he could feel her breath upon his snout. Her voice dropped to a whisper. "Look at me and speak truly. When did ye last see them?"

The fat stoat's face was trembling so hard that he could only stammer. "M-m-m-maj—"

The savage, fiery eyes penetrated his very being. "You never saw them at all, did you? The prisoners were already gone. I know they were. Tell me I'm right."

The fat stoat had totally lost the power of speech. He was only able to nod his head. She turned her gaze on his three companions, selecting the rat.

"What did he tell you? Have no fear, speak."

The rat was so relieved that he gabbled hurriedly, "Majesty, 'e said that they was asleep an' ter let the new guards wake 'em when they serves vittles."

She glanced at both the weasels, who were nodding furiously. Having heard what she wanted, Vilaya summed the situation up. "So, our prisoners have escaped. They never left this cave by the entrance. With sentries posted all over Althier, they would have been noticed right away. That means they left here by another way. What were they attempting last time, a tunnel? Search this cave for tunnels!"

The guards hastened forward but were halted by their ruler's upraised paw and her scornful voice.

"Fools, stay where you are. Dirva, you do it."

The old rat cackled as she toured the area, tapping the walls with a stick. "All solid rock. Ye said yoreself to put 'em in one where they couldn't tunnel out. So where've the liddle uns gone, eh?"

Dirva carried on around the walls, tapping high and low. "Like ye said, Mighty One, they ain't left by the entrance. So where . . . where . . . where . . . ahaah!"

Dirva stopped at the disguised rift, beckoning lanterns to the spot. "This must be it!" She rooted amongst the loose rubble which was blocking the exit. "I was right—lookit this!"

The ancient rat was holding up a small wooden spoon, which had belonged to one of the young fugitives.

Vilaya inspected the escape exit. "Unblock it. Use your spearpoints and knives, quickly!"

The fat stoat, thinking he could redeem himself by helping with the work, grabbed his spear.

Vilaya shook her head. "Not you. Give me that spear."

The stoat passed her the spear, pleading, "But, Majesty, I'll find 'em for ye. Forgive me, Mighty One!"

The other Ravagers present turned their eyes away as the Quean lunged with the weapon. Vilaya looked down impassively at the dying stoat. "Now you are forgiven. How does it feel?"

The fat stoat died without saying a single word.

Vilaya sensed rather than saw Zwilt the Shade enter the cave.

Old Dirva watched him sweep by. "Well, lookit who's back!"

The tall sable surveyed the scene quickly. "What's been going on here?"

Vilaya countered the question with one of her own. "Where are the runaways you said you'd bring back?"

Zwilt had his story ready. He could not tell his Quean what really happened.

"The runaways are all dead. I caught up with them out in the woodlands. They fought, but I slew them all."

Dirva sniggered. "An' what of the four Ravagers who were with ye? I see they haven't returned."

Zwilt did his best to ignore her whilst continuing with his original enquiry. "They were slain in the fight. Where are the captives?"

Vilaya nodded toward the rear wall, where the guards were trying to break through with their weapons. "Somewhere, at the back of there—we'll soon find out. Come on, you idiots, a few woodland babes did that. Put your backs into it, weaklings!"

Zwilt inspected the congested gap, noting the bent spearpoints and blades of the workers. "Hmm, that's because it was blocked from the other side. Instead of trying to pull those rocks out, why don't you try to push them back?"

Vilaya saw the wisdom in his suggestion. "Do as Commander Zwilt says. Jump to it, I want those captives found and brought back here!"

A sarcastic note crept into Zwilt's tone. "And what if they're not found? We're due back at that Abbey sometime soon. I think your captives will be long gone by now. So what'll you do then, O Mighty One?"

It was the insolent way in which Zwilt used her title that nettled Vilaya. Her eyes flashed angrily. "Tell me, O Great Commander who cannot bring back a few pitiful runaway guards, what would you do?"

Zwilt's eyes betrayed nothing although he was seething inside. He did, however, broach a solution. "I would do what I first wanted to—attack Redwall. You saw how few real warriors they have. We have almost two hundred trained fighters. I could do it if you wanted me to."

The Sable Quean paused as if pondering his suggestion. She gave her reply in a harsh regal voice. "I'll tell you what I want you to do. I want you to realise that I'm your Quean! Now, help to get that rubbish out of the way and get after those escaped prisoners . . . or else!"

Zwilt kept his distance from Vilaya wisely, knowing how swift she could be with her tiny poisoned dagger. He dropped his paw to his sword hilt. "Or else what? You seem to have forgotten that I've slain more beasts than you've eaten suppers. I'll obey you for now, but if the captives can't be found, then I'll conquer Redwall, with or without you!"

Vilaya smiled. "But for now you will obey me. So get to it, Zwilt. Bring the captives back here."

The tall sable smiled back at her. "As you wish, Majesty. Step aside, if ye please."

Vilaya stepped away from the blocked entrance.

Zwilt moved sideways to pass by her, remarking, "Now we know where we both stand, 'twould not be wise for me to turn my back upon you."

Vilaya touched the crystal sheath which held her lethal little blade. She was still smiling.

"Aye, Zwilt, 'twould not be wise at all, though sometimes you do not even have to turn your back on the Sable Quean. Ask him."

She walked gracefully off, pointing to the dead stoat.

It was a high summer day. From a cloudless blue sky, warm sunlight beamed down on the ramparts of Redwall Abbey. Abbess Marjoram peered out at the path to the south. It lay shimmering and silent. Diggs, Foremole Darbee and Granvy stood with Marjoram at the southwest wall corner.

Foremole wiped a spotted kerchief across his eyes, then looked away. "Hurr, moi ole eyes be wored owt a-starin' at ee parth. They still h'aint nobeast a-cummen, nay, marm, thurr b'aint, an' us'n's bee'd yurr since brekkist."

The Abbess was clearly worried. She expressed her fears openly. "Really, I'm at a loss what to do. The vermin and their Quean are supposed to be back today. I've got to give them an answer, but without Skipper and Buckler here, we're at a disadvantage."

Granvy turned his attention to the woodland area beyond the south common land. "We'd better just hope that Buckler's party get back here ahead of the Ravagers. It's only just midday—there's time yet."

Diggs was, as ever, cheerfully optimistic. "Indeed there is, marm. Lashin's o' the jolly old daylight left, eh, wot! Why, bless me snout if old Buck doesn't come bowlin' along at any blinkin' minute. I'll wager he'll be singin' a song an' dancin' a bloomin' jig, bearing good tidin's and happy news an' whatnot. Don't fret, marm!"

Marjoram could not help smiling at the ebullient hare. "You seem to put great faith in your friend."

The tubby hare chortled. "Well, the blighter ain't let me down yet, marm. Buckler Kordyne's as true blue an' trusty as anybeast alive, ye can take that from me!"

He turned to view the east and north walls, rubbing his paws in anticipation at what he saw. "I say, they're bringin' lunch around. Well, the bloomin' cheek, servin' those Guosim an' Witherspyks first, instead of me, their superior officer!" Cupping paws around his mouth, Diggs bellowed to Friar Soogum and his helpers, "Never mind servin' the rabble first. What about the quality chaps, eh? There'd better be loads o' scoff left when ye get over here . . . or!"

Sister Fumbril roared back in a fearsome voice, "Or wot, ye young lard bucket?"

Her reply did not seem to bother Diggs, who grinned winningly as he called back, "Or we'll starve, an' you'll never know the blinkin' pleasure of our company ever again, so there!"

Friar Soogum yelled, "That'd be a mercy, sir!"

Pushing their trolleys, Soogum and his servers trundled up. The Friar waved a ladle. "Summer veggible soup, celery'n'apple crumble, with damson tart an' blackberry cordial to follow. How'll that suit ye, Mister Diggs?"

Disguising his delight behind a mournful face, Diggs scowled. "Hmmph, suppose a chap could manage to bally well force a bit down, wot!"

Sister Fumbril nodded southward across the walltop. "Well, don't force too much down that famine face o' your'n. Mayhaps yore friends might like some?"

Abbess Marjoram wheeled about and spotted Buckler emerging from the fringe of the south woodlands. Whooping and yelling, she scrambled up onto the battlements. "Over here, my friend, over here!" She almost overbalanced, until Fumbril reached out and helped her down.

The big jolly otter laughed. "Calm down, Marj. He'd have a job to miss the sight o' Redwall Abbey. Though ye don't usually see a Mother Abbess dancin' on the battlements!"

Drull Hogwife and Cellarmole Gurjee hurried to open the small south wallgate. Buckler, Jango, Skipper and Bartij stood to one side as Flib led the four Dibbuns inside.

Word had gone round the Abbey like wildfire. Redwallers came flocking down to meet Tassy, Guffy, Gurchen and Borti.

The Log a Log's wife, Furm, threw herself upon the babe. "Oh, Borti, my liddle Borti, yore safe!"

Though still not fully recovered from her injuries, Clarinna had hastened down from the Infirmary. Pushing her way through the onlookers, she wailed, "My babes, Urfa, Calla, where are they? You said that you'd bring them back, Buckler. Where are they?"

Buckler signalled Sister Fumbril. Between them, they ushered the distraught mother back to the Abbey as Buckler reassured her in a hopeful manner. "Don't worry, Clarinna. I know exactly where they are. Now we have the vermins' location, I'll make sure that your babes are back with you shortly."

Abbess Marjoram, who had heard Buckler, whispered to Skipper, "Is that right? D'you know where the little ones are being held?"

The Otter Chieftain called out aloud, "No sense in whisperin' about it, marm. There's some here who'd like t'know where their Dibbuns are, right?"

Marjoram held up her paws as the assembly began a clamour. "Everybeast not on wall duty go to the orchard. We'll take lunch there and hear all the news from our friends."

Dymphnia Witherspyk blew her snout upon her apron hem. "Oh, I won't be able to eat a single bite until I know about my twins, Jiddle and Jinty. Are they alive an' safe?"

Oakheart put his paw about her comfortingly. "Now, now, my dear. Come along and we'll hear the news together. Forget the food."

Their impudent son, Rambuculus, sniggered, "Never mind, Ma. I'll scoff yore lunch for ye!"

Trajidia cast out a paw dramatically, which accidentally caught Rambuculus square on the jaw, felling him. Trajidia ignored his prostrate figure, giving theatrical vent to her feelings. "Oh, brother, you heartless wretch, have you no feelings for your kinbeasts and our dear parents?"

The Witherspyk grandmother, Crumfiss, prodded Trajidia with her stick. "Well hit, young un. Leave him there an' let's git some lunch. I'm famished!"

Passing over his command to the Guosim Divvery, Diggs came down from the ramparts to join his companion.

"What ho, Buck! As y'see, I've kept an iron paw on things back here, stemmed a shrew mutiny an' had the defenders on their mettle in good style. So, give us the news, mate. When do we launch a full-scale attack on the rascally old vermin types, wot? I've worked up a super ambush for when they run up here today. Now, what we do is this—"

Buckler interrupted him. "I don't think they'll be coming back today, Diggs. We had a small run-in with Zwilt an' a few others back there. Four of 'em went down, but Zwilt got away. Shame, really. I was longin' to cross blades with that evil scum."

Twilight was falling over the orchard by the time everything had been talked about.

The Abbess went over what had been said. "So what you're saying is that this Warrior mole Axtel knows exactly where the young uns are imprisoned."

Skipper nodded. "Right, marm. I know the place myself. In fact, I'm sure I could find it. That big oak, it's a whole pile o' caves an' passages under the roots."

Granvy interrupted. "It's the hideout which the vermin call Althier—but really it's the old Corim headquarters that was known originally as Brockhall."

Marjoram sipped some cold mint tea. "Then I take it you intend attacking the place to free the young uns. But what about the Sable Quean and the beast called Zwilt?"

Buckler shrugged. "It doesn't look like they'll be payin' us a visit today, but that doesn't mean they won't show up, marm. Maybe they're on their way here right now, though somehow I doubt it. Anyhow, if they don't show up by midday tomorrow, it ain't likely that they will. But the Abbey must still be defended, or at least, seem to be defended."

The Abbess put aside her tea. "What exactly do you mean by that?"

Skipper winked at Marjoram. "Let me explain, marm. Just after midday tomorrow, Buck an' Diggs are goin' to slip out o' Redwall. With them'll be the Log a Log an' all the Guosim fighters. They've laid their plans for a surprise attack on Althier, an' if'n it all goes well, the rest o' the young uns will be back at our Abbey afore long."

Marjoram looked slightly perplexed. "But doesn't that leave us short of defence here?"

Now it was Diggs's turn to speak. "Not at all, dear

marm, for I have worked out an absolutely spiffin' wheeze. Haha an' hoho, leave it to clever old Subaltern Meliton Gubthorpe Digglethwaite, the super tactician, an' be not alarmed, O Superior Mother of this Abbey!"

Marjoram turned appealingly to anybeast within earshot. "What in the name of all seasons is he talking about?"

Diggs was about to reply when his attention was distracted by the delivery of more food to the lunch table. With an adroit move, he commandeered a platter of rhubarb and apple crumble. This allowed Oakheart Witherspyk to take the floor.

Sweeping off his floppy hat, the portly hedgehog made an elaborate bow. "Allow me, Abbess. The defence force will be made up of my goodself, Skipper, Bartij, Sister Fumbril and such Redwallers and members of my troupe as are required. Not a lot, you may say, an' rather few warriors. But what will win the day for us? Why, subterfuge, illusion and trickery, what else? Look up to the west wall threshold. Tell me, what do you see?"

Marjoram stared up at the wall. "Three tall, cloaked figures armed with spears. Where did they come from?"

One of the tall figures swept back the surrounding cloak, shouting down to Oakheart, "Well, what d'ye think, Pa?"

It was young Rambuculus, holding up a window pole on which the cloak and hood were propped.

Oakheart called to him, "That's the style, you young scamp, but hold the spear higher and tell Trajidia not to start declaiming to unseen foebeasts."

Trajidia emerged from another hooded cloak. She stamped a footpaw moodily upon the parapet. "Oh, Father, I'll get no acting experience at all just standing here like this pole I'm holding. I can sound really fearsome, y'know—listen to this."

She waved the spear, which was, in reality, a hoe with a carrot stuck on top. "Begone, vile vermin! Back, back, to the shadow of your dark lairs, ere ye provoke the wrath of a warrior hogmaid and bring calamity upon yourselves!"

Oakheart clapped a paw to his brow. "No, no, my precious. Your voice is far too shrill an' ladylike. Try muttering it under your breath, fiercely, and in a gruff register."

Turning back to Marjoram, he reassured her, "Drull Hogwife has a double closet full of old habit cloaks, all hooded. Subterfuge, y'see, marm. We can make it appear as though the walltops are bristling with defenders, all well armed. A load of squinty vermin won't know the difference. An' we can bellow out orders, march back'n'forth, do a lot of stampin', salutin' an' commandin'. Well, what d'ye say, Marj, my old friend?"

Marjoram sighed. "It just might do at that, Oakie. If a couple of hundred Ravager beasts turn up outside our walls, I hope it does, for all our sakes!"

Granvy patted Marjoram's paw. "It'll work, don't worry. We won't just be yelling and rattling spears about. I'm working with Foremole and his crew. We're making some big ballistas to hurl stones and all manner of missiles. That should keep any invaders busy, right, Darbee?"

The Foremole nodded solemnly. "Ho urr, marm, us'n's wull give 'em billyoh, an' chuck gurt bowlders on they'm vurmint skulls, hurr aye!"

Somehow, the stolid mole's logic seemed to comfort Marjoram. She smiled briefly.

"So be it, then."

20

Down in the depths of the escape tunnel, two lanterns reflected weakly as they flickered over the dark water, which stretched away as far as the eye could see. Tura hitched the mousebabe Diggla higher on her back as she waded in. The squirrelmaid shuddered.

"Phwaah! It's freezin' cold!"

Jinty dipped her paw in, then leapt back. "I don't like this. Can't we go back an' see what it's like the other way?"

Trying to set an example, Midda splashed boldly into the water. "Oh, it ain't too bad once yore in here!"

Jiddle stood alongside his sister, loath to go in. "Maybe Jinty's right. Mightn't the other way be better?"

Midda turned on both Witherspyk hogs. "Listen, you two. I don't like this any more'n you do. But this is the way we chose, so this is the way we're goin', see? Now, come on, get yore paws wet!"

Jiddle and Jinty still did not make a move. Jinty commented, "I wish Flandor was here. He was an otter. They're used to water an' things like that. He could've gone ahead to see how far it stretches."

Tura was in over her waist now. She backed her friend up. "Midda's right. We've got t'go on. If'n ye turn back, it's just losin' valuable time. Besides, you'd prob'ly walk slap bang into the vermin. I'll wager they've found how we escaped, an' it won't take 'em too long to unblock the hole. Come on!"

Both hogs hesitated reluctantly at the water's edge.

Midda became furious, wading back toward them, yelling, "Go on, just think of yoreselves. Forget these little uns that we're tryin' to save. Look, either you make a move right now, or me'n Tura will double up our loads with those babes yore carryin'. Then you can do wot ye please. Either stay there an' moan about how scared ye are, or go back an' tell the vermin yore sorry for escapin'. Well?"

Rather shamefaced, Jiddle and Jinty waded into the water.

They pushed on into the gloom. The water got gradually deeper, until they were going on tippaws, holding their chins up. Then the tunnel took a turn. Midda had now taken the lead, with Tura slightly behind her. Two little ones were holding on to the squirrelmaid's tail, treading water, as it had become too deep for them. Suddenly Midda went under. There was a small hiss as the lantern she was carrying went down with her. Urfa the little harebabe gave a bubbling squeal.

The shrewmaid fought her way back to Tura. She was spitting water and wiping her eyes. "Here, stay where you are, mate, hold on to this babe. I've done a bit of swimmin', so I'll go ahead an' sound out how much deeper this is an' how much further we've got to go. Be back as soon as I can!"

The escape party stood neck high, shivering in the icy water as they waited for Midda's return. Diggla liked the echoing sound of his voice, so he made full use of it.

"Yoo-hoo, Middy, where are you? Yoo-hoo! She taken a h'awful longa time, innen't she?"

Jinty felt something strike her footpaw. She chided Jiddle, "Stop kicking me, it's not funny. I nearly fell over then."

Her brother replied indignantly, "I didn't kick you. What're ye talkin' about?"

Tura hissed urgently at the pair, "There's somethin' in the water—don't move. Stand where you are. It just brushed by me. Whatever it is, it's big an' strong. Don't move a muscle, it might leave us alone. Stay perfectly still!"

The little ones who were in the water hanging on to the squirrelmaid's tail, plus a few who were large enough to wade on their own, became frightened.

"Whoo, I felt it! Quick, let's get back onna dry bit!"

"Burr, ee'm feels loike ee gurt surpint!"

At that moment, Midda came swimming back, guided by the light from their remaining lantern, which Tura was holding aloft.

The shrewmaid waved. "It goes a little deeper further on, but not for long, then it gets shallower. What's up? Why are ye lookin' at me like that, mate?"

Tura could feel the thing curling slowly around her footpaws. Her voice became shrill, strained with fear. "There's a beast in the water, feels huge'n'slimy!"

Midda halted, feeling her footpaws touch ground. "A beast, ye say, where?"

Tura had both her eyes shut tight. The mousebabe and the little hare perched on her shoulders, clinging like limpets to her ears as she muttered, "Windin' itself round my leg—no, wait, it's let go now. See the water ripplin', Midda? It's headin' over to you. Listen, we're all goin' to back slowly out of the water, 'til we're safe on dry ground."

Midda kept her voice level as she replied, "Good idea, but afore ye do, d'ye mind tossin' me the lantern? Uhuh, it's nosin' round me now!"

Tura threw the lantern, holding it with both paws to keep it up straight. Midda caught it neatly, with one paw underneath and the other catching the ring on the top. Meanwhile, Tura and the others began performing a painfully slow retreat to the bank.

Midda held the lantern down so that its base reached the water's surface. The shrewmaid stood motionless, peering into the water. When she spoke again, her voice was tense with fright. "Oh, no, it's an eel, a bloomin' giant of a one. I've never seen one like it in river or stream. Wait, it's comin' up!"

Slowly at first, the eel surfaced, its smooth snout poking out of the water. It was a huge female yellow eel, with eyes like milk-hued pebbles. Seeking the warmth of the lantern's crystal glass, it nosed up against it. Midda held the lantern steady as she studied the creature. A feathery dorsal fin rippled down its muddy olive-hued back. As it rose further, the underside was exposed in the lantern light, creamy yellowish, the colour of old ivory. Midda moved her face closer to its eyes—it seemed to ignore her. Then the truth dawned upon the Guosim maid.

"It's blind, Tura. This eel can't see a thing. It was prob'ly born down here an' lived all its life in these dark waters. Look out . . . oooffff!"

Jiddle could not contain himself; he yelled out, "What is it, Midda? Did it bite ye?"

Midda, who had stumbled sideways, righted herself. She held the lantern up, pointing to the tunnel side. "Look, look over there. It's chasin' those little white fishes. There's a great shoal of 'em!"

Sure enough, the tiny fish reflected the lantern light. Silvery white, like frosted pine needles, they shot out of the water, scattering hither and thither to avoid the eel's hungry jaws. The icy water bubbled and splashed as the monster eel drove its coils along in a lightning pursuit of its sole food source, the tiny cavern fish which were as blind as their hunter. Off they went, in a splashing stampede, with the hungry predator making devastating forays into the teeming shoal.

Midda shouldered Urfa once more, urging the rest forward without delay. "Hurry now, everybeast, back into the water! Stick to the right side of the tunnel. We'll make a dash for it while that thing's busy with dinner!"

This time there was no argument. They waded quickly in, with Midda in the lead and Tura bringing up the rear. Jinty called out advice. "Pull yourselves along on the wallside—there's a ledge stickin' out. It's much faster!"

Her tip proved true. A thin rim of rock, level with the water surface, stuck out. It was ideal for pulling a body through the water. They practically flew along, spurred on by the fear that the big eel might return at any moment.

Gasping and panting, they emerged from their icy, wet ordeal onto a soily clay-mixed bank. Tura flopped down, relinquishing Diggla, who limped about, trying to rid his limbs of their stiffness.

Jiddle grabbed him firmly. "Sit still here, ye little scamp, an' don't go runnin' off, d'ye hear me?"

The mousebabe stuck out his lower lip ruefully. "I hungry. Diggla be hungry, want vikkles!"

Midda held up the lantern, inspecting their surroundings. "Hmm, should be somethin' hereabouts. Look at all those roots hanging from the ceilin'."

Jinty seized a molebabe who was stuffing her mouth with a soft white substance. The Witherspyk hogmaid began rooting it out of the babe's mouth. "What'n the name o' spikes is that stuff? Come on, spit it out—it might be poison!"

Tura saw the source of the molebabe's feast. "No, look, it's some sort of mushroom. I've seen these before—they're alright to eat."

The mushrooms did not have any stem. They stuck out amidst roots and soil like smooth white shelves.

Midda tasted one. It was quite pleasant, with a nutty, wholesome flavour.

Jiddle chanced a piece. "Hmm, not bad at all. This should keep us goin' until we get some proper vittles."

Diggla ate a bite or two of the white fungus, then started pulling chunks off and throwing them at Midda and Tura. "This not be nice vikkles. Diggla not eat it!"

Midda wagged a stern paw at the mousebabe. "That's good food. Stop throwin' it about this instant!"

Diggla stopped, warned by the shrewmaid's severity. However, that did not keep him from complaining sulkily, "You sayed we gonna getta h'apple pudden, wiv hunny an' meddycream. Huh, an' straw'bee fizz t'drink. You h'only a big fibberbeast!"

That was when Midda lost her temper. She leapt up, roaring at the hapless mousebabe, "Shuttup, you ungrateful liddle snip. If it wasn't for me'n'Tura, you'd still be eatin' slops an' drinkin' stale water in that vermin prison! I've had about enough of you. Yore nothin' but a spoilt liddle nuisance who has t'be carried everywhere! We should've left you behind!"

This caused Diggla to throw back his head and bellow piteously. "Waaaah! Waaaaah! She shouten at me, an' I h'only a likkle beast! Waaahahaaah! Worra she shouted at Diggla like that for? I never doo'd noffink!"

His cries set the other babes off, weeping and sobbing.

Tura clapped paws about her ears. "Please, somebeast, do something to stop 'em bawlin'. I can't stand it!"

Unexpectedly, it was the Witherspyk hogtwins who did the trick. They bounded forward and performed a comic duet from their troupe repertoire. It was a song in which they acted the parts of two spoilt babes. It caused merriment amongst the little ones, particularly Diggla, who had no idea the lyrics were aimed at him. Jiddle and Jinty cavorted about, pulling tongues and making funny faces as they sang.

"Yah boo, I don't like you,
an' I can cry all day,
if I don't get just what I want,
then you will hear me say,
'I . . . wanna drinka water, ain't goin' asleep,
waah waah boo hoo hoo!

If you ain't extra nice to me,
I won't breathe 'til I turn blue!
I'll stick me tongue out, curl me tail,
an' tweak the bab's snout,
kick Granma, annoy Granpa,
an' scream an' yell an' shout.
Yah yah boo hoo hoo,
see I can cry real tears,
an' make me eyes go funny red,
an' wiggle both my ears.
Now do's I say, or I'll whinge all day,
waah waah sob boohoo!
Yah yah yah! Waah waah waah!
An' I still don't like you . . . so there!"

The babes thought this was hilarious, falling about chortling and giggling at the twin hogs' antics, forgetting their previous woeful mood. After eating more mushrooms and drinking cold water, they began to doze off.

Tura blew a soft sigh of relief. "Thank the seasons for that. Let's hope they don't kick off agin soon."

Midda settled her back against the wall, eyes half closed. "I think we could chance a rest here. It seems fairly safe—what d'you think, mate?"

Tura let her bushy tail curl over her face. "Aye. Don't think we're bein' followed just yet. Besides, we'd hear the vermin splashin' through the water an' that'd give us warnin' enough. Ah, well, wonder how much further we've got to go afore we're out of here?"

Jiddle nodded up the passage. "D'ye want me'n'Jinty to go an' take a look?"

Midda opened one eye. "If ye really want to, but go carefully. If'n ye find anythin' interestin', then come straight back here an' tell us."

Jiddle broke off some dead roots, binding them together with rootstrands. He beat the end of the bundle with a stone. This caused the dead wood to bush and feather out.

The resourceful young hog lit it from the lantern flame, making a stout and useful torch.

He and his sister walked off down the tunnel, surrounded by a small halo of light. It diminished, then disappeared as they rounded a bend.

Midda settled back to rest, commenting, "Those two are gettin' pretty valuable to have around."

Tura sighed wearily. "Please don't talk t'me. Can't ye see I'm asleep? You'd better rest while ye can, mate!"

The Sable Quean was in a dangerous mood, which did not bode well for her minions. Vilaya sent out a messenger recalling all Ravagers from their woodland camp, deciding they could better serve her at Althier. Zwilt had no say in the matter, now that there was a rift between the two. He took command of the guards who were trying to break through into the escape tunnel.

Knowing Vilaya was watching his every move, the tall sable drove the guards harshly. "You, there, fool, are you leaning on that rock or trying to move it? Put some energy into it or you'll feel my blade. Come on, the rest of you idlers, shift this rubbish. I'm growing old standing here waiting on you!"

Dirva, having the Sable Quean's protection, scorned Zwilt mercilessly, watching him shake with rage. "I thought a big strong beast like you could move that rock yourself, Lord. Or don't ye want to get yore paws dirty with a bit of honest work?"

Zwilt moved suddenly. Pushing a guard aside, he lifted a big chunk of rock. He tossed it backward, pretending not to notice when the wizened rat had to leap aside to avoid being struck.

Dirva bared her snaggled fangs. "You did that on purpose!"

Zwilt bowed mockingly. "Forgive me. I did not see you there."

The rift was finally unblocked. It was widened also,

allowing fully grown vermin to pass easily through. Vilaya entered the tunnel with Zwilt and Dirva. She glanced both ways, consulting her old rat aide.

"To the left or the right, which direction did they take?"

Zwilt noticed some telltale traces showing which way the fugitives had gone. He nodded in that direction. "They went off to the left."

Vilaya ignored him, staring pointedly at Dirva. "Come on, I don't have all season. Which way?"

The old rat knew that if she gave the same answer as Zwilt, it would seem like she was backing him. " 'Tis hard to say, but the right looks more likely."

The Sable Quean gave Zwilt a scornful glance. "Bring the Ravagers through. We'll split into two groups. I'll take the right—you go to the left. Take Dirva with you. She is useful."

The tall sable bowed his head curtly. "Your wish is my command, Majesty!"

A full force of vermin marched off down the tunnel in different directions. Zwilt beckoned a lean, sly-faced stoat to his side. He held a brief, whispered conversation with the stoat, whose name was Gliv. She nodded, then melted back into the ranks.

Dirva caught up with Zwilt. "What did ye want with that one, eh?"

Zwilt the Shade kept his eyes on the passage ahead. "Just some business—pity you never heard it. After all, you were only sent to spy on me. Old Dirva, eh, the eyes and ears of the Quean. Dirty little spy!"

Dirva curled her lip at him. "I'll find out wot went on twixt you two, believe me. Aye, not only will I be watchin' you, but I'll keep a sharp eye on that stoat Gliv. Neither of ye will be stealin' a march on ole Dirva, ye can bank on that!"

Dirva dropped back, mingling with the marchers, until she was alongside Gliv. Prodding the stoat sharply in the side, she snarled, "Wot did Zwilt want with ye, eh?"

Gliv winked at her. "Wouldn't yer like t'know!"

The old rat gave Gliv another vicious prod. "Alright, keep yore little secret, but remember this. I'll be watchin' ye, Gliv. Y'won't be able t'make a move that I don't know about, 'cos I'll be watchin' ye like a hawk!"

Gliv chuckled slyly. "Then you'll be watchin' the wrong beast, won't she, Lugg?"

"Huh huh, dat's right, mate!"

Dirva tried to turn, but too late. Two meaty paws seized her, one lifting her clear of the ground, the other stifling her nostrils and mouth. Lugg was Gliv's mate. A huge bullet-headed stoat, massively strong, he held the old rat as though she weighed nothing. Gliv blew a sharp blast on a small bone whistle.

Zwilt heard the signal and issued orders, grabbing a lantern. "March on forward!" He dropped back until everybeast had passed him except Gliv, Lugg and Dirva.

Nodding to his henchbeasts, he watched the old rat. Forepaws and upper body pinioned in Lugg's powerful grip, Dirva kicked wildly as the big stoat's paw suffocated her. Her eyes were wide with terror.

Zwilt's dead black eyes stared into hers.

"Well, well, Vilaya doesn't know it yet, but she's deaf and blind here. How does it feel, old one, knowing you cannot spy on me any longer? Sweet dreams!"

He watched until Dirva's eyes clouded over and her limbs went still.

Gliv smiled. "Just as ye ordered, Lord, dead without a single mark on 'er!"

Zwilt nodded. "You did well, friends. I won't forget this little service you rendered me."

A Ravager guard came hurrying back, saluting with his spear. "Sire, we've had t'stop—the tunnel's flooded up ahead. They can't go no further 'cos there's somethin' in the water, a monster, they say!"

Zwilt the Shade drew his long broadsword. "A monster? Well, let's go and take a look at it!"

21

In her bankside cave, Mumzy the water vole was having trouble with one of her patients. It was Sniffy, the Guosim Tracker, who had recovered from his wounds. He was restless, wandering ceaselessly round Mumzy's cosy abode and speculating about when the contingent from Redwall would be arriving. Axtel, the Warrior mole, was content to rest up until such time as his injured footpaw grew more useful.

Mumzy waved a ladle at Sniffy, who was starting to try her patience. "Will ye not be still! Scuts'n'whiskers, yore sendin' me spare, clumpin' about like a useless ould omadorm. Sit still an' have a bowl o' this celery'n'turnip soup!"

The Guosim Tracker sat down, then sprang up again. "Where are they? Wot's keepin' 'em, eh?"

Axtel dipped a chunk of chestnut bread into his soup. "Yurr then, Sniff, whoi doan't ee goo owt an' take a lukk? You'm may'aps see 'em a-comen."

That was all Sniffy needed. He bounded for the entrance. "Thankee, mate, I'll do just that!"

Mumzy shook her head when he had gone. "Ah, sure, there's a creature in a rush t'get old, an' he's left this grand ould bowl o' soup untouched."

Axtel tugged his snout politely. "Doan't ee wurry, marm. Oi'll see et woan't bee wasted, hurr hurr, oi surrtingly will!"

Sunlight and shade dappled the noontide woodlands as Sniffy breathed in the sweet-scented Mossflower air. He stood with his snout quivering appreciatively, glad to be back out in the open.

"Yore ma named ye right when she called ye Sniffy!"

The Tracker turned swiftly to find Jango leaning on a sycamore watching him. The Guosim Chieftain waved a paw behind him.

"Afore ye ask, I've brought 'em all with me, threescore strong an' armed to the teeth!"

Sniffy saw the rest of his comrades break cover, along with Buckler and Diggs, who winked at him.

"Threescore an' two, actually, if you'll pardon me contradictin' your jolly old Logaface. Well, now, Sniffers, totally recovered, are we?"

Sniffy smiled. "As good as ever, Mister Diggs!"

Jango remarked sourly to Buckler, "Tell that lard barrel mate o' your'n that if he ever calls me Logaface agin, he'll be wearin' that liddle bobtail of his as a hat!"

Mumzy was all of a-fluster as the mob of shrews tried to crush into her dwelling.

"O, sweet seasons, are ye sure you've brought enough help along? There ain't enough o' me fine soup to dish out t'this lot!"

Buckler bowed gallantly. "Thank ye for carin' for the wounded, marm. There won't be time to sit about suppin' soup, though. We've got serious business to attend to, an' swiftly!"

Axtel pulled himself upright, thrusting the war hammer into his belt. "Aye, you'm roight, zurr. Let's uz bee goin'!"

Log a Log Jango saluted the water vole. "We'll drop by t'see ye here when this is over, darlin'."

Mumzy wiped her paws on her apron. She stroked

Flib's cheek fondly. "You take good care o' this young un. I would, if'n I had a daughter like her."

Jango smiled. "I'll do that, marm. Right, Guosim, move out quick'n'quiet, now."

Flib brought up the rear with Sniffy and Diggs.

Axtel stumped along in front with Jango and Buckler.

The young hare questioned him as they went stealthily through the silent sunlit woodlands. "You've been inside Althier, so you know what it's like, Axtel. What do ye think would be the best way for us to attack the place?"

The Warrior mole had been thinking of a strategy whilst he was laid up in Mumzy's home. "If'n you'm splitten yore h'army en two 'arfs, 'twould be ee best plan, zurr. Oi'll take wun lot wi' me, daown ee tunnel whurr I cummed out of. You'm an' Jango take ee h'uthers in by ee frunt door. Hurr, 'twill h'ambush yon vurmints frum both soides."

Buckler nodded. "Sounds like a good plan t'me—what d'ye say, Log a Log?"

Jango was in agreement, with one condition: "Aye, I'll go along with it, providin' that Axtel takes that nuisance Diggs with his lot."

At the rear of the column, Diggs was having his usual fit of chunnering. "Huh, the least we could've done back there was to stop for lunch, wot. Rank bad form t'just go chargin' off like that, an' on a bloomin' empty stomach, t'boot. That flamin' Logawotsisname, no manners at all, y'know."

Flib nudged him sharply in the ribs. "Watch yer mouth, flopears. That's my dad yore talkin' about. He's a chieftain, a Log a Log of Guosim, an' don't you forget it, see!"

Diggs grinned mischievously. "Oh, is he indeed? Well, hoity-toity marm, an' pardon me t'blue blazes! Is that why you jolly well run away from home, 'cos he was such a capital chap, wot?"

Flib countered, "Well, it wasn't him who refused to stop an' eat. It was yore pal Buck, so wot d'ye say t'that?"

The tubby hare answered blithely, "Oh, that's just Buck.

He's always doin' things like that. A stout friend an' true, but he hasn't got a grain o' sense when it comes to vittlin'. Needs me t'keep him on a steady course, if y'know what I mean. By the way, did ye happen t'smell that soup? Mmmm, leek an' celery, with just a smidgeon o' mint an' wild ramsons. Jolly good cook, that Mumzy lady!"

Flib admitted ruefully, "Aye, I could've scoffed a bowl or two o' that. Nothin' like a drop o' good 'omemade soup. Maybe she'll have the cauldron on when we go there agin, eh, Diggs?"

The tubby hare cheered up. "There's a thought t'keep a chap goin' through the dark task ahead, eh, wot!"

Late noon shadows were lengthening when Axtel told Jango to order a halt. They crouched down in the shrubbery within sight of the massive ancient oak.

The mole pointed with his war hammer. "Thurr she'm bee's yonder, zurrs!"

Buckler drew his long blade. "There should be some kind of entrance—a gap or a door in that tree. Right, me'n' Jango will take our gang closer an' wait on you. Where's Diggs?"

"Here, sah, ever willin' an' able!"

Buckler patted his friend's shoulder. "Listen, mate, you go down the hole last. Before you do, give me the old grass-blade signal!"

He turned to Jango. "I'll count to threescore when we hear from Diggs. That'll give Axtel an' his lot time t'get well in. Then we hit the opening hard an' attack from the entrance. Make our way toward one another, moppin' up any vermin on the way. We should have 'em on the run by then. That'll be the time to find the little uns an' get clear o' the place. Right!"

Buckler winced as Axtel's huge paw grasped his. "Gudd fortune go with ee, zurr. Yurr's to ee safe returnen of ee babbies!"

The young hare extricated his numbed paw. "Thank you, friend—an' luck be with you also!"

Sniffy crept forward. He made a circuit of the big oak before reporting back. "There's a nice liddle door leadin' in there. I couldn't stop t'see if'n it was locked, though."

Jango looked up from sharpening his small shrew rapier. "I don't think we'll be botherin' to look for a key, eh, Buck?"

Buckler chuckled. "No, mate. We'll knock just the once—a mighty big knock!"

They settled down to wait in silence.

Axtel soon located his former exit from Althier. He rummaged around with strong paws, and soon had a hole big enough to admit two at a time. The thirty Guosim vanished down the hole promptly.

Diggs waited until the last shrew had gone, then plucked a broad blade of grass. Folding it a certain way, he locked it tight between both paws and blew hard. A loud, piercing noise, like that of a hunting hawk, rang out sharp and clear. Then it was Diggs's turn to disappear down the opening.

Buckler and Jango heard the signal. The young hare began counting slowly to sixty. "One . . . two . . . three . . ." Jango murmured to his Guosim warriors, "Draw yore weapons an' wait on my word!"

The first streaks of twilight appeared in the sky. Somewhere off to the west, a few descending skylarks could be heard warbling as they came to earth. Paws gripped sword hilts tightly, jaws clenched, eyes narrowed; the Guosim crouched, waiting for the count to end. Buckler stuck to the plan, murmuring off the numbers steadily, neither slowing nor speeding up.

"Fifty-seven . . . fifty-eight . . . fifty-nine . . . sixty!"

The war cries mingled as they charged the door. "Logalogalogaloooog! Eulaliiiiaaaaaaa!"

Midda and Tura were wakened from their brief nap by the sounds of splashing and shouting coming from the flooded area.

The Guosim maid commented tersely, "Looks like those stinkin' vermin are back on our tails. Grab the little uns an' let's get goin', mate!"

The babes were quickly roused. They went willingly, their frightened little faces showing starkly in the lantern light.

Tura shouldered the awkward, leggy harebabes, grunting under the effort. "I wish you two would hurry up an' learn to hop along without fallin' flat on yore faces. Anyhow, where've Jiddle'n'Jinty gone to? They should've been back by now."

As if on cue, a light appeared down the tunnel. It was the young Witherspyk hogs, carrying their torch. Immediately they heard the noise of the vermin.

Jiddle's spikes stood up straight. "Oh, no, how long has that been goin' on?"

Tura tapped a footpaw impatiently. "Just long enough to worry us. Now take one o' these hares, an' let's see how fast ye can go!"

They went at a brisk pace. Midda caught up with Jinty, who had been saddled with the other harebabe. "Tell me, wot did ye find down there? Is there a way out for us?"

The hogmaid explained, "We went a long way, an' it was all like this, just tunnel. Then we came to a sort of fork—it turned into two tunnels then."

Diggla, who was seated on Midda's shoulders, expressed annoyance. "More tunnils, more tunnils, huh. Itta nothin' but lotsa tunnils down 'ere!"

Midda was anxious to hear more. "Well, go on. Wot sorta tunnels? Did ye explore 'em!"

Jinty shrugged. "Didn't have time. Jiddle said we should be gettin' back 'cos you'd be worried."

Midda tugged the mousebabe's tail to stop him from jiggling about. "Jiddle was right, I suppose, but didn't you even take a peek at the two tunnels?"

Jiddle caught up with her. "I did, but only a quick glance. One went in a slope, uphill. The other one went downhill, it looked pretty steep. That's why I came back. I knew you'd want to try the uphill one—it should prob'ly lead us out into daylight, d'ye think?"

The Guosim maid speeded up the pace. "It prob'ly will!"

Back at the edge of the flooded tunnel, Zwilt the Shade had several Ravagers holding torches close to the dark waters as he scanned them.

He saw nothing for a moment, then a wide ripple revealed the wavering fin and the dull sheen of the eel. He took a step back—it was truly a big thing. He nodded coolly, as if encountering a monster that size was an ordinary occurrence.

"Doesn't look like much t'me. What are ye all scared of? Here, Lugg, take a spear and slay it."

Wordlessly, the bulky stoat grabbed a spear from a ferret and a torch from a river rat. He sloshed into the water after the huge yellow eel. It turned and began swimming off. Some of the Ravagers shouted encouragement.

"Go on, Lugg, stick it good afore it swims away!"

"Aye, chop its 'ead off, an' we'll build a fire an' roast it. A fish that size should taste good!"

Lugg lunged forward. The water was now over waist high. He struck hard at the eel, misjudging the kill. The blade grazed its side, merely causing a deep scratch. However, it was sufficient to enrage the yellow eel. It charged Lugg and attacked him.

The bulky stoat was slow and ungainly in the cold, dark water. He yelled in pain as the eel's sharp teeth latched onto his stomach. The big slithery coils wrapped around Lugg, tugging him sideways. He dropped the spear, the torch hissed as it went beneath the water, and Lugg's head made a resounding thud as it struck the rocky tunnel wall. He gave a faint moan and vanished beneath the dark icy surface.

Zwilt watched the writhing coils rising above the water,

then shouted an order. "Throw your spears, quickly, while we can still see it!"

A salvo of spears embedded themselves in the monster's body. The hafts clacked together as it went into a frenzied death dance. More spears struck the eel, and several arrows from the Ravager archers. It took a long time before it finally floated limp upon the surface.

One of the river rats waded in, yelling, "Lend a paw 'ere, mates. This'll make good eatin'!"

Zwilt waded in after him, with drawn sword. "Touch it an' ye lose your head—that goes for everybeast. We're not here on a fishing trip. Now, get through this water an' pick up the prisoners' trail. Move!"

At the other side of the tunnel, Vilaya found herself facing a blank wall. The end she had chosen was nothing but a cul-de-sac. The Sable Quean viewed it philosophically as she spoke her thoughts to a weasel named Grakk.

"Well, at least we know the captives didn't come this way. We'll follow Zwilt—he might have had some luck."

She sent Grakk in the lead, following up by walking leisurely in the rear of the column. At one point, Vilaya called for a rest. Guards with food and drink attended her. She beckoned Grakk to her.

"Take two guards and scout ahead. Report back to me as soon as you find anything."

The weasel bowed, then trotted off with two other weasels in his wake.

Whilst sitting there eating and drinking, Vilaya began to relax. She assessed the situation. The fugitives were young and inexperienced, little more than babes, for the most part. They could not outrun vermin guards and trained warriors. Zwilt would recapture them. Which brought her to another point.

Zwilt the Shade, what was to be done with him? Now they were enemies, Vilaya could no longer trust or rely upon the tall sable. But he was serving a purpose at the moment. When he returned with the prisoners, she would hear all that went on from her faithful old rat Dirva.

The Sable Quean knew that Zwilt would be easy to trap. He was arrogant and headstrong, ever ready to use his sword instead of his tongue. Once he was out of the way, she would no longer trust any one beast with the sole power of acting for her. No, she would have three, maybe four, captains to carry out her orders. Play them against one another, just to keep them wondering. Divide and conquer was always a sound strategy. Vilaya's thoughts were disturbed by a guard.

"Majesty, Grakk is returned."

Seeing the weasel coming down the tunnel, she held up a paw, calling to him, "Grakk, what news?"

Grakk waved his paws in alarm, making a silencing noise. He did not speak until he was face-to-face with her.

"Hush, Majesty, keep yore voice down. There's beasts outside—just beyond the openin' we came through!"

Vilaya's claws dug into the weasel's shoulder as she pulled him closer. "Beasts, what beasts? Tell me."

Grakk winced. "There's other news you'll want to 'ear, Majesty, but first let me tell ye. On my way back along this tunnel, me'n' my mates 'eard noises from inside the caves. So I peeked through the break in the wall, an' I saw 'em. They was Guosim shrews, all armed an' ready, searchin' round everyplace. An' I saw one o' those fightin' rabbets, the one we met at that Abbey. Aye, an' he'd just met up with that molebeast who tunnelled in 'ere, you know, the big mad un who wields an' 'ammer!"

Vilaya gripped him even tighter. "How many of these warriors were there?"

Grakk groaned as her claws pierced his shoulder. "Aaaargh! Majesty, I dunno, but they'll soon be in this tunnel, the way they're scourin' round outside."

Vilaya released him, issuing an immediate order. "Listen carefully, Grakk. Tell our beasts to lay aside their weapons quietly. Go to the opening and block it up again. Be as silent as possible and make certain that opening is blocked completely, with solid rock and earth. Pack it tight, much tighter than those escapers did. Then stay posted there and listen. If they discover the blocked opening, let me know right away. Well, go on, what are you waiting for?"

Grakk brought his mouth to the Sable Quean's ear and whispered. Then he saluted and crept off to do her bidding.

Vilaya sat immobile awhile. Then she hugged herself, rocking back and forth as she keened in a hoarse whisper, "No, not Dirva, the only beast I ever trusted with my secret thoughts. Oh, he'll pay dearly for this. Zwilt the Shade will curse the day he was born by the time I'm done with him. Ooooohhhh, Dirva, my old counsellor!"

Under the impact of Jango and Buckler, the small door set into the oak trunk was knocked inward with a resounding slam. The Guosim shrews and Buckler went thundering into Althier, where they confronted their first handicap.

The whole place was in darkness, as the Ravagers had taken all the torches and lanterns to search the escape tunnel. Charging right in from daylight to complete blackout caused a certain amount of confusion.

Buckler roared out in his best Salamandastron parade-ground voice, "On my command allbeasts will stand still. Haaaaalt!"

Jango, who was standing close to Buckler, remarked, "Well, that did the trick, mate. Ye could hear a pin drop in here. Proper dark, though, ain't it?"

Sparks flew, illuminating the caverns in a brief flash. It was Sniffy, striking his rapier blade across a flint.

"Stan' still, Guosim—I'll get a glim goin' . . . there!"

A pale little flame grew out of the tinder bag, which the resourceful Tracker always kept with him.

The Guosim shrews moved with admirable urgency, dashing outside and chopping branches from the dead lower limbs of an old spruce. The makeshift torches burned instantly, crackling as they cast light amidst the subterranean shadows.

Buckler shook his head. "I don't like it, Jango. Something's not right—there's no sign of anybeast down here!"

The Guosim Chieftain held up a paw. "Lissen, Buck, I can hear sounds comin' this way!"

Suddenly Diggs charged in, yelling, "Lights ahead, chaps! Give 'em blood'n'vinegar, follow m—"

He ground to a halt. "Er, er, what ho, you chaps—oof!"

The tubby hare was knocked flat from behind when Flib and the others came hurtling in. Diggs sat up, dusting himself off. "I say, steady on. Who told you to charge in like a flippin' shower o' madbeasts?"

Flib put the blame right where it belonged. "You did!"

Straightening his tunic, Diggs wagged a paw at her. "Well, just be a bit more jolly well careful in future—that's classed as assault on a leadin' officer, I'll have ye know!"

Axtel arrived after the charge, stumping in on his injured footpaw. The mole waved his hammer at Buckler. "Yurr, we'm b'ain't see'd nobeast. 'Tis vurry h'odd."

Jango shrugged. "Same here, mate. Buck, wot d'ye say we splits up into groups? That ways we can scour this place quicker, in case they're hidin' away."

The young hare agreed. "Good idea—right, Jango, Diggs, Axtel, Sniffy, myself and er . . ."

He glanced around, noticing Flib standing to attention and putting on a brave face. "And Flib, you'll be group captains. Pick your teams, then get off in different directions. Make sure you search every corner o' this place. Go to it!"

Grakk had stayed at his post, listening on the other side of the blocked escape route. He heard Diggs passing through the former dungeon with his escort of searchers. The tubby hare did not linger long.

"Not a confounded thing in sight here, chaps, just another bloomin' cave. This Althier place is nothin' but a load of old caves'n'passages, wot. Come on, let's see where this passage leads to. . . ."

Grakk stayed, listening until there was complete silence from outside. Then he scurried off to make his report. The Sable Quean was waiting at the edge of the water in the flooded section. One look at her furious face warned the weasel to be careful. He waited until she looked at him and asked, "Well?"

He swallowed hard. "Majesty, it's safe. They passed right by the place that we sealed up."

She turned away, snapping at a group of guards. "Get me over this water. Do you want me to wade through in my robes?"

A nervous ferret bowed low. "If'n you'd like to sit on this litter, we'll carry ye, Majesty."

A pile of spears, spaced out into a square, had been bound together. Wordlessly, Vilaya perched in the centre of the structure. Half a score of vermin lifted it carefully, then entered the water, with two more going ahead, to sound out the depth. As the other Ravagers waded in, one of them stiffened with fright at the big dead eel floating near the wall.

"Wot'n the name o' Hellgates is that?"

His companion, an older river rat, touched the limp body with his spearpoint. "It's a big dead fish. 'Twon't harm ye. Huh, ye can always tell Zwilt the Shade's passed through by the deadbeasts lyin' about."

His companion grimaced as he steered a course away from the horrifically slashed eel. "Aye, that's true enough. Death seems t'foller Zwilt."

The river rat continued grimly, "Take it from me, mate. Try t'stay out the way when Zwilt an' Vilaya meets up. That'll be a sight to see, an' make no mistake. Those two are bound to go head-to-head, an' we'll be left to foller the winner!"

His mate tried speculating as they ploughed through the dark icy water. "Who d'ye think'll come out on top?"

The river rat shrugged. "Yore guess is good as mine!"

Torches and lanterns cast rippling eerie shadows on the damp tunnel walls as they advanced gingerly into the unknown. Hardened as he was to suffering and death, the river rat let out a horrified gurgle. He had stepped on something soft and slippery, lurching to one side as the mangled carcass of Lugg bobbed to the surface.

The stoat's body had been crushed by the maddened eel; Lugg's swollen tongue protruded obscenely. The river rat recovered himself sufficiently, hurrying ahead of his companion in a rush to be out of the other unknown horrors the water might conceal beneath its murky surface.

Zwilt by this time was back on dry ground, needing no damp pawprints to show the route of the fugitives. They only had one way to go in a tunnel, he reasoned. The tall sable had also been planning ahead, knowing whatever excuses he gave for the death of Dirva, he could expect no quarter from Vilaya. The old rat had been counsellor and confidante—almost a mother figure. Despite the way the Quean had treated her, she remained faithful only to Vilaya.

Zwilt pressed forward, touching the gold medallion around his neck. A good broadsword could outwit a small poisoned dagger. When he and Vilaya met, there would be only one left to command two hundred Ravagers. If he ever wished to attack and conquer Redwall Abbey, the survivor had to be him.

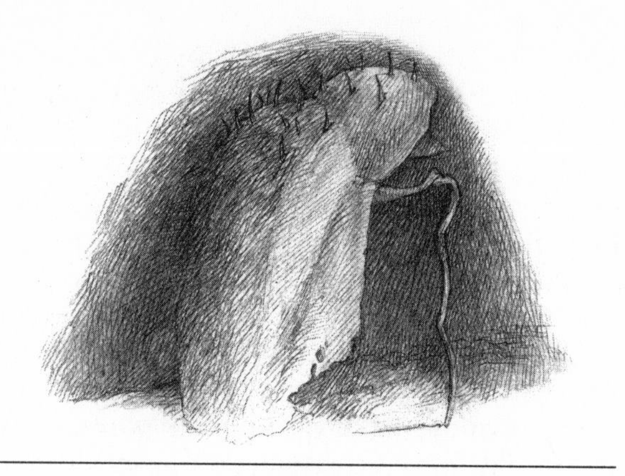

22

Midda lifted the mousebabe down from her shoulders. She massaged the back of her neck, which was sore from carrying Diggla—he was never still for a moment. The shrewmaid faced the fork, which Jinty had told her of. Tura relinquished her passenger, looking from one tunnel to the other.

"The one on the right goes downward. The other goes up. Which one d'you think we should take?"

Midda answered promptly, "The one that goes up, of course. That'll prob'ly get us out of here."

The squirrelmaid was still contemplating both tunnels. "Aye, that was my first thought, an' that's what the vermin'll think, too. Mightn't the downhill one be better? They won't expect us t'go that way."

Jiddle interrupted. "That's what I was thinkin', but I don't like the look of the one that goes down. I'll wager we'd run into more water that way. It might be very deep, then where'd we be, eh?"

Little Diggla pushed his way past them, snorting. "You all talkin' shoopid—Diggla goes up!"

The sight of the tiny mousebabe trudging busily away caused Tura to chuckle. "He's right. Up's the only way to go. Come on, mates!"

*

It soon became rather tiring trekking uphill. Jinty put Calla the harebabe down. "Come on, young un, time ye tried walkin', great sleepy lump, look at the size of you!"

Midda shook her head. "It'll slow us down if the youngest babes have to walk."

Jiddle allowed the other harebabe, Urfa, to slide down from her back. "Aye, an' if we keep carryin' 'em, it won't be long afore we're too tired to go any further. I vote we should all walk!"

Diggla nodded decisively. "All walk now. Looka me—I walk. Midda not have t'carry Diggla!"

The very small ones held paws, with Diggla at their centre. Jiddle and Jinty brought up the rear, urging them on with a simple chant.

"One two, one two, I will walk with you,
put your paw down on the floor,
now you've taken one step more.
One two, one two, keep on goin', me an' you.
Oh my, dearie me, what comes after one two? Three!
Three four, three four! We can walk a whole lot more!"

Jiddle called to Tura, who was at the front, "Look at us—they're gettin' along just fine!"

The squirrelmaid glanced back. "That's good, keep goin', but keep yore eyes'n'ears about you. Don't forget there's vermin on our trail."

After a while, the upward tunnel took a sudden bend. This culminated in an oval-shaped cave with two other tunnels leading off it.

Midda sighed. "Oh, no. Now which way do we go!"

She sat down to rest whilst Tura took a brief look at both passages. The squirrelmaid shrugged.

"They both look the same t'me. Don't suppose it makes much difference which one we follow."

"Oh yes it do, hahaaarr, believe me, it do!"

Tura jumped with fright as a figure emerged from the shadows, clad in a torn and tattered cloak.

It was a very tall and exceedingly skinny hedgehog. The little ones were scared. They huddled close to Midda and the Witherspyk twins. Tura took a step back from the hedgehog. There was something decidedly odd about him, but she determined not to be afraid.

"Well, tell me, which one would you choose?"

The beast threw back his hood, letting the shabby cloak fall open. He was not a pretty sight. Most of the spines on his body were missing, exposing a scabrous, unwashed hide. His left eye was wrinkled into a leaky slit, and what few teeth he possessed were blackened stumps. He carried an ash staff, which he twirled in the direction of either tunnel, cackling as he performed a shuffling jig.

"Which one? Which one? Hahaaarrharrr, beauty, ask Triggut Frap an' he'll know. Hahaaarrr!"

Midda countered boldly, "Well, she's just asked ye. So why not tell us, Triggut Frap, if that's yore name!"

The Guosim maid had obviously taken the wrong approach. Triggut Frap turned his back on them, no longer laughing or dancing. "Not tellin' yew. Why should Triggut tell yewbeasts anythin'? Nastybad, that's wot ye are, nastybad!"

Diggla was over his initial fear of Triggut. The mousebabe wagged a tiny paw at him. "We not nastybad. Us are good. You be nastybad!"

An instant change came over the strange hedgehog. He slumped down against the cave wall, weeping and whimpering. "I ain't nastybad. Nobeast likes pore Triggut, jus' 'cos I ain't pretty. Go 'way, go on, go 'way, all of yews. Triggut doesn't care!"

Jinty stifled a giggle. She whispered to Jiddle, "This one's crazy as a frog with feathers!"

Tura silenced her with a stern glance, also warning Midda in a low murmur, "I'll do the talkin'. Leave Triggut to me."

Turning her attention to Triggut, who had started scattering ground dust on his head, the squirrelmaid adopted a kindly voice. "Oh, come on now, friend. Of course we like you, but we've got to get out of here. So, please, will ye show us the way? We're tired an' hungry, an' we'd love to see daylight again."

Another mood swing came over Triggut. He rose, holding out a grubby paw. "Heeheehee! Get yew out, eh? Wot'll yews give me?"

Tura indicated the little group with a sweep of her paw. "I wish we had something to give you, friend, but we're poorbeasts without a drop o' water or a crust betwixt us."

Triggut's single eye narrowed. "Got nothin, eh? Then you'll just have ter work for me awhile. That'll be worth summat."

Tura nodded agreeably. "Sounds fair enough. What sort of work were ye thinkin' of, friend?"

Triggut's mood changed again. He poked Tura with the staff. "The sorta work that I say yew'll do!"

Jiddle sidled up to Tura, whispering in her ear, "Better make it quick. Think I can hear sounds from down the tunnel—it'll be the vermin!"

That decided the issue instantly. Tura bowed politely. "We're at yore service, Triggut. We'll work for you, no questions asked. Now can we go, please?"

The scabrous hog emitted his mad cackle. "Hahaarhaarr! Ravagers after yew, are they? Want t'move fast, do yew? Heeheehee! Foller Triggut, me pretty ones!"

Before they realised what was happening, he whipped out a length of cord, noosing it around Calla and Urfa.

Midda jumped up. "Hold on, there. Wot d'yer think yore doin'?"

Triggut fended her off with his ash staff. "Jus' makin' sure yew don't all run off on me. Now, d'yew want t'go or not? Jus' say the word, wibblesnout!"

That, and the distant sound of Ravagers, settled any further argument. They marched off behind Triggut Frap.

After a lengthy uphill walk, they finally emerged into welcome afternoon sunlight. Tears sprang to Midda's eyes—the woodlands looked so fresh and green after being underground for so long. Birdsong echoed cheerily from beech, oak, yew, sycamore and other familiar trees. Bees droned, insects chirruped, and butterflies flitted silently about. Sounds and sights they had all sorely missed in gloomy caverns. But it was the sky, that fluffy-cloud-dotted vault of light blue, which really gladdened young hearts.

Triggut did not give them long to gaze upon nature's beauty. Yanking the harebabes with him, he made off at a lolloping trot through the Mossflower greenery.

Midda caught up with him. "Which way is it to Redwall Abbey? We have friends there, you know."

The mad hog sniggered. "Don't know, heehee, an' if'n I did, I wouldn't tell yew. Not far t'the stream now!"

Midda held on to the cord, to stop the harebabes being pulled over. "Stream, what stream?"

She recoiled from Triggut's breath as he pushed his face close to hers. "Hahaaar hahaaaarr! Yew don't know where yew are, do yew?"

The Guosim maid shook her head. "No!"

He sneered in her face. "Good. Now, come on, move yerself!"

Tura sensed they were going southeast, by the position of the sun. They passed through a series of sandstone outcrops, travelling downhill through gorse-dotted scree into a valley between two high hills. Stumbling wearily into a grove of pines, they came out on a streambank. A ramshackle raft was anchored to a boulder in the shallows. Triggut giggled.

"All aboard, me beauties, quick as yew please. C'mon, li'l rabbets. We're goin' fer a nice sail."

The raft was ancient, with water springing through the

gapped logs which formed its deck. None of this bothered Triggut Frap. He tied the two harebabes to a mast which lacked any sail. Producing a fearsome dagger from his cloak, he drove it into the mast directly above the heads of Calla and Urfa. His single eye glared balefully at the others as he gave out orders.

"See them poles yonder? Pick 'em up an' get this raft movin'. Take 'er downstream, an' steer clear o' the banks. Yew'll do as I says, if'n yews wants ter keep these rabbets from 'arm. Now git polin'!"

Tura picked up a long pole, murmuring to her friends, "Do like he says. There's no tellin' wot a madbeast like this un will do next, so don't upset him."

Triggut, who had heard the squirrelmaid, snarled, "That's right. Don't upset Triggut Frap. Yew 'eard her. I'm a madbeast, see, crazy, crazy mad! Bees keep a-buzzin' round in my 'ead, all day an' all night, never stop. Buzz-buzzbuzzbuzzbuzz. . . ."

He carried on making bee sounds, his voice getting louder and higher. Then he reached for the knife embedded above the helpless harebabes. "Buzzbuzzbuzzbuzz. . . ."

Tura suddenly bellowed out, "Ahoy, Captain, we've got her goin' now, stayin' in midstream, just as ye said. Any more orders, Captain?"

Triggut's mood changed instantly. He ceased buzzing and chuckled happily. "Hahaarrr, keep 'er sailin' nice'n'smooth, mates!"

Tura winked at Midda, who caught on promptly. "Aye aye, Cap'n, nice'n'smooth it is. Well spoken, Cap'n!"

Triggut showed his snaggled teeth in an appreciative grin. "Hahaarrhaarrr! Cap'n, is it? I likes that. Cap'n of a fine ship with a good crew. Keep 'er steady, mates!"

Tura played up to the crazed hog shamelessly. "You heard the Cap'n. Keep 'er steady as she goes!"

Had it not been for the situation in which they found themselves, Midda would have wished for nothing more. Having spent most of her young life on Guosim logboats, she loved the feel of a fine summer day on a stream. The gurgle of meandering water, the fresh, clean smell of drifting banks and the swaying motion of the vessel, leaky as it was. She could watch the streambed as it slipped by. Crowfoot fronds, like flowing green tresses, swaying underwater; the flick of a minnow's tail, its red underside showing as it skimmed under the raft. A purple-scaled gudgeon, sucking pebbles on the streambed. Lacewings, delicately hovering over the current.

Tura glanced sideways at her friend. "D'you have any idea where we are, Midda?"

The shrewmaid shook her head. "No, I don't know this area at all, but by the lay o' the land, an' those tall rushes ahead, I'd say we're somewhere close to a watermeadow."

Triggut's voice cut in on them. "Ahoy, crew, stow yore gab an' bend those backs. Take 'er in to the right bank. There's a turnoff ahead that we'll be takin'."

The turnoff was a streamlet marginally wide enough to take the raft. Triggut halted them momentarily whilst he pulled out a woven reed net. It was a snare, full of small fish. Flopping it down on the deck, the mad hog winked at Tura. "Some vittles for my finny friends. Go on, keep polin' dead ahead. Be there soon now. Hahaarr!"

Just to keep his mood sweet, Midda replied, "Cap'n says straight ahead, crew. Did ye hear him?"

Tura, Jiddle and Jinty chorused back, "Aye aye, Cap'n!"

As Midda predicted, it was a watermeadow, and a very pretty one, at that. They punted up the sidestream, with tall reeds and bulrushes shielding either side, emerging into the meadow. There was a low rise at its centre, forming an island. It was a large expanse of watermeadow, breathtakingly beautiful. Orange-flowering bog asphodel, butter-hued bladderwort, white brookweed and pink-blossomed comfrey burgeoned amidst wide green platters of waterlilies.

Triggut Frap pointed. "Make for the island!"

The little ones were enchanted by the dragonflies and butterflies of many hues—skippers, whites, commas, admirals and fritillaries. The raft nosed into the island, where Triggut moored it, ordering them ashore.

Midda decided the time had come to dig in her paws. She acted as spokesbeast for her friends. "We don't go ashore without the harebabes, Cap'n. We always stay t'gether, y'see."

She watched the hedgehog, who took another change of temperament. He pulled the dagger from the mast, freeing Calla and Urfa with a few slashes. His tone was quite level as he pointed the dagger at Midda. "Right, all ashore, an' yew can stow that Cap'n talk, it don't fool me. This is my island, an' yew'll stop on it fer as long as I like, see!"

Midda faced him squarely. "You've got no right t'keep us prisoners. We're free creatures now!"

Triggut smiled nastily, cocking his sparsely quilled head to one side. "Yew made a bargain, an' I'm keepin' yew to it after 'elpin' yew to escape the Ravagers."

Then his demeanour underwent another change. He began his shuffling jig once more, cackling as he twirled the dagger and waved his ash staff.

"Heeheeheehee! Think yew kin escape my island, don't yew? Hahaarrharrr! Jus' watch this!"

He swished one end of his staff in the water, calling, "Come on, me beauties, come to ole Uncle Triggut, come, come!" Upending the reed snare net, he shook out numerous small fish, mainly minnows and sticklebacks.

There was a frightening rush of water, on and below the surface, with dorsal fins showing clear. Almost a score of big pike, those voracious freshwater predators, were there. Leaping and splashing in a feeding frenzy, their large, sharp-toothed mouths snapping and slashing as they tore the small fish into shreds and devoured them.

With a swift move, Triggut seized Diggla and held him over the roiling surface of the water. The mousebabe screamed; pike were leaping up, trying to grab him.

Tura shouted, "Alright, alright. We'll do as ye say, sir. Give Diggla back. We'll obey ye, I swear we will!"

The mad hog tossed the mousebabe carelessly back onto the bank. "Heehee, I knew yew'd see things my way. But just keep in mind, I can call on my friends anytime!"

Midda bowed her head. "What do you want us to do?"

Triggut scratched his chin, causing a few spikes to drop off it. "Hmm, what do I want? Lemme see." He swept over them with a grand wave of his ash staff. "I want yews t'build me a house. Aye, a nice, big house!"

Jinty Witherspyk looked concerned. "But we don't know anything about buildin' houses!"

Tura trod lightly on her footpaw, silencing the hogmaid. "Oh, I should think we can manage that. Now, wot sort of house will ye be wanting?"

Triggut repeated, "A nice, big house!"

Tura adopted the air of one who had been building houses all her life. "D'ye want it made of wood or stone, how many rooms must it have, d'ye want windows, would y'like a bark-shingle roof, or woven reeds?"

As Triggut shrugged, more spines rattled off his scrofulus body. "Er, I dunno. . . . Aye, yes, I'll have all wot yew said. Windows, wood, stone an' all that stuff."

Tura nodded. "Fair enough, friend, but first my workers need feedin'. Ye can't build houses on empty stomachs!"

The crazed hog curled his lip scornfully. "Yew kin fend for yerselves as far as vittles goes. Come an' I'll show yews."

It was a fairly substantial island. They followed him to its tree-covered middle.

Triggut pointed edibles out to them. "There's apple trees, pears, some acorns, bushes an' vines with berries. Plenty o' roots, too. Make the most of 'em, then get started on my house."

Tura sat down, shaking her head. "Not today, friend. These beasts need a rest an' vittles afore they're fit for work. Besides, I ain't drawn up the plans for yore house yet. No good tryin' t'build without some plans, is it?"

Midda, Jiddle, Jinty, even some of the little ones nodded in agreement. "No good at all!"

Triggut wiped a grimy paw over his damaged eye, which was constantly leaking. Then he laughed. "Haharrharr! Tomorrow it is, then, but let me warn yew. There's some thinks Triggut Frap's mad. Well, that's as may be. But don't ever think I'm stupid, 'cos I ain't, see? So, whilst yew clever lot sit there plannin' to escape from my island, remember that."

He darted forward and snatched Diggla. Looping a cord around the mousebabe's waist, he hauled him clear. "Haharr—gotcha! This un's too liddle t'work, so I'll take care of 'im for yew. Heeheehee, I always wanted a mousey fer a pet. Now I got one. Just in case yew lot get any funny ideas. Eat hearty an' sleep well, mates!" Kicking and wailing, Diggla was yanked off by Triggut.

The young friends could do nothing about it. Midda slumped down glumly.

"Well, here we are, prisoners again. But this time we're on a pretty island in the middle of a watermeadow . . . surrounded by vicious pike, an' watched over by a madbeast who's got little Diggla as a hostage. Tura, yore the brains round here. Wot d'we do now?"

The squirrelmaid stared levelly at the shrewmaid. "I'd say we don't start quarrellin' an' bein' nasty to one another. Let's work t'gether. There's got to be a way out o' this somehow. Any ideas?"

After a moment's silence, Jiddle spoke up. "Wot d'ye mean, ideas on how t'get Diggla back, or to get off this island, or how t'fix that rotten mouldy ole mad creature?"

Tura shrugged. "Any of those three will do."

Young Jiddle dropped his voice to a whisper. "Let's deal with Triggut Frap first. It'll soon be night, an' he ain't so different from any other beast that he doesn't have to sleep. . . ."

Midda smiled. "I think ye may have somethin' there!"

*

Buckler Kordyne stood in the open air with his party of Guosim warriors. He pounded his paw on the great oak trunk in frustration. "Not a blinkin' trace of the young uns anywhere!"

Log a Log Jango put up his rapier. "Nor the vermin. They've vanished, gone, disappeared!"

Axtel Sturnclaw held up a huge digging claw. "You'm a-wanten oi shudd go back in thurr, an' search agin, zurr? Us'ns may've missed summat."

Buckler shook his head. "I can't see there's much point. What d'you think, Jango?"

The Shrew Chieftain affirmed his friend's view. "We rooted that place out from top t'bottom. Sniffy couldn't find 'em, an' if'n he can't, then nobeast can. Right, Sniff?"

The Tracker assented wearily. "Right, Chief. Oh, they've been there, but the stink o' vermin, burnt torches an' all those pawprints overrun by ours—no, sir, 'tis no use goin' through those caves an' passages agin. They've fled the place for sure!"

Buckler's quick mind was racing as Sniffy spoke. He formed a swift plan and gave out orders. "Then we search the woodlands for a half day's march all around. Axtel, Jango, take a group of Guosim apiece. I'll lead the rest. Where's the best place to meet up again?"

"That ole Mumzy vole's place. We all knows how t'find it."

Buckler clapped the Tracker's shoulder. "Good idea, Sniffy. Let's get on the move—the longer we hang about, the further away they'll get. Right!"

Zwilt the Shade paced the streambank. His scouts had tracked the fugitives that far, but there the trail ended. The tall sable watched anxiously as two river rats came hurrying from different directions along the stream's edge. He pawed at his broadsword hilt. "Well?"

The rats were of the same opinion. "No signs of 'em on the stream, Lord." "They could've gone either way, up or down!"

Zwilt called across to another three on the opposite side. "Any traces over that way?"

A stoat who had swum across waved his paws. "Lord, they never went this way!"

Hearing a twig crack in the woodlands at his back, Zwilt turned, blade at the ready. The Sable Quean emerged from a sheltering beech trunk. Her eyes betrayed nothing, though her voice was heavy with contempt.

"The great Commander Zwilt can't even find some runaway babes, it seems."

Zwilt moved as she came forward, not wanting Vilaya any closer to him. "I'll find them. 'Tis only a matter of time. You can return to Althier and await my arrival with the prisoners."

She replied almost casually. "When I left Althier, it was teeming with Guosim warriors. Forget Althier—we can no longer return there. So, what are your plans now, or are you ready for further orders from me?"

Vilaya took a step forward, but Zwilt took a pace back. His long blade swished as it cut the air keenly.

"Stand where you are—come no further!"

Danger crackled on the air like forked lightning. The Ravager army spaced themselves out, staying clear of any confrontation between their leaders.

Vilaya chuckled humorlessly. "Quite a time you've had, Zwilt. I followed you and what did I find along the way? My old friend Dirva, a monster eel and one of your beasts, the big stoat Lugg, all dead. Very careless of you!"

The tall sable's dark eyes flashed briefly. "I am used to death in my trade. Stay! Come no closer, Vilaya. My blade is longer than your poisoned toy."

The Sable Quean opened her paws to show she was unarmed. "I see you no longer call me Majesty. Remember,

Zwilt, I could have stolen up on you. The snake can strike swiftly, you know."

She began circling sideways, her paw reaching for the tiny dagger. Zwilt's swordpoint followed her every move.

"It would have to be a brave snake to take its chance with me. Remember, Vilaya, I am not some slow, thick-headed vermin. Now, do ye wish to challenge me?"

The Sable Quean knew she could not. She had witnessed Zwilt the Shade's bladework. It was only the unsuspecting that she could take advantage of. She tried another tack.

"It is foolish quarrelling amongst ourselves when we should be concentrating on recapturing those young ones and using them as a lever to defeat Redwall."

Zwilt kept her menaced with his bladepoint as she inched almost imperceptibly forward. He sneered. "The foolishness was in your ridiculous plan to take that Abbey by stealing some babes. Well, I went along with it for a while, but no longer. Look around you, Vilaya. There are two hundred warriors, armed and trained for battle. With me to command them, Redwall will be conquered by invasion. War is the only sure thing to decide a victory."

Raising his blade, he called to the Ravager army, "My warriors, are you with me?"

That was when the Sable Quean made her move.

Vilaya sprang at Zwilt. Sidestepping her, he thrust the broadsword in a blurring flash. The point was protruding from the back of her cloak. The blade was withdrawn as fast as it had struck. Vilaya staggered, openmouthed, clutching the regal purple cloak about her. She looked from the rapidly spreading stain on its silken folds, to Zwilt.

Vilaya gasped in a halting voice, "Y-you . . . have . . . s-slain . . . a . . . Quean!"

She toppled forward, facedown on the streambank.

Zwilt placed a footpaw upon his fallen foe. "Now let us conquer the Abbey of Redwall!"

Spears, blades and various weapons were raised as the vermin horde yelled aloud, "Zwilt! Zwilt! Zwilt the Shaaaaaade!"

A smile of triumph lit up the tall sable's saturnine features. He raised the broadsword, intending to behead the Sable Quean, but halted as he felt somebeast tugging at his cloak. It was the ferret Gliv.

" 'Twould be a bad omen to cut her again, Lord. Let me bury this so-called Sable Quean here on the bank. I'll bury her deep, where worms will feed on her carcass—'tis all she deserves. Vilaya, ruler of worms, beetles and insects, she can feed her subjects!"

The tall sable stayed his sword paw. "Aye, Gliv, we'll never know how many of them she can kill with her little poisoned dagger. Bury her where the earth is cold and damp."

Log a Log Jango and Axtel Sturnclaw, along with their patrols, sat with their footpaws in the cooling streamwater, outside of the water vole's home. Mumzy bustled about, replenishing their platters with weighty portions of her damson and apple turnover. She shook her head sadly.

"An' ye didn't find any o' those liddle uns out there. Sure, I wonder where the pore babbies have got to?"

Jango washed the turnover down with some elderflower cordial. "We ain't found 'em yet, marm, but soon as we've fed our faces an' cooled our paws, we'll be off lookin' for 'em agin, ye can take my word for that!"

Axtel was already up and alert, testing his wounded limb. "Yurr, ee streamwatter bee's gurtly coolen, moi ole futtpaw's ready t'go agin, marm."

"Ahoy, the camp—friends comin' in!"

Jango shielded his eyes, peering to where the shout had come from. "It's Buckler an' his crew. Looks like they ain't had much luck either, though they're comin' pretty fast."

Buckler and his followers were breathing heavily. Jango moved along the bankside.

"Looks like ye've been coverin' some ground, mate. Here, siddown an' cool yore paws. Try some o' Miz Mimzy's vittles. She can bake a fair ole turnover."

The young hare remained standing, gathering his breath. "No time for that, Jango—we nearly ran into the full pack o' Ravagers back there. Lucky they never saw us, but they're on the move, an' that Zwilt beast is leadin' 'em. They're headed for Redwall, we heard the shouts. Get Diggs an' the rest. We've got t'get back to the Abbey, double quick!"

Casting aside his empty plate, the Guosim Chieftain stamped streamwater from his footpaws.

"Ravagers marchin' on Redwall, ye say? Form up an' move out, Guosim, there's no time t'waste! Er, about Diggs, he ain't with us. I thought he was with you, Buck?"

Buckler looked distracted for a moment, then he sighed. "Well, he ain't. I haven't clapped eyes on Diggs since we were searchin' the caves at Althier. Well, Diggs'll have to look out for himself. We can't stop now—got t'go!"

Mumzy picked up a half-finished chunk of turnover. "But wot about the liddle uns, Mister Buck?"

The young hare shook his head. "No sign of 'em yet, an' they weren't with the vermin, so we'll have to call off searchin' for 'em until after we've defended the Abbey. If'n either the young uns or Diggs turns up here, I've no doubt you'll take 'em in an' care for 'em, marm. We'll be indebted if y'do. Take care of yourself, friend!"

Buckler gave the water vole a swift salute with his blade and hurried off with Axtel and the Guosim.

Diggs was still wandering about in the caves and tunnels beneath the great oak. The plain fact was that the tubby hare was lost. He had become separated from the group he was searching with. Unwittingly, he had ambled into Vilaya's personal chamber, where he found some wine, a cooked trout and wheat bread, all intended for the Sable Quean's private consumption. Not wanting to share his find with the others, he settled down to a lucky repast, munching away and chunnering as he justified his actions.

"Bloomin' Guosim chaps wouldn't share it with me if they'd have found it, rotters! Well, yah boo, shrews, you can go an' blinkin' well whistle for your share. Mmmm, not too bad, if I say so m'self, rather tasty, in fact. Huh, this must be the officers' mess. Treat themselves pretty well, these vermin cads, wot. Oh, bother'n'blow, the confounded torch has gone out now!"

After trying unsuccessfully to blow the sparks back into flame, he did what he would normally do after a meal—took a short nap.

Subaltern Meliton Gubthorpe Digglethwaite's idea of a short nap was rather lengthy. He woke in complete darkness and silence. Yawning and stretching, the portly young rogue felt his way out of the cave, calling to his fellow searchers for assistance.

"I say, buckoes, fetch a light here, if y'd be so kind?"

There was no response to his cries, which annoyed Diggs.

"Huh, dratted spiky-headed fiends, it's just like you t'leave a chap in the dark, an' it's prob'ly suppertime, too. Right, desert me. I don't jolly well care. Hah, but wait until I catch up with you, laddie bucks. I'll have a word or three t'say about comradeship an' all that. By the right, left'n'centre I will, believe me!"

How long he rambled through the darkened underworld of caves and tunnels, Diggs could not say. It was only by pure accident that he managed to find himself at the broken-down door in the big oak trunk. Diggs staggered out thankfully. "Ahah, good old fresh air again, wot!"

He heard a rustle in a nearby bush. Drawing his sling, Diggs loaded a heavy chunk of rock into it. He advanced on the bush, twirling his weapon purposefully.

"Front'n'centre, come on out an' face me, you lily-livered maggot. Yowoooh!"

A stone hit his slinging paw, causing him to drop it. A

dark form thundered out of the brush, laying him flat with a mighty body charge. Diggs struggled to rise, but a footpaw, which felt like a stone shelf, held him pinned to the ground. He found himself staring up into the fierce brown eyes of a large, powerful badgermaid. She was twirling a sling twice the size of the weapon he carried. It was loaded with a boulder. She growled menacingly, "Tell me where my friend is, and I might allow you to live!"

23

Moonless night had settled over the watermeadow. The young beasts were huddled together sleeping soundly. Midda and the Witherspyk twins were wide awake. They lay stomach down, scanning the darkened landscape.

Jiddle murmured, "What's keepin' Tura? She's been gone for ages."

Jinty rubbed her eyes. "Well, she's prob'ly searchin' around the island, right, Midda?"

The Guosim maid nodded. "Aye, first she's got to find where old bees in the bonnet has his den. That's where he'll have taken Diggla. Mad ole beast like that, 'twouldn't surprise me if'n he made his nest up in a tree, like a bird. Jiddle's right, though, Tura's been gone a long time now. Too long for my likin'."

"Shall we go an' search for her?"

Midda rejected Jiddle's suggestion. "No. It might cause confusion, an' if the babes wake to find us gone, they'll bawl the place down. Hush, now, I thought I heard somethin'. . . ."

Triggut's wild laughter caused them to jump with surprise. "Hahaaarrhaaaarrr! Heard somethin'? So yew did, but don't fret, 'twas only me. Here's yer liddle bushytail friend. Yew kin have 'er back this time. . . ."

Tura, gagged, bound and stunned, was flung into the captives' camp. When Triggut called out of the darkness again, his temperament had changed. Now the mad hog was irate and threatening. "Next time yew try any clever tricks, I'll send yore mouseybabe back to yew. His ears first, then his tail an' snout. Maybe the followin' night yew'll get his paws an' tongue. Do I make meself clear?"

A groan of defeat came from Midda. "Alright, we understand—it won't happen again!"

With a final burst of insane merriment, Triggut skipped blithely off into the night.

Jinty Witherspyk loosed the squirrelmaid of her gag and bonds, bathing her face with some cool water. Tura was totally miserable.

"You wouldn't believe it, but that crazy creature has a crew of toads guarding him. I was creepin' up to his den, when suddenly they were all over me. Yurgh! Damp, slimy beasts, they sat on me an' croaked until the madbeast came runnin' an' cracked me over the head with his staff. Then he tied me up like an ole bundle o' washin'. I thought he was goin' to kill me!"

Midda inspected the bruise on Tura's brow. "But he didn't. You'll live. Did you get to catch sight of little Diggla?"

Tura shook her head. "I never even got into Triggut's den. Well, wot's our next move, mates?"

Jiddle Witherspyk yawned wearily. "I dunno. Just sit an' wait, I s'pose. Wot else can we do, eh?"

His twin sister agreed glumly. "Not a lot. Triggut Frap might act crazy, but he's certainly outsmarted us."

Midda stared at both young hogs in disgust. "Defeated already, are we? Seasons o' slutch, you two should hear yoreselves. Ye make me feel ashamed to know ye!"

Tura shot her friend a reproving glance. "They're right, though. We ain't got much to sing'n'dance about, now, have we?"

The Guosim maid glared at all three, launching into a

scathing diatribe, which brooked no argument. "Where were we a day ago, eh? Locked up in an underground cave, all dark'n'gloomy. We were eatin' slop an' drinkin' dirty water. Vermin with spears were standin' over us. One of our mates, a fine young otter, was murdered by that Sable Quean. So tell me, wot did ye have for supper tonight? Fresh fruit an' berries, with clean water t'drink. An' where are we now? I'll tell ye! Out in the open air, under the stars on a summer night, without vermin watchin' every move we make. Hah, lookit yore faces! Oh, poor ole us, ain't we the unlucky ones, still alive an' kickin'. It ain't right, I tell ye. Shouldn't we all be dead like poor Flandor? Huh, you lot make me sick!"

Tura had taken enough. She stood snout-to-snout with Midda, giving the Guosim a piece of her mind. "An' you make me sick, with all yore shoutin' an' yellin'. Who do ye think ye are, scraggymouse?"

Midda bristled. "I know who I am—a Guosim shrew, ye jumped-up bushtailed boughbender!"

Jiddle and Jinty rubbed their paws gleefully. They sensed an insult bout starting, so they called encouragement to the pair.

"Don't let her call ye that, Tura. Tell Midda wot ye think of her, go on!"

That started the contest in earnest. They stood paw-to-paw, hurling insults at one another.

"Ho ho, boughbender, is it? Ye wet-bottomed waterwobbler!"

"Hah, listen to ole weasel whiskers the nutnibbler!"

"Huh, I'll bet ye wish ye had a real tail, an' not a damp piece o' string, Guosimguts!"

"If'n I had a tail like that thing o' yores, I'd hire it out to sweep dusty caves!"

"Aye, an' if'n I had a face like yours, I'd change me job to frightenin' frogbabes!"

"Bottlenose! Baggypaw! Bumptious bum!"

Tura tried hard to hold a straight face, then broke out

into a fit of the giggles. "Oh, heeheeheehee! Hahahaha! Bumptious bum? Hahaha! Where'd ye get that one? Bumptious bum. Heeheehee!"

Midda could not resist joining in her friend's merriment. "Hahahaha! I just thought it up. Hohoho! It's a good un, ain't it? Bumptious bum, hoohoo!"

Jiddle and Jinty were chuckling, both holding their ribs.

Tura wiped tears from her eyes. "Heeheehee, oh, stop it, please. Bumptious bum, that'd be a good name for old madbrain. Bumptious bum!"

Midda corrected the squirrelmaid. "The way all his spikes are fallin' out, maybe we'd better call him bare bumptious bum. Heeheehee!"

Triggut's insane cackles halted the merriment. From somewhere nearby, he called to them, "Haharrharr, may'aps yew'd best stop all yore noise an' get some rest. Yew start on my new house tomorrer!"

They held their din momentarily, lying down with closed eyes until they heard the crazy hog retreating.

Jiddle opened one eye and waved a paw in his direction. "Good night . . . bare bumptious bum!"

The smothered giggles continued until they finally dropped off to sleep.

Vilaya the Sable Quean awoke slowly, her left side ablaze with pain. Gliv the stoat was bending over her doing something.

"Lie still, Vilaya. Your wound must be sealed, or you'll bleed to death. This is goin' to hurt."

Gliv drew the spearblade from the fire she had built. Vilaya screeched in agony as the red-hot spearhead pressed against the broadsword gash under her ribs. Smoke wreathed up. A stench of scorched fur and flesh permeated the air.

Peering close, the stoat inspected her work. "That's done the job. Now all ye've got t'do is live an' get well agin. I ain't no healer, so I've got no potions or lotions to give ye."

The Sable Quean watched as Gliv bandaged the injury with strips torn from her silken cloak. Vilaya was mystified by the stoat's behaviour.

"I know you. I've seen you whispering with Zwilt. You're one of his spies, aren't you?"

Gliv nodded as she tied the dressing securely. "Aye, I was one of those who did his dirty work."

Vilaya posed the question. "Then why are you helping me now? You probably don't even like me. What's your name?"

The stoat raised the sable's head, bringing a beaker of water to her lips. "Drink this, but take it slowly. I'm called Gliv. I don't like you, Vilaya, but I've got my reasons for helping you. Zwilt thought he'd slain ye. I stopped him choppin' yore head off by sayin' I'd bury ye for the worms an' insects to eat. I will, too, if'n ye don't get over that wound."

The sable pushed the beaker away. "Don't fret—I'll live. So, in what way did Zwilt offend you, Gliv?"

The stoat's eyes hardened at the memory. "He had my mate, Lugg, killed. Lugg was his loyal servant. Zwilt should never have sent him into the water to battle with the giant eel. It was Zwilt's fault. I blame him for Lugg's death. He was a big, trustin' lump of a stoat, but Lugg was my mate. I loved him."

The sable winced as she lay back and relaxed. "And what do you want me to do about it?"

Gliv stared into the flickering fire. "Yore goin' to kill Zwilt soon as y'get well. I've seen ye use that poison blade, an' I knows ye want him dead now. You got yore reasons—I got mine. I don't care, as long as I can live t'hear the death rattle in Zwilt the Shade's throat! That'll be yore thanks t'me for savin' yore life, Vilaya."

The injured beast spoke imperiously. "Vilaya is my

name, but to one such as you I am the Sable Quean. You will address me as Majesty!"

Gliv curled her lip scornfully.

"Huh, Quean o' nothin' is wot ye are t'me. When ye slay Zwilt an' command the Ravagers agin, then I'll call ye Majesty. But right now, yore just a beast carryin' out my orders so that ye can stay alive!"

Gliv watched Vilaya's paw straying toward the slender thing she kept slung about her neck. The sly stoat held up the little poisoned dagger in its crystal sheath. Dangling it from its necklet, she shook her head mockingly.

"No ye don't, Vilaya. I'll take care o' this liddle toy until the time comes."

A wry smile hovered about Vilaya's lips. "My my. You are a crafty stoat!"

Gliv nodded. "Aye, an' yore a dangerous sable, so betwixt us we're the right pair for the task. Now, git some sleep, 'cos as soon as ye can stand without fallin' over agin, we'll be on the trail of Zwilt the Shade."

On the streambank, the small fire burned down to grey ash in the woodland night. Two creatures went to sleep, each dreaming of deathly revenge.

Morning broke overcast and sullen, with the rain silencing birdsong. This mattered little to Oakheart Witherspyk, who had the security of Redwall Abbey to oversee. Donning an old cloak and putting his flop-brimmed hat on over the hood, the portly hedgehog mounted the west gatehouse steps. Trudging up onto the battlemented walkway, he looked left and right, blowing rainwater from his snout tip. He snorted disapproval to the leaden skies.

"Bah! Not a single beast on sentry. Where in the name o' spikes'n'spillikins are they?"

He strode the ramparts in high dudgeon, knocking down unattended cloaks, which were propped up on poles to give the appearance of a heavily guarded Abbey.

Granvy the Recorder emerged from the gatehouse, pulling on his hooded cloak. He shouted to the Witherspyk patriarch, "What'n the name o' seasons are you doing up there in this weather? Get down here before you get soaked!"

Oakheart gestured theatrically about him. "There's not a confounded guard up here. Where've they all gone, may I ask?"

Granvy set off across the rainswept lawn. "Everybeast is where any creature with a grain o' sense should be right now—taking breakfast inside. Come on!"

Great Hall glowed warmly with myriad candle and lantern lights. The air was redolent with cheerful sounds of Redwallers breaking their fast. Friar Soogum and his helpers bustled twixt the long tables, ladling out hot oatmeal and honey. Fresh fruits, golden-crusted ovenbreads, hot mint tea—an array of delicacies to please even the most jaded palate—graced the tables. Abbess Marjoram sat with two Dibbuns perched on her lap, trying to teach them rudimentary manners.

"No no. Put the beaker down. You can't eat and drink at the same time—finish what you have in your mouth first."

She saw Oakheart stamp in and fling off his wet cloak. "You look drenched, Oakie. Come and have some hot food!"

The hedgehog shook water from his hatbrim. "Hot food, is it, marm? How could I sully my dutiful lips with hot food when my blood runs cold at the thought of all those deserters!"

Foremole Darbee dipped an oat farl into a bowl of melted cheese. He wrinkled his button snout at Oakheart. "Doozurrters, zurr? Whut do ee mean?"

The portly hog shook a damp paw in a circle, denoting the outer walls. "Our sentries, m'dear sir. All those volunteers who are supposed, at this very moment, t'be protecting all we hold dear from vermin onslaught! I make it my morning chore to check the walltops, an' d'you know, there's not a single guard to be seen up there!"

Sister Fumbril commented blithely, "Why, bless y'spikes, Oakie, is there a vermin onslaught goin' on out there? Nobeast told us!"

A ripple of laughter echoed from the diners. Oakheart stemmed it by pounding a paw upon the table. "That's just the point, don't ye see, marm? There could be a vermin attack, even as you're jokin' about it. Where would we be then, eh?"

Abbess Marjoram nodded gravely. "Point taken, Mister Witherspyk. You are quite right! Attention, everybeast. All those supposed to be on wall duty, leave what you are doing and get back up there on guard immediately, please!"

Baby Dubdub waved a honey-smeared paw, echoing Marjoram. "Meejittly, please, meejittly!"

Young Rambuculus rose sulkily. "But it's rainin' out there. Can't we wait'll it stops?"

His sister Trajidia leapt up, declaiming, "Alas, to pour shame upon the noble name of Witherspyk with churlish remarks. To your post, O errant brother!"

She was about to sit down again when Grandmother Crumfiss prodded her. "Aye, an' you, too, missy—off y'go!"

Oakheart mounted the wallsteps with the guard detail behind him. On reaching the walltop, he was surprised to see Skipper leaning on a battlement.

"Great seasons, Skip—where did you pop up from?"

The Otter Chieftain pointed to the east wickergate. "I was down checkin' the wallgates. Aye, an' I took a turn round these ramparts. I would've raised the alarm sharpish if'n any vermin showed up."

Rambuculus smirked at his father. "So it was alright for us t'have breakfast, see!"

Skipper tweaked the insolent young hog's ear. "No, it wasn't, young un. What if'n I'd chose to join ye, eh, what then? Yore pa's right. Stick to yore duty, obey orders an' ye can sleep easy at night, remember that!"

The guards took shelter under the old long cloaks, brandishing makeshift weapons as they patrolled up and down. Bartij peered out into the rainswept woodlands. Skipper caught the big hedgehog's sigh.

"Wot's the matter, mate? Ye don't look too happy."

Bartij shook his head as Auroria Witherspyk stumbled on the hem of a cloak, dropping her make-believe spear with a clatter.

"Look at 'em, Skip. They're nought but young uns playin' a game. Oh, I grant ye they might look like warriors from a distance. But they ain't! So wot d'we do if a couple o' hundred Ravagers comes marching up?"

The otter blinked rainwater from his eyelids. "I dread t'think, matey, I dread t'think. Let's just cross our paws an' hope it don't come down to that."

Cellarmole Gurjee came ambling up the wallsteps.

Bartij nodded to him. "Gurjee, 'ow are ye gettin' on with that weapon ye were plannin', the big cattypult wot throws rocks. Is it ready yet?"

The Cellarmole shrugged. "Not yet et b'ain't, Bart. Hurr, 'tis a gurt 'eavy tarsk. Y'see, me an' ee molecrew, we'm gotten 'er near ready, but us'ns got to getten et up out of ee cellars."

Closing his eyes, Skipper leaned his head on the battlement. Foremole Darbee joined them.

"Yurr, you'm feelin' alroight, zurr?"

Skipper explained. "The siege catapult, Gurjee tells me yore moles are buildin' it in the winecellars. Tell me, Foremole, wouldn't it have been better t'build it up here, where we'll be usin' it from?"

Foremole Darbee nodded his velvety head. "May'aps you'm roight, zurr, tho' et bee's turrible weather t'be a-wurkin' out o' doors."

Bartij took Skipper to one side, whispering to him, "It

ain't the rain, Skip. Wot Darbee means is that moles an' high places don't go together, see?"

The Otter Chieftain nodded understandingly. "Yore right, of course. Lookit Darbee an' Gurjee, they're goin' down the wallsteps already. I should've thought o' that. Moles are frightened o' heights. It ain't their fault, just their nature."

Oakheart, who had been privy to the incident, made a helpful suggestion. "Ahem, pardon me, friends, but wouldn't it be better for the moles to unjoint the thing? I'm sure if we had all the relevant parts, then we could assemble the catapult up here, what d'ye think?"

Foremole Darbee caught the gist of Oakheart's scheme. He touched a digging claw to his snout three times at the hedgehog (a mark of high esteem and admiration amongst moles). "Oi thankee, zurr. You'm gurtly woise!"

The Witherspyk hog bowed deeply. "An unexpected compliment, my dear sirrah. I'll go and see if the Abbess can spare any creatures to help with the transportation of your weapon's parts."

Zwilt the Shade had been driving his Ravagers hard. He had almost reached the southern walls of the Abbey by midday, despite the worsening rainfall. The tall sable called a halt in the southern fringe of Mossflower woodlands. From there he could make out Redwall's south wall. It was barely visible through the sheeting rain curtain. Zwilt beckoned a Ravager to his side. Fallug, a tough-looking weasel, was not too bright, though he was trustworthy. On the march to the Abbey, Zwilt had been forming a plan, to which the inclement weather was an unexpected boon. He outlined his orders to Fallug.

"Listen, now, I'm putting you in charge of half of these Ravagers. How does that suit you, my friend?"

A smile formed on the weasel's hard, knotty features. "Suits me fine, Lord. Am I a gen'ral or summat?"

Zwilt managed to return the smile. "You can be a captain for now, Fallug. Once I take that Abbey, then you can be a general. Now, listen. Take spearbeasts and any who carry an axe. I need a tree, a good, big, solid one. Go away from Redwall, so you won't be heard, pick a beech or an elm. When you've chopped it down, trim it off but leave plenty of bough stubs so it can be carried."

Fallug racked his brain for a moment, then caught on. "Goin' to burst yore way in through the front door, Lord?"

Zwilt patted the weasel's shoulder. "Exactly, Captain. So make sure you get a tree that can do the job. Can I leave that to you . . . Captain?"

Proud of his new title, the weasel threw out his chest. "Aye, Lord, ye can trust me!"

Zwilt nodded. "I do. Now, once you have the tree—or should I say, the battering ram—carry it out of these woodlands but try not to be seen. Take it over the path and across the ditch. Travel out on the flatlands a couple of miles, stay low. Out there, that's where I'll be with the rest. Directly on a straight course to reach the big gate at Redwall. Understood?"

Fallug saluted. "Unnerstood, Lord. A tree shouldn't weigh too much with fivescore Ravagers t'carry it."

Another idea occurred to Zwilt. "Better still, once you've got the tree, wait until nightfall before you bring it to me. That way you won't be seen."

With the rain still providing cover, Zwilt set out from the woodland fringe along with his warriors. Outwardly, he was the same enigmatic, tall sable that his Ravagers feared and obeyed. However, inwardly, Zwilt the Shade was quivering with anticipation at the prize which lay ahead. Unlike Vilaya, he did not need slaves and subdued woodlanders to serve his needs—an army of two hundred was sufficient. Zwilt had always followed the trade of death, and plenty of slaughter was what he was looking forward to.

24

Diggs lay flat on his back, staring wide-eyed at the magnificent figure of the badgermaid who had him pinned down with a single paw. Never short of an answer or explanation, the tubby hare smiled winningly up at her.

"Er, beg pardon, marm, but could you repeat the question?"

She increased both the pressure of her footpaw and the volume of her voice. "I said, tell me where my friend is, if you want me to spare your life. Where is he? Speak!"

Being the resourceful creature he was, and fearing for his young life, Diggs took what he considered to be the appropriate course of action. He bit her footpaw sharply.

The huge badgermaid roared, instinctively raising her footpaw. Diggs shot off like a rocket, straight back into Althier. Heaving the broken front door upright, he blocked the entrance with it, yelling out in panic, "I say, steady on there, old gel. I'm not a bloomin' foebeast—I'm a friend. I'm searchin' for some young uns. Why d'you want to jolly well slay me, wot?"

A terrific thud from outside knocked the door flat—Diggs found himself laid out under it. Then the door was lifted and flung to one side. With awesome strength, the badgermaid reached in and lifted him bodily out. She sat Diggs down against the oak trunk.

This time she sounded calmer, a mite penitent even. "Er, if you're not a foebeast, then who are you?"

Diggs gingerly touched his snout where it had been hit by the fallen door. "Name's Meliton Gubthorpe Digglethwaite, Subaltern of the Long Patrol, late of Salamandastron. An' I think you've broken my flippin' hooter, beltin' that bloomin' door down like that. Couldn't ye have knocked?"

The badgermaid sat down beside him. "Salama . . . what?"

Diggs plucked a dockleaf and dabbed at his snout. "Salamandastron, but don't concern y'self with that right now. Y'can call me Diggs, everybeast does—an' pray, what do they call you, when you ain't knockin' doors down atop of 'em, wot?"

She wrapped the outsized sling around her shoulders. "I'm Ambrevina Rockflash of the Eastern Shores, but I get called Ambry a lot."

Diggs was about to shake paws with her, but he saw the girth of Ambry's paws and thought better of it. "Well, pleased to meet ye, I'm sure, Ambry. I say, you don't happen to have any vittles with you? I'm absoballylutely famished, ain't eaten in ages, y'know."

The badgermaid went back to the bushes where they had first encountered each other. She brought out a large satchel with shoulder straps. Opening it, she produced a few pears, some ryebread and a chunk of yellow cheese.

Forgetting his bruised snout, Diggs tucked in. "Good grief, a chap could lose a few teeth on this bread'n'cheese. Still, the pears are soft, wot. Now, who's this friend you seek, a family member, mayhaps?"

Ambry passed Diggs another pear. "Do you ever have strange dreams, Diggs?"

The tubby hare nodded. "Cheese'n'pickles for late supper in the jolly old mess, that always does it. Huh, dreams, flippin' nightmares, more like. But why d'you ask?"

Ambry's brown eyes took on a distant look. "Back on the far Eastern Shores, I was having the same dream for some seasons. It's a journey I want to take. I've got this yearning to be in a certain place, I must go there—yet I've never set eyes on it, except in dreams."

Diggs held up a paw. "Stop right there, Ambry. Don't tell me, let me guess. This place you're wearin' your paws out t'see, is it a big mountain on the shores of the sea?"

The badgermaid was thunderstruck. "How did you know?"

Diggs took a bite of the cheese, probing with a paw to see if he had loosened a tooth on it. "Remember that word y'couldn't get your tongue around? Salamandastron, that's the name of it, Mountain of the Mighty Badger Lords an' headquarters of the jolly old Long Patrol. Beg pardon, carry on with your story, wot."

Ambry continued. "After my father died, I could never get along with my brothers. So, early one morning I packed my satchel and set out to find the place of my dreams. That was at the start of spring season, and I had no real direction, just wandering willy-nilly. Well, I had been roaming for some time when one day, it was at the beginning of summer, I noticed I was being followed by a young riverdog."

Diggs cut in. "By riverdog, I take it y'mean otter?"

Ambry nodded her handsome striped head. "Aye. He had no kin to speak of, and not much to say for himself. Still, we got on well enough, sharing the cooking and foraging, watching out for one another. One night, we made camp by a river, slept under some rock ledges not far from it. I woke the next morning, and he wasn't there.

"So I thought he'd gone to fish for our breakfast—he was a good fisherbeast. I lay about a bit, then went to find him along the riverbank. He was nowhere to be seen. Then

I saw signs of a scuffle. I found the light javelin he had made for himself. I found the vermin pawtracks, too, and I knew he'd been taken. So I had to find him. The trouble is, I'm no great tracker, I lost the trail many times. How I stumbled on this place I'm still not sure. Diggs, do you think he's somewhere around here?"

The tubby hare tossed away a pear core. "I'm pretty sure he was, Ambry, but he ain't now, matter of fact. None of 'em are. What you were tellin' me was a familiar story. Y'see, there's a horde of vermin call themselves the Ravagers. They've been stealin' young uns left, right an' flippin' centre. I'm with some shrews, a Warrior mole an' a chum of mine called Buck. We trailed the vermin an' the others to this place—Althier, they call it. Trouble was, by the time we got here an' mounted a surprise attack, the blighters had all taken off. Don't know where they are, or the young uns. My lot went to track 'em, an' I got left behind, lost, like y'self, wot. I say, it'd be a super idea if we teamed up an' got on the trail, wot. We'd stand as much chance of findin' them as Buck, an' that confounded Jango Logathing, he's the Guosim Chief. Huh, Jango ain't too fussy on me, y'know."

Ambry stood up, helping Diggs to his paws. She smiled at the tubby hare, to whom she was taking a liking. "I think you're right, Diggs. We may be the very pair to find them. Let's scout around until we find some tracks. You take charge. Which way do we go?"

The irrepressible hare waggled his paw in the air, then bent his ears backward. "Er, that way!"

They pushed off into the undergrowth with Diggs leading the way, though he did not have a clue where they were going—small details like that did not concern him. He called out cheerily to his newfound friend, "I say, Ambry, what's this friend of yours called? Just so I can shout to him if I see a young otter in the distance."

Ambrevina Rockflash unwound her long, hefty sling. "Flandor, that's what he's called. Flandor!"

*

The unexpected rain at dawn spattered down on the young ones at the watermeadow island where they had been sleeping out in the open. It started the littlest babes crying. Midda rose grumpily. With the help of Tura and the Witherspyk twins, she herded the infants beneath the leafy canopy of a weeping willow, where it was relatively dry.

Tura glanced up at the bruised, heavy clouds. "Wonder how long this lot's goin' to last?"

The Guosim maid moved into the tree shelter. She was not in a good mood, never having liked rain. "Don't matter if'n it lasts all season, we've still got t'get some food for the little uns. That'll mean a proper soakin' an' no mistake!"

Trying to be helpful, Jinty snapped off a fern at its base. She held it out to Midda. "My granny Crumfiss always holds one of these over her head when it's raining, like an umbrella."

Grabbing the fern, Midda snapped it in two and flung it from her. "Oh, does she now? Well, I ain't no granny hog, traipsin' about holdin' a stupid fern over me head. I'm a Guosim, see!"

"Hahaharr! Ye look more like a wet mousey t'me."

Triggut Frap had been watching them. He stood a short distance away, with mousebabe Diggla tucked beneath his ragged cloak. The mad hog made an exaggerated bow. "Good mornin', friends, an' wot are yew doin' wid yerselves on this fine day?"

Tura glared at him. "We're tryin' t'keep dry—shelterin' from the rain, that's what we're doin'!"

Triggut patted little Diggla's head. "Did yew hear that, liddle mousey? Shelterin' from the rain, if y'please. Ole Triggut thought they'd be hard at work, buildin' my fine house."

Jinty had plucked another fern. She held it over her head. "Build a house in this downpour?"

Triggut underwent a sudden mood change. He snarled,

"Aye, that's wot yew lot are here t'do. Now, get to work. A drop o' rain won't kill yew!"

Midda pawed Jinty to one side. She faced Triggut belligerently. "Lissen, y'can go an' boil yore crazy head. We ain't workin' in this weather, an' ye can't make us. Go on, wot are ye goin' t'do about that?"

Triggut yanked the mousebabe up on his rope lead. "Heeheehee, not a lot, but I think I'll do a spot o' pike fishin'. This un should make good bait. Heehee!"

Diggla struggled helplessly as the crazed hog jiggled him up and down on the rope.

"Waaaah! Don't let 'im throw Diggla t'the pikers!"

Tura stepped quickly out into the rain. "Alright, you win. We'll start work right away. But we'll need tools—spades to dig, an' axes to chop down trees, an' sharp blades to trim 'em up with."

Triggut wiped his leaky blind eye, shaking his head until a few spikes rattled from it. "Axes, spades an' sharp blades? Hahahahaaarrr!" He bared his blackened tooth stubs viciously. "Triggut Frap might well be mad, but he ain't plain daft!"

Jiddle, who had not spoken until now, shrugged. "Well, sir, how d'ye expect us to build this house of yours without any tools to do the job?"

Triggut answered flatly, leaving no room for argument. "Yew kin dig with y'paws. Yew've got paws, haven't yew? An' there's plenty o' fallen trees on this island without havin' to chop any down. Anythin' else yew need, well, I'm sure yew can think of a way to get it done. After all, yews are the bright young uns with brains. Me, I'm only a pore crazybeast. Go on now, get to it, afore I decide t'go fishin' for big, wild, starvin' pikefish. They'll rip anythin' to bits, even a nice liddle mousey like this un. Hahaha ooo hahaarrr!"

Triggut lingered near the water's edge, stirring the surface and watching the pike rise. They had long, sinister greenish-brown bodies, with lime-hued spots; their ravenous jaws gaped wide in search of food. The sleek monsters gathered, waiting.

Mousebabe Diggla tugged on the rope to get as far away from the water as he could, pleading with his friends, " 'Urry h'up an' builda big 'ouse, Diggla not likes this beast. Whaw, 'e smell h'orful, pew stinky!"

Jinty saw Triggut beginning to tug on the rope, eyeing the water. She called sternly to Diggla, "You naughty liddle snip, don't talk about Mister Triggut like that. Mind your manners, please!"

It was an uneasy truce, and a very wet one, at that. On the tacit agreement that the smallest babes would be more hindrance than help, the main participants began work. With a pointed twig, Tura scratched out a rectangle on the ground. Inside of this shape, they commenced clearing grass, ferns, brush and other vegetation. They toiled away, with steam rising from their sodden coats.

After a while, Jinty complained, "Ooh, my back's killing me. I can't carry on like this—I'll have to lie down and rest."

Midda muttered gruffly to the young Witherspyk maid, "Just keep goin', mate. Try not to think of yore aches an' pains, but just imagine wot we'll do to that scabby nutbag when we get the chance. That'll help!"

Surprisingly, it did. Midda smiled inwardly, listening to the hogtwins gritting savagely in low voices as they tore out roots and stones from the muddy ground.

"I'll strangle Triggut Frap with me own paws when I get hold of the brute!"

"Aye, workin' us like slaves an' threatenin' to have our mousebabe eaten by pike. Oooh, just give me a short time an' a long stick. By thunder, I'll show him!"

Tura rubbed shoulders with the seething pair. "Not if'n I gets to him first, ye won't. I'll feed him, not Diggla, t'the pikefish, scrap by scrap!"

Midda chuckled. "Who, that dirty, filthy ole scum? Huh, the fish'll spit him back as soon as they get a mouthful of Triggut, believe me!"

Jinty could not suppress a giggle. "Teehee, maybe that'll be our way off this island. Feed the crazy hog to the pike an' poison 'em all!"

Jiddle did a fair impression of a pike which had tasted Triggut's flesh. "Yurk! Oh, 'elp me, I'm poisoned, goin' mad an' dyin' all at the same time. Hahaha!"

Tura joined him. "Yaarggh! An' t'think we imagined he was our friend. Gurrrgh!"

Triggut Frap's harsh voice cut into their merriment. "Sharrap an' keep workin'. I don't know wot yew lot 'ave got to laugh about. Now, work, or I go fishin'!"

Saturated, mud-spattered and sore-pawed, the young captives laboured on in silence. However, Triggut could not stop them thinking their vengeful thoughts.

BOOK FOUR

The Battle of Redwall Abbey

25

It was late evening before the rain ceased. Buckler, Axtel, Jango and the Guosim shrews emerged from Mossflower's dripping woodlands at the east wallgate of Redwall. Their progress had been somewhat hindered—Axtel's footpaw wound had slowed him down considerably.

Following the code of the Long Patrol, Buckler never left a wounded comrade behind. In fact, he had spent most of the march from Althier assisting the Warrior mole, whose injury had left him with a permanent limp. The worry uppermost in the young hare's mind was that Zwilt might reach the Abbey before he could. However, he felt reassured by the relative quiet and calm which surrounded Redwall.

Log a Log Jango was also relieved. "Well, at least we didn't arrive in the midst of an invasion, mate. Wonder wot happened t'the vermin?"

Buckler took a pace back, peering up at the walltop. "Here comes a sentry—we'll soon find out."

Jango shouted to the figure patrolling the battlements, "Ahoy, you, there, let us in, will ye? We're Guosim!"

It was Furm, Jango's wife, carrying a long cloak and hood propped up on an oven paddle. She peeped over the ramparts at the group below. "Is that you, Jango Bigboat?

Well, I ain't lettin' ye in unless you've brought our little uns back with ye!"

Buckler answered sharply, "Don't fool about, marm. Redwall could be under attack at any moment. Open this wallgate on the double!"

Furm pattered speedily down the wallsteps and drew back the bolts, admitting the group.

Buckler and Jango rushed past her without a word, up the steps to the walltops, with the rest following them. Buckler rapped out orders. "Spread out along the walkways. See if ye can catch sight of the Ravagers before night falls!"

Skipper and Oakheart were on the west threshold above the main door. The Otter Chieftain noted Buckler's anxiety as he hurried up.

"Buck, wot's happened? Did ye get the babes back?"

The young hare shook his head. "Not yet, Skip, but we know that Zwilt an' his vermin are marchin' on the Abbey. Thank the seasons we arrived back ahead of them!"

Shielding his brow with a paw, he peered out into the setting sun on the western plain. Blinking and rubbing his eyes, he repeated the action. "Look out there, Skip—follow my paw. What d'ye see?"

The otter gazed keenly at the crimsoning sky and darkening horizon before speaking. "There's somebeasts there, I think. A bit far off to tell."

Oakheart Witherspyk drew an elegant crystal monocle from his belt pouch, declaring vainly, "I don't really need this, as I have perfect eyesight. However, I sometimes use it for long-distance objects. Hmm, let me see now, out there, y'say?"

Buckler continued pointing. "Aye, sir, due west."

Squinting his right eyelid around the monocle, he gazed steadily westward. Returning the monocle to his pouch, the florid hedgehog nodded gravely. "I fear you are right, sirrah. Even though they are trying to conceal themselves, there appears to be quite a number of creatures out there. Whether they are vermin, alas, who can say from this distance?"

Buckler questioned Oakheart further. "About how many would you say there are?"

The Witherspyk patriarch shrugged eloquently. "Fourscore, mayhap five. I wouldn't venture to say accurately. But it seems only half the number who turned up outside our walls latterly."

Buckler nodded. "Thank you, Oakie. Oh, by the way, you haven't seen anything of Diggs yet, have you?"

Skipper shook his head. "No, mate. He ain't turned up here yet. Listen, you look tired'n'hungry, Buck. Go with Jango an' his Guosim. Get some vittles in ye an' take a breather. Go on, I'll double the guard on this wall an' keep an eye on the flatlands. If the vermin make a move, you'll be the first to know."

Buckler went gratefully, though as he approached the Abbey's main door, he was intercepted by Abbess Marjoram, who cautioned him, "Supper's being served in Great Hall at the moment. I've sent Jango and his shrews to take theirs down in Cavern Hole. I suggest you join them, Buck."

The young hare was puzzled. "Why's that, marm?"

Marjoram explained, "Because Dymphnia Witherspyk and your brother's wife, Clarinna, and many others who are concerned to hear news of the missing Dibbuns are supping in Great Hall. I know you don't want a lot of questions and tears, especially from Clarinna. But I have faith in you, Buck. You'll find them, if anybeast can. Go on now, off to Cavern Hole with you."

Foremole and Big Bartij joined the diners in Cavern Hole. Over barley broth and mushroom and gravy pasties supplemented by tankards of October Ale, they discussed the imminent danger.

Buckler finished his supper hastily; he already had a solution. "We'll need some of those long old cloaks they're usin' on the walltops. Once it's dark, I'll sneak out by the north wallgate. Maybe if I get close enough, I can learn what they're up to. Those old cloaks should give good cover—the dark'll help, too."

Jango rose, patting his stomach. "Right, mate, me'n my Guosim are with ye!"

"Hurr, an' oi, too, zurr. We'm bain't in no rush, so ee h'injured futtpaw won't cause ee no bother." Axtel Sturnclaw shoved the heavy war hammer into his broad belt. Everybeast saw from the look in his fierce eyes that it would be foolish to try stopping him.

Foremole Darbee nodded his admiration of Axtel. "Burhoo, oi'd foller a wurrier loike ee anywheres, zurr. You'm a gurt h'example to ee molers."

Big Bartij chuckled. "He surely is. Mind if'n an ole hog tags along, Mister Buck?"

Buckler bowed courteously. "Only too pleased, my friends. Sniffy, would you do the honour of being front scout?"

The Guosim Tracker licked gravy from his chin. "It'd be me pleasure, sir, an' I 'opes when we gets back 'ere that brekkist'll taste as good as supper did!"

Darkness had descended over the west flatlands as they forded the ditch on the far edge of the outside path. The party plunged waist deep into the channel, which was swirling with water from the recent rains. Crouching low, with drawn weapons, they scurried over the plain, travelling due west.

Slightly ahead of the group, Sniffy scouted the land, pointing out ground-nesting birds, so they would not step on them and startle them into flight.

Buckler spread his force out into a skirmishing line, staying in front of them but behind Sniffy. He tried to concentrate his mind on the task at paw, though his thoughts kept straying to Diggs. The tubby rascal, where had he gone? Was he in any trouble? Would he be safe?

The tick and cheeping sound of distant buntings brought him back to reality. He glanced about, judging the distance they had travelled from the Abbey. Again, his thoughts strayed, this time to the stolen babes. Pitiful little mites, how they must be missing their friends and families! Were they still alive? He banished the idea from his mind, plodding onward.

"Mister Buck, a word with ye, sir—you, too, Chief."

Log a Log Jango and Buckler both heeded what Sniffy had to say.

"I feels we're gettin' close to 'em now—best keep our 'eads down. Go bellyflat'd be better!"

The word was passed along. Everybeast began crawling along the flatlands, through the still-wet grass.

Zwilt had not let his vermin light any fires, lest the glare betray them. The Ravagers slept soundly on the open ground, damp as it was. Even their three sentries were slumbering, hunched in sitting positions.

Buckler and his group were only a very short distance from the foebeast. The young hare crouched with Sniffy and Jango, trying to attain a tally of the enemy's numbers. That was when everything went wrong.

Fallug and his party had not chopped down a tree for the battering ram. They found an old sessile oak, which had been blown askew by the winter storms. The ground was loose soil, so the fivescore vermin only had to rock it back and forth, felling it with a final mighty shove. The sessile oak had a fine straight trunk, which was soon trimmed into shape. Fallug left most of his contingent to carry the long timber.

Taking eight runners with him, the Weasel Captain set off at a loping trot to bring the good news to his superior. He speeded up as he spied the forms of creatures out on the flatlands, right where Zwilt had said they would be. Unable to contain himself, Fallug called out as they neared the encampment, "Lord Zwilt, I gotta fine oak trunk, just wot ye wanted, Sire!"

He tripped over a figure crawling along the ground. The

weasel stumbled and fell; his paw reached out and came into contact with a huge digging paw. He shouted, "Huh, wot the—you ain't no Ravager!" Axtel's hammer strike missed Fallug but wiped out a river rat who was running behind him. A vermin screamed as Jango's blade plunged into him. Then everything became chaos on the darkened plain.

Buckler took out a stoat with one strike of his rapier. Aware that they were vastly outnumbered, he yelled, "Gather t'me—retreat to the Abbey!"

Zwilt was upright now, whirling his broadsword. "On guard, Ravagers! Strangers in camp! Kill them!" Zwilt struck out, missing his target in the dark. His blade went sideways, smacking down on Jango's head and stunning him. Sniffy lugged his fallen chieftain clear, yelling, "Mister Buck, our Log a Log's down. 'Elp me!"

Buckler rushed through, his blade scything a deadly path as he helped Sniffy to support Jango. They stumbled away with the other Guosim rallying around them.

One or two of the bolder vermin tried to strike at their rear. They met Axtel Sturnclaw. The Warrior mole seemed in his element, pounding vermin with his war hammer, butting with his rocklike skull and lashing out with a mighty digging paw. He began roaring his war cry.

"Hooooaaaargggggh! Cumm to ee Deathmoler! Hoooo-aaarrrgh!"

Buckler grabbed Flib. "Here, help with yore pa. I've got to get Axtel out of here. Bartij, over here, mate!"

Bowling vermin aside, the big hedgehog found Buckler.

The young hare grabbed his paw. "We've got to get Axtel away afore he's mobbed an' brought down. Come on!"

Bartij booted a weasel aside. "I can hear him. Has he gone mad, Buck?"

Buckler dodged a spearpoint, running its owner through. "Aye, mate. I didn't know it 'til now, but Axtel is a berserker. He's got the Bloodwrath, like a Badger Lord. We've got to stop him fightin' an' make him retreat with us, or he'll battle to the end. There's too many for him!"

Axtel was scarred from ear to tail, bellowing and battling with no thought of defence or safety. Buckler confronted him, clearing a space with his long rapier. He pointed behind Axtel in the direction of Redwall, shouting in his face, "Over there—the enemy's over there!"

The Warrior mole halted for a brief moment, glaring at the young hare through blood-misted eyes. Buckler knew he was taking an awful risk, but he grabbed Axtel and spun him around, yelling urgently, "They're attackin' the Abbey. The Redwallers will be slain if they don't have a warrior to save 'em. Quick!"

Axtel lumbered off toward the Abbey, roaring his war cries and pounding the air with his war hammer. Buckler and Bartij defended his back as they retreated over the flatlands.

Guosim fighters turned every few paces, slinging stones as hard as they could at the Ravagers. Most shrews carried a sling and a pouch of round stream pebbles. Their throwing was so intense and accurate that the vermin slowed their pursuit, trying to stay out of range. Flib was particularly good. Even in the dark, her rapidly hurled missiles found targets amidst the vermin ranks.

Sniffy grabbed Flib, dragging her along with the retreating Guosim. "Back off, ye young rip, or you'll be left alone outside the Abbey. C'mon, you've done enough, Flib!"

Zwilt had not taken part in the fight. He reasoned that there was little sense in a commander being faced with a crazed, hammer-wielding mole or cut down by a chance slingstone.

Fallug ventured forward with the Ravagers, but only as an observer. He trotted back to make his report to Zwilt. "They fight fiercely for such a small force, Lord, but they're in retreat now, back to their Abbey. Hah, woodlanders can't stand against our Ravagers!"

Zwilt regarded his Weasel Captain with cold scorn. "Where are the beasts I left you in the woodlands with?"

Straining his gaze into the darkness, Fallug pointed. "Comin' right now, Sire. They're carryin' the tree trunk ye wanted. It's a big 'eavy one!"

The tall sable issued fresh orders. "Quickly, now, go to them, leave the battering ram. Tell them to drop it—I mightn't need it if they're fast enough."

Fallug was perplexed, but he saluted dutifully. "Right away, Lord, but how'll we get into Redwall without battering the door down?"

"Come!" Zwilt pulled him along, explaining as they ran. "We'll split into two more groups. Take yours off to the left—I'll take mine to the right. If we're fast enough, we can cross the ditch, get onto the path and cut them off. The ones inside the Abbey are bound to open the big gates to let their friends in. My Ravagers will be coming in from three sides—from the left, the right and the back. We'll slay all those outside and rush in before they close the gates, but only if we act fast!"

Skipper and Oakheart had the west walltop covered with guards, who were mainly composed of older Redwallers, some mothers, Foremole and his full molecrew. They could hear the sounds of a running skirmish.

The Otter Chieftain tightened his jaw grimly. "Buck'n'Jango's gang are in trouble. They must've been seen by the vermin."

Oakheart dabbed at his eyes with a spotted kerchief. "Indeed, 'twould seem so, but 'tis confounded dark out there—too dark to give them any help. Can't tell which is t'other, it's all a mass of shapes. Very confusin', sirrah. Let's just hope they get back safely, eh?"

Foremole Darbee furrowed his velvety brow. "Hurr, an' us'll 'ave to h'open ee gates so they'm can coom h'insoide. 'Ow'm uz a-goin' t'do that, zurr?"

Skipper thumped his rudder down fretfully. "Aye, mates, that's the problem. If'n we throw our gates open, we'll get all manner o' vermin chargin' in here!"

Granvy the Recorder emerged from the wallshadows. "Light a fire in the gateway."

Skipper frowned at the ancient hedgehog. "Wot are ye doin' up here, mate? Yore far too old for this sort o' thing. An' wot good will a fire in the gateway do?"

Granvy outlined his plan. "It's worth a try, for want of a better idea. We build a large fire not far from the main gate, surround either side of it with pike or javelin beasts, then at my signal, open the doors."

Oakheart scratched his headspikes. "It might just work! That way we can sort out the riffraff—let our friends enter and fight the vermin off. Keep the villains out, then as soon as Buck an' the others are in, we slam the gates!"

Skipper was already descending the wallsteps. "Get anythin' that'll burn. Come on, mates, pile it up but leave enough space for the gates to open an' shut. Oakie, get the word around. There ain't a moment t'lose!"

Sniffy shouted to the Guosim as they fought their retreat over the nighttime plain. "We'll be at the ditch soon. If'n ye falter, we're deadbeasts. Try an' jump o'er it in one bound!"

Buckler, who was having problems keeping Axtel from turning to face the Ravagers, called to Flib, "Get yore pa over here to me. You get across the ditch an' leave him to me. Wait, Axtel, come back here, mate!"

The Warrior mole had charged off down the path. He met Fallug and his vermin as they tried to cross the ditch lower down. Standing at the edge of the path, Axtel caught the first pair, two river rats. They splashed back into the ditch, their lives snuffed rudely out by the mighty war hammer. However, he could only hold one spot on his own, and they began crossing further down.

Buckler heaved Jango up onto his shoulders and was rewarded with a clout over his ears. The Shrew Chieftain had suddenly wakened and was struggling wildly.

"Git yore paws off'n me, I ain't no babe t'be carried. Where are we? Is young Flib alright?"

Buckler dropped him in a heap, relieved at his friend's recovery. "We're at the Abbey—get over that ditch. Come on, ye'll have t'jump, they're almost on us!"

Flib, who had leapt the ditch, saw vermin coming down the path on her left side. She turned and ran for the gate, with Ravagers hard on her paws.

Buckler, Jango and Bartij had gathered the remaining shrews in front of the main gate when Skipper's shouts came from the walltop. "Ahoy, mates, hold fast, there!"

Granvy's shrill call rang out. "Light the fire!"

There was a loud whoosh as lighted torches were tossed onto the hill of wood, moss, straw-filled mattresses and dead vegetation, all soaked in vegetable oil. The night lit up over the gates as red-gold shafts shone through the doorjambs, lintels and bottom space of the oaken west portal.

A shrew standing next to Buckler gave a sigh. He sagged forward, pinned to the door timbers by a vermin spear.

Jango bellowed into the night, "Hellgates an' bloodfire, we're sittin' targets if'n they don't open these gates! You in there, git the doors open, fer pity's sake!"

26

More by luck than judgement, Diggs and his badgermaid friend arrived on the banks of the stream previously visited by both the young ones and Zwilt's Ravagers. The tubby young hare had found ramsons growing in the treeshade. Uprooting a bunch, he munched on the pungent plants as he cast about.

"Hmm, been a bit of to-ing an' fro-ing around here. Tracks are still here'n'there, despite the bally rain, wot."

Ambrevina turned her face from Diggs's overpowering breath. "Whew, d'you have to chew those things?"

Diggs took another mouthful of the wild garlic plant. "Whoever 'twas prob'ly took t'the jolly old water. Bally rain swelled the current—no point tryin' t'go upstream. Er, beg y'pardon, would y'like some ramsons?"

The badgermaid never answered. Loosing her huge sling, she whipped out with it, neatly snagging an old willow trunk which had been washed into the stream.

Diggs nodded admiringly, watching her haul it into the bank. "Oh, I say, well done, that, gel, wot! Do I take it we're goin' for a bit of a sail downstream?"

Ambrevina snatched the malodorous ramsons from his grasp. Flinging them away, she wiped her paws on the damp grass. "Wrong, Diggs. I'm going downstream on this trunk. You aren't going anywhere until you've washed out your mouth and given me your solemn word that you'll stop eating that stinking weed. So, that's my offer, take it or leave it!"

The tubby hare looked aggrieved but wilted under her determined gaze. He thrust out his lower lip, chunnering. "Chap's got to eat, ain't he? Nothin' like some fresh ramsons, y'know. Good for the digestion, wot wot!"

Ambrevina scowled at him, holding up a massive clenched paw. "Aye, though it's been known to cause sudden unconsciousness if eaten within a certain distance of me!"

Diggs blinked owlishly, clambering aboard the willow trunk. "Hmmph! No need t'get so bloomin' cut up about it, miz. One'd think that what a chap scoffs, or chooses to scoff, is his own bally business, wot!"

With a mighty heave, she lifted the log end clear of the water, causing Diggs to cling on for balance. "Now, are you going to wash out your mouth, or shall I shake this log about a bit and do it for you?"

The going was easy, with a smooth, fast-flowing current. Ambrevina straddled the front of their makeshift craft, using a broken-off branch to paddle and steer. Diggs occupied the stern, giving her the benefit of his nautical experiences.

"Spent quite a while on a raft, y'know. I'm no beginner at this sort o' thing. Oh, yes, luff your tiller, sink your sail an' swoggle your midriff. Whoops! Go easy there—you nearly tipped me off into the flippin' drink!"

Ambrevina kept her face forward, smiling. "Then you should have learned to swoggle your midriff a bit better. Hmm, there's a sidestream coming up, I see."

The badgermaid steered their craft to the opening of the inlet. Diggs sniffed, unimpressed by his friend's observation.

"I'd stick t'the main current, if I were you, then we may get some flippin' where, wot!"

Ambrevina parted the reeds as she replied, "Well, I'm not you, and I want to look about here before we carry on. Hmm, look at this, my friend."

She pulled out a dripping reed net, squirming with stream life and tiny fishes. Diggs inspected it. "Very clever, I'm sure. Who d'you suppose it belongs to?"

Ambrevina put the net back into the water. "I've no idea, but my feelings tell me we may find out more by following this sidestream."

The irrepressible Diggs winked at her. "Indeed we may, marm, an' we might stumble over some vittles, too. D'you know, I'm blinkin' famished!"

The badgermaid blinked in mock astonishment. "You don't say. I'd never have believed it if you hadn't mentioned it. Now, get paddling and keep quiet!"

Whilst Ambrevina poled their craft through the reedy vegetation, Diggs dabbed at the water with a twig, muttering darkly, "Never have believed it? Huh, shows how much you know. Of course you wouldn't remember old Wuffy Cockleshaw, Sergeant in the Long Patrol, he was, an' a jolly nice chap, too. He missed dinner three times on the run! Faded away to a mere shadow. Ended up no more'n a pair of ears with bony paws stickin' out. Old Wuffy couldn't abide rhubarb crumble, y'know. Used to give me his when they served it in the mess. A friend right t'the end was Wuffy. It's prob'ly those extra bowls o' rhubarb crumble that've kept me goin', wot!"

The badgermaid was about to give her talkative companion a sharp prod with the paddling pole when an odd sound reached her. She turned to Diggs.

"Hush, did you hear that? There it goes again!"

It was a mad, high-pitched cackle. Diggs made what he deemed to be a shrewd observation. "Comin' from up ahead, wot. Well, at least somebeast sounds t'be jolly well enjoyin' themselves. Just listen t'that. Bloomin' chap must be sittin' on a feather!"

Ambrevina backed water, halting the willow trunk at

the end of the channel. The island stood out plainly in the midst of the watermeadow. She and Diggs stayed hidden, peering from the shelter of a bulrush patch at the strange scene.

Triggut Frap was holding Diggla the mousebabe by his tail, dangling him over the water. The young ones were pleading with him, with Tura calling out, "Alright, alright. Stop that an' we'll do as ye say!"

The scabrous hedgehog began striking the pond surface with his staff, shouting insanely, "Hahaarrrharr, I'll teach ye to obey me! Once a day, at eventide, that's when yew eat, when I tell yews to stop work. Is that clear?"

Jiddle replied anxiously, "We hear ye, sir. Please don't do that to Diggla. He's only a babe!"

Diggs recognised the young hedgehog. "I say, that's young wotsis spike. I know his family."

Ambrevina clapped a paw over Diggs's mouth. "Sshh, not a sound!"

Triggut watched as the pike began gathering. "Heeheehee! Maybe I'll let my pets have a nibble at him, just t'make sure yew pays 'eed t'my orders!"

The pike began leaping as he bobbed Diggla up and down above their predatory snouts.

The mousebabe was yelling, "Lemme go, ya bad naughty stinkybeast. Put Diggla onna shore!"

Ambrevina readied her sling, loading it with a sharp lump of shale. Diggs voiced his alarm.

"What are you up to? Don't sling that rock. If you hit that barmy-lookin' hog, he might fall into the drink an' take the little chap with him!"

Rising slowly, Ambrevina began whirling the huge sling. "Trust me, I know what I'm doing. It's not the hog I'm after."

Placing one paw straight out, she squinted along it, whirling the sling until it thrummed. Then she threw.

The largest of the pike was halfway out of the water in a leap at the mousebabe. With deadly accuracy, the shale chunk hit it like a thunderbolt, completely ripping off its lower jaw. The fish flopped back with a splash, thrashing and crimsoning the water. Tasting blood, the rest of the pike shoal hurled themselves upon the dying fish. The water boiled and bubbled red as the voracious pike cannibalised their leader, rending it to shreds.

Reloading her sling, Ambrevina jumped into the water. She started wading toward the island, whirling the weapon and roaring thunderously, "Put that young un back on dry land or my next one will smash your skull. Put him back . . . now!"

Midda raced forward, grabbing Diggla from Triggut's grasp.

Diggs seized the badgermaid's paddle, poling the willow trunk energetically toward the island. "What ho, little chaps. Fear not no flippin' more, we're here to save you. Pretty nifty, wot wot!"

The young creatures were laughing and crying at the same time, leaping about wildly and cheering. Triggut stood stock-still, shocked by the sudden turn of events.

Ambrevina strode swiftly ashore, batting away at the pike with her loaded sling. She smiled at the captives, towering over them. "Don't worry. You're all safe now!"

Triggut made an attempt to cut and run, but Tura tripped him. The freed captives threw themselves upon the mad hog, pounding at him with their paws. Diggs picked Diggla up, chucking him under the chin.

"Good day to you, little sir. Any eats around here? You know, vittles, scoff, tummy treats, food!"

The mousebabe spread his tiny paws wide. "Lotsa lotsa vikkles all over d'place onna trees!"

The tubby hare sniffed. "Huh, I'm the last chap t'say he doesn't mind livin' off the blinkin' land. The odd apple, ramsons, an' a few berries are better'n nothin', wot! But, dash it all, I'd give my left flippin' ear for some properly cooked vittles again. Er, I wonder what that rascally old scruffbag fed himself on?"

Midda, Tura and the rest were still dealing out rough justice to Triggut Frap when Diggs strolled across. He nodded to them. "I say, chaps, don't knock the blighter's block off just yet. I've a question or two for him, y'see, so pardon me, an' leave off kickin' the villain's bottom for a while, if you'd be so kind. Thank ye!"

No sooner had the young ones ceased beating Triggut than mousebabe Diggla hurled himself upon the miscreant, squeaking shrilly as he pummelled him. "Yarr, bad naughty villin, t'row Diggla to d'pikes would ya? Take dat'n'dat'n'dat'n'dat. . . ."

With one paw, Ambrevina lifted the still-kicking mousebabe off his victim. She was shaking with mirth. "Oh, you great fierce warrior, spare him. Allow Diggs to talk to the rascal."

Distastefully, the young hare hauled Triggut up by one dirt-crusted ear and commenced his interrogation. "Now, then, y'foul smellin' brute, where's your cookin' gear? Oven, cauldron an' whatnot, eh?"

The mad hog spat out a loose tooth, mumbling, "Don't need that sorta thing. I eats everythin' raw!"

Diggs nodded understandingly. "Hmm, I can see 'tis doin' you a power o' good. What sort of things d'you eat raw, wot?"

Spines fell from under Triggut's shabby cloak as he shrugged. "Anythin'—fruits, roots, fishes, frogs, worms."

Diggs held up a paw. "Stop right there. I've heard enough, thank you! Huh, fat chance of a decent feed here, chaps. What d'you suggest we do with this curmudgeon, wot?"

Midda had taken the knife from Triggut's belt. She brandished it. "Kill him—that's what he deserves after the way he made us suffer. Kill the scum, I say!"

Diggs wrested the knife from the shrewmaid. He smiled wanly at Ambrevina. "Typical Guosim, eh? Not very bloomin' maidenlike. I know one just like her, name o' Flib."

Midda grasped the hare's paw. "She's my sister. Is she still alive?"

Diggs nodded. "Aye, missy, an' just as jolly well feisty as you, if I ain't much mistaken." He pointed the knife at Triggut. "Well, then, me stinky old scout, looks like you ain't too popular this season."

The crazy hog grovelled at Diggs's footpaws, wiping at his leaky eye as he wailed, "Waaah haaah! Don't kill me, kind sire. I never meant to 'urt 'em. 'Twas all a joke. Spare me, I beg yew!"

Diggs, whose mind was still on food, posed a question. "Right, I'll see what I can do if you can tell me this. The mainstream yonder—does it run twixt some high rocky banks where a good old water vole has her home, wot?"

Triggut's bare head bobbed up and down furiously. "Aye, sir, I've seen 'er, though we ain't never talked together. Ole water vole, wears frilly aprons an' bonnets. Just follow the stream down a ways. Yew'll see 'er place. On the right bank it is, sir. Now, will yew spare me?"

The chubby hare grinned cheerfully. "Why, of course, my dear chap! I say, young uns, wait'll you taste old Mumzy's vittles, real first-class scoff!"

Tura gave Triggut a none-too-gentle shove. "An' what do we do about this rotten thing?"

Triggut began giggling insanely. "Heeheehee! Don't yew fret, missy. Jus' leave pore Triggut Frap 'ere. I won't never 'arm another creature. Yew kin take me word on that! Heeheehee!"

Ambrevina uncoiled the rope which the mad hog had used to restrain Diggla. She began binding Triggut until he could not move a paw. Tossing the rope over a branch growing midway up a nearby hornbeam, she hoisted him into the air. Securing the rope's end around a lower limb, she left him dangling.

Jiddle yanked on the rope, watching the unfortunate beast bounce up and down. The Witherspyk hog smirked. "There now, laugh that off!"

Having reinforced Triggut's old raft with the willow trunk, the entire party boarded it. They pushed off onto the watermeadow, in full view of their former tormentor, waving mocking farewells.

"G'bye now, don't forget an' finish that nice big house off someday after you're loose!"

"Aye, an' don't go paddlin'. There's still some pike left. They aren't too fussy about what they eat!"

"Haha, nothin' worse than hangin' about, is there?"

Diggs was in such high spirits at the prospect of good food that he composed a shanty right there and then.

"A-sailin' off on the watermeadows
fills us coves with glee,
think of all those hot baked scones,
an' dainty things to scoff at tea!

"Yo hoho let the wild winds blow,
as we roar hungrily,
Belay, cast off, set a course to scoff,
for my little mates an' me.

"A pasty'll do an' a tart or two,
served by a maiden fair,
but long as the tuck keeps comin' fast,
by golly, we don't care!

"Yo hoho let the wild winds blow,
an' fish swim in our wake,
Ahoy, set sail for nutbrown ale,
an' a chunk of ole fruitcake!"

Jinty fluttered her eyelashes at the tubby hare. "Did any-beast teach you to sing, Mister Diggs?"

Diggs puffed his chest out proudly. "No. Why d'you ask?"

She smiled innocently. "Oh, nothing, really, but it might've been nice if they had."

Diggs thought about this for a moment, then gave the hogmaid an icy glare. "See here, marm, I've seen creatures thrown overboard for remarks like that. It's bloomin' mutiny, y'know!"

Midda nodded as if in agreement. "I know what y'mean. My pa's a Guosim Log a Log, an' I've seen him do the same to awful singers."

Everybeast aboard laughed heartily. Life had suddenly become good for them after so long.

Apart from keeping a weather eye out for high-sided banks, there was little to do. The fast downstream current meant they did not have to row or punt. Diggs, having promoted himself to captain, steered with a paddle from the stern. The rest took their ease, allowing the cold water to run through their paws, watching speckled trout through the clear stream.

Ambrevina judged Midda to be the young ones' leader. The badgermaid spoke to her. "I suppose it was a lot worse than that island, being held underground in those caves?"

The Guosim maid turned her face to the sun, closing her eyes, enjoying its summer warmth. "It was all bad, being held prisoner—in the caves or on the island—until you and Diggs rescued us. I can't thank you enough, Ambry."

After a brief silence, the badgermaid continued, "When you were taken prisoner, did you chance to come across a young otter? His name was Flandor."

Midda did not speak. She opened her eyes, letting the tears run down her face. She nodded.

Ambrevina felt a sudden sadness, like a leaden weight pressing on her heart. "He's dead, isn't he?"

Midda wiped the back of a paw across her eyes. "Flandor was murdered by the Sable Quean. He was trying to defend us. I'll never forget him. He was a very brave otter. Did you know him, Ambry?"

Ambrevina stared at the passing fields and woodlands, radiant with bright summer. She sighed deeply. "I was searching for him. Flandor was my only friend."

Diggla, who had been using the huge badgermaid as a hill, clambered over her shoulders and stared into Ambrevina's deep-brown eyes as they softened with unshed tears. The mousebabe placed a tiny paw on each side of the big striped muzzle.

"Don't you not cry, now. Us all yore mates."

Ambrevina was a very large creature, so she took special care as she hugged Diggla. "Thank you. I couldn't wish for nicer friends."

A nautical shout from Diggs broke the spell. "Avast an' ahoy, ye lubbers, there's the place, a-hovin' up on our por . . . starb. . . ." He pointed. "On that side with the tall rocky bank! Now listen, crew, this good volemum is called Mumzy. So I want you all to call out to her, jolly loud. Right, one, two . . ."

"Muuuuummmmzzzeeeee!" the young ones bellowed at the top of their voices.

Suddenly, there she was, standing on the high banktop, waving a tablecloth. "Ah, sure, an' doesn't that sound like young tubgutt Diggs. So, now, I see ye've brought company for tea with Mumzy. Young uns an' babbies are always welcome at my ould fireside for a sup an' a bite. Corks an' cloudbursts, will ye look at the size of that fine badgermaid? Faith'n'mercy, don't eat me out of house an' home, miz, will ye?"

Ambrevina cheered up, waving back to the water vole. "I'll try not to, Mumzy, but I can't answer for Diggs!"

Inside her comfortable dwelling, Mumzy sat the young ones down. Rubbing her paws gleefully, the water vole addressed her guests. "Sure, an' it does me ould heart good t'see such a grand lot o' babbies. Just ye bide here whilst Mumzy fixes up such vittles that'll put a shine in yore eyes an' a sheen to yore fur. Miz Ambry, you, too, Diggs, I've got news to report, so lissen careful, now."

Diggs and the badgermaid paid attention to Mumzy as she began chopping nuts into honey for a pie filling.

"Buck an' Jango were here with their crew, but they got word that the Ravagin' vermin were marchin' on Redwall, aye, the full shebang o' the villains. So yore friends didn't wait about—they went off at the double. I think they were tryin' to beat that ould Zwilt an' his rascals to the Abbey. So, ye'd best be on yore way, if ye wish to help 'em out."

Diggs saluted her. "Naturally, marm, call of duty an' all that, y'know! Oh, corks, does that mean we'll miss a decent spot o' scoff, wot?"

Ambrevina reminded him sternly, "What would you rather do, sit here stuffing your face, or go to the assistance of your comrades?"

The tubby young hare shrugged. "I know what I'd like to jolly well do, but I also know what I've bloomin' well got to do. Forward the buffs, true blue an' never fail. On to Redwall, posthaste!"

Mumzy threw a few things into a small flour bag. "Here, now, take these t'help ye on yore way. 'Tis only an' ould chestnut'n'mushroom bake an' a bite of blackberry tart, but 'twill keep ye goin'!"

Diggs grabbed the bag. "Grateful t'ye, marm, but what about those little blighters?"

The motherly water vole smiled fondly at the young ones. "Ah, don't fret yore fur about the babbies. They'll come t'no harm with me. Sure, I'd keep 'em for good if'n I could. Just do what ye've got t'do, then send for 'em whenever 'tis safe t'do so. Go now, an' may kind breezes be ever at yore backs an' fortune smile kindly on ye!"

Ambrevina was immediately off, though Diggs lingered a moment as Mumzy told her young guests what she was planning for their lunch. "Right, me liddle darlin's, how'd ye fancy a honeynut tart with hot arrowroot sauce, some raspberry cordial an' a fine ould bowl of apple'n'pear crumble?"

Diggs gritted his teeth as he climbed to the bank top.

"Lucky blighters. Serves 'em right if they scoff too flippin' much an' end up with tummyache, wot!"

Ambrevina had to wait for Diggs to catch up. "Which way to Redwall?"

He took the lead. "Follow me, Ambry, old gel. By the left, though, you look jolly keen for a crack at the vermin, wot?"

Keeping hot on his footpaws, the badgermaid hastened him on. "I just want to catch up with those who murdered my friend Flandor. Can't you go any faster?"

The gluttonous hare fed on pawfuls of food from the flour bag as he panted forward. "You've prob'ly heard that hares are built for speed. Well, not this bloomin' chap, I can tell you. My pal Buck can deal with the vermin until we arrive—he's a Blademaster, y'know. There's him, Jango, Skipper, Axtel, Bartij an' absolute scads o' Guosim shrews an' useful Redwallers. They're sure t'keep a firm paw on things 'til we arrive. I say, d'you want any o' this tucker, Ambry? Jolly tasty stuff, wot!"

Ambrevina cast a jaundiced eye over the mixed mess of congealed chestnut and mushroom bake mingling with blackberry tart. "Aye, give it t'me, will you?"

Diggs reluctantly passed the bag to her. "Have a bite or two, but leave some for a famished young chap—share an' share alike, wot wot?"

She flicked the lot off into the undergrowth. "This is not the time for meals. We'll eat when we get to Redwall Abbey. Now, shake a paw, will you!"

Diggs increased his pace, knowing it would be unwise to argue with a badger of his companion's size. However, that did not stop him chunnering to himself. "Huh, shameful waste, that's what 'tis. Chuckin' good scoff away to the blinkin' insects. By the left, if my old mess sergeant caught y'doin' that, marm, you'd be on a real fizzer, quarter season in the bloomin' guardhouse. Hah, an' you'd richly deserve it!"

They passed on, leaving the half-finished bag of food

hanging from a bramble in the undergrowth. A scrawny paw reached out and retrieved it.

Gliv clutched the bag to her, crawling back through the bushes to where Vilaya lay resting.

The sable's glittering eyes watched the stoat keenly. "Who was that passing by? What did you steal from them?"

Gliv sat down just out of reach. She began eating from the bag. "It was just one of those rabbets an' a big stripedog. From wot they was sayin', I think they're bound for that Abbey. Looks like Zwilt will have a fight on his paws if'n 'e has t'face the stripedog. She was big—looked like a fighter t'me."

The injured Sable Quean was inching closer. "And they gave you those vittles?"

Gliv stuffed a pawful of Mumzy's food down, licking her blackberry-stained mouth. "'Course they never gave me it. The stripedog slung it away, said they didn't 'ave time fer meals."

Holding her wounded side, Vilaya rolled rapidly over, seizing the bag from Gliv. Casting aside any pretence to daintiness, she wolfed the remainder down. "Go and find me some water. I'm thirsty."

The stoat sneered. "Feelin' better, are we? Ye'll soon be up an' about. I thought you was gonna die for a while back there."

Vilaya stood up, leaning against a sycamore. "No time for dying. I've got a score to settle!"

Gliv grinned coldly. "Huh, so have we both!"

27

Seeing his friends with their backs to the west wallgate, illuminated by the shafts of firelight, Skipper roared out the order. "Open the gates! Everybeast to the entrance! Quick!"

The main entrance was pulled open in a trice. Ducking down, Buckler, Bartij, Jango and the Guosim crew retreated hurriedly inside. The defenders hurled a salvo of javelins, rocks and slingstones at the advancing Ravagers. Temporarily blinded by the sudden burst of light from the bonfire in the open gateway, the vermin were taken by surprise. They scattered both ways along the path, seeking to avoid the onslaught of missiles, some slipping backward into the ditch.

Zwilt lashed about him with the flat of his broadsword, yelling hoarsely, "Forward! Forward! Keep going, can't you see the gates are open? Forward! Chaaaaarge!"

Something struck his blade like a thunderbolt. It flew out of his grasp, over the ditch, onto the flatland. Zwilt the Shade was strong—he was also fast and agile. However, the tall sable was not about to face the hefty hammer-wielding mole who had disarmed him so savagely.

Knowing instantly that the attempt had failed, Zwilt leapt the ditch in a single bound, calling out, "Retreat! Back, Ravagers, back! Retreat!"

Blinded by the firelight and assailed by slingstones from the gateway and walltops, the vermin were only too ready to obey their commander. They fled westward to where the sessile oak trunk lay abandoned outside their camp.

Now that Zwilt had regained his blade, the need for secrecy and concealment was over. He squatted down by the fire his vermin were building. The weasel Fallug, whom he had promoted to captain, knelt alongside him, nursing a swollen jaw—a stone had hit him.

"Wot next, Lord? Do we still use the batterin' ram?"

The tall sable blinked as he stared at the fire. "As soon as it's ready. We'll charge those gates and smash them, in daylight if we have to. There'll be no mistake a second time, I swear it!"

Abbess Marjoram came to the main outer gate. Skirting the fire, she sought out the defenders, congratulating them. "Thank you, friends. 'Twas a brave thing you did here."

Granvy wiped his face with a clump of dewy grass. "Good idea that fire, eh, Jango?"

The Guosim Log a Log crouched down by a gatepost. "A masterstroke, I'll grant ye. Though if'n ye hadn't got the gates open when ye did, we'd have been slaughtered out there. Sniffy, how many did we lose?"

The Tracker wiped smoke from his bleary gaze. "Two slain, four wounded, Chief. I was goin' to check south down the path, but that berserk mole's still out there. Nothin'll stop that un—Axtel will smash anybeast wot stands in his path!"

Buckler put up his long rapier. "That's how Bloodwrath works, mate. We'll just have to hope he comes to his senses. Marm, stop, where are ye goin'?"

The Abbess had walked out onto the path. "Stay where you are, everybeast. I'll deal with this."

Jango started after her, but Sister Fumbril drew him back. "Marjoram knows what she's about, sir, trust me!"

Skipper nodded. "Do as the Sister says, matey, an' trust our Mother Abbess. That goes for all of ye. Now, how about dampin' this blaze down. We could be sittin' targets stannin' in the firelight!"

The blaze was subdued with a bit of effort. Some of the embers were pushed into the open ditch, some scattered to the inside wall, the rest were damped down with water from the Abbey pond. Dawn was streaking the sky when Abbess Marjoram passed through the gateway, ordering Foremole Darbee and Cellarmole Gurjee to close and lock the doors. Axtel was limping alongside her. She was giving him advice on his wounded footpaw.

"I'm sure that Sister Fumbril can treat your injury. She's very skilful at such things. I guarantee you'll be walking normally by the season's end, running, too. Oh, Bartij, would you take Axtel's hammer? The poor beast shouldn't have to limp about carrying that great heavy thing. It's not doing him a bit of good."

Buckler watched in amazement as Axtel Sturnclaw, the berserk warrior, meekly surrendered his weapon to Bartij.

"Hurr aye, mum, ee war'ammer do gets gurtly weightful at toimes. Hoo urr, but et bee's a wunnerful vermint stopper, even tho' oi says et moiself, mum!"

Buckler shook his head. "Well, I've seen everything now!"

Bartij winked. "Yore at Redwall Abbey now, young mate—you h'ain't seen nothin' yet!"

Friar Soogum bustled up with two kitchen helpers in tow. "Er, Abbess, marm, where do I serve brekkist today?"

Marjoram was never at a loss when it came to prompt decisions, unlike the hesitant Friar. She rattled off instructions, including everybeast. "Serve it up on the west ramparts to those who'll be keeping an eye on our foes—Mister Buckler, Skipper, Bartij, Log a Log Jango and his Guosim. Redwallers and Dibbuns will eat in Great Hall. I think it would be wise for those not engaged in defence of the

Abbey to stay off the walltops until any threat of attack has gone. Sister Fumbril, Axtel and myself will dine in the Infirmary. Foremole, would you and your molecrew dine in the gatehouse with Granvy, just in case you're needed?"

Darbee tugged his snout respectfully. "Ut'd be moi pleasure, mum!"

Marjoram patted Soogum's paw fondly. "That's your problem solved, old friend. Now, is there anything else, please?"

Buckler had a request. "Marm, could you have the good Friar serve an extra portion on the walltop? Make it a big helping."

The Abbess nodded. "I'm sure our Friar could arrange that, but what do you require another breakfast for?"

One of the young hare's ears drooped thoughtfully. "Just an idea, really. It's been my experience that whenever fine vittles are served, Diggs is usually somewhere about. Oh, I'm not worried about the tubby glutton, wherever he is. But I'd be easier in my mind if he were here where I could keep an eye on him."

Marjoram smiled. "Oh, I think we can manage that, Buck."

Buckler made a quick, elegant bow. "Thankee, marm. An' I apologise for not bringin' the little uns safe back to Redwall. As soon as this Ravager matter's settled, I vow I won't rest 'til the babes are all inside these walls an' peace is restored."

The Abbess nodded. "I'm sure you speak truly, my friend."

Out on the flatlands, work was progressing on the battering ram. Zwilt had supervised his vermin in the making of the weapon. One end of the sessile oak trunk had been hacked into a blunt point and burned several times in the fire. This had the effect of sharpening and hardening the ramming end. Fallug and his crew had returned to the woodlands. Now they were hauling in heaps of thick green-leafed boughs. Zwilt outlined their use to his captain.

"I want a frame built, a canopy to go over the ram. The carriers underneath it will be protected from anything those Redwallers heap down upon them. Now, we'll have two shifts of ram carriers, one relieving the other to keep the attack going full pelt. I want archers and sling throwers constantly on the go. That'll keep the woodlanders' heads down below the walltops."

Fallug grinned crookedly. "Aye, Lord, an' 'twill 'elp our ram beasts from bein' attacked!"

The weasel was pleasantly surprised when Zwilt patted his shoulder heartily. Something resembling a smile stole across the inscrutable sable's features.

"You're a beast I can trust, Fallug. Tell me, how do you like being a captain, eh?"

Fallug puffed out his narrow chest. "I'm enjoyin' it, Sire. Ye can rely on me—I'll do me best for ye, Lord, on me word, I will!"

Zwilt toyed with the medal about his neck. "Good. I knew I could, so I want you to be in charge of all my Ravagers from now on."

Fallug looked fit to burst as he puffed in more air. "Me, Lord?"

Zwilt nodded. "You'll need a bit of help, so why not pick out a few trusty comrades and make them captains?"

A worried look furrowed the weasel's brow, but Zwilt reassured him, "Of course, you won't need to be a captain any longer. I'll promote you to chief, or general. Which title d'you think suits you best?"

Fallug replied without hesitation, "Chief, Sire! Sounds good, don't it? Fallug, Chief of all the Ravagers. Aye, chief suits me fine, Lord!"

Zwilt watched the ram point shaping up. "Right, Chief Fallug, these are your orders. You'll be in charge of this whole attack—archers, slingers, ram carriers, everything!"

The new chief looked slightly perplexed. "But where'll you be, Sire? Wot'll you be doin'?"

Zwilt stared at the distant Abbey walls. "I'll be doing what I do best—being Zwilt the Shade. You just carry on obeying orders. Don't look for me. I have a plan of my own. If it goes the right way, I may be inside Redwall whilst you're still knocking on the doors. Leave me now. I'll put the word about that you are in command here."

Back on the ramparts, Bartij, who had no experience of warfare, shielded his eyes against the sun, peering at the distant vermin encampment. "There's smoke a-risin'. See, they've lit a fire. Looks like they're burnin' one end of the big log. Why d'ye suppose they'd do a thing like that, eh?"

Jango dipped a crust of toasted nutbread into his hot mint tea and sucked it with relish. "I'd say they're makin' a batterin' ram, eh, Buck?"

Buckler put aside a bowl of oatmeal. "Yore right, mate. Skipper, fetch Foremole, please. I need to speak with him."

Foremole Darbee did not like high walltops. He sat down with his back to the battlements, concentrating his gaze on the walkway. "Hurr, 'ow can oi 'elp ee, zurr?"

Buckler sat down next to him. "This stone-throwin' catapult thing your crew are making in the cellars, can we get it up here?"

Darbee shook his velvety head glumly. " 'Tis all in bits, zurr. Oi knows nuthin' abowt cattypults, but if'n us gets it up yurr, 'twill need t'be resembled."

Skipper quaffed off what was left of his hotroot soup. "Granvy's the beast who'd know about assemblin' it. Come on, we'll lend a paw to carry it up here."

It turned out to be a far harder task than they had expected. Some of the timber donated by Cellarmole Gurjee was huge and weighty. Long-seasoned lengths of elm, beech and oak, devoid of bark or branch, were hauled laboriously up to the walltop.

Old Granvy the Recorder inspected the material doubtfully. "Hmm, wish I'd bothered to look at this lot earlier. I'm afraid most of it is far too ancient and dried out t'be of any use. It'd snap under pressure."

Bartij flicked a woodlouse off a chunk of beech. "Can't we make any use of it, Granvy?"

The old hog sighed wistfully. "I wish I knew. I dug out an ancient parchment which had the plans for a ballista—that's what they're called, you see. But I've never seen a real one, and I'm not sure how it works. What we need is a creature who knows all about such weapons."

Oakheart Witherspyk mounted the battlements, dramatically gesturing toward the vermin foe. "Hearken, comrades, our present dilemma is how to counter a battering-ram attack. What to do, eh? If I may be so bold as to make a suggestion, what about fire?"

Skipper assisted the portly hog down onto the walkway. "I knows wot yore thinkin' of, mate, hurlin' fire down on it, to set the ram ablaze. Well, it won't work, Oakie. Once that batterin' ram was on fire, they'd lean it up agin' our gateway. Then they'd just sit back an' watch the whole thing burn down. No, sir, we'll have to come up with somethin' better'n that!"

Foremole Darbee had a typically molelike solution. "Zurrs, 'ow abowt soil'n'urth. Hurr hurr, they'm villyuns wuddent git far a-tryen to shuv ee rammerer through a gurt 'eap o' soil'n'urth!"

Buckler's ears stood up in admiration of the mole's scheme. "Now, that's what I call a great plan! We'll tip loads of everything over the wall, right here over the main gate. Aye, an' we'll shore it up from the inside, too. Hah, it'd take an army of vermin a couple o' seasons to ram their way through that lot!"

Skipper slammed his rudder down on the walkway. "Ahoy, mates, we'll have t'get started real sharpish, afore the vermin git their ram up an' runnin'!"

Redwall Abbey immediately became a hive of activity. Foremole and his trusty crew began digging up the lawn and some flower beds. Oakheart got an earth-moving chain in motion. Improvised stretchers were loaded up with soil, gravel, clay, stones and turf. The biggest and sturdiest creatures carried these to the walltop. Meanwhile, Flib and Trajidia Witherspyk rigged a rope and pulley up on the walkway. A line of the young, helped by some old ones, bore an assortment of vessels. Bowls, pails, ewers, cauldrons, anything that could be filled with soil and debris, was passed from paw to paw. Sniffy hooked them to the pulley, whilst Flib and Trajidia hauled away energetically. Jango got a work song going, something of a shanty. Everybeast soon caught onto the chorus, roaring it out lustily, even the Dibbuns. Anybeast who was not sure of the verse just kept chanting the "haul up" bits. It all worked rather well.

"Haul up! Haul up!
Haul up, d'ye hear me call,
the strong of heart must play their part,
for the sake of ole Redwall . . . haul up!

"Dig up that earth for all yore worth,
fill all those pails again,
an' just let me catch one of ye,
complainin' of a pain!

"Haul up! Haul up!
Haul up, d'ye hear me call,
the strong of heart must play their part,
for the sake of ole Redwall . . . haul up!

"Come on now, mateys, bend those backs,
there's loads o' work to do,
if you don't toil an' tote that soil,
you'll let down all this crew!

"Haul up! Haul up!
Haul up, d'ye hear me call,
the strong of heart must play their part,
for the sake of ole Redwall . . . haul up!

"So haul 'em up an' lower 'em down,
no time to moan or weep,
'til every mother's whelp o' ye,
can roar out in yore sleep . . . haul up!"

Oakheart laboured alongside Buckler, heaving rubble over the wall. Together they tipped the contents of an old wheelbarrow onto the growing heap in the gateway below.

The florid hedgehog spat on his paws, reaching for a heaped cauldron. "Y'know, the higher that hill gets, the more I worry!"

Buckler emptied a pail over the edge. "What's worryin' you, Oakie?"

His friend pointed at the growing heap. "If it gets much higher, the vermin will be able to climb up here on it. Have y'thought of that?"

The Salamandastron Blademaster smiled wolfishly. "Aye, the thought had crossed my mind. I hope Zwilt the Shade is the first to try it. I wager he'll be dying to meet me!"

28

At the same time the vermin party were cutting boughs in the woodland, two beasts were watching them from a hiding place nearby. It was Vilaya and Gliv. The Sable Quean's wound was healing nicely. It had scabbed over and was not causing her any great discomfort. She was being disguised by the female stoat, whilst keeping an eye on the work party.

"Here, tear a strip off my cloak, a bloodstained piece. Now tie it around my brow, Gliv, good. How does that look?"

The stoat knotted the material beneath Vilaya's right ear. "Take off yore cloak. I'll smear some soil on yore face." Gliv did this, leaning in close to check the effect. "Aye, ye look the part now. Anybeast'd take ye for an ole Ravager who's taken a scratch or two. Come on, let's gather some leafy branches an' join 'em."

The Sable Quean drew her helper closer, murmuring to her, "No, you stay here. I'll go with them—it's better that I go alone."

Gliv glanced uneasily at her. "But what about me? What am I supposed to do?"

Vilaya was smiling now. The stoat had seen that smile before. She tried to pull away, but Vilaya held her tight.

"You've been a lot of help to me, Gliv, but I don't need you anymore. Be still, now!"

Gliv felt the sudden sting at her throat—she gazed in frozen horror at her killer. Vilaya was still smiling as she clamped a paw over her victim's mouth.

"I took back my little dagger while you were tying that rag about my head. Go to sleep now. Your work is done."

Gliv died with her eyes wide open, still staring at the smiling face of the one whose life she had saved.

Fallug snarled at the branch carriers as they lugged their burdens back into the vermin camp. "You lot took yore time. C'mon, move yerselves—that stuff's needed. Shift yore lazy paws along, c'mon!"

A river rat muttered to Vilaya, "Huh, lissen to ole swollen 'ead throwin 'is weight about."

Vilaya replied in a sullen whisper, "We should only be takin' orders from Zwilt. Where is he?"

The rat shrugged. "I dunno, but he's left Fallug in charge. We've got t'call 'im Chief now. Weasels, eh, they're all the same, bossy an' thick'eaded, ain't that right, mate?"

Vilaya spat on the ground. "Right! But I wonder where Zwilt's got to. Ain't 'e goin' to attack the Abbey with us?"

A stoat who had overheard the pair nodded northward over the flatlands. "I think ole Zwilt's got 'is own plan. I saw 'im goin' off over that way with four others. They was carryin' ropes an' some 'ooks."

Before he could elaborate, Fallug cuffed his ear roughly. "Yore not here to chat. Now, git those branches tied t'that frame an' fix it over the batterin' ram."

He turned irately to Grakk, a weasel he had promoted to captain. "Wot is it now, eh?"

Grakk saluted with his spear. "Chief, that lot in the Abbey are tippin' stuff over the wall in front o' the gate, I think!"

Fallug stared at him pityingly. "Who told you y'could

think, mudbrains? Leave the thinkin' t'me or Lord Zwilt. Yore here t'carry out orders, that's all!"

Vilaya moved away from the group until she was behind a small rise. She crouched there until the moment was right. With everybeast facing the Abbey or preparing the ram, she stole quietly off into the flatlands, heading north until she crossed Zwilt's trail. He and his escort were travelling in an arc. Vilaya knew they would cross the path into the woodlands, then go south to Redwall Abbey. After all, what else was Zwilt the Shade interested in?

Diggs had lost his way, but the tubby hare was not to be put off. Peering intently at the woodland floor, he shuffled slowly onward, chunnering relentlessly. "Ahah, wait now, I think we're on the right blinkin' track. Never lost for long if you're a bally Long Patrol chappie, wot!"

Ambrevina idly twirled her long sling. The huge badger maid leaned against a sycamore, observing ironically, "Never lost for long, eh? Then it's just as well I've got you for a guide, friend."

Without looking up, Diggs chunnered on. "Oh, yes, did a half season y'know. Learnin' trackin', sign readin' an' whatnot from old Corporal Broomscuttle. Jolly good old type Broomie was, taught me a heap of useful stuff. I was his bloomin' star pupil, y'know."

His badger companion was trying hard not to smile. "Were you, really? That's good to know!"

Studying the ground intently, Diggs chuckled. "Haw haw, you can bet your grandma's marchin' boots it is. See this small, faint track here? That's a sort o' wotsit beetle. Forgotten the blighter's name, but the thing is this, it always travels south. Hah, an' by my reckonin' that's where the Abbey is. Er, or was it west? No bother, Tracker Diggs'll soon find it, wot!"

The garrulous hare got no further, owing to the fact that Ambrevina lifted him up bodily. Perching him on her shoulder, she pointed to her right. Above the trees—directly in the opposite direction Diggs had been taking—Redwall's Belltower stood out like a pikestaff. She enquired calmly, "What d'you suppose that is, Tracker Diggs?"

For the first time in quite a while, Diggs fell silent. He twiddled his ears this way and that, sniffed the air and tested the breeze with a damp paw.

Then he spoke. "Well, of course, it's jolly old Redwall. Top marks, marm. You passed my little test. I was wondering when y'd finally notice the confounded thing!"

Ambrevina dumped him down unceremoniously. "That must be the back of the Abbey—east wall, do you think?"

Diggs brushed himself off without turning a hair. "Oh, undoubtedly. Well, forward the buffs an' pip pip. Here's to some of the finest scoff that ever passed a chap's lips, wot. Now, I wonder if it's lunchtime, or midmornin' snack break. I say, there, wait for me, Ambry, old gel!"

Zwilt the Shade emerged from some bushes with the four Ravagers at his back. They watched the hare and the badger hurrying off toward the Abbey. Though Zwilt felt like heaving a sigh of relief, he showed no emotion to his escort. The obvious size and power of Ambrevina made him feel quite puny in comparison. She presented a problem he had not anticipated. However, Zwilt was not about to allow anything to get in the way of his Abbey conquest, not even a massive badger.

Following the pair at a safe distance, the tall sable moved amongst the trees like a noon shadow. The four Ravagers followed in his wake, fearful of putting a single paw wrong, each trying to breathe noiselessly.

Further intrigue was added to the moment by Vilaya, who had caught up with Zwilt. The Sable Quean crouched behind a guelder bush. She spied on Zwilt as he, in turn, watched Ambrevina and Diggs. Then they all moved off toward the east Abbey wall.

Diggs went straight to the small wicker gate and tried it several times. "Huh, might've guessed the flippin' thing'd be locked. Let's see if we can't raise some sentry types, wot!" Standing back a few paces, he yelled up at the walltop, "I say, anybeast at home?"

The big badgermaid peered at the battlements. "Apparently not. Shall I give it a try?"

Without waiting for Diggs's permission, she cupped paws about her mouth and bellowed thunderously, "Come on, stir your stumps, we're friends!"

There was a sudden patter of paws, followed by some scrabbling as somebeast climbed up the battlements.

Young Rambuculus Witherspyk poked his head over the top. Not noticing Diggs, the first thing he saw was Ambrevina. The young hog was obviously overwhelmed by the sight of such a massive beast, never having seen a badger before.

"Whoa! Corks'n'crivvens, who are you?"

Diggs stepped into view, making reply. "Who d'ye think she is, a ferret or a bally stoat? Now get down here an' open the gate, you little pot herb!"

Zwilt had heard all that went on. He and the Ravagers were lying amidst nearby ferns. Deeming it a chance he could ill afford to miss, Zwilt drew his broadsword, murmuring to his escort, "Don't make a sound. No shouting out or charging. But as soon as that little door opens, follow me. If we're swift and silent, they'll be ambushed. Two of you take the hare and the young hog. I'll run the badger through before she has a chance to fight. You two grab her paws, and I'll stab her from behind. . . . Ready!"

Diggs was irked by Rambuculus's insolence. The young hog could be heard calling out as he descended the east wallsteps, "How'm I supposed t'know who you are, eh? We're fightin' a war in here, y'know. There's vermin all over the flatlands, comin' with a batterin' ram, an' my pa sends me off patrollin' the bloomin' back wall. It's an insult, that's what it is! Then you two turn up shoutin' an' tellin' me that you might be a ferret an' a stoat. Now this flippin' lock's stickin'!"

Diggs yelled at the door, "Well, unstick the bally thing an' let us in or I'll kick your flamin' tail!"

Rambuculus tugged the lock loose. Opening the door, he poked his head around it. "Hah, y'can't kick a hedgehog's tail. Didn't anybeast ever tell ye? You'll get a pawful o' spikes, so there!"

Ambrevina entered, with Diggs right on her heels. To show his displeasure, the tubby hare slammed the door shut quickly, waggling his ears at Rambuculus as he shoved the bolt back into place.

"Listen t'me, laddie buck. One more word from you an' I'll whack you over the cheeky snout with a loaded sling. Here, what was that blinkin' noise?"

The "blinkin' noise" was Zwilt's swordpoint hitting the door with a thud. Rambuculus glared accusingly at Diggs. "That was you slammin' the door. Nearly took it off its flippin' hinges. No need for that sort o' thing!"

Ambrevina ignored the squabbling pair. Hearing the distant noise of conflict, she set off over the back lawns. "Sounds like there's trouble at the front wall—come on!"

Zwilt stood stock-still, his swordpoint still stuck in the door timbers. He waited until the pawsteps inside receded, then began levering his weapon free.

One of the Ravagers, a lean river rat, commented, "Another wink of an eye an' ye'd have got 'em, Lord. 'Twas a close thing." His voice trailed into silence as Zwilt fixed him with a basilisk stare.

"Shut up and get the ropes and grapnels fixed. We'll go in the way I planned."

Vilaya watched from the cover of an elm trunk, with new schemes hatching within her conniving mind. She craved revenge, wanting to slay Zwilt . . . and yet. He had a horde of Ravagers attacking the Abbey from the front, and he himself was forming a secret entrance from the rear. It was a plot worthy of the tall sable, of any sable. What if he conquered Redwall? Would it not be better to kill him then?

This would give her back command of the Ravagers, plus make her the new ruler of this magnificent Abbey.

Two pairs of grapnel irons, thrown by the vermin, clanked onto the battlements. Tossing his cloak to one of the guards, Zwilt grabbed a rope in either paw. Using his footpaws against the joints in the sandstone, he hauled himself energetically up to the walltop. He was followed by his escort of four, who wasted no time scaling the ropes.

Vilaya watched them disappear from view, pulling the ropes up after them. Any opportunity of entering Redwall from its east side was gone. The Sable Quean skulked off through the woodland, intent on assessing the attack on the west wall. No doubt it would present further chances of attaining her goal.

Meanwhile the battle at the front had begun. Fallug sent almost a hundred Ravagers forward with the battering ram and met with his first hurdle: the ditch. Beneath its cover of leafy-boughed framework, the front of the war machine dipped sharply as the front carriers, shoved on by those behind them, tumbled into the ditch. Yells of scorn rang out from the walltops, accompanied by many missiles.

Buckler shouted out a command. "Don't waste weapons on that thing—they're sheltered under the cover. Get down, everybeast, they're shooting back!"

Arrows, slingstones and javelins rained up at the defenders from the vermins' ground force. In the midst of all this, Diggs arrived with Ambrevina at his side. He threw a crouching salute to his comrade.

"Subaltern Diggs an' jolly large friend reportin' for duty, sah. I say, are we late for midmornin' snack, or early for a bite o' lunch, wot?"

Buckler grinned at his irrepressible friend. "Sorry, bucko, but we've got a war on our paws, or didn't you notice? Vittles will have to wait until later." He thrust a paw of welcome at the huge badgermaid. "I'm Buckler Kordyne. Sorry I haven't had the pleasure of meetin' ye, marm!"

He grimaced as the badger returned his paw shake.

"I'm Ambrevina Rockflash from the Eastern Shores. I met up with Diggs back at Althier."

A javelin clattered on the walkway beside Diggs. Seizing it, he leapt up and hurled it back. His aim was greeted with a scream from a Ravager. Diggs ducked back down again.

"Oops, sorry. Haven't made my flippin' report yet. We found the young uns, all safe an' unhurt. At the moment, they're with old wotsername, the waterthingy, Mumzy. You'll be pleased t'know they're all fit an' fat as bumblebees. Or at least they jolly well will be when she's finished feedin' their little faces!"

Buckler clapped his friend's back soundly. "That's great news, Diggs—we couldn't have asked for better. Ahoy, down there, Trajidia, run an' give the word to the ladies, your mum, Jango's wife, Furm, an' Clarinna. Tell them the babes are safe an' well!"

Diggs interrupted. "I say, Traji, ole gel, don't forget to report who it was that saved 'em—meself an' this fine badgermaid, Ambry. Any rewards in the shape of vittles by the cartload will be acceptable, wot!"

Trajidia skipped off blithely, shouting the news to all. "Rejoice, rejoice! Our lost infants are found and will soon be restored to their beloved kinbeasts! They will sleep in their own little beds once again!"

Some of the vermin had clambered out of the ditch and scrambled back to report the disaster to Fallug. The weasel whom he had promoted to captain, Grakk, shook his head.

"Zwilt ain't goin' t'like this, Chief!"

Fallug peered across at the ram. It lay at an odd angle, its point dipping down into the ditch. "I knows wot Zwilt ain't goin' t'like. Can't ye lift it over that ditch?"

Grakk shook his head. "We could if'n we wasn't under attack, Chief, but every time we shows our faces out in the open, we takes a right poundin' off those beasts on the walltop. An' another thing—have ye seen the pile o' rubble they've tipped in front o' the gate? Take my word, it'd take us ten seasons to try an' charge a ram through that liddle lot! So, wot's yore orders, Chief? Wot d'we do now?"

Fallug sat on the ground scratching at his tail. Zwilt's plan had fallen flat, and he would either have to find a solution or answer to Zwilt on his return. Irately, he stalled for time. "Gimme time t'think up a plan, will ye. I don't like bein' rushed!"

Grakk shrugged. "Alright, but wot do I tell all these Ravagers t'do while yore thinkin', Chief?"

A sudden ghost of an idea flashed into Fallug's head. "Call the ram crews off. Tell 'em to join up with the slingers an' archers. Don't stop attackin', keep the Redwallers' 'eads down, pepper the walltop an' don't stop. Once it goes dark, we'll make our move."

Grakk smiled slyly. "An' wot'll that be, Chief?" Fallug leapt up, shaking with temper. "It ain't none o' yore business. You just carry out orders, see!"

Zwilt and his four Ravagers had concealed themselves in the deserted orchard. The tall sable knew he could not make a move until the attack, and the battering ram, were fully underway. Chewing on a near-ripe russet apple, he watched from a spot where he could see the defenders on the west wall. They were all able-looking beasts. Two hares, two big hedgehogs, a brawny otter and a fair number of armed Guosim shrews and Abbeybeasts. Added to that was a solid-looking mole armed with a war hammer and, finally, the huge young badger. Anybeast with only four at his command would be committing suicide going against such odds. However, Zwilt was growing impatient. He flung the half-eaten apple from him. What were Fallug and all those other Ravagers up to? Why could he not hear the booming thuds of a battering ram pounding the Abbey gates? Had something gone amiss with his plan?

The tall sable turned to his vermin escort, explaining his next move, to avoid any mistakes. "Listen carefully. I need to know what's happening on the other side of the west wall. The only way I see of doing that is to get inside the Abbey. I can look out one of those high windows. From there I'll be able to judge what's happening at the main gate. You four follow me. There should be hardly anybeast inside—they're all out on the walls—but we'll take no chances. Go quietly, keep your eyes open and guard my back."

Avoiding the front door of the Abbey building, they explored the south side, where Zwilt found a window with its shutters open. Judging by the mouthwatering aromas emanating from it, this could be only one place, the kitchens. Nobeast seemed to be in attendance. It was the work of a moment for all five creatures to slip inside.

Even in the present situation, it was far too tempting to ignore the food laid out there. Realising how hungry he was, Zwilt posted one of his Ravagers at the door. He fell on the food like a wild beast, as did his escort. Pasties, bread, pies and scones, still warm from the ovens, were laid out to cool on the worktops. With scant regard for choice, they grabbed anything at random, cramming their mouths full, spitting out what they could not gulp down, moving from one thing to another, knocking over platters and trays of food.

Fazdim, a river rat, upended a flask of blackberry wine, gurgling gleefully as it splashed over his chin, staining his lean chest. "Be plenty more o' this good stuff when this place is ours, eh, Lord?"

Zwilt snatched the wine from him, throwing up a cautionary paw. "Hush! What was that?"

The rat Zwilt had left guarding the kitchen door, tippawed back to make his report. "Lord, it's somebeasts singin' an' dancin' out there!"

Zwilt tasted the blackberry wine, nodding his approval. "Let them sing and dance. What harm can that do? Fazdim, you take a turn guarding the door, but get me some of this wine first. I'll have to wait here until the coast is clear, then I'll go upstairs."

Though he would not admit it openly, the tall sable was enjoying his first taste of Redwall fare. He wanted more.

Out in Great Hall, Trajidia had delivered the joyous news to the ladies. They began singing and dancing with happiness, knowing the babes were alive and safe. The transformation in Clarinna was remarkable. She joined in with the celebrations immediately. Friar Soogum and his kitchen helpers provided the music, singing lustily as they drummed on an assortment of upturned pots and bowls. A molemaid scraped away on a small fiddle as the dancers threw up their paws, laughing and jigging gleefully to the jolly song.

"Oh, whoopsy doo, one two three,
happy jolly beasts are we,
clap your paws, three four five,
what a day to be alive!

"The sun never shone so warm and bright,
my paws never felt so free and light,
good news never was so comforting,
whirl around, my friend, let's sing.

"Oh, deedle doo, and doodle die,
no more tears from you or I,
kick those paws up in the air,
joy and bliss be everywhere!

"Our hearts are filled with joy and cheer,
goodbye to anguish, grief and fear,
whirl me round now, tralalaa,
raise your voice and shout hurrah!"

29

Vilaya stayed close to the north wall, making her way through the woodlands. She had removed the blood-stained rag from her brow, cleaned up her soil-stained face and donned her silken cloak. She was once again the Sable Quean.

The fight was going back and forth twixt the ramparts and the flatlands further down. Nobeast noticed as she crossed the path and slid into the ditch. She strode slowly and regally toward the useless battering ram. The Ravagers knew she was dead—had they not seen it with their own eyes? Zwilt the Shade had slain her with his broadsword. With Zwilt somewhere inside the Abbey and the vermin army being run by mere minions, it was high time for the resurrection of their real leader, the Sable Quean.

The recently appointed Captain Grakk was issuing orders to the ram bearers, who were taking cover beneath the bough and leaf canopy in the ditchbed. Using his spearhaft none too gently, Grakk routed the vermin out.

"Leave this ram, now. Git yoreselves outta there! Boss Fallug needs all of ye to attack the walltop. Move, ye worthless bunch, come on, shift yoreselves! Hah, fancy droppin' a batterin' ram into a ditch after all the 'ard work we put in makin' it, eh? Leave it there. Boss Fallug says he's got plans fer it once it goes dark!"

The Ravagers were starting to scramble from the ditch when one, a stoat, fell backward. His paw was pointing, and his face a mask of fear as he wailed, "Waaaaaahhhhh! Eeeeeeyaaaah!"

Everybeast turned to see what had caused this weird effect on the stoat. Eyes popped wide, jaws dropped, the vermin and their captain stood transfixed by the apparition. Vilaya walked unhurriedly up until she was facing the Weasel Captain, whom she addressed by name.

"Are you in charge now, Grakk?"

The weasel was trembling uncontrollably as he managed a stumbling reply. "Ch-charge, y'Majesty, er, er, no, I'm only a cap'n, marm. Er, er, it's Fallug's in charge, er, Lord Zwilt made 'im a boss, er, Majesty!"

Vilaya repeated the name. "Fallug. I don't know that one. Take me to him, Grakk. Bring these Ravagers with you."

Fallug was revelling in his newfound authority, which had many benefits. Some of his foragers had brought in a large clutch of partridge eggs, of which he would take the largest share. He sat watching them roast the eggs in hot ashes, well out of range from Redwall missiles. Fallug was retrieving the first of the cooked eggs with a twig when a ferret pointed out what was going on.

"Lookit, Boss, they've left off fightin' an' they're all comin' over 'ere. . . . An' the Quean's with 'em!"

Fallug shaded his eyes, staring hard at the lead figure. There was no doubt about it—the Sable Quean was unmistakable. Murmurs ran through the foraging party.

"But I thought Zwilt killed 'er!"

"Aye, 'e did. I saw Zwilt do it meself, mate!"

"Then why's she 'ere? Why ain't she dead?"

"Maybe . . . maybe she's a ghost, come back to slay us all!"

They began edging back, ready to break and run off.

Fallug was not about to relinquish his new high office, nor was he about to show fear in front of his command. "Git back 'ere, ye ole frogwives, she ain't goin' to slay nobeast. Lord Zwilt'll sort this out when he gits back. Meanwhile, I'm the boss o' this army, an' I ain't afeared o' nobeast, livin' or dead!"

When Vilaya arrived at the smouldering fire, all the Ravagers stood to attention. All except Fallug, who was still crouched over the ashes, pulling roasted eggs clear with his twig.

Vilaya looked down at him. Her voice held the ring of authority as she spoke. "Are you the beast they call Fallug?"

Dropping the twig, Fallug drew his dagger, making a show of cracking a partridge egg with the blade. He replied boldly, "Aye, I'm Boss Fallug, an' I'm in charge around 'ere until Lord Zwilt gits back!"

The onlookers to this confrontation were surprised when Vilaya smiled approvingly. Her tone was almost cheerful. "Well said, Boss Fallug. That's the way it should be! But the Sable Quean has always ruled over all Ravagers, so I'll take charge now. You won't be needed anymore." Reaching down, she patted the back of his neck.

Oakheart Witherspyk had mounted the battlements once more, trying to assess the new situation, which was puzzling them all.

"D'ye think somethin's going on out there, Skipper?"

The otter leaned on the walltop. "Aye, mate, I do, an' I just wish I knew exactly wot it was."

Buckler climbed up alongside Oakheart. "They've all gathered round that campfire over yonder, too far t'see what's goin' on."

Axtel drew the war hammer from his belt. "You'm wanten oi to goo an' take ee lukk, zurr? Et woan't bee no trubble to oi."

Diggs interposed hastily. "No need for that, old lad. Rest that jolly old footpaw of yours, wot. Besides, who are we to argue if the bloomin' wretched vermin want to chuck in fightin' for the day? Maybe they've decided to take afternoon tea. Jolly good idea, don't y'think, eh, Buck?"

Jango shook his head at the gluttonous young hare. "Don't ye think of anythin' aside o' vittles? We've not long eaten lunch!"

Diggs gave his ears a cavalier wiggle as he set off down the wallsteps. "Pish tush, sah. That's alright for you t'say—shrews don't need as much bally nourishment as hares do. I'll just toodle off down t'the jolly old kitchens an' see what the Friar is fryin' up, wot! Oh, I say, that was rather a good un, the Friar fryin' up stuff, wot?"

Glancing back, he saw his pun had not been appreciated. With that, he strode off, chunnering. "No sense o' humour. That's the trouble with you mouldy lot. Thought it was pretty funny m'self, Friar fryin' an' all that. My old aunt Twodge was right, where there's no sense, there's no bloomin' feelin'. Huh, she was right!"

Flib climbed up alongside Buckler. She nodded toward the Ravager army. "They might've stopped fightin', but that don't mean the dirty scum ain't hatchin' summat up. Take my word, mate, we'd do well t'keep an eye on that lousy lot!"

Buckler hid a smile, nodding vigorously. "Right, marm, I'll take yore advice, marm, good of ye to mention it, marm, thank ye kindly!"

The Guosim maid eyed him coldly. "Marm me jus' once more an' I'll shove ye off'n this wall . . . rabbet!"

Buckler tweaked her ear. "Aye, try callin' me rabbet again an' I'll take ye with me, cheekyface!"

Pulling free of the hare's grip, Flib eyed Buckler with a face like thunder.

Jango winked at Buckler. "Growin' up into a proper Guosim lady, ain't she?"

Sniffy the Tracker nodded over at the foebeasts' position. "Sounds like they're fixin' to start somethin'. Lissen t'that. Sounds like a war chant to me, Chief."

Log a Log Jango cupped an ear in the direction. "Aye, they're yellin' somethin', I can't make out wot it is, though. Ahoy, Flib, me darlin', can ye make out wot those vermin are chantin'?"

After standing for a moment in rebellious silence, Flib relented, complying with her father's request.

"Vilaya, Vilaya, Sable Quean! That's wot they're callin'. Prob'ly workin' themselves up for action."

Buckler nodded courteously toward her. "Thankee, mate. You've got good sharp ears!"

She smiled, her sullen mood fading. "I've got better ears than my pa or Sniffy. You'd be surprised at some o' the things I can hear."

Buckler nodded. "I'm sure I would."

Flib looked toward the Abbey building. "I just heard a noise from over there—bet you didn't!"

Buckler was concentrating more on the Ravagers' shouts, which were growing louder, but to humour Flib, he asked, "What sort of noise was it?"

She shrugged. "Came from the south side o' the Abbey. Sounded like wot you yell out sometimes. Eu-lowly-oh!"

The Salamandastron Blademaster was suddenly alert. "Y'mean *Eulalia,* the Long Patrol war cry? That'll be Diggs—he must be in some sort of bother! Skip, Jango, keep a close watch on those Ravagers. I'll be back as soon as possible. Guard that rubble pile in front o' the gates. If they charge, they'll try to come at us straight up it. I've got to go!" Drawing the long rapier from its back scabbard, Buckler sped off down the wallsteps.

Grakk had replaced the slain Fallug, who lay stiff on the ground, his face fixed in a hideous grin caused by the adder venom from Vilaya's lethal little knife. She stood to one side, nibbling daintily on a roasted partridge egg, watching her new commander whipping the vermin into a battle frenzy. Grakk used thrusts of his spear to emphasise words.

Zwilt was temporarily forgotten, now that the Ravagers had fallen under the spell of their Sable Quean. One who could rise from the dead, and the bars of Hellgates. She who could slay a warrior like Fallug with a single touch of her paw. What else could they do but follow her? En masse, they thundered out their replies to Grakk's questions.

"Who do we serve? Who do we serve?"

"Vilaya! Vilaya! Sable Quean! Yahaaaaaarrrr!"

"An' who are we? What do we do?"

"Ravagers! Ravagers! Kill! Kill! Kill!"

They began the advance, waving spears, axes, pikes and all manner of weaponry. Stamping hard with their footpaws, until the open flatlands thrummed like a great drum, as they repeated over and over, "Vilaya! Vilaya! Sable Quean! Yahaaaaar! Ravagers! Ravagers! Kill! Kill! Kill!"

Buckler instinctively knew where Diggs would be—around the kitchen area. If it was not a usual mealtime, the tubby rascal would make his way to the kitchen window. Pasties, pies, scones and tarts were often taken from the ovens and left to cool on the open window ledge. Cutting along the south side of the Abbey building, Buckler sensed right off that something was amiss. He drew his blade, running to the window. One glance was all that was needed.

Amidst the welter of broken dishes and scattered food, Diggs lay slumped on the floor. Vaulting over the windowsill, the young hare went straight to his companion. Turning Diggs over, he cradled his head, leaning close to his nose. Thanking the seasons that Diggs was breathing, Buckler reached for an oven cloth to stanch the deep wound on his unconscious friend's head. Binding it tight, he reached out a footpaw, pulling a half-empty sack of flour close. Resting Diggs's head on the makeshift pillow, Buckler suddenly became alert.

There were cries of alarm from within Great Hall, coupled with the sound of a little one wailing. Grabbing up his long rapier, he charged out to confront the intruders.

Buckler skidded to a halt. Abbess Marjoram, Clarinna, Jango's wife, Furm, Drull Hogwife and Dymphnia, Witherspyk, clutching Dubdub to her, were surrounded by Zwilt the Shade and his four Ravagers. Buckler knew that only by keeping cool could he rescue them.

Leaning on his sword, he shook his head at the foebeast, commenting scornfully, "Making war on ladies and an infant now, 'tis a brave thing t'do. What a great pity a real warrior's turned up. So, what'll you do now, coward?"

Zwilt's broadsword was already drawn. He drove his Ravagers away from him. "Stand clear and keep a watch on the others, lest they try to run outside and give the alarm. Well, rabbet, come for a lesson in swordplay, have you?" He began circling, his blade swishing the air as he limbered up his paw.

Buckler circled in the opposite direction, holding his weapon lightly. He smiled coldly. "Always ready to learn, if you think you're the master, though I thought babe stealing was your chosen trade."

Both beasts continued circling, drawing closer to each other. It was obvious Zwilt and Buckler were skilled swordbeasts. They locked eyes, never letting their gaze stray. Moving nearer, they walked side on, to present the narrowest target. Footpaws braced nimbly, each seeking an opening.

Herded to the side of the stairway by their captors, Marjoram and her friends watched the duel.

Zwilt, feeling he was close enough, made the initial move. Bounding at his opponent, he struck out with the broadsword, hissing viciously, "Tizzzzz death!"

Buckler sidestepped, countering with a single slash

which deflected the broadsword. As he passed Zwilt, he flicked out his blade, nicking his enemy's ear.

Zwilt lashed out on the turn, laying a wound across Buckler's cheek. The young hare knew that stopping to consider a cut was fatal in a fight to the death. Ducking low, he scythed out with the long rapier, slashing Zwilt's left footpaw.

With his blade cutting whirring arcs, the sable warmed to the attack, pacing high, stepping forward, seeking to drive the hare back.

Buckler, familiar with the move, stood his ground, jabbing with his swordpoint between Zwilt's swings. The sable felt the rapier tip jab his sword paw—he was forced to back off.

Now Buckler came forward. Step! Jab! Parry! Lunge! Zwilt went sideways, one of his swings catching the young hare's side at the waist. Grabbing the big broadsword in both paws, Zwilt battered away at Buckler, who was forced to crouch.

Using this position to his advantage, the hare came upward in a leap, shouting his war cry. "Eulaliaaa!" He drove his adversary backward with a speedy display of figure-of-eight maneuvers.

Steel clashed upon steel. Zwilt was driven backward; he bounded onto the stairway, but Buckler was there first. Skipping up a few steps, the hare gained the advantage, coming down on the sable like a thunderbolt. The clang of weapons striking each other echoed about Great Hall.

Both contestants were panting heavily as they hacked and thrust, each desperate to finish off the other. They battled upon the sweeping flight of stairs, up and down, neither giving an inch. Zwilt was swinging wildly when a fierce slash from Buckler scored his muzzle. He retreated downstairs, leaving a blood trail behind him. Clamping a paw to his wounded side, the young hare hastened to the attack.

Zwilt was losing the fight. He knew he had met a swordbeast who was more than his match. For the first time in his life, the sable felt the broadsword was becoming too heavy to lift. The hare was still light on his paws, wielding the rapier with skill and vigour. So Zwilt the Shade made the only move left open to him.

Hurtling down the stairs, he grabbed baby Dubdub from his mother's paws. Holding his blade against the tiny hog's throat, Zwilt rasped viciously, "Get back, or this one's a deadbeast!"

Dymphnia Witherspyk tried to snatch her baby back. "Don't hurt him, give him to me! Oh, please!"

Abbess Marjoram pulled Dymphnia away. "Stay clear, friend, or he'll hurt the little one, I know he will. His kind are evil—stay clear!"

Dubdub squealed as Zwilt squeezed him. The sable gestured at the ladies, snarling savagely, "Get out of here, you lot. My business is with the rabbet, not you. Begone quickly or the babe suffers!"

Buckler beckoned the ladies away. "The babe will be alright. Go now. I'll settle things with this vermin!"

Abbess Marjoram shepherded them away to the other end of the hall. Still keeping his blade ready, Buckler confronted his foe. "So, now what?"

Zwilt moved out into the open, holding the baby hog tight. "Throw your sword away, rabbet!"

The young hare hesitated.

Zwilt raised his voice. "Cast that blade away or I'll have this one in two pieces!"

The long rapier clattered on stone floor as Zwilt ordered his four Ravagers, "Get him—take hold of him, now!"

Buckler called out as they seized him, "Are you going to let the babe go free?"

Zwilt's smile was cold evil. "Of course I am. As soon as I've slain you!"

Dubdub wriggled, squealing, "Leggo me, nastybeast!"

Buckler held out his paw, cautioning the infant hog, "Be still, now, and stay quiet. You'll soon be back with your mamma."

He nodded at the tall sable. "A life for a life, then. Is that the bargain?"

Skilfully, Zwilt flicked Buckler's fallen rapier with the blade of his broadsword. It skittered away to where it was totally out of the young hare's reach.

The sable eyed his captive coldly.

"The time for bargaining is over. You are in no position to bargain. This babe may live, then again, he may not. A lot of your friends will die before Zwilt the Shade and his Ravagers are done here."

Enraged by his captor's treachery, Buckler bounded forward, trying to reach Zwilt, but the vermin guards clung to him. Sinews stood out on the hare's neck as he yelled, "Coward! Liar! The old sayin' is right! The best vermin is a dead one! Zwilt the Shade? Hah! Zwilt the Scum, more like it!"

The sable was shaking with rage at the insult. He passed Dubdub to one of the Ravagers.

"Get him to those stairs. Kneel him down and grab his ears. We'll see what he has to say when his head is decorating the point of a spear!"

The guards dragged Buckler, struggling wildly, to the stairs. Forcibly, they made him kneel, two holding his forepaws from behind, with the remaining one tugging on his ears, stretching his neck taut.

Zwilt stood over his victim, raising the big broadsword aloft to judge the strike. "Well, rabbet, you don't look so brave now, do you?"

Craning his head sideways, Buckler stared with loathing at his enemy. "I don't answer to cowards!"

The broad blade flashed in the candlelit hall. Then it stopped in midair. Zwilt was still grasping it, but his mouth was wide open, as though he was silently screaming.

Buckler watched in amazement as the sable lost his grip on the sword. He swayed once, then fell to a kneeling position, facing his intended victim. A hoarse rattle issued from Zwilt's throat; his eyes held a look of surprise as he stared at Buckler. Then he toppled sideways on the stairs. Dead!

Clarinna was bent over him still holding the hilt of Martin the Warrior's legendary sword, which she had driven deep between Zwilt's shoulder blades. The harewife stood dry-eyed, her voice unusually harsh for such a gentle creature.

"That's for Clerun Kordyne, the father of my babes, who you murdered!"

Baby Dubdub lay on the floor where the guard had placed him before running off with the other Ravagers, who had quickly released Buckler. He seemed none the worse for his recent ordeal, repeating the last word he had heard, over and over.

"Murdered, murdered, murdered!"

Leaving Martin's sword protruding from Zwilt, Clarinna picked up little Dubdub. She wept into his tender spikes.

Abbess Marjoram came hurrying with her friends. Buckler stood, rubbing the back of his neck to ease the stiffness. He gathered the broadsword and the medal from his fallen enemy's neck, passing them to Clarinna. "These belong in your family. I'm sorry I couldn't have slain Zwilt for you, marm."

Abbess Marjoram had retrieved Buckler's blade. She held it out to him. "Don't be sorry. You did something far braver than slaying a vermin—you offered to sacrifice your life to save another."

The young hare did not stop to dispute the point. He sped off, rapier in paw, for the door.

"Maybe so, but there's four vermin loose within Redwall, and we're being invaded from the west flatlands!"

30

Buckler came running up to the walltop, thinking to use it as a viewpoint to seek out the four vermin guards. He was almost knocked flat by Bartij, who bustled past him carrying a boulder.

The big hedgehog beckoned to the stones piled on the walkway. "Lend a paw here, Buck. We need more stones. That young badgermaid's got our cattypult goin'. Hoho, ye should see it lobbin' stones at yon vermin!"

Skipper was alongside the ballista, waving. "Ahoy, mate, come an' see this thing workin'!"

Ambrevina had made a few alterations to the weapon. Now it had two thick young alder saplings, sturdy trunks, culled from the Abbey grounds. Between these, an old canvas groundsheet was laced. She had rigged the whole thing up on the original timbers. Ropes were attached to the tops of the alders. These were secured to a heavy baulk of oak, which had a hole drilled in it. A team of moles and Witherspyk hogs hauled on the ropes, leaning their weight on the oaken baulk. This bent the alder saplings backward until a wooden peg, anchored to the timber base, could be inserted into the baulk hole.

Four good-sized rocks were laid in the canvas sling. Jango stood on the battlements, watching the oncoming

Ravagers. The Guosim Log a Log called the range. "Back! Stop! Left a bit! Stop! Ready, Ambry!"

Using a bung mallet, the badgermaid knocked the peg out with a sharp tap, releasing the stone load. There was a whoosh of air as the four rocks shot off over the battlements and out over the flatland into the ranks of the advancing vermin. Even though they scattered, the missiles fell so swiftly that two were slain and three more lay injured, screaming in the dust.

Skipper nodded at the Abbey building. "Everythin' alright down there, Buck?"

The young hare moved out of the way, allowing a mole to stumble past under the weight of a big sandstone chunk.

"Zwilt was in the Abbey, but he's been slain. There's four vermin loose in the grounds, an' Diggs is lyin' wounded in the kitchen!"

Skipper picked up his javelin. "I'll see t'the vermin. Sister Fumbril, will ye go an' attend our mate Diggs? He's been injured."

The Warrior mole Axtel had been listening. He stumped off down the wallstairs, brandishing his war hammer. "You'm leave ee vurmints to oi, zurrs. They h'aint a-goin' nowheres twixt ee four walls. Oi'll see to 'em. Hurrr!"

Sister Fumbril joined Axtel. "Then ye can walk me as far as the kitchens, sir."

Buckler took a rock from old Granvy. It was far too heavy for the aged Recorder, who smiled his thanks.

"Thank the seasons we have a creature who knows about these ballista things. Dame Fortune must've sent the badgermaid to us. Apparently, the beasts where she comes from, on the eastern coastlands, use them all the time. Both she and her family have sunk many a searat galley before it ever came to shore."

Oakheart Witherspyk leaned on the threshold wall, watching the vermin advance. "The scoundrels are still comin', sirrah. It strikes me that one ballista ain't enough to stop all of 'em. What say ye, Buck?"

The hare came to join his friend on the threshold. "Aye, Oakie, this is where the final battle will be—on this point, where the hill is piled in front of Redwall's gate. Once they cross that ditch, they'll try an' force an entry by chargin' us. Unless . . ."

The Sable Quean stood at the back of the slow-moving advance, urging the Ravagers forward. "They can't get us all with a few boulders. Double-march them, Grakk. The quicker we reach that hill of rubble, the sooner we'll make an end of it. The woodlanders are still outnumbered. We can do it with one good charge. Speed up the chant, get them moving."

Grakk could see great things ahead for himself. Boldly, he marched along with the rear ranks, roaring out, "Wait'll we gets in there, bullies! Ye can eat all ye like, sleep on soft beds an' be waited on tail an' paw by woodlander slaves! Sable Quean Vilaya! Kill kill kill!"

Not committed yet to a head-on charge, the Ravagers broke into a shambling trot, waving their weapons and taking up the call, which spurred them on.

"Kill! Kill! Kill! Victory to Vilaya, Sable Quean!"

Having left Redwall by the small north wallgate, with a heavily armed force, Buckler, Jango and a crew of Guosim warriors sped silently along to put the plan into action. Emerging from the woodlands north of the Ravagers, they hurried over the path, then slipped quietly into the ditch. A short time thereafter, they were in the main gate area, peering over the ditchtop at the unsuspecting vermin advance.

The Guosim were in two lines, one behind the other. Buckler commanded the front line.

"Put shafts to bowstrings, an' make every arrow count. On my word now. Stand! Draw! Shoot!"

The front rank of Ravagers were taken by surprise. The sudden volley of barbed shafts hit them hard.

Buckler signalled his archers to stand back; Jango took

over. "Back row, forward! Slings an' javelins! Stand! Throw! Fall back!"

This time it was a salvo of stones and fire-hardened ashwood javelins which hit home, thinning the Ravager horde. They fell flat, returning the missiles with their own stones, spears and arrows.

Vilaya lay facedown on the flatland, striking at Grakk's footpaws. "Get them up, keep going, we're almost there!"

Orders rang out from the ditch. More shafts, javelins and slingstones pelted down on the vermin. Grakk was about to rise when a dull *whump* rent the air. Black smoke billowed out, followed by sparks and flames.

Jango tossed the empty cauldron of dirty kitchen fat on the blazing battering ram. Slapping his ears with a paw, he blinked through the billowing haze. "Scorched me ears, whiskers'n' blinkin' eyebrows to a frazzle, there. Ahoy, Buck!"

Buckler shoved the Shrew Chieftain ahead of him, along the ditch bottom with the rest of his Guosim fighters. "Hurry, mate, back to the Abbey while they're still won-derin' what happened!"

Cellarmole Gurjee and Axtel Sturnclaw met them at the north wallgate. As they piled in, Buckler locked the gate behind them.

"Anything to report here?"

Axtel's eyes were still blood-tinged from the berserk fury. He was limping about in circles as he touched his snout in a brief salute. "Oi h'accounted furr three o' they vurmints, zurr. Ee fourth un throwed hisself frum ee wall-top an' perished without offerin' a foight. Oi 'm h'awaitin' further orders, zurr, thankee koindly!"

Jango glanced up at the twilight sky. "Best git yoreself up atop o'er the gate. There'll be battle aplenty for ye there soon!"

Buckler bounded onto the north wallsteps. "Right, mates, no time to waste now!"

Some of the defenders had wrapped damp cloths about their faces to counteract the black smoke billowing up from the ditch. The ram was blazing; the flames had taken hold. From down below there was silence—not a Ravager could be seen anywhere.

Trajidia Witherspyk lowered her face cover, trilling, "Hoorah! Victory is ours. The rascally foe have been routed! Rejoice, brave friends, rejoice!"

Oakheart fixed her with a withering glance. "Cease your foolish prattle, daughter dear. Well, my comrades in arms, what think ye?"

Skipper watched the dark, oily smoke clouding the setting sun. "I don't like it. Somethin's goin' on."

Jango nodded agreement. "Aye, they ain't just upped stakes an' left. They'll be back, y'can be sure. But when?"

Axtel gave an experienced warrior's opinion. "When ee doan't bees 'spectin' et, zurr, that's when."

Buckler paced back and forth, framed in the last rays of daylight. "Right, sir, it'll be sometime durin' the night. Vilaya will try to catch us nappin'. So we must be alert an' on guard all through the darkness."

Abbess Marjoram came up on the walkway. "Is everything under control? How are we doing?"

Skipper saluted with his javelin. "We've beaten 'em off once, marm, an' we're fit'n'ready for any vermin wot wants a second try. No need for ye to worry, marm."

Marjoram smiled warmly at the Otter Chieftain. "Why would I ever worry, with such brave warriors to keep my Abbey safe? I just came to tell you that Friar Soogum and his helpers will be arriving soon with supper."

Oakheart patted his rumbling paunch. "Kind of ye t'be so considerate, friend Marj. We could all manage a bite or two. It's been a long, weary day, an' the night will be far more tiresome, I suspect."

The Abbess tapped Buckler's paw. "I think perhaps you'd better come to the Infirmary. I'd like you to look in on Mister Diggs."

Buckler gave the matter some brief thought before replying, "Er, much as I'd like to, marm, I rather think my place is up here—in case of trouble, y'see. I'm sure Diggs would agree if he were here, marm."

Skipper gave the hare's shoulder a nudge. "Go on with ye, Buck. If'n anythin' breaks, we'll let ye know loud'n'clear. Right, mate?"

Axtel winked at Buckler. "Roight, zurr. Us'll raise a gurt showt that'd be hurd ten leagues off'n. You'm go an' see ee friend Diggsy!"

As Marjoram and Buckler passed through Great Hall, a song that was almost a dirge echoed out. It gave the Abbess a start. "Good grief. What's that?"

Buckler knew. He pointed out Clarinna, who was seated in a corner beside the body of Zwilt the Shade. She had a bowl of water, with which she was cleaning the blade of Martin's sword whilst singing the dirge to the slain enemy.

Buckler explained this to Marjoram. "Clarinna could not properly grieve the murder of her mate, my brother Clerun, until his killer was punished. It's an old Salamandastron custom."

Pausing, they listened to the eerie sound. Clarinna carried on singing, oblivious to their presence.

"Sleep now, my love, rest quietly in peace,
the cost of thy blood now is paid,
for I with mine own paw, fulfilled the warriors' law,
exacting vengeance with this shining blade.
Thy son and daughter, too, who'll grow not knowing
  you,
I'll tell them that you dwell by tranquil streams,
amidst the silent trees, mid fields of memories,
mayhaps sometimes you'll visit them in dreams.
Sleep now, sleep now, my love, sleep on,
for time will dry all tears and ease the pain,
now justice has been done, sleep on, my love, sleep on,
until the day when we shall meet again."

As they mounted the stairs, Buckler observed, "Clarinna won't recover properly until her babes are back with her. They're happy enough for the moment with Mumzy the old water vole, thanks to Ambrevina and Diggs. How's the old rascal doing, marm?"

Marjoram led the way up to the Infirmary. "See for yourself. Sister Fumbril has taken care of that dreadful head wound he took, but at the moment, he's drifting in and out of consciousness."

Diggs lay very still on his sickbay bed, his head swathed in a turban of herb salves and bandages. Buckler stood staring at his friend as he spoke to Sister Fumbril. "How's he doing, Sister?"

The jolly otter healer shook her head dubiously. "There's no way of knowin', sir, he's been like that since he was carried up here. It was a terrible wound, a stroke of a big sword, I think. He's lost an ear an' been scarred for life. I'm waitin' on him t'wake up, but he ain't respondin'."

Buckler eyed a table laden with food of all sorts. "Bring that table closer, Abbess. I've never known the tubby fraud to sleep through any mealtimes. Let me try."

Seating himself by the bed, Buckler started into the delicious repast, commenting loudly, "Mmmm, hazelnut'n'apple bake with arrowroot sauce. I wonder, should I save some for old Diggs? No, he never saved any for me back in the Long Patrol mess. Hello, what's this? Mushroom, leek and gravy pasty! I say, Diggs, d'you fancy a bite o' this? It's yore favourite. Yummy, still nice'n'hot, too!"

Diggs groaned. Opening one eye, he glanced quizzically at Buckler and said in a voice like an old officer, "Wot . . . wot? An' who are you, sirrah? Speak up!"

Buckler smiled. 'C'mon, you great fat fraud. It's me, Buckler, your mate!"

Diggs opened the other eye, staring scornfully at his lifelong companion. "Buckler, eh? Bit of an odd handle for a chap. 'Fraid I've never had the pleasure of meetin' ye. An' who in the name of snits'n'scuts is Diggs, eh?"

Buckler poured himself a beaker of October Ale. "Diggs is you, y'great lardsack, that's yore name!"

Diggs snorted. "Piffle'n'balderdash, laddie buck. I'm Colonel Crockley Sputherington—known as Sputhers t'my friends, but you ain't no chum of mine, sah, so show a bit of bloomin' respect to a superior officer, wot, wot!" His friend held out a slice of the pastie.

"Oh, right y'are, Colonel, sah. How about tryin' a bit of this scoff? It's very good, y'know."

Diggs wrinkled his nose. "Take it away, this very instant, y'greedy buffoon. It looks disgustin'!"

Buckler appealed to Sister Fumbril. "It ain't like him to refuse vittles. What should I do?"

The cheerful otter shrugged. "Be thankful he's still alive, I suppose. I'd try humourin' him, if'n I was you."

Diggs glared at the Sister—he was outraged. "Humour y'self, y'great grinnin' planktail. One more word an' I'll have ye slapped on a fizzer for gross insolence, marm! Now, take y'self jolly well off, go on! An' take this gluttonous oaf with ye. Aye, an' all this mess y'call vittles. The very sight of it makes me ill!"

Deciding to take Fumbril's tip, Buckler stood to attention, throwing the patient a stiff salute. "Right y'are, Colonel Crockley Sputherington, sah. Come on now, marm. Let's shift all this stuff an' let the good officer get a spot of shut-eye. He must be tired."

Any further discussion was cut short by a thunderous war cry from out in the grounds. "Redwaaaaaaaalllll! Redwaaaaaallll!"

Buckler hurtled from the Infirmary, calling to Sister Fumbril, "That's it, the attack! I'm needed on the walltops, they've made their move!"

As the sickbay door slammed behind him, Diggs cast a pitying glance at the Abbess, sighing. "Chap's off his rocker, gone bonkers, I'd say. Dearie, dearie me. How sad for a beast so blinkin' young, wot!"

*

The battle of Redwall Abbey really had started in earnest. Like a foul tide, the Ravagers charged over the remainder of the nightdark flatlands, bellowing bloodcurdling war cries. Buckler came bounding up the wallsteps to join Skipper and Jango on the threshold battlements. The Guosim Chieftain was honing his rapier on the smooth sandstone.

"I knew that cattypult wouldn't stop the scum forever. They've still got more'n enough vermin to overrun us."

Buckler's long rapier swished as he drew it. "Aye, but the ballista bought us a bit o' time. Pity it can't be used for close-up work. Well, this is it, mates—we need everybeast that can fight right here!"

Jango, Skipper and Oakheart began bawling orders.

"Logalogalogaloooog! Guosim to me!"

"Redwaaaaaallll! Come on, buckoes, let's show 'em!"

"Gather to me, brave beasts! Woe unto they who would face a Witherspyk!"

Axtel Sturnclaw began pounding a baulk of timber with his war hammer, roaring, "Woooohuuuurrrr! Cumm an' meet ee choild o' death, vurmints! Woooohuuuurrrr!"

Vilaya caught up with Grakk, who was at the centre of the first wave. She yelled at him above the noise, "Get them across that ditch an' straight up the hill onto the wall. Don't stop—keep up a full charge. Once our Ravagers are on the walltops, we'll eat them alive. Don't fail me, Grakk! You're in command now!"

Flib joined the second row of archers and slingers. Trajidia Witherspyk, armed with a sling and stones, stood shoulder-to-shoulder with her. Flib's blood was up—she bounced up and down, whirling her sling in anticipation of the action.

"Yaharrr! We'll show that scummy lot the way to Hellgates. First vermin that shows his nose over the wall's a flamin' deadbeast, eh, Traj?"

Faced with the reality of life and death in warfare, the hogmaid's dramatic nature suddenly deserted her. "Oh, er, right, Flib, we'll show them. . . . But what are we supposed to do? I mean, do we actually have to kill other creatures, face-to-face?"

Flib laughed recklessly. "Well, o' course we do, ya blinkin' wiltin' lily! If'n ye don't kill Ravagers, they'll kill you. Just sling'n'whack'n'batter as hard as ya can. Stick by my side. I'll show ya how!"

Streaming to either side of the burning ram, vermin fighters scrambled out of the ditch. Grakk urged them up the sloping hill of rubble, waving his spear, and firing them up.

"Take the Abbey, ye bold buckoes! Let's conquer the place an' live the good life. Go to it if'n ye want enough vittles t'stuff yoreselves, aye, an' slaves to serve ye! It's all there for a night's killin'!"

The first score mounted the pile, their footpaws sinking in as they scrabbled upward. Buckler waited until he could see their villainous faces rising through the smoke and darkness. He raised his blade, steadying the first row.

"Stand ready. . . . Wait now. . . . On my command . . . Shoot!"

A hail of shafts and slingstones whined through the air like angry wasps. Screams and gurgles rang out from below, followed by a salvo of thrown spears and javelins. Three Guosim fell to the missiles, two wounded, one dead.

Now the second wave of vermin came climbing up over the bodies of their fallen comrades. This time, there were more of them, and the ascent was faster. Jango heard Buckler calling his row to fall back and reload. The Guosim Chieftain leapt onto the battlements, shouting, "Second row forward. . . . Stand ready. . . ."

Flib whirled her sling, winking at Trajidia. "Here we go now, Traj. Good huntin', mate!"

Jango's command rapped out as they stepped to the threshold. "On my command . . . Shoot!"

Trajidia was about to loose her slingstone when the scarred head of a rat poked over the top at her. She whacked the loaded sling down hard on her enemy's skull. The rat stumbled, grunted and kept coming. The hogmaid hit him again. And again. And again! An insane strength seemed to fill her limbs. She was screaming like a madbeast, "Eeeeeyaaaaah! Get back, back, baaaack!"

The rat reared to his full height on the walltop, then fell lifeless in front of her. She slung off her stone at a stoat who was following the rat. He toppled backward, struck full in the throat. Trajidia heard the order to fall back and allow the third row forward. She retreated, loading up her sling, laughing hysterically in Flib's face. "I did it, I did it, mate! See that! Two of 'em—I got two Ravagers. Eeeeeyaaaaah!"

The rows of defenders had now fallen into disarray, so fierce was the vermin onslaught. Buckler was everywhere at once with his commanders. Thrusting, kicking, slashing and stabbing at an endless stampede of vermin attackers. The Redwallers were sure to be overwhelmed as the tide of Ravagers swept upward. Some were even now fighting on the walkway, in paw-to-paw combat with the lesser force.

Then the unexpected happened. Ambrevina smashed the ballista to smithereens with a fusillade of blows from her mighty paws. Timber went flying everywhere as she grabbed both the young alder trunks, with the canvas sling tied between them. Skipper saw what was coming. He acted swiftly, ordering the defenders to retreat south along the walltops.

"Back to the south corner, everybeast. Stay out o' that badger's way or ye'll be slain!"

Buckler, Skipper, Jango and Oakheart put their backs to the retreat, fighting off the Ravagers who were pursuing them. There was, however, not much need for this when Axtel arrived on the scene.

The Warrior mole was in roaring Bloodwrath, hurling himself joyfully into the advancing Ravagers. His war hammer rose and fell, as if he was a mighty smith working at an anvil.

Ambrevina swept the walkway clear, wielding both the supple young trunks, bellowing in fury. Vermin flew through the air, right over the walltops, left, right and centre. The drastically thinned ranks of the foebeast could not, nor would not, face two such beasts consumed with the urge to slaughter. Even those climbing the heap fell back. However, this could not save them. Having cleared the threshold and west walkway, Ambrevina and Axtel jumped over the wall. They came thundering down upon the Ravagers like twin thunderbolts.

Buckler grabbed Jango. "Come on, Log a Log, get your Guosim and let's finish this! Skipper, Oakheart, stay up here and guard the Abbey. See to the wounded!"

Seeing the battle lost, Vilaya took to her paws and fled across the flatlands, with panic lending speed to her footpaws. Grakk ran, too. Panting and gasping, he caught up with the Sable Quean.

"Majesty, did ye see that? The big stripedog an' that other thing, the madbeast with the hammer? Once they came at us, we stood no chance. We need a new plan now."

Vilaya threw a paw around the weasel's shoulder. "I plan to get far away from here, travelling alone."

Grakk sensed what was about to happen—he knew Vilaya, and knew what he had to expect for the failed conquest. He tried to pull away, but too late. The Sable Quean was already thrusting with her small venomous blade.

She released him then. He collapsed to the ground with a small sigh. Vilaya stared down at him.

"Mayhap you never heard me say I travel alone."

She sped off into the night, leaving Grakk staring at her retreating figure. It gradually grew dim, as did his eyes.

*

The once-fearsome army of Ravagers was defeated on the path twixt the ditch and the Abbey's west wall. Leaderless and totally unnerved by the ferocity of the counterattack launched upon them, they scattered and stumbled off in disarray. Buckler chased after a small group, but only for a short distance. Putting up his blade, he returned to the Abbey.

Skipper was sitting on the hill in front of the main gates, watching the burning battering ram. He nodded to the hare. "I think that's the last we've seen of the Ravagers, mate. Take a seat an' rest yore paws."

The young hare sat down beside him with a sigh. "I chased after one or two of 'em, but they were runnin' scared. No point in catchin' vermin who've lost the will to fight, so I gave up."

Skipper probed at the debris with his javelin tip. "Hah, try tellin' that to Jango an' his Guosim. Those shrews don't take no prisoners, mate!"

Buckler rose, dusting himself off. "Well, you know what they say. The only good vermin's a dead un. It's hard to break a lifetime's habit. Did ye see anythin' o' Axtel or Ambry? Are they off huntin' vermin, too?"

Skipper pointed west over the flatlands, which were tinged with pale reflections of early dawn from the eastern sky. "Went over yonder, both of 'em, though ole Axtel was goin' a lot slower'n the badgermaid. Somebeast said the Sable Quean had run off that way."

Buckler leapt the ditch with a single bound. "I'm goin' after 'em, Skip. Keep yore eyes peeled on things around here, mate!"

The Otter Chieftain shrugged. "Not much t'see now the battle's over—ahoy, go easy up there! Can't a beast sit in peace for a moment?"

He dodged to one side as a Ravager carcass rolled down from the walltop, followed by several more.

Foremole Darbee poked his homely face over the wall.

"Oo hurr, moi pololojees, zurr! Me'n moi crew bee's shiftin' ee slayed vurmints offen ee rampits t'be buried."

Skipper climbed nimbly to the threshold, his dignity still intact. "Well done, good sirs. The ole place could do with a tidy-up. Don't want Abbess Marj seein' this lot lyin' about Redwall, do we?"

The Abbess appeared at the top of the gatehouse steps. "We most certainly don't, though I'll excuse it this time, seeing as how you restored my Abbey to me. So, what can I do to reward you goodbeasts?"

Oakheart came panting up onto the parapet. "A smidgeon of breakfast wouldn't go amiss, my dear Marj."

Marjoram curtsied, smiling. "Then breakfast it shall be!"

A crowd of defenders made their way across the lawns, with Oakheart Witherspyk, in fine baritone voice, giving a rendition of a song he had written many seasons ago for one of his renowned Witherspyk productions. He remembered it well, because he had cast himself in the role of the conquering hero. Everybeast soon caught on to the chant which opened each verse, and the repetition of the final verse line.

"We won we won we won we won. . . .
A victory's like the finest of wine,
I can say this without conceit.
We left our enemies to dine
on the bitterness of defeat.
The bitterness of defeat!

"So hey sing ho as we merrily go,
no warriors happy as we,
for every beast will share a feast,
of the fruits of victory!

"We won we won we won we won. . . .
Oh, see the foe as away they go,
all battered an' beaten full sore,

we wave our swords an' shout hoho!
They'll never come back for more.
No, they'll never come back for more!

"Let's cheer out near an' far hoorah,
brave comrades, rally to me.
Not a moment to waste, come on an' taste
the fruits of victoreeeeeee!"

Drull Hogwife met them at the Abbey door. She was looking flustered. "Ooh, er, beg pardon, Mother Abbess, but is Mister Diggs with ye?"

Skipper answered for her. "No, marm, Diggs ain't with us. He was lyin' wounded in the sickbay last I heard."

Drull threw her apron up over her face. "Oh, corks, he ain't there now. Diggs 'as gone!"

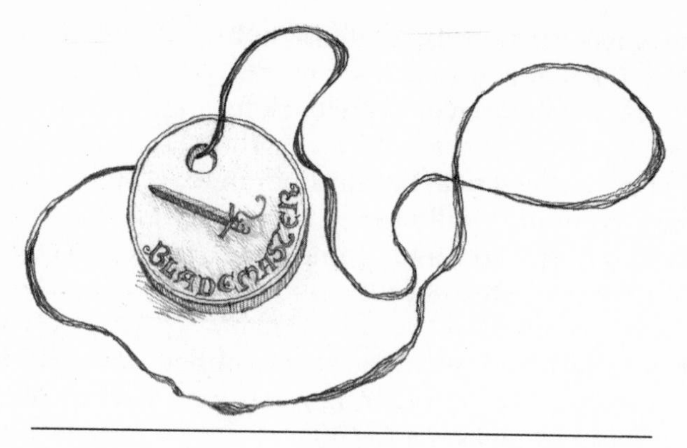

31

After ridding herself of Grakk, Vilaya pressed on awhile before settling down to rest. The Sable Quean lay behind a small hummock. The defeat of her forces at Redwall rankled her, though not for long. Ever an opportunist and a creature of whim, she chose to stay alone for some time. If and when she needed another following, it was a simple matter.

Vermin had always been in awe of Vilaya. She was quick, ruthless and intelligent—all the qualities which made her a Sable Quean. Maybe the next band of roving barbarians she might meet up with would prove suitable to serve her. Redwall to her was nought but a bad dream, which she pushed to the back of her mind. She was far away from the Abbey now. She would not worry about the severe lesson she had learned at the paws of simple woodlanders. However, a lesson learned was a gaining of knowledge. She drifted off into a light sleep.

Daylight was fully up when she woke. She stretched, standing up as she gazed around. Larks chirruped in the high azure sky, grasshoppers rustled, bees hummed, and myriad-hued butterflies flew silently upon the high summer morn. All this natural beauty was wasted upon

Vilaya—she was hungry and thirsty. Then she saw the distant figure coming over the flatlands toward her.

The Sable Quean cursed herself for a fool. Always having Ravagers on guard, ready to report any movement, it was strange having to shift for herself. Her eyesight was keen; she stood still until she identified the unmistakable bulk. The big badger was tracking her, moving at a steady lope.

Ambrevina plodded doggedly on. She had slowed her pace to accommodate Axtel and his injured footpaw. In the half-light of dawn, the Warrior mole had rallied somewhat, even running slightly ahead of her. Then he stumbled, tripping over the huddled body of Grakk. Axtel sat rocking back and forth, his velvety face creased in pain as he hugged the damaged footpaw. Ambrevina knelt by his side.

"Are you hurt, my friend? How can I help?"

The sturdy mole would not look at her. He waved a mighty digging claw, grunting, "You'm carry on, marm. Oi'm h'only 'olden ee back. Catch ee up wi' ee villyun. If'n you'm wanten to 'elp oi, do that. Leave yon evil vurmint in such ee way that she'm carn't 'urt any more pore likkle uns. Hurrr!"

The huge badgermaid clasped her friend's digging claw briefly. "You rest here, I'll pick you up on my way back. Don't worry about the Sable Quean. Death marked her well on the day she murdered a young otter called Flandor. I took an oath she'd pay for his death."

Axtel Sturnclaw watched her lope off westward, with pale dawn light on her back.

Ambrevina kept the same pace, conserving her huge strength. Dust pounded off her paws, which sounded like dull drumbeats on the plain. She emptied her mind of everything, concentrating only on her mission. Almost a league further on, she was finally rewarded. The slim lone figure stood out on a hummock in the distance. The drumbeats speeded up as the badgermaid burst into a run.

Vilaya took off like a startled hare, telling herself she could outdistance such a big, lumbering beast. After a while she ventured a backward glance. It struck fear into her heart. Framed by the golden summer sunlight, her pursuer was still coming, vengeance lending speed to her scorching pace. The Sable Quean sobbed, a dry lump rising in her throat as she sucked in the warm air. Now she could hear the badger's footpaws—*Whump! Whump! Whump! Whump!*—coming onward at a ground-eating rate. Then she heard the hunter's breath, hard and hot, but with no sign of weakening.

Vilaya tried to put on an extra spurt of speed, which she actually did for one brief interval. Then it was as if she was moving waist high through water. She had run out of breath; her pace began flagging. Devoid of energy, she felt her adversary's hot breath on the nape of her neck. Quick as a flash she loosed her long silken cloak. It billowed out and fell, catching the badger's footpaws, snarling her up so that she stumbled.

Ambrevina felt her balance go. Automatically, she threw herself into a headlong leap. She collided with Vilaya's back, sending herself and her quarry thudding to the ground. Being on top, the badgermaid was first up. Swinging her loaded sling, she hefted the sable with a footpaw, turning her over.

The Sable Quean's face was tight with horror. She gasped, "You . . . you've killed me!"

Her paw clasped the crystal poison holder and the lethal blade which it sheathed. It had broken and pierced her chest. Vilaya could smell the sickly aroma of serpent venom as it oozed around the wound. Her eyes blazed hatred at the badgermaid standing over her.

"Y-you . . . k-killed . . . the Sable . . . Quea. . . . !"

Ambrevina saw Vilaya's body contort once, twisting like a corkscrew. It went stiff; she died like that.

Flandor, the young friend of Ambrevina Rockflash, had been avenged. She turned and walked away without a backward glance, blinking as the sunlight shone into her eyes, mingling with her tears.

Redwall Abbey's twin bells, Matthias and Methuselah, boomed out a warm brazen message of peace over Mossflower Country. In the aftermath of a temporary breakfast, with the promise of an afternoon feast, Redwallers and their allies flooded joyfully out into the Abbey grounds.

Buckler, Jango, Oakheart and Skipper accompanied the Abbess, gathering on the gatehouse steps to deal with current matters. Marjoram looked to Buckler for assistance.

"First there's the problem of your friend Diggs. Where do you think he's gone? Maybe you can organise a search party. He could be anywhere in the Abbey, even in the grounds. Very odd, him going off like that."

Buckler did his best to sum up the situation. "Aye, marm, I'll arrange a search locally. As y'say, it is odd, but Diggs was acting strangely after his head wound, as you saw. But I don't care if he thinks he's some old officer." Here Buckler chuckled. "Colonel Crockley Sputherington, wasn't it? Huh, Diggs is Diggs, basically—he can take care of himself. An' as for not wanting vittles, he'll show up faster'n a scorched frog as soon as his stomach tells him it's dinnertime. Leave the problem of Diggs t'me, marm. Now, what next?"

Oakheart held up a paw. "What's become of our two friends, the real heroes of the battle, Ambrevina an' Axtel? They seem to have disappeared, too."

Jango did not seem unduly worried. "There's a pair that don't need any lookin' after. I pity any score o' vermin wot gets in their way, mate."

Skipper nodded agreement with his Guosim friend. "Right, matey. Ambry an' Axtel are two fearsome warriors. They'll come back if'n they feel like, but if they wants to wander an' travel, well, fortune be with 'em both, an' may the sun shine warm on their paws."

The gatehouse door opened. Big Bartij strode out, wielding a shovel. He was followed by Foremole Darbee, plus a procession of moles, all suitably geared out with picks, shovels, hoes and rakes. Darbee gave orders to his crew.

"Go ee an' foind summ wheelybarrows. They'm prollibly bee's in ee h'orchard. Discuse oi, marm, us'ns gotten wurk t'be dunn!"

Marjoram shook her head in wonder. "I didn't know that many creatures could fit into our little gatehouse. Must've been quite a crush in there!"

Bartij tugged his headspikes respectfully. "Oh, it was, marm, but we're all about our tasks now. We're goin' to open the gates an' clear that pile o' rubble away. Then there's the lawns an' flower beds t'be set right an' proper agin. One thing me'n the Foremole can't abide is untidy Abbey grounds!" He strode off without awaiting a reply.

The Mother Abbess's smile lit up the summer morn. "Right, that's one problem we don't have to worry about! Shall we adjourn to the walltops and keep out of their way?"

Trajidia Witherspyk, who was already on the ramparts with Flib, sang out shrilly, "Ahoy, below, I see two creatures approaching from afar!"

After a moment's pause, Flib called, "It's Ambry an' Axtel. She's carryin' him on 'er shoulders."

Shortly thereafter, a Guosim crew went racing out to meet them. The shrews were carrying a stretcher, on which Axtel was placed, despite his protests. Flib commandeered the warrior's war hammer, granting herself the honour of carrying it back to the Abbey. Sister Fumbril met them at the south wallgate, shaking her head at the mole.

"Mister Axtel, sir, wot've I told ye about travellin' on a wounded footpaw? It'll never get better at this rate!"

Axtel Sturnclaw treated the Sister to one of his rare grins. "Oi'll take ee h'advice then, marm. Frum naow on, oi'll goo everywhere by stretcherer. These yurr shrewbeasts'll carry oi. B'aint that roight, mateys?"

A groan of despair arose from the Guosim bearers. Axtel was no small wispy beast.

Not expecting to find Diggs within the Abbey, Buckler had organised a party of Redwallers to search the building. He was in the upper dormitories when he accidentally bumped into Clarinna. She was slipping out of the Infirmary with a bundle on her back. The young hare halted her progress.

"Good day t'ye, marm. Forgive me, but I didn't get time to thank you for savin' my life. It was a brave thing you did, slaying Zwilt."

She curtsied, trying to get past him. "I only did what I saw as my duty. You were the one that acted bravely. Now would you stand aside, please?"

Buckler stayed where he was, indicating the bundle. "Where are you going in such a hurry, and what's in there?"

He saw her jaw tighten. "I'm going to get my babes, Calla and Urfa. I know they're safe, but they've been gone for so long. They need me—please, let me go!"

Taking the bundle, he set it down. "But you haven't the faintest idea of where to go. You'll be lost before you get far. Listen, I've got to find Diggs, he's missing. But if I haven't found him by tonight, then tomorrow noon I'll take you to get the babes myself. Ambrevina will come with us. She knows exactly where she and Diggs left them. That's on my oath as a Long Patrol Warrior. Agreed?"

Clarinna nodded. "Agreed. Come on, I'll help you to search for Diggs."

Late afternoon shadows were lengthening when the Abbess went to the orchard. Friar Soogum was there, supervising the feast preparations.

"Mother Abbess, d'you think this'll do?"

Marjoram clapped her paws in delight. "Oh, Friar, it's perfect. What a feast this will be!"

The table linen was spread upon the orchard grass, with

pretty blossom arrangements decking the fruit trees. Lanterns hung, ready to be lit by evening. Casks of strawberry fizz, October Ale, dandelion and burdock cordial and jugs of mint tea or pennycloud brew were placed in the tree shade. Scones, tarts, pies and pasties were there in abundance, alongside trifles, broths, oven-baked breads and delicate almond wafers. The entire effect was magical or, to quote the Abbess, "the setting for an evening's delicious enchantment!" And it really was just that.

Glowing from their day's chores and tasks, everybeast trooped into the orchard. Early evening twilight was enhanced by lighted lanterns of pink, gold, blue and green, circled by fluttering moths of varied hue. Over excited Dibbuns were issued with beakers of strawberry fizz and warned to keep a modicum of silence whilst the Abbess said grace.

Decked out in her best pale-fawn habit, belted with a spotless white cord and sporting a small circlet of woodland flowers round her brow, Marjoram recited the special words, penned earlier that day by her friend Granvy.

"We meet in happiness this day,
to celebrate our victory,
not to boast of fighting ways,
but just the joy of living free.
Oh, may that feeling never cease,
for you, my true and honest friends,
enjoy this feast, in love and peace,
and hope our freedom never ends!"

A tiny squirrelbabe held up his beaker. "I drink to dat!"

Laughter echoed round the orchard as they fell to in earnest. Skipper blew on a bowl of his favourite freshwater shrimp'n'hotroot soup, winking at Buckler. "D'ye think all this scoff might tempt ole Diggs out from wherever he's stowed hisself?"

The young hare picked up a slice of greengage tart.

"Well, if he doesn't, I'll wager he's at least three leagues away, the great lard barrel!"

Clarinna passed a long cheese'n'hazelnut roll to Ambrevina. "It was kind of you to say you'd accompany Buckler and me tomorrow. Thank you so much!"

The badgermaid accepted the offering with a nod. "I've seen your babes, marm, Calla and Urfa. Two charming little creatures. I can see why you wish dearly to be reunited with them. My pleasure!"

Baby Dubdub sprayed crumbs about as he spoke through a mouthful of honeyed scone. "My pleasure! My pleasure!"

Oakheart beamed over the rim of his October Ale tankard. "The babe's learnin', Dymphnia. Did y'hear that? A real actor in the makin', a true Witherspyk!"

His wife brushed crumbs from her apron, then wiped Dubdub's face with a corner of it. "Indeed, Oakie. I just wish he wouldn't practice his lines at mealtimes."

Jango speared a hunk of cheese with his blade. "I'll come along with ye on the morrow, Buck, just for a walk, chance to stretch me paws, eh!"

Flib was over her war shock now. She winked at Jango. "An' I'll toddle along with ya, Pa, t'make sure ye don't get into any trouble!"

Axtel had joined the molecrew in seeing off a huge cauldron of the mole's speciality, deeper'n'ever'turnip'-n'tater'n'beetroot pie. He held up a piece in his paw. "Oi'll goo with ee, zurr'n'marms. Thurr may bee's vurmints a-lurkin' in ee wuddlands. Oi'll give 'em ole billyoh!"

Marjoram put on a face of mock despair, managing a wail. "If any other beast volunteers to go, there'll only be me left behind here!"

Friar Soogum poured a tiny crystal goblet of elderberry wine. "Here, marm, drink this—you'll feel better. Don't fret, marm. I'll stay here with ye. I'll make a special liddle supper, just for me'n'you. We'll sit up in the belltower an' share it. Oh, an' more o' this fine wine, eh!"

Trajidia Witherspyk fluttered her eyelashes at the Friar. "I never said I was deserting this beautiful Abbey. Will you find room for a young un like me at your table, oh, kind and handsome Friar, sir?"

All those who heard Soogum mention the special supper suddenly expressed a fervent desire to remain at Redwall.

"Er, me, too, please, could I come?"

"Hurr, an' oi h'also. Oi carn't walk too furr wi' moi paws!"

"An' can I bring a few of the Dibbuns? They'd enjoy a treat, bless their liddle paws!"

'I'd like t'come, too, but only t'keep an eye on the babes!"

Marjoram waved her paws, miming alarm. "Stop, stop. We'll never get you all into one belltower!"

In the softly lit orchard, the sound of woodlanders laughing drifted up to the starry night sky which had now cloaked Mossflower.

It was high noon of the following day. The sun hung like a burnished gold medallion in the cloudless sky. Abbess Marjoram was on the path outside the newly cleared west gate. Other Redwallers were with her to wish a hearty goodbye to the travelling party. Friar Soogum and his kitchen helpers fussed around the group, passing out haversacks of food and drink.

The good Friar's constant worry in life was that anybeast would not have enough to eat. He pressed a further package upon an already overloaded Clarinna. "Just some dainties, candied chestnuts an' crystallised fruits, for your little uns, marm. Oh, an' I slipped in two small flasks of best pear cider—babes always like that."

The Abbess was forced to intercede on behalf of those leaving the Abbey. "Friar, you've provisioned them handsomely, but that's quite enough now. Any more and they won't be able to move. Buckler, are you ready to go?"

Adjusting the shoulder straps of a huge haversack,

the young hare managed a quick salute. "Ready, marm! Ambry, Axtel, Jango, let's march!"

With Buckler and Clarinna following Ambrevina, and an escort of twenty Guosim backed up by Jango, Axtel and Flib, the column moved out, going south down the path. The remaining Redwallers cheered them on their journey.

Skipper shouted out, "Come on, Buck, mate, get 'em goin' with one o' yore Long Patrol marchin' songs!"

Buckler promptly obliged with an old parade-ground air, which could be speeded up or slowed down to accommodate the marchers. They soon picked up the rhythm, as it was not a difficult song.

"Y'place yore left footpaw
in front o' yore right footpaw,
then y'do it over'n over'n over again!
Remember, left right, left right,
chin up high an' eyes bright,
don't fret about the sun, the wind or rain.
Keep those ranks good an' straight,
don't tread on yore matey's paws,
or he might just turn around,
kick yore tail an' tread on yores!
So place yore left footpaw,
in front o' yore right footpaw,
then do it over'n over'n over again!
Remember, left right, left right,
never argue, never fight,
keep goin' 'til you think you've gone insane!"

Axtel wound a spotted kerchief around his mouth.

"H'it bee's ruther dusty marchin' at ee back!"

Once they were out of sight from the Abbey, Ambrevina turned off into the woodland. Buckler shepherded them across the ditch, patting backs and mouthing words of encouragement.

"Well done, mates, a nice little walk so far, eh?"

Unused to his parade-ground pace, they were all quite breathless. Flib was heard to mutter, "Huh, a nice liddle walk fer you, y'great lankypaws!"

Buckler glared at the shrewmaid. "What was that, miss?"

Axtel, who had grown rather fond of Flib, placed a heavy digging claw on her shoulder. "She'm just sayin', zurr, that moi ole h'injured paw b'aint wurkin' vury gudd."

Buckler's attitude changed instantly. "Oh, I'm sorry to hear that, friend. Right, we'll rest an' take a spot o' lunch in the woodlands. Pass the word along, Jango."

It was pleasant, being off the dusty open path on such a hot summer's day. The wood of Mossflower provided lots of cool, green shade. Buckler chose a spot beneath an old crack willow on a tiny streambank. Everybeast sat with their footpaws in the muddy shallows as Clarinna distributed food.

Buckler winked at Jango as they watched their crew. "Just look at 'em. You'd think they'd been on a season-long slog. Have you ever seen anythin' like it?"

The Guosim Log a Log plumped down on the bank, squidging his footpaws into the mud. "Whaaaaaw! That's better. Pass me that ale flagon, Sniffy." He held out a paw, looking around. "Sniffy? Where's that beast got to—who's seen ole Sniffy?"

Ambrevina sighted the Tracker coming through some bushes.

Jango found the ale and took a swig. "Where've ye been, Sniff? Siddown an' git some lunch."

The Guosim Tracker beckoned to the east. "Just scoutin' o'er thataway, Chief. Beggin' yore pardon for disturbin' yore lunch, but there's somebeasts there."

Buckler was at his side, blade drawn. "Whatbeasts? Where?"

Sniffy went into his customary crouch, reentering the bushes. "Foller me an' I'll show ye."

Buckler went after the Tracker, with Jango, Flib and Ambrevina in his wake. Sniffy could mutter out of the side of his mouth quite well. He kept up a running commentary as Buckler caught up to his side.

"Don't know wot t'make of it, Chief. There I was, a-nosin' through the shrubbery, when I 'ears 'em. Voices, sounded like they was arguin', then they started laughin'. I never saw 'em, though, sounded like too many beasts fer me t'be spotted by. So back I comes to report to ye. Hah, afore I was outta earshot, I 'eard 'em singin'. Stop! 'Earken, mates, there they go agin! Can ye 'ear them, Chief?"

They halted suddenly. Jango and Ambrevina ran into their backs. The Guosim Log a Log almost got Sniffy in the rear with his drawn rapier. He whispered, "Aye aye, wot's the holdup?"

Buckler stifled him with a paw. "Listen!"

Somebeast was singing lustily, with shrill voices joining in discordantly.

"She's the sergeant major's daughter,
Miss Floosabia Grugsby Lee,
And anybeast who woos her gets
a medal for bravery.
Her nose is blue, her eyes are red,
she's got a laugh that'd wake the dead,
an' I'm the one she's chose to wed.
Floosabia Grugsby Lee, please stay away from me!
Go to your left two three,
now to the right two three,
'tis forward on the double,
an' get me out of trouble,
so I can run away to sea.
Far far away from . . .
. . . Floosabia Grugsby Lee!"

Another voice complained to the singer, "Sure will ye give yore ould gob a rest. That's no song t'be singin' in front o' liddle uns!"

The singer gave a brusque reply. "One more peep out o' you, marm, an' you'll find your insolent self on a fizzer so fast your paws won't touch the bloomin' floor, wot wot!"

The motherly figure of Mumzy the water vole emerged from the shrubbery, giving as good as she got. "Arrah, go an' fizz yore tail, an' see if'n I care a jot!"

She was leading a long double file of young ones. They were bumbling along holding on to a rope, which kept them in an orderly line. The harebabes, Calla and Urfa, were walking quite well now, holding paws with Jiddle and Jinty Witherspyk. Midda and Tura brought up the rear. Mousebabe Diggla was strutting behind Diggs, who was patrolling the line. Diggla was first to spot Ambrevina standing in the bushes. He raced to her, squeaking, "Ambee! Ambeeeeeeee! It be me, Diggla!"

The badgermaid swept him up with one huge paw. "So it is! Diggla, my little friend, how are you?"

Diggs raised a hazel twig, which he was using as a swagger stick. "Column! Haaa . . . alt! Stand easy an' be still now!" Marching briskly over to Buckler, he prodded him with the stick. "Hmm, I remember you, sah. Buckley, isn't it? Well, now, laddie buck, what are ye doin' in this neck o' the woods, eh, wot wot?"

Aware of Diggs's unfortunate identity crisis, Buckler came to attention, throwing up a smart salute. "Leadin' a patrol to escort you all back to Redwall Abbey, Colonel Crockley Sputherington, sah!"

Diggs looked thinner and paler than his former self. His head was still swathed in bandages, and his left ear was missing. Tapping his open paw with the cane, he nodded several times.

"Rather tardy of ye, Bucklow, but better late than never, eh? Not flippin' many for an escort. Got any more with ye?"

They trooped into the camp on the muddy streambank, whereupon, catching sight of her babes, Clarinna swept both Calla and Urfa off their paws. Kissing and hugging them, she wept and laughed wildly.

Midda, who was being embraced by Jango and Flib, smiled at the sight of the harewife being reunited with her babes. "Well, ain't that a sight for sore eyes!"

Jango patted her back. "No more than you are, darlin'!"

With the babes still clinging to her, Clarinna launched herself upon Diggs, knocking him flat. "Oh, my wonderful friend, you kept your promise and restored these two sweet babes to their mother's paws! How can I ever thank you, gallant Subaltern Diggs?"

Her benefactor was horrified. "Restrain your blinkin' self, marm. Remove y'self an' these two little blighters from me before I'm drowned in slobberin' kisses. Unpaw me, I say!"

Extricating himself, Diggs stood up, brushing off his tunic. "Who in the name o' scuts'n'scallywags is this creature Diggs? Mistaken identity, I fear, marm. I'm Colonel Crockley Sputherington, I'll have ye know!"

Not wishing to upset his friend, Buckler played along. "Attention, everybeast. Allow me to introduce this brave officer. His name is Colonel Crockley Sputherington, an' I hope you'll all address him as such. Understood?"

The "colonel" bowed formally. "My thanks t'ye, Bucklepaw! Right, form up in order now. On my command, back to Redwall Abbey, quick march!"

Jango indicated the open food haversacks. "Ain't ye goin' to take a bite o' vittles afore ye go?"

Diggs walked a circle around the Log a Log, sizing him up. "An' who in the name o' blue blinkin' blazes are you, sah?"

Jango returned his stare. "I'm Jango Bigboat, Chieftain an' Log a Log o' the Guosim!"

Diggs viewed this statement with no evident surprise. "A shrew, eh? I thought so." He turned to Buckler, murmuring confidentially, "Greedy little blighters, shrews.

Get him back into line, Buckleton. We ain't wastin' time on scoff, wot!"

Without further ado, Diggs swaggered off at the head of the column. Jango scratched his beard in astonishment.

"Well, don't that sink the logboat? Ole greedy lardbucket Diggs refusin' vittles—I don't believe it!"

Mumzy sorted out some candied chestnuts to give the little ones on their march. "Ah, sure, pay no heed t'the beast friend. He's as mad as an ould boiled frog, but he means well."

The line of little ones holding on to the rope was still filing past Buckler, which caused him to remark, "There's about twoscore an' five young uns here, Mumzy. Where did they all come from?"

The water vole filled her apron pockets with tit bits. "Some found their way to my cave, an' the rest we found wanderin' round the woodlands. Orphans, their parents slaughtered by the Sable Quean's lot. I been gatherin' 'em in whenever I could. They were cryin' their eyes out, hungry an' lost. Sure, I couldn't leave 'em to fend for themselves, now, could I, sir?"

Buckler pressed her old paw affectionately. "You certainly couldn't, marm. Come on, let's go to Redwall Abbey. There's room for everyone there!"

32

Over the western flatlands, swallows flitted and swooped against a sky aflame with crimsoned evening glory. Slim narrow clouds, lilac and pearly grey, hemmed the far horizon. Redwall Abbey was bathed in soft rose light from eaves to gables. It was a sight which would be forever emblazoned in the memories of those young creatures seeing it for the first time.

The column trudged wearily along the path in a haze of fine dust sent up by their footpaws. Some of the babes, too exhausted to march, were carried on the backs and shoulders of their rescuers.

Trajidia Witherspyk, balancing on the southwest edge of the battlements, espied them first. She hallooed out in full dramatic style. "Hearken, one and all. I see them, I see them yonder!"

This set off the twin Abbey bells, booming out their message of home and safety for all.

The Abbey gates swung open as cheering creatures rushed down the path en masse to greet the travellers. Swaggering martially at the column's head, Diggs (alias Colonel Crockley Sputherington) bellowed out orders in fine parade-ground style. "Eyes front! Hold the line, back there! Mind your dressing, watch your pace, keep in step! No breakin' off an' dismissin' 'til I give the command!" His words were suddenly lost as both sides met.

Dymphnia Witherspyk seized Jiddle and Jinty, squeezing them until they were gasping for breath. "Oh, my beautiful liddle hogs, I've not slept a wink since you've been gone. Oh, my dears, y'don't know what this does to a mother's heart!"

Diggs pushed roughly past the trio, trying to restore some order to the happy chaos. "By the left, right'n'centre, discipline's gone to flamin' pot. They're nought but a bloomin' rabble!"

Dymphnia gave him a hefty pat on the back, which nearly knocked him flat. She steadied him, gushing, "Oh, well done, Mister Diggs, well done!"

He stood quivering with rage from ear to scut. "Mister Diggs, marm? Confound Mister flippin' Diggs an' all his blinkin' ilk. D'ye know whom you're addressin'?" He strode off, waving his swagger stick, yelling, "Back in your ranks, you slab-sided puddle-pawed cads!"

Dymphnia was perplexed. She turned to Buckler. "What did I do? Did I say something wrong?"

The young hare drew her to one side as the jubilant crowd flooded through the gates into the Abbey grounds. "You'll have to forgive him, marm. It's that wound he took to the head. Thinks he's some otherbeast now, wants t'be called Colonel Crockley Sputherington."

Dymphnia allowed Jiddle and Jinty to run off and be reunited with the rest of their family. "Oh, dear, I never guessed that. I knew he'd been injured, but nobeast told me about Mister Diggs thinkin' he was some other creature. Ah, well, not to worry, Buck. I'll soon fix him."

She hurried off after her babes, not explaining how she could effect a cure for Diggs.

Fortunately, the orchard decorations had been left up, and thanks to the good efforts of Friar Soogum and his staff, a further feast was set up, waiting. When everybeast was gathered there, Abbess Marjoram mounted an upturned wheelbarrow.

Skipper called the chattering, laughing crowd to order. "Ahoy, mates, silence one an' all for Marjoram, Mother Abbess of Redwall. Stow the gab an' quiet, please!"

Visibly moved by the sight of the freed captive young ones, Marjoram wiped a habit sleeve across her eyes and sniffed several times before starting her speech.

"Welcome to Redwall Abbey, my friends, both old and new! You are all free to live here in peace and safety. Please treat this place as your home for as long as you wish. Now, I won't waste a beautiful and happy summer's eve with lots of boring talk. I see you are hungry and tired. Sister Fumbril, Drull Hogwife and other helpers—not forgetting our new friend, Mumzy Water Vole—will tend to the babes. They will have fine new clothes, a dormitory with soft little beds and, who knows, maybe a good bath in our Abbey pond tomorrow. But for now I want you all to enjoy the feast. Eat, drink, sing, dance and be merry. And once more welcome, twice welcome and thrice welcome to Redwall Abbey. Let the celebrations begin!"

Everybeast tucked in with a will. The appetite of the newly arrived young ones was so hearty that Friar Soogum stood wide-eyed.

"Goodness me, I'll have to get extra supplies from the kitchens if they carry on at this rate!"

Drull Hogwife shook her head in wonderment. "I thought those liddle uns was wearied out an' more'n ready to sleep. Good grief, lookit them eat!"

Tura lifted her smudged face from a bowl of blackberry sponge in arrowroot sauce. "Beggin' y'pardon, marm, but if'n you'd never seen vittles like this, wot'd you sooner do, eat or sleep?"

Smiling at the squirrelmaid's logic, Skipper filled himself a bowl of his favourite shrimp'n'hotroot soup. "Well said, missy, they can always sleep later. Ahoy, Colonel, d'ye want to try a bowlful o' this?"

Diggs had not touched food thus far. He had been wandering about the orchard, chunnering to himself. Curling a lip at the Otter Chieftain, he snapped, "Doesn't anybeast think of anythin' but stuffin' one's flippin' face? A disgustin' exhibition, sah! Those young uns should be abed now, catchin' up on their shuteye, wot, wot? Well, alls I can say is that they'd better be up bright'n'early on the morrow. Ho, yes, I want t'see them all on parade, ready for a long route march! I'll lick 'em into shape, sah, see if I don't!"

Cellarmole Gurjee objected strongly. "You'm'll do nuthin' of ee sort, zurr. They'm likkle uns needs carin' furr!"

Dymphnia Witherspyk did not seem in agreement with Gurjee. "Oh, tut tut, sir. I'm sure a good long march'll do the babes a power o' good. Ain't that right, Oakie?"

Putting aside a hefty fruitcake, Oakheart nodded. "Quite right, m'dear! Oh, Colonel, might I have a private word with ye, a whisper in your good ear, sir?"

The Colonel strutted over to where Oakheart was sitting. Leaning down, he bent his unbandaged ear at the florid hog. "Whisper on, sah. What d'ye jolly well want?"

With a chunk of the cake clutched in one paw, Oakheart swung out, catching the hare a stunning blow to the back of his head. Colonel Crockley Sputherington fell to the grass, knocked out cold.

There was an immediate uproar. Buckler ran at Oakheart, his paws clenched. "What'n the name o' blood'n'vinegar did y'do that for?"

Trajidia wailed, "Oh, Father, what a cowardly thing to do, striking down a poor beast in such a sly manner!"

Oakheart merely grinned, consulting his wife's opinion. "How was that, m'dear? Did I do it right?"

Dymphnia clutched his fruitcake-filled paw. "Couldn't have done it better myself, Oakie. You hit him right on the button, just as I did to you, darling!"

The Abbess hurried forward with a pail of cold water and a cloth. "Will somebeast pray tell me what's going on?"

Dymphnia obliged willingly. "My Oakie once struck his head on the tiller of our raft, knocked himself clean out. When he came to, he thought he was an owl. Egbert Whootfellow, we had to call him. We put up with him for six days, sitting perched on top of the mast making owl noises. In the end, I could stand it no longer. So, I climbed the mast when he was asleep one night and shoved him off. He wasn't really an owl, you see, couldn't fly. Fell to the deck headfirst, knocked out again. Would you believe it, when he came around again he was Oakheart Witherspyk once more. I think it was the second knock to his head that cured him."

Abbess Marjoram rolled up her habit sleeves. "Right, let's see, shall we?"

Whoosh! She emptied the bucket of cold water over the head of the senseless hare. He sat up groaning. Wiping water from his eyes, he swiftly viewed the splendid feast, then launched into a tirade.

"Yah, you rotten bunch o' cads, helpin' your bally selves to all this bloomin' tuck while I was asleep! I hope your scringey tails wither an' drop off!"

Buckler threw a paw about his friend. "Diggs, is it really you?"

Wrenching himself loose, his companion began heaping a plate with all he could lay his paws on. "Of course it's me, ye great blitherin' oaf! Who did ye think it was, a duck with a top hat on? Call y'selves friends, wot! Rotten, the whole bunch of you are, lowly bounders'n'cads. What a slimy trick t'pull on a starvin' young subaltern. I'll never speak to you again, never! Specially you, Buck Kordyne!"

Without warning, his mood changed. He smiled. "I say, that summer salad looks jolly nice. Mind passin' me a goodly portion, Buck old lad, wot?"

Everybeast laughed, cheering at the transformation. Diggs was Diggs once again, gluttonous as ever.

The feast continued until dawnlight, when lots of young ones fell fast asleep where they sat, bowls and spoons still in paw. Mumzy, Sister Fumbril and other dedicated helpers began carrying the babes off to their dormitories. Ambrevina wandered by, laden with four young creatures. She nodded to Buckler. "I think Clarinna would like a word with you. She's over in Great Hall."

Dawn rays were shafting through the tall windows, tinted by the stained glass. Buckler found Clarinna sitting by the tapestry of Martin the Warrior. He sat down beside her.

"Are Calla and Urfa both asleep now?"

Clarinna nodded upward. "Tucked up in the dormitory, bless them. Here, Buckler, these are for you." She placed the great broadsword and the coin medallion in front of him. Buckler sat staring at them awhile, then pushed them back to her.

"These are my poor brother Clerun's birthright. By family tradition, they belong to Calla, his eldest son."

Clarinna shook her head. "I and my little ones won't be returning to Salamandastron. It's my wish that they grow up here, with me at Redwall Abbey. I don't want to see them being raised under a Badger Lord, joining the Long Patrol and learning warriors' ways of war, regiments and weapons. Redwall is a place of peace, gentleness and wisdom."

She hung the medallion around Buckler's neck. "You must wear this. You have always been the true Blademaster. Clerun was a farmer at heart."

Buckler touched the bright gold emblem. "But it was you who slew Zwilt the Shade. You were the brave one, Clarinna."

She pointed to the figure of Martin the Warrior. "No, it was he who did it, really. Martin bade me to take his sword. After that, I remember nothing, only seeing the sable lying dead in front of me. I think Martin would not allow that evil beast to murder a babe in his Abbey. Nor would he see a bravebeast like you sacrifice his life to save that babe."

Buckler picked up the broadsword. "Martin was very

wise. He knew Zwilt would have killed us all if he had gotten the chance. I'll wear the medal, Clarinna. But what of this sword? It's not a weapon that I'm suited to. I have my own long rapier, which Lord Brang forged for me."

The hare mother stared at the blade with something like loathing in her eyes. "I'll have no more to do with that thing. As far as I'm concerned, you can throw it in the sea!"

Buckler patted her paw understandingly. "Leave it to me, Clarinna. I know the very beast it will suit. A broadsword forged at Salamandastron by a mighty Badger Lord is far too precious to throw away." Wearing the medallion and shouldering the hefty blade, Buckler strode from Great Hall, out into the sunlight of a new summer day.

Soft autumn mist lay in the hollows and vales of the dunelands by the far west coast. It would be fully midmorn before the sun's warmth evaporated it. A young hare, Windora Rowanbough of the Long Patrol, stood atop a high hill. Leaning on her slender javelin, she peered intently at a distant dunetop. Having ascertained what her keen eyes could see, she wheeled, shooting off like a shaft from a bowstring in the direction of Salamandastron.

Windora was a Runner, the swiftest and best on the mountain. She was poetry and grace in motion, limbs moving like silent pistons, ears blown flat back by her remarkable speed.

Lord Brang was at his anvil, putting the final touches to a helmet. It was a work of great beauty, a polished steel dome with a bright copper spike at its centre. A curtain of fine steel mesh, both functional and simple, hung halfway around it, protection for a warrior's neck and upper shoulders. The huge badger polished away at the helmet with a piece of greased silk, making it shine in the forgelight.

General Flurry Flackbuth entered, giving a small cough to make Brang aware of his presence. The Badger Lord did not even look up.

"Don't you bother to knock anymore, Flurry?"

The old bewhiskered hare shook his head. "Beggin' y'pardon, m'Lud, I knocked twice!"

Brang placed the helmet carefully on the windowsill. "Didn't hear ye, my friend. I must be gettin' old."

Flurry replied almost apologetically, "We're none of us gettin' any bally younger, sah. You were busy, let's say, er, occupied with your work, eh?"

Brang filled two tankards from an ale cask. Taking a red-hot dagger blade from the forge fire, he quenched it in the tankards, passing one to his friend.

"Mulled ale. Always makes the morning a little more bearable. Well, then, General, what news?"

Flurry savoured a sip of his drink, standing with his back to the forge fire. "Young Runner Rowanbough just reported in, sah. Seems there's three bodies approachin' here from the east."

The Badger Lord looked over his tankard rim, speaking as though he were talking to himself. "Two of our own, and a long-overdue badgermaid. My dreams were right, Flurry. Send out a score of our Long Patrol in full fig to meet them. Bring all three right here to me."

The autumn mist had died to milky wisps as the three travellers halted on the hilltop, where the haremaid had stood earlier.

Buckler drew his rapier, pointing at the great mountain on the coastline. "Well, there it is, Ambry. Salamandastron!"

The badgermaid stared at it for a long moment. "Incredible! It's exactly as I used to see it in my dreams. Can you believe that?"

Diggs twirled his sling idly. "Don't see why not, marm. You're a bloomin' badger, aren't ye? Who are we to question your flippin' visions an' whatnot, wot!"

Ambrevina's paw strayed to the hilt of her broadsword. "Look—we've got company approaching, maybe twoscore."

Diggs set off downhill, calling back, "That'll be the jolly old reception committee, wot. All good friends an' stout comrades. Huh, I bet they didn't think to bring a measly plum pudden to welcome returnin' heroes, famine-faced bounders. Hah, look who's leadin' the parade, old Flackers! An' there's Skinny Swippton, Algie Bloggmort, Tubby Magrool an' Lancejack Cudderfauld. All in their best number ones, just to meet Sub Digglethwaite, wot! I don't know whether t'feel flattered or battered. Hi, there, you chaps!"

The escort kept pace with General Flurry, who was limping slightly, favouring a gouty footpaw. Then he halted, awaiting the arrival of the trio, exchanging the customary salute with Buckler.

"Blademaster Kordyne, welcome back."

Keeping his eyes to the front, the young hare replied, "Thankee, General, sah. Afraid we haven't had the chance to spruce up appearances, sah!"

Flurry noted their travel-stained tunics and dusty appearance in contrast to his escort's smart turnout.

"Hmmph! No matter, laddie buck, no matter. Er, Subaltern Diggs, can't ye do anythin' about that left ear? It's floppin' about like a flag in a breeze, wot!"

Diggs managed a stiff heroic grin as he explained, "Oh, that, sah. 'Fraid I can't. Lost the ear in battle, doncha know. Only left me with one dainty shell like, see?"

He unfastened the chinstrap, holding the false ear out for inspection. "Charmin' old hedgehog named Crumfiss Witherspyk knitted this for me. Rather fetchin', ain't it, sah? Flops about in the wind a bit, but it looks jolly well like the real thing from a distance, wot wot!"

He slipped the chinstrap back on, adjusting the ear to a rakish angle. This brought many admiring remarks from the young hares, to whom there was nought like a real battle-scarred warrior.

"I say, top hole, Diggs. That's really the duck's nightie!"
"Rather. I love the way it sort of flops halfway!"
"Didn't you get anythin' chopped off, Buck? Bet you wish you had. Old Diggs looks absolutely dashin', wot!"
"You could win all kinds of wagers in the mess with an ear like that, old lad. Chaps'd give you all their pudden ration just to try it on!"
General Flurry cut sternly through the banter. "Silence in the ranks, there!" He saluted Ambrevina courteously. "My 'pologies, Milady, ignore these young rips. Lord Brang awaits you in his quarters, soon as possible."
The badgermaid gave him a brief, gracious nod. "Thank you, General. Please, lead on!"

There were banners staked out along the beach and an honour guard of Long Patrollers leading up to the fortress entrance. The Regimental Band, complete with fifes and drums, belted out a brave marching air named "Hares in the Heather." Resplendent in burnished armour and a magnificent cloak of carmine velvet, Lord Brang emerged to greet the trio.
Standing either side of the badgermaid, Buckler and Diggs saluted. Brang acknowledged them with a nod. He stood facing Ambrevina, who though not having the Badger Lord's powerful bulk, was taller than him by a half head. The music halted.
Brang held forth his paw, treating the new guest to one of his rare smiles. "Lady, I am Lord Brang Forgefire, Ruler of Salamandastron. Your presence here gives me great pleasure. Welcome!"
The badgermaid accepted the outstretched paw graciously. "I am called Ambrevina Rockflash, from the far Eastern Shores, Sire. I deem it an honour to be here."
With Ambrevina's paw resting upon his, Lord Brang turned, leading the procession into the mountain. The

band began playing a stately measured piece, entitled "Heart o' the Western Shores."

General Flurry whispered to Buckler, "Lordship wants to see all three of ye up in his Forge Chamber before the feast."

Diggs's eyes lit up. "Oh, I say, a jolly old feast, wot! You go on ahead with Ambry, Buck. I'm not much flippin' good at reportin' back. I'll stop down here with the chaps!"

General Flurry's moustache tickled Diggs's good ear as the old officer murmured threateningly, "You'll do no such thing, sah. Go on, straight up to the Forge Chamber with ye!"

Diggs groaned and carried on upstairs, managing to twitch his good ear savagely at one of his regimental comrades. "Beware, Tubby Magrool. Touch a single festive crumb before I get back, an' I'll box your fat head!"

The mist had cleared now, leaving a fine autumn day. From the broad, low window of the upper chamber, the mighty sea was smooth as a millpond right out to the hazy western horizon.

They sat on a cushion-strewn ledge, savouring the rosehip and almond-blossom cordial which Flurry served liberally. The Badger Lord could not take his gaze away from Ambrevina.

"You carry the name Rockflash. I knew one or two of them in my young seasons. They were experts at wielding slings."

Ambrevina produced her own sling, a big, formidable thing. "Aye, Lord, I can use one. I was brought up amongst kin whose only weapons were slings."

Brang indicated the broadsword she wore. "Yet you carry a blade, one I made at that forge yonder. I recognise it as belonging to the Kordyne clan. How so?"

Buckler interrupted to explain. "My brother Clerun was slain by a sable beast, Zwilt the Shade, and his vermin killers.

I'll mention all that in my report, Sire. But his wife, Clarinna, gave me the sword and this medal, of which you know. She lives at Redwall now, with her twin babes. They wish to be peaceful creatures, so she gave me the sword. I have my own blade, so I thought Lady Ambrevina could use it."

Brang nodded. "And can you use it, Lady?"

The badgermaid smiled. "I am learning, Lord, and what better teacher do I need than Blademaster Kordyne?"

Buckler flushed to his eartips, remarking, "She doesn't really need a sword, being so brilliant with a sling, Lord. Perhaps she could instruct you in the slinger's art, Sire?"

Brang took the sling, weighing its balance. "Perhaps she could. I'd enjoy that!"

Diggs blanched as his stomach growled aloud. "Not as much as I'd enjoy a flippin' feast!"

Brang's reproving eye fixed upon the tubby subaltern. "What was that—I beg your pardon?"

Diggs giggled foolishly. "No need t'beg my pardon, Sire. 'Twas my tummy makin' all that commotion. Er, I, er, was just sayin' how jolly spiffin' it is t'be back home, eh, wot wot?"

The Badger Lord's eyes softened indulgently. "Aye, I suppose it is good to be back home, and talking about that, I hope you'll treat this as your home, Lady?"

Ambrevina curtsied lithely. "I would be delighted to call Salamandastron home, Sire! I've seen this mountain many times in my dreams."

Brang nodded. "I know you have, and I've dreamed of having you here. When one gets old, the young must take their place. Salamandastron would be safe in your paws, Ambrevina. General Flurry and I will one day pass all this over to you. I think my mountain would flourish under your rule. Though you will have much to learn. Maybe you need a General Buckler Kordyne at your side?"

Buckler shook his head. "You know how I feel about such things, Sire. I'm well content with being a Blademaster, if that's alright with Lady Ambrevina?"

The badgermaid paused a moment before replying, "Of course, Buck. I know I could always count on you if I needed to. That is, providing I could have a faithful assistant, a Colonel Diggs maybe?"

General Flurry huffed through his mustachios, " 'Pon me scut, marm, that young blighter an officer! What would he know about bein' a confounded colonel?"

Ambrevina could not resist chuckling. "Oh, he's had previous experience, eh, Buck?"

Buckler stifled a laugh. "Aye, marm, that he has!"

Lord Brang looked from one to the other. "I think you'd best make your reports. You first, Diggs!"

The homecoming feast lasted a full three days, with little letup. The amount of food and drink a regiment of hares got through was truly legendary. Ambrevina sat between Lord Brang and Buckler. She enjoyed every moment of it, even the bawdy barrack-room ballads—she joined in as she learned the choruses.

All the young hares voted her tremendously popular, especially after she gave an exhibition of slinging out on the beach. They were filled with awe at the distance and accuracy of the badgermaid's throwing. Diggs had the company in peals of laughter, wearing the false ear in various positions: under his chin as a beard, or across his nose as a moustache, when he performed a hilarious imitation of General Flurry.

Lord Brang and Buckler took a break from the festivities on the third afternoon. Away from the hurly-burly, they sat on a sun-warmed rock just above the tideline. The Badger Lord stared out at the placid sea gently lapping golden sand as it ebbed westward. Brang sighed.

"You know, Buck, I wish you'd reconsider that post as a senior officer. Lady Ambrevina would welcome a fine brain such as yours when she takes over from me."

Buckler tossed a pebble at the receding tide. "I didn't say I wouldn't help her, sir. I'd give my life in her service, she knows that. But this thing about bein' a general, well, that's not really my style."

The big old badger chuckled. "In some ways you never change, just like your grandsire, a true Kordyne warrior. Though, listening to the report of your mission, I can see that you've altered greatly in other things. Experience, that's what you've gained, Buck."

The young hare picked up some sand, then let it sift through his paw. "Aye, I've seen a few things and learned a bit. Travelling with a companion like good old Diggs, friends such as the Witherspyks and the Guosim. Discovering the wonders of Redwall Abbey and its honest creatures. Huh, even meeting my first Bloodwrath mole, Axtel. Losing my brother Clerun, seeing his two little babes, knowing what it means t'be an uncle. Freeing the young uns, battling with the Ravagers, watching friend and foe alike slain. You don't live through those things without addin' to your knowledge of life, sir. Thanks to you, who sent me off that day. It seems so long ago now."

They sat in silence a moment, then Buckler arose. "Beggin' y'pardon, Lord, but I've got to go. It's time for the Lady Ambrevina's fencing lesson."

Brang nodded, drawing a parchment from his cloak pocket. "Of course, off y'go, now. I'll read this letter you brought from my friend Marjoram."

Buckler saluted and trotted off. The Badger Lord watched him draw his long rapier as he went, ready to begin the lesson. Before he unrolled the parchment, he called after the young hare, "Before you go, d'you remember what I told you about travelling?"

Buckler turned in a swirl of sand, shouting his reply, "Indeed I do, Sire. You said travelling was an adventure—an' it was, too. A real adventure!"

Bounding up onto a rock, Buckler twirled his blade on high. With all the joy and vigour of his growing seasons, he roared the Long Patrol battle cry.

"Euuuulaliiiiaaaaa!"

Epilogue

Herein is the contents of a letter sent by Abbess Marjoram to Lord Brang.

To Lord Brang Forgefire, Ruler of Salamandastron and Lord of the Western Shores
From Marjoram, Mother Abbess of Redwall Abbey

Dearest friend,

I send you heartfelt greetings and best wishes for your continued good health. My thanks for the gift of the beautifully crafted bellropes. I am sure they will help to toll our Abbey bells for untold seasons to come. I hope you are pleased with the enchanting young badger Ambrevina. Her presence will grace your mountain, and I am certain that one day she will become a worthy successor to you.

It is a delight for us to have two young hares with us. Only last afternoon, I took tea in the orchard with their mother, Clarinna. What a remarkable creature she is, having started a gardening and nature study class for our Dibbuns. Calla and Urfa are dear little babes. They will grow into fine leverets.

What brave and courageous hares you have at Salamandastron! Buckler and Diggs are a credit to your Long Patrol. I was sorry, as were a lot of others, to see them leave us. Our population at the Abbey has swelled somewhat, since now we have Axtel Sturnclaw, Mumzy Water Vole and the entire Witherspyk Company staying with us permanently. Come one, come all, as long as they are good and honest beasts, that's what I've always said. We are blessed by the seasons, happy to live amidst peace and plenty and strengthened by growing numbers of friends. What more could one ask?

Log a Log Jango sends you his good wishes. I think you and he have met before.

My chief desire would be to gaze from Redwall's west battlements one morn and see you marching at the head of your gallant Long Patrol, roaring out a stout marching song as you come to visit us. Do you think this would be possible? Next summer would be nice. We would love to have you all here with us. Friar Soogum has promised a feast that will go down in the Annals of Redwall. I myself will toll the bells specially for you.

Brang, old friend, I know you will honour us with your presence. You and any other one who is honest and true will find joy, happiness and peace at my Abbey. Redwall will always be here with a welcome for all.

Marjoram, Mother Abbess of Redwall
Abbey in Mossflower Country